Melabeth

Book 3

Purification Through Fire

By: E.B. Hood

This book is dedicated to my brother Nick Hood. Wish you were here bro. R.I.P 4-12-1978 to 11-18-2009.

Melabeth The Vampire (Melabeth Series, Book 3)
(www.melabeth.com)

Copyright © 2012 by Eric B Hood.
(melabeththevampire@gmail.com)

Alley Cat Publishing
alleycatpublishing@gmail.com

Paperback, ISBN **978-0-9884100-4-6**
Paperback V.3
Editing by: Bill Stanton
Cover: photography by Wendy Hood.
Cover Art By: Mirella Santana
Digital artist and genius, Thanks for all your hard work!
You can find Mirella Santana at
https://www.facebook.com/mirellasantana.digitalartist

Contents

Chapter 1 Breaking Things

It had started out such a great day. We had just stopped at a Pizza Hut to have lunch after church. My grandfather had been preaching, and from what I remember it was a pretty good sermon. He joined the family a little late, but I had saved him a seat right next to me.

"Sit next to me grandpa." He joined me on my side of the bench. On the other side sat my mom, dad and my brother in a baby carrier.

He smiled down at me, "Not a better seat in the whole world. How is my almost six year old?"

I smiled, "Good." It was always odd when someone reminded me that I was six. Trapped in the body of a child, would I ever get used to it?

Idle chit chat erupted from the adults. They talked about the sermon that my grandfather had just given. It was cold outside and was starting to snow. By the time the waitress came, the conversation was deeply entrenched in weather conditions of past, present, and future. She took our order and, in the blink of an eye, we had food in front of us.

Mindy complained about how little I ate. I really couldn't stomach too much human food, but I could eat it, and it would digest. My heartbeat sped up for nothing. I could run laps around the house; not only would my heart stay steady; so would my breathing. Unlike being a vampire, breathing was necessary, but I never felt short of breath. Pizza was my favorite, probably why we were here a lot. I would eat more pizza, than anything else.

It was cold outside as small flurries of snow came down. My grandfather gave me a quick hug before hurrying off to his car. He needed to get ready for Sunday evening services. My parents and I busied ourselves putting on our jackets as my father finished paying the bill. We rushed across the parking lot as the cold wind sliced through us. Unlike being a vampire I got cold. Still, it seemed to me that I handled extreme temperatures better than most. We rushed into my Dad's Tahoe. I jumped into my booster seat while my dad started the vehicle.

I was just putting on my seat belt as my father started to back out. The windows were icy and hard to see out of. My father didn't see the small Honda shooting through the parking lot. When the Tahoe hit the car, my head banged against the back of the seat as the SUV came to a stop. There was a screeching sound as the little car dragged across the bumper before coming to a stop. The car had been moving fast.

My dad asked, "Is everyone ok?"

Mindy and I said in unison, "Fine."

"I'll be right back," said Dad as he hopped out of the truck.

Mindy unbuckled and stretched her whole body in-between the front seats. She was busy inspecting my little brother for damages. Mindy just shook her head, "This is just great."

I had known she wasn't speaking to anyone, but I answered just the same. "This isn't dad's fault."

Mindy gave me a dirty look, "I know. Why don't you sit quietly until we get home?" She crawled back to her own seat once she had determined that the crash hadn't even woken up my brother.

His breathing came easy as he lay in silence. It was strange looking down at him; I loved him so much. Even with all that love, it was tinged with fear. Is he safe to be around me? What will my blood do to him? I could feel him; he was a part of my blood circle. Apparently not all of my blood left my sister with my birth.

I should have taken her advice; I should have sat in my seat quietly and minded my own business. I could hear everything, and what I heard outside of the Tahoe was causing me to tighten my hands into fists. The young man was cursing my father and threatening him.

What happened next is the very thing that is now my unraveling.

It was like an out of body experience. My eyes sharpened as my senses heightened, and the world felt like it slowed down. I took off my seatbelt and spun around on my knees so I could see out the window. What I saw made me lose what little control I might have had. The young man was much larger than my father; he stood menacing in front of him. He had two friends with him. One was standing behind him watching him tell my father off. The other was half watching him and inspecting the damage on the car. The car itself was torn up pretty bad.

It was slow motion as I watched the young man push my father with one hand.

My father threw up his hands, "What do you think you're doing?"

"About to kick your ass… that's what I'm doing. Maybe next time you will watch where you are going." As he said this, my father had taken a step back, but the young man quickly moved forward, closing the space.

The next thing I knew I was out of the Tahoe standing behind my father. I moved around him right between him and this man. The man looked down at me in surprise, but my father had not yet noticed me. Before anyone could react to my presence, I swung.

I punched hard, straight into his knee. I was surprised that the sound of breaking bones filled my ears. The man fell like a tree, landing on his ass. He grabbed his knee and began to scream.

The next thing that filled my ears was the surprise of his buddy, "DAMMMNNN, did you see that shit! She cold-cocked Buster, in one punch he went *down*." The kid was laughing at his hurt friend. "Come on dude! She's like five. You ain't hurt."

"What happened?" The other friend hadn't been paying attention, but with the screaming he was now on the scene.

The next few minutes were kind of funny as both these guys teased their downed friend. When they finally came to the conclusion that he was really hurt, they knocked it off. My father picked me up and took me into his arms. He quickly returned me to the Tahoe and shut the door. There Mindy was staring at me with wide eyes. She turned her head away from me and said, "Oh, this is bad. What is she?" She had said it quietly; she had not meant for me to hear it, but I did.

The next few hours were pure hell. After the conversation with the police officers (who were sure that my father had hit him) I began to slowly realize the gravity of what I had done. Still, the worst part had yet to come. After some time my father returned to the truck and started it. Mindy asked, "What's going to happen?"

My father sounded tired, "Well, nothing really."

Mindy sounded exhausted, "Nothing?"

My father went on explaining, "The officer didn't want to believe that Molly hit that man. Hell, I don't want to believe it. After forty five minutes of Ralph telling him, that's what happened, the officer decided that Bert had a bad knee. The officer agreed with me that the car accident was Bert's fault. Of course it happened in a parking lot so it really doesn't matter. In parking lots they call it no fault accidents."

Mindy asked, "Bert is the kid who hit us? Who is Ralph?"

"Bert hit us; Ralph was his buddy who witnessed Molly hitting Bert." My father clarified.

Mindy still sounded worried, "What does this mean? Will they be pressing charges on Molly?"

My father shook his head, "No, no charges. I think everyone is going to chalk this up to Bert having a bad knee."

Mindy sounded a little bit relieved, "Is that why he was so hurt then?"

My father shook his head again. He turned his head back and looked at me for the first time since he got back into the Tahoe. It was that look, the look that had me shaking in the corner of my room in fear, the fear of being rejected, tossed out for being a freak. I never wanted him to look at me like that... like I was an alien.

"I don't know, hard to tell," His voice said it all as my sister fell silent.

I hadn't said a word all the way home, and no one really talked to me. They didn't talk about me or how my father witnessed me hit a man with unbelievable strength. Now, here I am sitting in my corner full of fear and anger, fear of rejection, of my new family and anger at my own actions. I lost control and now what will come of it?

My body shook; breath was shallow as my heart sped away. Holding myself tight in a ball, my body pressed tightly into the corner of my room, I could feel it, the panic rising in me. My eyes were squeezed tight, but the tears found their way out, flowing down my cheek.

Every noise in the house sounded like elephants with high heels walking on tile. Tomorrow was January 8th, 2003 - my birthday. I would be turning six, and even though I looked to be six... I was not; I was trapped, and the last six years have been... difficult. I thought about my life and how things had developed. I hoped it would help me calm down. I needed to work it out in my head. I was afraid, but I didn't know why. My feelings were so jumbled up. I couldn't even express to myself why I felt the way I did. Maybe thinking it out, starting from the beginning, it would help me figure out this fear.

In the beginning, Alice came to see me almost every night. Her ability to make me see anything she wanted really helped with the craziness of being a baby. At night she would make my world come to life and give me someone to talk with. She was very nurturing, always wanting to be a mother. This was her strange way of being one, a strange baby for a strange girl. It didn't take long to find that I was very attached to Alice. I could feel what she was feeling, and I always knew where she was. It was weird; I didn't know her exact location, but I did know how far away she was and in what direction.

As soon as I awoke in this new body, I knew we had a new connection. A week out of the hospital and Alice came to see me. I was asleep, but I knew she was coming. Seeing through her eyes and feeling her body move as she became closer to me was amazing. I soon learned I could do it even more when I was awake. It was a real out-of-body experience, and it was a great distraction from the boredom of being a baby. Still Alice slept a lot during the day, and during the day I couldn't even feel Alice. It was like someone shut off the lights as soon as she fell asleep. Months later Alice had figured out my trick and came up with one of her own; she could block me. Alice was deeply private and only let me enter into her head when she was aware and willing. I didn't like it but couldn't say I blamed her.

In many ways this rebirth was like a second chance at life for me. I knew I wasn't human; there were lots of signs. I ignored anything that was inhuman about myself. I so longed to be normal, to relive my life. It was strange having my sister for my mother. My grandfather was my real father, Jack. In the womb I had time to forgive him. Now it's like I have, my father back. I had forgotten what all the drugs and alcohol had done to him. Now when he comes over (which is almost every day), it's like my father from my childhood, full of love and warmth.

My father was John Brook, and he was great. So calm and patient, I loved him as much as my real father. Or is he my real father? Of course, there is Nicks... wow, I have daddy issues. It was still hard to remember that now I was Molly Brook, not Melabeth. I missed my name. Nicks and Alice still call me Melabeth, so now I have many names along with many fathers. It's good to be loved!

I do believe that is what I am afraid of - losing my new family. I am afraid of being discovered, being found out, that I am not human and then being tossed out. It has been hard to hide what I am, and Mindy is not completely fooled. She knows I am not normal, but she has no idea to what extent. Nor does she understand that it is me, her sister, inhabiting her baby's body. I have heard her speak to John on many occasions about how strange I am. He has always reassured her.

Mindy told John about the time I kidnapped her and what I was. I really don't think he believed her. He would say things like, "Well, this vampire, she's dead now. She can't hurt you, and I am sure she hasn't affected Molly at all."

Mindy would say, "But she put her blood in me. I have never been right since that night. I have never gotten sick; I have been stronger. You can't deny the way I heal, can you?"

John would speak to her like a child, "You can't blame good health on vampires."

Mindy would give up, defeated. I felt bad when it sounded like her husband thought she was a little nuts. When she talked to my grandfather, it was like the same conversation with some minor changes. Instead of not believing her about what happened (because he was there), he would try to change the conversation not wanting to talk about it. He was also under the same opinion as my father that I was alright and perfectly normal. This line of thinking was a lot my fault.

I didn't mean to make my sister crazy. It just kind of worked out that way. She is a stay-at-home mother, and my father was a hard worker in a factory. Hiding my true nature was easier with my father and grandfather. It helped that they were away most of the day. I was home all day with Mindy and often got caught doing things that no baby or toddler would do... like reading books, or making a sandwich without making a mess, or just making a sandwich.

Even with all this, life was good, and I was not going to do anything to mess up my second chance at it. Life has a way of falling into a pattern until an event changes it. My life was in a pattern; I fought with Mindy while I was loved by my grandfather and father. I hung out with Alice at night, and she made sure my special needs were met.

The fact that I still needed blood bothered me, but at least for now I didn't have to hunt it down myself. Alice brought me blood, and I was always hungry for it. In fact, when she missed a night, the next day was horrible. All I could do was think of blood, always hungry. When I think about it, I didn't miss too many nights without feeding before my rebirth.

Of course, there Nicks and his library, I visit both often. Nicks felt horrible about killing me, but I wasn't mad at him. I had forgiven him. He thought that after he destroyed my body that my spirit would come to the library and there we would be together. He freaked out when he couldn't find me.

My sister, Mindy didn't meet my new father, John, until a few years after my death. She got pregnant, and they rushed off to get married. He was twenty, and my sister was almost nineteen. She soon became Mindy Brook, and, on January 8th, 1997, a child was born, me, Molly Brook. My blood had been floating in Mindy for seven years, and for seven years Nicks had no idea what had happened to me.

Nicks had looked everywhere and fell into a great depression when he could not find me. He felt me about the same time Alice did. In fact, Alice and Nicks met coming to see me at the same time. They met at a Target, those two meeting at a store; it always made me laugh. They both came looking for me, they both could feel me, but what they found was my sister.

Mindy was looking at baby stuff when she was approached by a strange woman and a man. Alice knew what Nicks looked like from the memories she had stolen from me. I am not sure how Nicks knew Alice, but he did. At first, Mindy didn't even notice the strangers staring at her. She looked a lot like me, so both Alice and Nicks stared in wonder. Alice had used her mind powers to make herself into someone different. She turned and saw Alice, but what she saw was an average middle age woman. Nicks was wearing a dark gray suit with his hair in a pony tail. He truly had a friendly face, and Mindy found herself smiling at the odd couple standing in the aisle with her. I am sure she believed they were there just shopping, trying to see some piece of merchandise that she was standing in front of.

Alice asked, "How are you doing?"

Mindy responded, "Good, am I in your way?"

"Not at all, my dear," Nicks said with a smile.

I do believe it took them a second to realize it was not me they were talking to. Alice asked, "Are you expecting?" This was not a bad question, for she was shopping in the baby aisle.

"Yes, I am only a few weeks."

With a nod, Nicks said, "Congratulations."

"Yes, congratulations," Alice added.

"Thank you both."

Both Alice and Nicks wished my sister a nice day and then walked off together. I wasn't there, but I bet I can guess what they talked about. After that, both Alice and Nicks took personal interest in Mindy's care. The day I was born, my doctor was Nicks, and Alice appeared as one of the nurses. Even my blood test at the hospital was taken care of. They had made sure that they were engineered into my life. When I was about three I went to a dinner with my parents. They were going out to dinner with my dad's boss. My dad's boss was really excited to meet me, and I was only a little surprised to find out it was Ezra.

I slept most of the day because I was always up at night with Alice. As I became older, this became somewhat of a problem. It didn't help at all when I went to preschool or first grade. I was always tired and wanted to sleep during class. It didn't help that I didn't get excited about what normal children get excited about, like when the teacher would say, "Ok class, let's all sit in a circle. We're all going to play a game." All I could think was, "Oh joy."

And then my brother was born, Jeffery. Born on April 5th, 2000, he just turned nine months old. I love my brother and love everything about him. Still, he made things harder for me. It didn't help me when my father and grandfather could really see the difference in behavior seeing how normal babies act and remembering how I acted. Of course it just confirmed everything my sister had been saying.

It was utter shock when she discovered how much work a baby really was. The baby cried in the middle of the night because no one else was feeding him, a baby who hadn't learned to walk in four months. And I suppose being potty trained at six months was a dead giveaway, but, hell, I couldn't stand diapers.

I tried to calm my mind and stop the anger. I felt as if I were losing it. I looked out my bedroom window and what I saw, only upset me worse. There on the ledge of the window was a gray cat; it was my cat, Spooky. She reminded me once again how far away, I was from a normal life.

I remember it like it was yesterday. Michael came out of the woods carrying a cat. I had just finished killing Alex. My mind was already racing toward payback with my father. The cat Michael carried was a five year old shifter. She was the child of two shifters I had killed that day. We couldn't leave a witness, so it was decided she would come with us.

After we returned to camp and before I left to take revenge upon my father, Alice asked me to blood the girl. By giving her my blood, she would be under my power. I would know where she was and be able to influence her. At least that was the plan; it didn't happen exactly like anyone would have thought. I died, but my blood never did. The blood lived within Alice and the shifter. Alice had not known that I was alive until my rebirth, so she took it upon herself to raise the child.

Luckily for the shifter, Alice lost interest; Ezra did not. After the death of Charlotte, Ezra was down in the dumps. He took on the job of raising the Shifter and gave her the name Spooky White. They were close.

By the time I came back, Spooky was eleven years old and powerful. She could take the shape of any cat, a big tiger or a small house cat. She was a fifth generation shifter. That alone made her strong. With my blood, she was "Something else entirely," according to Ezra.

Strong and loyal to Ezra, she had known how I had killed her father, mother and uncle and some cousins as well. Ok, I killed her whole family, but they were not my target. I tried to make excuses, but deep down I felt awful. Worst of all she knew this, yet she still hated me. She hates me and loves me. The blood in her makes her seek me out, feel what I feel.

I know deep down, she wishes me dead. I killed her family and enslaved her, and the last thing I wanted right now was her to see me. She knew this, so she came. She wanted to laugh at me, but was forced to care. We stared at each other through the window, in love and hate, linked to one another, another reminder of who and what I was.

My hearing was still amazing. My second sight had never left me. I could hear the sound and see the world as if I had radar. I could hear my mother talking to my father, "I am taking her to the doctor."

My father's voice, full of worry, "I don't know… I'm not sure that's such a good idea. What are you going to say?"

On the edge of tears my sister said, "I don't know… maybe I can get them to run some blood work. That way we know if she is sick or something."

"I don't know, sweetheart," My father started to say.

He was interrupted as my sister hissed, "What would you have me do?"

My father sounded defeated, "Just don't mention vampires."

"I'm not stupid, John," and with that they went quiet.

Mindy was heading toward my room. I knew the sound of her footfall against the carpet. I got up and wiped the tears off my face. As she came in., the look on her face was surprisingly soft. With a gentle voice, she reminded me, "Time to go to bed, sweetie. We have a big day tomorrow. We are going to go see Dr. Cummings. That will be fun; you like Dr. Cummings."

I shook my head and said, "Yes, I like Dr. Cummings." Then I crawled into my bed while my mother tucked me in.

She kissed my temple, "Goodnight, sweetheart. Don't worry… everything is going to be ok."

I answered with a weak voice, "Ok."

"Goodnight," she said as she crossed the room and shut off the light. She closed the door behind her and left me alone again with my thoughts.

I thought about going to the library to see Nicks, but I was too ashamed of my actions. Alice would not come tonight; I knew this, but I didn't know why. She had been coming less and less, hiding more and more from me. Spooky had been delivering my blood for me of late.

I got up, went over and open the window for Spooky so she could come in. She was a large gray house cat, and she had one bag of blood strapped to her belly. It was all nice and warm. She hated delivering my blood, but tonight I'm more grateful than usual. The stress made me irritable, and the blood helped calm me down.

She hopped up into my bed. I sat up and unstrapped the blood. As I drank, Spooky turned into a pretty young lady. She was fifteen, with dark skin and long black hair. She stood five eleven with legs that made me think, supermodel. I missed being a woman. She was nude, so she wrapped herself in a blanket as she sat upon the edge of my bed. The look she gave me said it all, disapproving.

She decided that she couldn't wait for me to finish feeding before telling me off. "Your parents deserve so much more than a little monster like you. Don't you understand what kind of stress your shit does to them?"

I ignored her. She had been playing the role of Ezra's adopted daughter. Ezra, my father's boss, just happened to live right down the street. He had two daughters, Alice and Sierra, aka Spooky. Some female vampire named Lily, played his wife. She was an older-looking vampire. She looked to be in her thirties like Ezra. Spooky had quickly become my babysitter; in short, she had become very close to my father and mother. I understood why she was upset, but, at the same time, I wished she would mind her own business.

After a few more minutes, Spooky added, "So, what's the new plan, genius?"

I licked my lips, savoring the last of the blood. "Go away Spooky. This is my problem and my family."

She gave me a dirty look, "You are so selfish." With that, she tossed off the blanket and turned into a gray cat. I was a little surprised. She normally could tell me off for hours.

Chapter 2 Dr. Cummings

The next morning Mindy woke me from my restless sleep. Father had already left for work. After breakfast we jumped into the car and were off to see my doctor. We had barely left the house when Mindy started with me, "Your father is so upset. I have never seen him this upset. Maybe the doctor can help. Can I count on you? I need you to help me today, Molly."

"Do what I can," I answered. What did she expect from me? I would do nothing to help her and she knew it.

Mindy was tense as we sat out in the waiting room. She about jumped out of her seat when they called our name. We were directed into a small room and asked to wait. The girl informed us that the nurse would be with us in a second.

With my hearing I could hear the nurse speaking outside the door. I could hear one saying, "She's here, Mrs. Brooks. I can't wait to hear about what's wrong with Molly this time."

Another nurse commented, "I have never met someone *so* sick look *so* healthy at the same time."

Another voice snickered, "I'll take care of it."

I chuckled and Mindy asked, "What's so funny?"

"The nurses," I didn't explain further, and Mindy just huffed at me.

The nurse came in and went through the normal line of questions. Of course, my sister's reasons for being here didn't make much sense. The nurse stayed professional, but I could tell she was struggling. The nurse finished and said on her way out, "Dr. Cummings will be with you in a minute." Once again, I sat in silence with Mindy.

I could overhear the conversation that the nurse was having with the doctor. The nurse was telling Dr. Cummings, "I have no idea what she thinks is wrong with her daughter. She seems to be pushing for a blood test, but real evasive about why, or what may be wrong with Molly. Of course, it's usually nonsense, like how advanced she is for her age."

The doctor said with extreme sarcasm, "Has Mindy hinted at what kind of blood work she might need?"

The nurse laughed, "I should have asked her. I bet she would know what's wrong."

With that, I could hear the light footsteps of the doctor heading our way. Dr. Cummings came in. She has been my pediatrician since birth. She is an avid runner and keeps her blonde hair in a ponytail. With blue eyes and a bright smile, she is always very happy to see me. It was hard to ignore that kind of enthusiasm, and I always looked forward to my doctor appointments.

The doctor smiled at me as she asked me, "How are we doing today?"

I couldn't help but smile as I replied, "Good." This response, with my open excitement, that won me a dirty look from my mother. I guess I was supposed to play sick, but I hadn't been sick a day in my life.

The doctor then turned to Mindy and asked, "So Mrs. Brooks, what seems to be the problem?"

Mindy was having a hard time explaining, "Well, I think that Molly might need some blood work. She has been acting a little strange, and I don't think she's feeling right."

Dr. Cummings followed up, "Not feeling well, poor thing. So, Molly has been showing signs of sickness; what kind of symptoms?"

Mindy answered with, "She hasn't complained, but she has been showing some signs of physical abnormalities."

The doctor asked, "Can you see them when you look at her?"

Unable to make eye contact, Mindy was almost mumbling, "Well, it's more about how she acts... like too physically strong. She's agile and capable of more than a five year old should be. "

To the credit of my doctor, she showed no signs of emotion on her face. If it wasn't for the fact I could hear the change in her heartbeat and the fact that she blinked a few times more a second, I would have thought she hadn't even heard Mindy speak. Dr. Cummings let a few extra seconds go by before asking, "There are a lot of choices when it comes to blood work. Can you elaborate on what has been happening?"

Mindy, "It's hard to explain; let me see..."

The doctor tried to help her clarify, "Is this a daytime problem, night time or both?"

"Both... maybe night," Mindy looked strained as she searched for a logical answer.

The doctor questioned, "What's the problem at night?"

Mindy explained, "Well, I hear her up at all hours, sometimes running throughout the house, but, when I get up to check on her, she is always back in her bed. She's really fast, and I don't know how to keep her in bed."

Once again the doctor surprised me, for the only physical sign of change was a few more blinks. How she held a straight face was amazing, what good bedside manners. She asked the next question as if my sister wasn't acting like a nut, "And what is the problem during the day?"

Mindy was nervous; she knew how crazy this sounded. She was trying to get the doctor to test me, but didn't know how to fake some strange disease. She went on trying to sound sure of herself, "She shows signs of being, well, physically gifted. She is strong… I mean stronger than me. She also moves, well, it's hard to explain, but I worry that something is wrong. She also hears everything… I just want to make sure her blood looks human… I mean normal."

Dr. Cummings didn't blink. But I do believe her eyes widened, but other than that she was perfectly professional. The doctor's tone changed just a little, "Mrs. Brooks, some children don't need as much sleep. It can be exhausting for parents. I wish I could bottle the energy your little girl has, but it is important to have a soothing bedtime routine and avoid caffeine."

Defeat filled Mindy's voice as she gave it one more try, "What about the daytime?"

Dr. Cummings held fast to her demeanor, "I do remember Molly's early crawling and walking. It sure does sound like she's physically gifted from what you have said. This would be a great age to sign her up for martial arts class, or gymnastics."

Mindy sounded even more defeated, "So, you don't think she needs any test?"

Dr. Cummings replied, "Well, let's give her a good look over."

Dr. Cummings started her examination of me. She did all the standard things, check my eyes, throat and ears. She had just finished listening to my heart when she said, "How have you been feeling?"

I knew Mindy would be mad, but what choice did I really have? Alice wouldn't let the blood test be checked, and even if they were to check it, it would only cause problems for my sister, "Fine."

The doctor turned when Mindy asked, "Does everything look good?"

The doctor replied, "She looks very healthy from my exam. There really is no lab work for the questions you are asking. You are asking good questions, and I know you are doing your best to take care of your kids. Now if you see Molly running a fever, not eating, or losing that boundless energy, make sure you give us a call back."

The doctor had given her an idea, Mindy quickly added. "She really doesn't eat, but last time you told me not to worry if she is still gaining weight."

Dr. Cummings smiled and, with a very reassuring voice said, "Well, some kids seem like they don't eat. Or eat so little you would think it wouldn't be enough to keep a bird alive, but she has gained 4 pounds and grown 2 inches in the last year. You are doing a good job… do you have any more questions?"

"Thank you, Dr. Cummings," Mindy looked like she might cry.

"Bye," I said with a wave.

The doctor gave me a big smile, "Have a good day, and Molly it was good to see you."

After the door shut, Mindy gave me a dirty look, "You are not going to martial arts."

The ride home was quiet. The strangest thing was my birthday. No guest, just family, cake and a few gifts. My grandfather was the most lively of everyone, acting as if this was a six year old's birthday. Mindy and dad couldn't even fake it, I was glad when the party ended. The next few days were filled with much of the same silence as we all fell into life's routines.

Chapter 3 Nicks

My father and Mindy were indifferent to me. At night they barely spoke with one another. Grandfather hadn't come by the house in three days, which was weird, but then he called. He reminded me over the phone he had a convention out of state, and it had been on the calendar for over a month. As soon as he said it, I remembered, but it did little to take away the uneasy feeling growing in the back of my mind.

It was the fourth night after I had broken that man's knee, and, for the fourth night, my father had not come to tuck me in. I waited and waited for my father or Mindy to come say good night. I waited for Spooky, or better yet Alice, but no one came. It was after midnight that I fell into a restless sleep. Worse yet, the hunger for blood was filling my dreams.

When I opened my eyes, I knew instantly that I was in the library. I had been putting off talking to Nicks. In the last six years I had been spending a lot of time at the library. When I traveled to the land of the dead, I left my body sound asleep. I was more like a spirit now. I could look how I wanted to look. Of course I choose my adult form; who wants to run around as a child, especially if they have a choice?

I found spirits who were not afraid of me. I really enjoyed talking to all the different spirits; you never knew what you might learn. As these thoughts crossed my mind, I couldn't help but think how they brought no solace to my present situation.

Nicks was in his seat before a giant fireplace. The fire crackled, and large flames jumped upward. Around him there were hundreds of books, lying on tables and lining the walls. He sat with a large book in his lap while he wrote in it with a quill. He looked up and smiled, as he put his book away. He got up with grace and embraced me. "Sit, it's been too long. I have much to counsel you on."

Nicks sat, and I sat in a chair across from Nicks, "I have screwed up royally. I broke a man's knee right in front of my father. If only Mindy would have seen it, at least I could be driving her crazier than I already have. Now my father looks at me… with those eyes."

Nicks inquired, "Does anyone know about it? Other than your family, that is."

"Yes, the police, but that doesn't matter; they didn't press any charges." The look on Nicks face went dark. He wasn't mad, but worried, so I quickly added. "I don't think anyone will pursue it."

"This is not good. It's not your fault; you couldn't have known. I am afraid we might need to act sooner than later."

"*We*," Frustration shot through my whole body. I knew Alice was up to stuff that she didn't want my involvement in, but now I found that Nicks had been planning, too. I felt so left out. I tried to hide my irritation, "What's going on? And how does this change anything? Great, now I sound like Carrie."

Nicks' voice was calm and gentle, "You know Carrie went to a better place?"

"I know… I just miss her and wish she would have stayed here in the library."

Nicks explained what I already knew, "Only spirits with fear stay here. Spirits, who are ready to go, do. Carrie was ready. The only thing that ever held her on this plain was magical items such as that necklace. You know this. We have other things we must discuss."

"All ears," and took comfort in a big chair.

Nicks nodded and explained further, "I know. While you were missing, I got a little sidetracked. I stopped paying attention. A dark and powerful Necromancer rose up in the ranks empowering the other necromancers. It wasn't long after your birth that a war broke out. The man who leads the Necromancers calls himself Necro-Z, and he plans on ruling the world. He has made powerful allies, such as werewolves, ghosts, and vampires. The only thing that stands in his way is the Council of Twelve and The Order. In light of The Orders situation, they have joined forces and now go by the Council, or the Council of Twelve. The Order was in no condition to take on this new threat… someone had severely weakened them."

"Oops, my bad," I said offhand.

Nicks shook his head, "As I was saying, Necro-Z is trying to destroy The Council. At first The Council didn't take his attacks seriously, not until they saw his new weapons. Ghosts that attack and kill the living, corpses that will remain animated even after the casters were killed. This has been among some of his new resources. There are very few spells to defend against a spirit. The necromancers themselves seem to be twice as powerful.

No one knows why, but I have some ideas. I believe that they have found the *Book of the Dead* - a powerful magical book that The Council of Twelve was guarding."

I added, "I remember that book. That is the book Alice and I tried to get it back to the Council... and I met the lovely vampire, Peter." I did a full body shudder. "You remember the one you put a love spell on, and he became my personal stalker."

Nicks chuckled at the memory, "Yes, if I recall, you had to jump out of a plane to get away from him."

Nicks was laughing at me, "Oh yuck it up. I don't remember it being that funny." I said this, but I was laughing too. It is always strange how situations that were not funny, become funnier with time. "What does this have to with me?"

Nicks had a thoughtful look as he pondered my question. "Not sure, not sure what it has to do with you and how much I should tell you. And before you ask, the only reason I don't want to tell you is because a lot of what I think is nothing more than guesswork. I would rather not concern yourself with theories, but more solid information. This is what we do know. First, Alex was better known as Richard Alexander Longaeva the son of Luna Longaeva."

"You mean Luna the head of The Council of Twelve? Sounds like I have made some new friends."

Nicks nodded, "Yes, she is indeed the head of The Council, and she knows you killed her son. The fact you killed him put a price on your head, but then you burned to death shortly afterwards. They sent witches to ensure you died in that fire. I think it is best for all involved that you stay dead. The second thing we know for a fact is that The Council lost the book, *Necronomicon*."

"*Necronomicon*?"

"Yes, simply it was better known as the *Book of the Dead* and filled with black magic. It was written by a man who, in his own way, believed he was doing good. The Red Adder wrote the book. He was a powerful man who, among many things, practiced death magic. It is believed that the book is the reason for World War One and Two. To say that the book was the sole reason would be... well incorrect, but it was a weapon sought after and fought for by both sides. After World War Two, the book fell into the care of

The Council, the reason The Council was formed. The original twelve wizards started The Council to protect the book.

"One of the founding wizards, who happened to reside in the United States, hired you and Alice to steal the book. He didn't ask you just to steal it, but to steal it from one of the high ranking wizards of The Council itself. Luna's and her son Richard control The Council of twelve."

That brought back memories, "Are you talking about Dan?"

"Yes," Nicks replied.

"I remember him. I only met him once in a hotel room for a minute. It was right after we had gotten back from stealing the magic book from Alex. I remember him because he was pissed when he found out we botched the job. Come to find out we had brought back a fake, a copy of the Bible. I don't understand Alice sometimes. How can she work for Dan? And why did Dan have to hire vampires to steal something that The Council is entrusted to guard?"

Nicks corrected me, "You are asking the wrong questions. What did Alex want with the book? How long had he had it? And how did he get it? Why hadn't The Council known it had been stolen? The biggest question of them all, where is it now? When you killed Alex, he did not have it on him. As for Alice trusting Dan, well, they go way back. In fact, they were married long ago."

"WHAT? Alice, married... to Dan, seriously."

Nicks laughed, "Yes, she was. I don't know the whole story... they were married sometime in the seventeen hundreds I think. Back to the matter at hand, I don't think Dan knew just how deranged Alex really was. Dan dare not go against another Council member, so he hired Alice. He was trying to keep the book out of the wrong hands, but I am afraid he has failed in that mission. To share one theory, the leader of the Dark Covent, Necro-Z, has the book. That is the most likely reason for the increased power of the necromancers."

I let out a puff of air, "I see. Everyone is looking really hard at Alice because she was implicated in the attack of the Atlantic Sun. She is also my only friend and everyone knows that she was involved with me, and now being watched, because I killed Alex. Even if they don't know if she was there, she knew me. To top it all off, she has taken in my sister who was the last one to see me alive. With the war going on and everyone looking for the book, some might think Alice has it. When I hit that guy, I just let a lot of people know that I am supernatural. I am putting my whole family in danger."

Nicks gave me a funny look, "I hadn't really thought about it quite like that, but you have some valid points. I do believe that we will need to be extra careful, for we do not know who might be watching. I believe it's time to begin your training, for you are the daughter of death, and that means that there will be requirements of you in the future, and you will need to be prepared.

"Seriously?" I gave Nicks the full eye roll with the head swing. "What is that?"

Nicks was not bothered by my attitude, "Do you remember Bow?"

I did remember her. I had met her some time ago. She was something special to Nicks, but I had not ever figured out what. She played the violin, and it was amazing. Nicks could have kept her around just for that, but I had a feeling there was more to it. Even though I was curious about her, I had the feeling I would regret it.

Bow floated in gracefully. She was a tall, slender girl in her late twenties. Her face was sharp and angular, but that did nothing to take away from her natural beauty. I couldn't tell how long her dark brown hair was, for she always kept it pinned up tight upon her head. Everything about this ghost was serious. She always dressed as if it were still the late eighteenth century. The only thing I knew about her was that she owed Nicks and It had something to do with her murdering her husband. I had tried to get more information, but she was a closed book.

"It is good to see you again," Bow said with a slight head nod.

"Good to see you, I think. What is it that I must learn?" I asked bluntly.

Nicks spoke, "How to be a reaper… you must learn how to harvest the spirits. They are stuck in the world and need help to find their rest. Some just need guides, some will need a push. Yet others you will need to destroy the rest of their spiritual energy to send their souls to the land of the dead. In that you will need weapons, spirit weapons. The bow will be your weapon, and she will teach you how to use the power that you have yet to unlock."

I moaned, "Well, that sounds like fun."

Nicks gave me a big hug, "Well, I won't keep you from your fun. Listen to Bow; she will help you achieve the greatness within you."

I smiled over the top, "Thanks."

Nicks had started to walk away. He stopped and turned around, "One more thing… about your family."

"Yes, what is it?"

"Maybe, honesty? That might help." Nicks turned around and left me with Bow. I wasn't entirely sure what he even meant by that. Did he expect me to come clean? The thought made me do a full body shudder.

Things got strange after Nicks left. Bow gave me a violin and a bow and asked me to play. I told her I had no idea how. That is when she commanded, "That is what I am here for, to teach you. You must learn to play. You must learn to work with me, to use my skills as if they were to be your own."

I had no idea how learning to play a violin would help me, but I didn't really mind. I had always wanted to learn. We worked together for a few hours before my time was up. I wished her well; she informed me that I would need a lesson every night. There was something strange about the lessons and the fact that Nicks wanted me to learn this. I could ask, but right now I really didn't care.

Chapter 4 Late Night Visitors

I was awake, lying in my bed, after returning from the library. I looked over at my clock, 11:48pm. I hadn't been away long, but I woke up hungry. I needed blood and had hoped that Spooky would have already delivered.

I saw the cat jump to my window from outside. "It's about time." That's when I noticed that the cat was not carrying any blood. I felt, Alice's arrival. Alice tried to block me, but I always knew when she was near.

She came into the house and came straight to my room. Alice never worried about waking anyone. Even if they did get up and wander out of their room to see what it was, Alice would control their minds and they would see what she wanted them to. Alice was so used to manipulating people it was second nature. I had just opened the window and let Spooky in when Alice came through my door.

She was dressed in a baby blue dress full of ruffles. She looked like a doll, and, to top it all off, she even had a blue umbrella. I realized as she came closer that she had a little blue top hat hanging on one side of her head. I asked, "Why dressed up?"

Alice embraced me, "We're going out. Get dressed. Spooky will make herself useful for once. She can fill your bed just in case your parents check on you."

"Why are we going out?"

Alice pouted pushing her bottom lip up, "You have become a real child. Get it, because you know... you're a child."

I moaned, "Yeah, I get it."

"*Anyway*, you need to get out and hunt. I can feel your emotions and, well, they're telling me you need to party. Get dressed and hurry up. We have people to kill and meet. Or vise versa, we can meet them and then kill them. I guess it doesn't really matter."

Spooky took her human form and crawled into my bed. I knew how she felt about Alice. Alice scared her; she was careful when speaking to her. Spooky simply said to both of us, "Have fun."

It only took a second before Alice tore up my closet, finally settling on an outfit. It was a red blouse with a black skirt. Alice complained, "Your sister doesn't know how to buy clothes. Oh well, I will be making you look older tonight, so I guess it doesn't matter how you dress. I will make you beautiful."

"Great, then I can wear jeans!"

Alice looked at me with daggers in her eyes, "Don't be ridiculous. Hurry up and put on the outfit I picked out for you. We have a long way to go and lots to talk about."

I knew better than to ask; she wasn't going to tell me where we were going. It wasn't long before I was chasing after Alice through the woods. My little legs had a hard time trying to keep up with her. We traveled and moved with amazing speed. Coming upon a clearing, Alice had come to a stop. I came to rest standing next to her, looking over the field in the same direction she was. Across the wide field, there was a small farm house with one large oak tree growing beside it. Around the house sat an assortment of barns and sheds. There were old cars and tractors rusting outside of the buildings... stuff everywhere.

"Where are we?" I asked.

Alice grinned, "Food. Three men… our favorite, two for me and one for you. These three I've been tracking for a while."

My powers had been changing, something I tried my hardest not to think about. I wanted to be normal and free of the supernatural world, but that was just a dream. I had come to notice that I was able to see… for lack of a better word, souls. You could call them auras if you wanted to. When I looked at someone I could see them radiating outward. It was very similar to a ghost, only with a solid center. Vampire auras were different; instead of radiating around the vampire, it appeared to be trapped within. I could feel auras, be it a ghost, or the living. I could see there was only one aura at this house. I told Alice, "They're not here. I believe there's a ghost home, but the house is empty."

Alice gave me a strange look, "New tricks. You know I like to know everything about my favorite reborn vampire girl. I know they're not home, but they will be soon. Let's go make ourselves comfortable."

We moved quickly and entered the old house through the back door. Once inside, Alice made herself at home on the couch. I could feel the spirit more clearly now that we were inside. The ghost was a mean one, full of malice. I whispered, "I'll be right back."

I went up the staircase and followed my senses down the hall to the last room on the right. I could feel a strange hunger come over me. I was human, a vampire and a reaper. I fed on food, the living and now even the dead. Alice and Ezra even seemed like food, but I hadn't told them that. I walked into the room.

It was very dusty, and the room seemed unused. It wasn't a very big room and piled full of boxes and junk. There might have been a bed, but I couldn't tell under all the stuff. Against the other wall was a dresser, then a rocking chair which was sitting in front of the only window. In the rocking chair was the ghost. She was an elderly woman who looked as mean as she felt.

The old lady had gray hair that hung around her face as if she had been sweating. She was looking at me with hatred in her eyes. She mumbled to herself, "Not mine, not my child. Where are my boys? My boys are good boys. It's those whores who cause all the problems, not my boys. Who is this little brat... and why is she in my house."

I moved into the room and toward the ghost. She quit speaking; instead she settled for staring at me with a mix of confusion and hatred. I stopped walking just a few steps in front of her and, looking over my shoulder, I noticed that a mirror hung on the wall over the dresser. In the mirror there stood a small girl with a pretty red dress. Over the years I had learned from Nicks how to control some of my powers. I found that I could make the ghosts solid, so they couldn't travel through the walls. Ghosts are bound to objects, such as this house. Even so, they are hard to catch if they can fly through solid objects and you cannot. I could hurt them when their bodies had substance. Nicks had explained that what was really happening was that I drained them of their life energy. No matter what the reasons, I could destroy them.

I let my power out. It was like a caged animal. My teeth elongated, and my fingers grew longer with long black nails. My eyes now glowed with an eerie light. Ezra couldn't stand it when my eyes lit up; it freaked him out. I was still looking in the mirror as my image changed into some kind of little monster. It looked as if someone was shining a flashlight through the back of my eyes. My eyes were blue and big... I could see what Ezra was talking about; it was unsettling. My eyes only glowed when I reached for this strange power, the power to devour the dead.

The ghost was now aware she was in trouble. She screeched at me, "Go away devil... leave me with my boys."

I bluntly informed her, "Your boys will be joining you shortly." Without another word, I attacked.

She was not a strong spirit; I ripped her apart. Like all ghosts she didn't bleed. Instead, she fell apart into black dust, which floated a few feet up towards the ceiling and then disappeared. It felt good, like a light snack, but I was still hungry. I went back downstairs to join Alice and wait for the main course.

Alice smiled at me, "I love your eyes... they're so pretty." Her eyes began to glow just like mine. The difference was that she was just making me see it. Being around Alice, I became used to seeing things that were not really happening. Only my second sight would see around her mind games.

I pulled the power back into me. Alice gave me a pouty lip. I laughed, "Oh, stop. It feels uncomfortable to let the power out for too long."

"Maybe you need to practice. I have to say, it's creepy, but I like it."

I quipped, "You wouldn't like it if I told you when my eyes glow you seem like food. I can feel your power and life."

Alice giggled, "I like the pretty eyes."

I dropped down onto the couch next to her. When she acted like this, there was nothing anyone could do but go along with it. She asked, "So, is this house off the Haunted Tour?" I simply nodded my head. Alice's voice went serious, which it seldom did. "Tell me what's wrong."

I was harsh, "Don't play stupid. You know Alice... you know."

Alice was quiet for a few minutes before she spoke again. "You're right; I know. I know, because unfortunately, I can feel your emotions. I know because I live down the street, I get hourly updates from Spooky. And you want to know what else I know?"

"Not really," I grumbled.

"I'll tell you anyway. Your problem is you're afraid."

I gave her my best death stare, but it didn't scare her at all. "Afraid? Afraid of what?"

Alice was animated as she told me, "Afraid of losing what you love. You are afraid of losing your parents again. You had everything taken away from you and you're afraid it will happen again. You have so much more; you have Nicks and Ezra, too. You need to stop being a coward."

I was angry, "What *do you* know about it?"

"What do I know about it?" Alice stared at me like I was crazy. "I'll tell you. My power... it's a curse. I use it to manipulate everyone; even those whom I wish to have a real relationship with. Then you come along, the first time, in a long time, and you could see around my power. That alone was one thing, but then… well… you cared. You cared for me when you didn't have to, when you shouldn't have. Then we bonded by blood, your blood, and we became true sisters. The only person who has cared about me for over a *hundred years*… dies, you died. How could you leave me?"

Alice turned her head away. I was stunned into silence, for, in her emotional outburst, I watched a tear slide down her cheek. I froze. I had never really thought about how Alice felt about anything. "Sorry, I didn't mean to leave you. I didn't choose to die."

Alice's face went from upset to serious. She wiped her tear away, "You didn't? That's what you say. I say you did; it was your choices that lead you to your death. I blame you." She crossed her arms and huffed really loudly.

"Ok, my fault. Sorry… again, now what? Since I don't want to die… again, what should I do? Oh, wise one."

"Be brave, not such a coward."

That upset me, "I'm no coward."

"I am not talking about your willingness to throw yourself headlong into battle. You are one of those rare souls who react to intense situations with action. Or it could be your compulsive OCD personality when it comes to doing whatever you deem needs to be done. I am talking about your fear of loss. All your life things have been taken from you… so it is of no wonder why you fear it. Still, it rules over you. I know why you fear loss, but others fear losing you. I fear losing you."

I was shocked and quietly and try to reassure her, "Well, I don't plan on getting into fights. I'm done with revenge."

Alice laughed, "Wake up, sweetheart. Your fighting days are about to begin, not end. Nicks is starting your training because he knows something is coming. There is talk of the end of the world and The Council is at war with the Necro Z. There's more we haven't told you. The Council was out to capture you before you killed Alex. I hadn't known it, but afterwards, after you were killed, I found out.

"After your death, they sent witches to insure your death. They went to the place where you burned, and they knew you died there. I was crushed; I had hoped that you had survived. They still watch your sister and your family. That is why Ezra hired your father and brought your family to this neighborhood. It's Ezra and my attempt to keep an eye on you and make sure that The Council doesn't learn who you really are.

"I feel it in my bones. I know it's coming. War, death - we will have it all. You may lose me; you may watch your new family die. Learn to live in the moment without fearing the future. Learn to enjoy every day. Stop trying to have a life that wasn't meant for you. I know I am being hard on you, and you have lots to lose, but I only have you. I will see you fight, and together we will kill. We will become what justice should be cold, and never bending. We might even die."

I shook my head, "Who are you and what did you do with Alice?"

She stuck her tongue out, "Pain in the ass. This is why I don't get serious."

I laughed, "Oh, is that why?" She smiled a wicked grin. I said, "Ok, I know you're right. I'm not deaf, and I heard over the last few years what has been going on. Nicks even brought it up and wanted me to train with Bow, but she just started to teach me how to play the violin." Alice's gave me a confused look, I had forgotten she didn't know who Bow was. "Never mind that, the important part is that I stopped trying to be human. I need to prepare myself… for whatever might be coming."

This made Alice happy, "It's about time. You need to be honest with your family. Let them choose to be with you or without you, but you can no longer keep them in the dark."

That reminded me of what Nicks had said. I whispered, "Honesty."

Alice asked, "What did you say?"

I spoke louder, "Nicks said I should be honest with my family. You basically told me the same thing. You're right; I'm a coward. I am afraid they will reject me when they learn that I am not their child. Worse, when they realize that I have stolen their child… how cruel am I?"

Alice leaned in and said with a wicked tone, "Not as cruel as me."

"I said I was cruel, not sadistic."

That made Alice laugh, she stopped laughing to say, "Dinner's here." I could hear the truck pulling up the driveway. We would eat soon.

I looked over at Alice as she sat with that look, the look of wickedness. She was not just going to kill these men; she was going to torture them. If I were honest, *we* were going to torture them. She was evil, or had evil in her. Why did I love her so? Why did I trust her? Until this very night I had no idea why she treated me differently. I was honored that she cared so deeply for me, but did I feel the same? I did; I just couldn't figure out why. I guess that is what love is, caring for someone without having a list of reasons why - trusting that person, when they give you no reason to.

Love made me feel naked, but, on the other hand, there was emptiness in hate. It was the same emptiness that threatened to swallow my soul... the hatred that I used to drive everyone away. The hatred that filled David's eyes until it destroyed us. At this moment I realized how much it mattered that someone cared that I died. I will find courage, courage to love. I must not fear loss... I took a deep breath.

Alice asked, "Don't over think everything. You will have a brain hemorrhage. For now, enjoy the moment."

I cleared my head and remembered how hungry I was. I asked, "What's the plan?"

"When they come in, they will see us as children they murdered. You will be playing the part of a small boy... it's ok to put your own spin on the character. Just remember to have fun with it."

I laughed, "Oh yeah, I can't wait. This was always the best part of being a vampire. Thanks Alice; I missed this and what you said..."

"Shut it," Alice took her hand and put it in front of my face. She used her hand mimicking a mouth opening and closing as she said, "This is what you are doing." Her hand closed tight, "And this is what you should be doing."

Alice was done being serious. I had learned long ago that once that ship sailed there was no point talking to her with any real meaning, but she gave me a quick wink, and I knew she understood my appreciation of her.

The men came into the front door, flipping on the light. They looked like regular guys. All three of them were middle aged with beards. They all had brown hair with speckles of white in them; they were brothers. One of them was overweight, while the other two looked pretty lean.

What surprised me was the boy that followed them in. He looked to be about eleven or twelve with black hair and olive skin. I was doubly surprised when a girl followed him in. She was similar in appearance - they could be related. She looked to be older, maybe thirteen or fourteen. The strange thing was that these two kids walked into a home without two very gifted vampires knowing about it.

Alice was now standing and alert. The men moved into the living room where we sat. I was sure that they couldn't see anything but what Alice wanted them to. I was sure until I saw Alice's face. I had never seen a look on her face like that. She looked frustrated and, at the same time, she appeared to be concentrating really hard. Alice whispered, "Damn, a trap."

Chapter 5 A Quick Bite

Alice's worry freaked me out, for whatever spooked Alice shook me to the core.

 The men entered the room in a V pattern with the big man ahead of the other two. The children stood near the front door where they came in with their backs against the wall. They appeared to be scared out of their minds. At that same moment I noticed something else about the boy, his eyes. They were purple - an *electric* purple.

I hadn't noticed until then that all the men were wearing the same jacket, long and black that hung past their hips. They pulled weapons out of them. The men all held hatchets, the men in the rear held a cross in the other hand. The man in front pulled out a red crystal. They were wizards and, worst of all, they were prepared.

I had felt the power of the priest's crosses before. The power of the crosses felt like I was being burned to death, even though it was all in my mind. Ezra had told me that the more powerful the vampire, the more skilled the magic user must be to affect them with the cross. He had told me that Alice hadn't felt the effect of one of those weapons for over a hundred years. With all of Alice's mind powers, it was impossible to concentrate the power upon her.

The purple-eyed boy stared at Alice. She fell on the ground and lay as still as a corpse. The boy looked away from her, and she started to move, slowly coming to her senses. The men all aimed their crosses at her, and she flopped around on the floor screaming in pain.

Rage rose up in me. I had been sitting; now I was standing on the couch. I felt my sharp teeth and my fingers becoming claws. The men had been looking at Alice when they walked into the room. There was no such thing as a child vampire since you have to go through puberty to be changed. They had dismissed me when they entered the room, and, at this very moment, they concentrated on the known threat, Alice.

Since I was a child, I did not have all my vampire powers. I could not fly, nor could I flash. Sunlight did not really affect me anymore. I had a heartbeat, but did not know if being struck in the heart might kill me. I was not as strong or fast, but Alice had found that I no longer needed to be invited in. That same power that protects homes is used in the crosses; Ezra had believed the crosses would not affect me. I was about to find out.

I attacked.

I jumped through the air straight at the man in front of me. I grabbed his outstretched arm that was holding the cross. I pulled on his arm and propelled myself right at him; with one quick slash my claws found their target. Blood poured from his throat as I flew over his shoulder immediately spinning into a flip so that I would land on my feet. As my feet softly touched the ground, I could hear and see in my second sight the man falling to the ground behind me. He grasped his throat, trying to stop the blood.

During the next few seconds I would have liked someone to have videoed the event. I fought two men wielding weapons. My size made it hard for me to strike them, but it also it made it hard for them to strike me. At one point I rolled between one of the men's legs, then I kicked his knee causing him to fall forward. His friend who was in mid-motion trying to cleave me with his hatchet took a nice chunk out of his buddy's shoulder.

The man screeched, "What the hell?"

"Sorry," the man said in a short gasp.

His friend, who was holding his shoulder, stood and yelled out, "Kill her."

With a hatchet in one hand, he still held the red crystal in the other. This time, instead of using the hatchet, he held out the hand with the crystal and said, "Pyro." The crystal burst into flames. I knew what was coming next as a line of fire jetted out of his hand toward me.

I did exactly the opposite that most would do in this situation. Most vampires, and people for that matter, would dive away from the flames. Not me, I dove towards the flames. I had been burned before; as long as I didn't stay in the fire too long, it would only burn my skin; I healed fast. Diving through the flames I rolled headfirst across the floor. I came out under his arm and now the stream of flames was behind me. He couldn't shoot the flames at me without hitting himself, so he swung down with his hatchet. I came to my feet, and, with one hand, caught his swing by grabbing his wrist. My free hand, full of sharp claws, found his balls.

I pulled down; blood came out as I tried to rip his balls off. He screamed and jumped back; as he did, his flaming hand dropped down to his crotch, as a reaction to me trying to rip his dick off. I realized his mistake before he did and jumped back and rolled backwards across the floor as the man lit himself on fire.

His friend yelled, "Aqua." Mist formed around his hand, then water shot forth putting his friend out. He had been too late because his friend lay on the ground screaming in pain and covered in burns.

The man, whose throat, I cut, was now standing up. His throat was full of scars, but he had somehow managed to heal himself. He pulled out a gun, "Let's kill this one." He said this to his friend who had already begun to work his way over to me.

I laughed and this gave the men pause. "You guys forgot something." In the fight the whole room had been turned around. I now stood between the two men and the children who were pinned against the far wall. The kids were scared shitless. The boy was hiding his face in the girl's chest. The two men now had their back to Alice and she was no longer under the power of their crosses.

I watched as both men tried to spin around, realizing their mistake... their last mistake. He yelled at the boy, "Use your power."

The boy was frozen in fear as Alice ripped them to pieces with blinding speed. She sliced and diced them a thousand times... she was mad. It was moments later, and the whole room looked as if a red paint can had exploded.

Alice was covered in blood; her face was full of rage. I had never seen her look so animalistic before. Her voice sounded as if she growled out the words, "Kill those two." She pointed a bloody finger at the children. She grabbed the burned man and picked him off the ground as if he weighed nothing. Then she began to feed.

I turned to the children; they huddled together, holding each other tight. I could feel their fear and smell their blood and sweat. I looked at their faces and something stirred in me. I felt... love, no, maybe. I couldn't say how I felt, but I knew in a second that I wouldn't allow anyone to hurt these children. They were just coming of age, and, judging from their fear, they hadn't wanted to come here. Alice would calm down; these two will not die tonight. Plus, I don't kill children... strangely, neither does Alice. She was normally killing those who would hurt the children.

Alice tossed the dead man, down; wait, she left me nothing. I was so hungry, damn! She looked at me with her big blue eyes, "What's the hold up? Kill those two."

The kids stood behind me and Alice in front of me. I stepped back firmly putting myself between Alice and the kids. The girl squeaked, "Please, don't."

I stared at Alice; she looked mad. Then her face changed, almost understanding, almost. Her voice was full of venom, "What's wrong, Melabeth? He is not a child… he is a demon."

"I don't care; I'm not killing them, and, even if he is a demon, why would we kill the girl?" Even if she left me no blood and I was starving. I was trying my hardest not to let the hunger affect my decision.

Alice gave me a tight smile, "I'll do it. I will let the girl live, but the boy must die."

"I meant to say, no one is killing them, either of them."

Alice's head tilted to one side, "That sounded like an order. I'm in charge, and I say the boy dies. Before you get bent out of shape, I'll tell you why. When magic folks have babies, most of the time they are magical, but every once in awhile they are not. Even less likely they are born a demon. Is he a real demon… no. They call all creatures they fear demons, even vampires. Still, their power is a menace to both sides. He cannot be allowed to live."

I questioned, "A menace how?"

"Well, for starts, you use your sound like sonar to see around my mind powers. The sonar has a weakness; you can only see shapes and movement. You can't see color and detail, like the color of my dress or the words in a book. Look at me now; what do you see?"

I looked at her; she was covered in blood. Then I realized what she meant. Her hair was a mess; there was no blue hat. She hadn't been wearing a blue dress; instead, it was an old white nightgown now covered in blood. Her skin was pale from age; vampires' skin started to look white as stone, after enough centuries passed. Her eyes were blue and huge. She was less human-looking than she had been when she came to get me tonight. During the day I noticed her power waned, and I was able to see through her web of lies. I realized Alice's fear of this child; he blocked her power. That is why these men were able to attack her in the middle of the night. "Just because he can block your power doesn't give you the right to kill him!"

Alice shook her head in disgust, "I really don't want to argue with you on this. If we don't kill him, a wizard or magic-user will. They aren't like necromancers who just happen to specialize in a particular type of magic. These… creatures, demons, whatever you want to call them... are cursed. Most of the time, they are killed at birth. They can see things with those eyes, and they destroy magic. You and I are magical creatures… they are a threat to all."

She was afraid. I had never seen her scared before. I had to wonder, "How many of these demons have you fought?"

Alice scrunched her eyes together, "None, but I have read all about them."

How superstitious, I thought. "No, you will not kill him… and that's final." Deep down I knew I was prepared to fight to the death for the well-being of this boy. They were children, and both deserved to be protected.

Alice stomped her foot, "Don't be like that, Melabeth. I really think it best we kill them. Once they see you, they can always see you. I will never feel safe again."

"No," I couldn't help but think that I was about to get my ass kicked.

Alice didn't resort to violence; instead, she proposed, "Ok, let's say we don't kill them. I don't believe it would be wise to let them go, for me, or for your family. What do we do with them? Are you going to take care of them?"

"Me?"

"Well, we can't very well just let them wander around. I don't even understand what his powers are, and we're talking about the safety of everyone. We are talking about keeping your baby brother safe."

"I don't know what we will do, but I still won't allow you to kill him… or her." I crossed my arms and gave my best death stare.

Alice's face tightened, "Oh, so it's my problem. I have to deal with it, but I can't kill them. Well, I won't; I won't do it." She spun around and turned her back to me. Crossing her arms and stomping the floor, Alice was in full fit mode. I was losing control of the situation and had no idea how I could save these children from Alice.

I was about to try to make an argument when I felt Spooky. I felt her panic; Alice felt mine. She spun around to face me. The child was gone and once again an ancient vampire stood before me. She spoke with urgency, "We are under attack."

I was stunned into silence as my mind raced. My family was in danger. Alice took charge and barked, "Bring your demon with you. You will slow me down." She flew out the door and jumped into the air. Vampires couldn't fly, but they could go weightless and jump amazing distances. Not all vampires could do it; you had to be powerful enough. She would be back at my house in minutes, for the first time I regretted not being a vampire.

I looked over at the two children still huddling against the wall. "How fast can you run?"

The boy's eyes grew bigger and the girl held him tightly, "I… I… don't think we can keep up."

I demanded, "I need you to keep up. I plan on keeping you safe, but I need to get home. My family is in trouble."

The girl nodded, "We can run pretty fast. We'll do our best."

I gave them my best smile. I don't think I was too reassuring, but I was too stressed to care. I commanded, "Come on then, let's go."

I may have not had all my vampire powers, but I was still strong and fast. The two children had a hell of a time keeping up as we weaved through the trees and underbrush. More than a few times I had to stop for them to catch up. The first time I heard the boy really speak was the third time I had to come to a stop. Panting for air the boy said, "Can we… stop… let me catch… my breath." The boy was chubby and more than a little out of shape.

I was impatient as I felt that not only was Spooky in a fight, but so was Alice. I could enter one of their heads and see what was going on, but then I would be unable to run. Since the boy needed a second to catch his breath, I turned to them and said, "Rest for a minute, and don't bother me. I need to see what's going on."

They gave me a strange look as I took a seat on the ground Indian style. I closed my eyes and willed myself to Spooky. Alice was harder to enter; she naturally blocked me, but Spooky was unable to. I entered her mind and found it strange and uncomfortable. I knew she was a cat. I hated being in her mind when she was in animal form. No matter, I must know what's going on, so I would endure.

It took a second to realize that she was no longer a house cat. She had turned into a great tiger and moved with strength and power. You would be hard pressed to find a gun or rifle that would pierce her hide. Her mind was not one of a beast or animal; she kept her self awareness. She had come to realize I was in her mind and she was glad. Neither with Alice or Spooky, could I communicate complex thoughts, but we could communicate feelings. She gave me strong impressions of worry, fear and anger. Spooky had grown close to my father and mother and loved my brother as if he were her own.

I could see through her eyes and feel her body move. She was moving around the side of my house, searching for intruders. For such a large creature she moved with great agility and without sound. I could taste blood in her mouth; she had already bitten someone. I wished I could understand what had happened and if my family was safe. I needed to help; I needed to be there. I couldn't wait; I came back to my body, and my eyes flew open. The children were sitting quietly in front of me still slightly out of breath. I asked, "Ready?" They both nodded and we all got up and began to run. I was close to my house, running through my neighborhood. There was a small patch of woods that lay between me and my house. I slowed to a walk as I entered the woods. The children caught up and were struggling for air. Using a hand gesture, I whispered to the children, "Stay here. I'll be back for you."

I entered the woods and moved toward my house. I was following a natural path in the woods. I came around the trunk of a large oak and ran face-to-face with a strange man. He was dressed all in black with a large hood so I could not make out his face. My reaction was slow; his was not. He had a gun in his hand.

I saw the sparks, but the shot barely registered as I fell on my back. My chest felt as if it had exploded as the world spun around. Seconds felt like minutes as the man moved in slow motion. He moved to where he stood over me. Slowly he brought the gun up and aimed at my face.

Before he could fire, a giant black tiger with red stripes pounced on him. The jaws clamped on his head, he couldn't have screamed even if he wanted to. The world fell out of my vision as the tiger took him down. The last thought I could remember was I hadn't realized that Spooky had turned into a black and red tiger...

Chapter 6 The Truth

My first thoughts were hazy as my mind awoke.

Flashes of memories and images were the first things to let me know that I was still alive. How much time had passed? Had they saved my family? I was even a little concerned about the children that I had promised to return to. Will Alice kill them without me around to stop her?

I had the strangest feeling of being in a coffin, probably just bad memories from my past. I felt Alice, shortly after Spooky. Their feelings were glad, happy. We must have won the battle. Does that mean we saved everyone? I felt my *consciousness* slip backwards into a dreamless sleep. In my next moment of consciousness, I found myself floating in black nothingness. I knew this place; it was part of the doorway, from life, into the library. The library itself was just a place souls pass through before true death.

I floated up toward the light and there was the door, the door into the library. I entered and found myself in my adult body. I headed into what looked to be a gigantic room. I had not been to this part of the library, but then again, I had no idea if the library had an end, or a beginning. This room was huge with a beautiful stone floor. It was a giant pattern. I was sure if I was looking from a higher location that I would be viewing a giant mural. It looked to be a plant of some sort, but hard to tell from ground floor. The room itself was a rectangle surrounded by eight floors of balconies. Columns stood every ten feet with arches on top holding the floor above it. The roof was a giant dome with a huge picture outlining some battle long past. The strangest part was there were no books, but, in the middle of the giant room, sat a chair. In the chair sat Nicks with Bow standing by his side.

I came to him, and he smiled, "My daughter, it is good to see you."

I was in a panic, "I need to leave. I need to get back to my body… my family was attacked. I don't know if they're ok."

Nicks stood and came to me. He gently took my hand, "Have no fear. Your family is safe and so are you."

I couldn't stand not checking on them, but what I said next came out all wrong. "Are you sure?"

Nicks' eyes never held anything but kindness, "Trust me, they're fine. Bow has checked on them personally. In fact, they are with you now, worrying about you."

"Why?"

Nicks shrugged his shoulders, "Who can tell? Maybe… and this is just a guess, but it could have to do with you being shot, and your body is now hooked up to life support."

"Smart ass. Wait... life support! Will I survive?"

Nicks once again calmly explained, "You were shot in the heart. Until now I did not know if you could survive that, but you don't really need your heart to live. Your body is repairing quickly, faster than I could imagine. It is my belief that you are becoming a new creature. You will be the first true Dhampir. By the time you're fifteen, you will return to what you once were. Vampire blood always returns the body back to the original state. That is why vampires never look like they are aging, but, in fact, they are. Their blood ages, even as the person infected looks the same. That is why vampires never change, not even the length of their hair. At least not on the outside, but they do become more powerful, so, in fact, that is change. In short, we now know that heart failure will not kill you, kind of a rough way to find out, don't you think?"

"I didn't plan it. I thought Dhampirs were half human and half vampire?"

Nicks laughed, "Yes. You are human and vampire… and death. The first reaper with a mortal body. I guess you will be many firsts, just as you are my first and only daughter."

What he said brought a big smile to my face, "Well, so much for a normal life."

Bow cleared her throat, "Speaking of which, it's time for your next practice."

It made me mad that she interrupted my time with Nicks for violin lessons, "Later Bow."

Nicks frowned at my dismissal of Bow. He stepped around to my side, putting his arm around my shoulder. Then he led me to the chair; he sat me down. Another chair came out of thin air for him to sit on. Bow stood quietly behind him, "It's time you understood. It is time I explain what I need from you. First, you must understand your power."

I was sure I didn't want to hear it, but what choice did I have? I made myself comfortable in the chair and then announced, "All ears."

Nicks explained, "I have had a violin shipped to your house. It is no normal violin, but in fact, it is the violin that Bow haunts. One of my powers is to use the knowledge of the dead. This is done by reading the books in the library. Everyone who died passed through the library, and, in doing so, left knowledge behind that was stored in the books. We can also use the gifts of willing spirits. This is what Bow was really trying to teach you. She was a master at playing the violin. If you could learn to use her skills, you would play the violin as well as her."

This, of course, amazed me, and I could see the endless applications. I couldn't help but think if he would have just said this in the first place, I would have been more willing to come to my lessons. I asked him, "Why didn't you just tell me that to begin with?"

Nicks responded with, "Well, there is a good reason I have been hesitant about telling you. Melabeth, you're a smart girl, and it wouldn't have taken you long to realize that, with your power, that... how do I put this?"

I understood, "With my power it will force me into some life, a life that I didn't choose."

Nicks' face was full of compassion, "Yes. Still you have my power, to destroy spirits that have refused to move on. You can use spirits who choose to help you. With this power I need your help. There are so many dying, and now there is a new power in the world. These necromancers are blocking me and keeping spirits from moving on. This is unnatural and will bring great evil to mankind. I am limited to what I can do in your world, but you can fight death, and life. You can go where I cannot."

"You were right not to tell me. I don't want that life. I want to go to high school, maybe meet a boy, have kids." I felt the tears, but held them back. "I really don't want to be a hero."

Nicks got up from his chair and embraced me, "You have too much on your plate. Try not to worry about what you will become. Go now, train later. You must go talk with your family. Just remember this, when you turn fifteen you will once again be a force to be reckoned with. You have not defeated all your enemies."

I narrowed my eyes, "I thought I killed them all?"

"Did you?" Nicks asked.

I thought about it. I had killed all the men who were involved with my rape and murder. I had learned on the way that all of them were high ranking Order members. I also learned that Alex was one of the wizards who sat on the Council of Twelve and that his mother Luna was the head of that council. A memory popped into my head, a memory of watching my own death. I remembered how the whole thing was a spell gone wrong… or did it? I blurted out, "There's someone behind the curtain."

Nicks nodded, "Justice must be served. It seemed likely that Alex was not acting alone. If so, they need to be stopped. We must know who really created you and why."

I huffed, "You're right. I have a lot of thinking and a few years to do it in. For now, I must face my fear… I need to tell my dad the truth."

Nicks' face was kind and full of confidence when he said, "He will understand."

"He'd better," I teased nervously.

I said my goodbyes and left the library. I wasn't looking forward to telling my family the truth about me, but I needed to.

I awoke to the sounds of beeping. The first thing I felt was a needle in my arm; it really didn't hurt, but it was uncomfortable. The wires came out from somewhere under my blanket; my whole body was wrapped except for my right arm with the IV in it. At first from the stack of equipment next to my bed, I thought I might be in a hospital, but, upon closer examination of my room, I was not. I was in a beautiful bedroom; it was huge with a tall ceiling. The walls were a soft green color with white trim. The furniture, including the bed, matched the walls down to the white trim. I knew at once I had never been here, but wherever it was, it was upscale.

Two people were in the room with me, Alice sat at the end of my bed with her doll in her lap. She was reading a book, Alice was always reading something. The other person in my room, sat in a chair, well, not really sat, but slumped. My father, John slept with a slight snore. The room was quiet, so it did not surprise me when I shifted my weight that Alice turned to me, "About time, sleepy head. You have been out of it for five days."

"Five days?" my voice sounded hoarse and broke. My mouth was dry and my vocal cords didn't like being awakened so suddenly. Alice read my mind as she moved swiftly and brought me a glass of water. Between sucking gulps of water through the straw I said, "Thanks... tell me everything."

"Well, to start off, you owe Spooky *a big* thanks. She saved your whole family and killed the nasty hit men. I did a fair part myself, you know."

"Thanks Alice... I mean it."

Alice smiled, "I don't mind killing. Where was I... Spooky, she killed most of the men. I came late, and you just got in the way. The man that shot you, was the last man. He had used some kind of spell to hide himself and escape Spooky and me. You flushed him out, sort of. Apparently you were their target. He took the chance of giving away his position to kill you. Afterwards we had a funeral for you; it was nice."

"Funeral?" I asked confused.

"Yes, it was sad. Your father cried, both of them. Even your mother wept openly. How does it feel to be dead... again?"

I was still confused, "Is that why I thought I was in a coffin? And why did you have to kill me? I see my dad, so did they know that I wasn't really dead?"

Alice cocked her head to one side as if she was thinking, "Yes, because it was fun... and no." I narrowed my eyes at her for not being clear. "Don't be moody. Yes, you were in a coffin. I didn't think you would remember any of it; you were mostly dead. We had to kill you, don't you remember the part where I said you are the target. The safest thing for your family right now is that the people who hired the hit men believe they succeeded. Your parents didn't know you weren't dead until last night. They are confused as to why they went to a funeral. Now they found you, days later, hooked up to life support. Well, let me restate that your father is confused, although your grandfather and sister took it well."

Well, it explained that bad dream. And now I am awake and must face the real nightmare. I must tell my father the truth and worst of all I was going to lose my family. Even if they were okay with all this, Alice didn't fake my death so that I could be with my family. She had done it to protect them, which could mean a couple of different things. Either she has no idea who wants me dead, or she cannot protect my whole family against whatever force is out to get me. I sat up, "I want some time with my dad."

She nodded, "I'll be back to check on you later. I'll let the rest of your family know you are ready to see them."

"Alice," she knew I was about to ask something of her. She nodded and I continued, "Delay telling the rest of my family, I would like to talk to my father first... please?"

Alice looked at me with understanding, then she stomped her foot, "What do I look like? Your maid?" She stomped out of the room and slammed the door.

I laughed, I knew she was joking. Knowing how she really felt was handy, so it didn't bother me when she acted out. What her fit was meant to do, it did; my father was awake and sat up alert. Once he was awake enough to realize I was laughing, he jumped to his feet and rushed to my side.

My father, John, was a big man, standing six feet four. He was well built and loved his football. Everyone loved him; he was kind and smart, but most of all, he was patient. My voice was small, "Are you scared of me now?"

He wrapped his large arm around me, "Afraid of you, never."

That brought a smile and tears..., "I think I owe you the truth."

"The truth," he chuckled. Humoring me he asked, "And what would that be?"

I couldn't look him in the eyes as I spoke, "Mom is right. I am a vampire, but there is much more to it."

My father was now angry. His voice raised an octave, "I knew you would overhear her. How many times I've told your mother if you hear that crazy talk... well, what would you think? Listen to me, you *are not* a vampire. Your mom... well she, it's hard to explain, but she is wrong. You are a normal little girl. I don't know what they have done to you... I don't understand what's going on."

I shook my head, "Please hear me. There is more to this. My mother has told you about the night her vampire sister kidnapped her."

I could see my father wasn't about to listen to me. He was now verbally correcting me, "Molly, you need to listen. Your mother has put some crazy thoughts in your head, and that Alice, well she isn't right. You need..."

What I did next was for Mindy; I owed it to her. She didn't need to be crazy in her husband's eyes. I also did it for me, for I couldn't hide who and what I was. I let my teeth grow long and sharp. My fingers elongated as my fingernails grew and become as sharp as razor blades. My father was still going off about me not being a vampire when he came to realize the changes that had overcome me.

"You are not a..." my father broke off in mid-sentence. I gave him my best I am not going to eat you grin. I don't think I did it right as my father recoiled almost falling down.

I quickly stopped showing off my teeth, "Don't be afraid. I won't hurt you."

I sat up and gently laid my hand on my father's arm. He froze in shock as he tried to reason it all away. He looked down at his arm where my hand lay. He pulled his arm away; my claws were still out, and the sudden jerk had raked my sharp nails across the top of his arm. Four lines of red rose from his arm, and the air smelled of blood.

I gently took his arm back, "Let me." I licked the wounds, and by the time I pulled my head back my father was staring at four pink lines. "There's more I must tell you."

My father's eyes were harsh, "No more. Goodnight." His voice was full of hurt, but at the same time he was commanding me. I knew better than to cross my father.

On the verge of tears he said, "Goodnight, you will be better soon." My father stood and left the room with a strange blankness on his face. He looked confused as he left.

He came back and stuck his head into the room. He stood there silently, then after what felt like hours, "I love you… we will talk about this later." He shut the door.

The tears fell now. The only good thing that came out of that was the fact he said he loved me still. I was surprised when Spooky spoke, "What you did was brave, foolish, but brave. I can't say I agree with you telling him, but I understand what you're doing. Well, I think I do."

I didn't know Spooky was in the room. She was naked, so she must have been curled up in the corner of the room as a cat. Now that I was thinking of her I could feel her, and I knew she had been by my side the whole time. She was hungry and tired, and yet she would not let me out of her sight.

I explained to her why I did what I did, "I can't let my sister be crazy, not to her husband. I am so afraid of losing my family. The truth will set me free, one way or the other."

For the first time I could ever recall, Spooky's voice held no venom in it. I could feel her, and I understood that was the first unselfish thing she had witnessed me do. She loved my family. She also cared deeply for me… of course, that was partly the problem. She had trouble with caring for me; how much of it was real? How much was because of the blood? For these reasons it had been so hard for her to be nice to me, but tonight she was. Spooky commanded, "Sleep. Tomorrow you will need your strength. Tomorrow you will find out if they can handle the truth."

I whined, "I can't sleep. After everything…"

Spooky did not argue with me; instead she turned into a large gray cat. She curled up right on my chest. I ran my fingers through her fur as she purred. I whispered into her ear, "Thank you… for everything." I was sure I would not find any sleep, but sleep found me.

Chapter 7 A New Start

I awoke with a start; I had had a bad dream.

I could not remember what it was; the more I awoke, the further away the dream was. Some time had passed, and night had come. The room was much darker than it had been. Lamps glowed dimly and machines that were attached to me now sat quietly turned off in the corner. Someone had unhooked me while I slept; they had left the IV in. At the end of my bed, sitting like a stone statue was my father. The look on his face was unreadable, but I took it as a good sign that he was here at all.

His voice was kind as he asked, "How are you feeling?"

"Fine," we sat in the quiet, staring at one another. Like an untied balloon, it all came out at once, "I'm so sorry. I'm not your daughter, your wife Mindy, my sister… she told you the truth. I tried to kill my father and… and… I…" the tears burst from my eyes. Crying made it so hard to speak.

"Shh…" he whispered in my ear. He pulled me into his large arms and held me tight. I could hear his heart as I sobbed. My father's voice was full of comfort, "Quiet now, you're safe."

He hadn't heard me. Between sobs, "I'm not your daughter; I'm nothing to you."

Again with no anger, his voice was calm and soft. "Mindy and your father have told me everything. I never believed them, but now I know the truth."

"Then you know I lied, but they don't even know the full truth of it. I'm not Molly, I'm Melanie."

My father's voice was full of conviction, "I know that you *are* my daughter and you are very special to me. You just happen to have the memories of Mindy's dead sister. Who do you want to be? It's up to you."

It was too good to be true, to be accepted, to be loved. "I want to be your daughter… and love you like my father."

He held me as I cried, humming softly rocking me back and forth. I cried for my suffering; I cried for my father, but most of all I cried because I was free. It was then when I became aware of the fact the room was not empty. Two other bodies joined our group, my mother and my father/grandfather.

"Mindy…" I tried to explain myself to my sister.

Mindy interrupted, "Don't, I have always wondered. It's better that I know the truth."

She had heard me admit who I was. Somehow she didn't hate me. I couldn't believe my ears, "Why?"

I couldn't see her face because we were all hugging, but from her voice I could tell that she was crying as she said, "Because I have always loved you but not as my daughter. I couldn't help but think that there was something wrong with me because of the way I felt. Now that I know the truth, now I understand. The fear of what you really could be and what I should do about it. I couldn't handle that. I don't have to worry about you. No longer do I need answers to questions I don't understand."

I never thought of it that way, how she might feel that it was *her* problem to deal with the supernatural side of me. My grandfather spoke in a soft voice, cracking with pain and suffering. "Can you find it in your heart to forgive me for what I did? This curse you bear, it should be mine."

"Forgiven, can you forgive me for almost killing your daughter?"

"Forgiven," he said, and we laughed, cried at the same time. What pain we all shared, what fear we all shared and what love we all shared.

The next hour was the happiest I could remember being in a long time. We sat around on my bed talking and laughing. It wasn't long before we were telling stories. My sister was telling the story of the first time she caught me reading. "Then I told John, and he was like, she wasn't really reading Mindy. Of course dad was no help at all; he just wanted to pretend that nothing happened. I really felt alone…"

Before she could finish, the door opened and Alice made her way into the room. My whole family stiffened and went quiet. I narrowed my eyes at Alice. She defended herself without me saying a word, "What? I didn't do anything. I don't know why they are so scared of me… Melabeth, I wouldn't scare your family." The grin on her face said otherwise.

"Alice why…." Before I could finish my sentence I remembered something. "What ever happened to those kids? You know the boy with the purple eyes."

Alice let out a big huff, "They're fine. I sent them to Dan; he'll take care of them."

I narrowed my eyes and asked, "In what way?"

"In a good way," Alice insisted. "Dan has helped out the children and their family before. He was really glad to see that I returned them… alive, which I shouldn't have."

"Thank you," I smiled, "You did the right thing."

Alice gave us a tight smile as she took a seat on the one free side of the bed. The rest of my family readjusted, away from her. "What did she do to you guys?"

My grandfather answered, "Nothing big, other than being creepy and scaring us a little with childlike pranks, just a little nervous about what I might see."

My father added, "Really, we are not being fair. I have known Alice for a while now. Of course I thought her to be the child of my boss… who is also a vampire. It's not what she did to us, but rather what we witnessed her do to others. See Molly…"

"Melabeth," Alice interrupted. "Her real name is Melabeth and it is the name I like best."

I gave Alice a dirty look, "They can call me Molly if they want; it is the name they gave me. Go on, Dad, I'm listening."

My father cleared his throat, "When the men came looking for us, a few of them gathered us in the living room and held us at gunpoint."

I clarified, "You mean just you and mom?"

"No, they came with your grandfather in tow. They had kidnapped him earlier and brought him along. They didn't want to miss anyone."

Mindy jumped in, "It all started when we heard a terrible beast, then screaming. It was coming from outside. The men became scared and started to scream at us. They kept asking what it was, but we didn't know. This infuriated the men and they were shoving their guns into our faces."

As my mom shook her head back and forth from recalling the memory, my father went on. "I was calm, or rather in shock by this point. I knew they would snap soon and start killing us. If they didn't kill us, the beast outside surely would. I was trying to figure out what to do and how to get upstairs and find you, before they could. I have never felt so powerless in all my life. That's when it happened; they became confused and started walking around the room saying crazy things. Then one of them shot the other one; we all hit the floor.

"While I lay on the floor awaiting my death, I felt your mother take my hand, and I knew it wouldn't be much longer. The last thought I could recall was… that I had failed you. The room filled with screaming, and I came to realize that neither your mother nor your grandfather were the ones screaming. We must have all realized it at the same time. We all sat up to witness the men tearing each other apart, digging their fingernails into each other's flesh, biting and clawing… and there in the middle feasting upon them, a little girl covered in blood. She was dripping from head to toe with sharp teeth." My father's body quivered at the memory.

I thought about it and added almost absent mind, "Most of the blood was from earlier."

My sister laughed nervously, "Well, that makes it all better… thanks for the clarification."

I chastised Alice, "You could have blocked that from their site."

Alice got up to leave, "I didn't come to interrupt. I spoke with your lovely family over the last few days. I have filled them in on so much; I just wanted to remind them of the time."

A look passed over my family's faces, "What?" I asked. "What's going on?"

Alice answered, "They need to say their goodbyes."

It took me a minute, "No!"

The next hour with my family went by like the blink of an eye. They explained how everyone in town had come to my funeral and how devastated they were at the thought of my death, but then Ezra and Alice snuck them away and explained what really happened. It came to light that I was the target, and it hadn't taken Alice and Ezra long to put together why.

I summed up what I knew. Alex was Richard Alexander Longaeva, the son of Luna Longaeva. He had somehow stolen a book from the Council of Twelve, which he himself was a part of. To further that, I found that the Council of Twelve was formed just to keep that very book safe. The Council was formed by twelve wizards at the end of World War II. After using the book in some kind of ritual spell, he created me.

Dan Caster, a founding wizard of the Council of Twelve was a good friend of Alice. He was a representative of the United States. Dan hired Alice to retrieve the book back from Alex, not wanting to go directly against Luna. Well, we failed to get back the book and thanks to the fact that Luna didn't seem to have any end to powerful evil children, namely Peter. She was the mother of the Lionhearts, three men who were turned into vampires during the crusades.

Apparently someone was still watching my family. After my death, they still kept tabs on them. After I hit and broke that man's knee, they knew I wasn't a normal little girl. Not only did someone put a hit on me, but it looked as if they might take out my whole family just to get to me. Alice is very powerful and very well connected in this country. They would most likely be wondering what was so special about my family that she would spend so much time watching over them.

This of course meant that, in order to protect my family until we find out who is behind this, I needed to stay dead. Alice needed to ignore my family and pretend they no longer held any interest to the Whites. This being said, this was the last night with my family.

My worst nightmare was when my family found out about me, they would fear and hate me. Now they have found out, and they don't fear or hate me. The fear of losing my family and once again be thrust back into the supernatural world, had indeed come true. My little brother hadn't even turned one. How could I choose to stay, putting him in harm's way? I couldn't. My father and grandfather talked for at least an hour trying to figure out what else could be done, but I knew what had to be done. Until that book was found and the people behind this were brought to justice, I would never be free.

After saying goodbye, I watched tearfully as my family left with tears in their eyes. Mindy was eager to get back to my brother. She still loved me and forgave me; wow, there is nothing I wouldn't do for her in return for that gift. My grandfather and father were both devastated, and I had never felt the way I did this very moment as the door shut. This time there was no hate to bury the hurt.

No fear, no hate, just loneliness, it was a feeling I was used to. I had grown up with family until my father had kidnapped me. I've known loneliness; this was my old friend. Ezra came in the door, followed by Alice and Spooky. Spooky was dressed which was strange. She was mostly a cat, and, when she shifted, I couldn't recall too many times she bothered to get dressed. I noticed she was carrying bags.

"Time to go," Ezra announced.

Alice added, "You two should leave before light. Oh, one more thing," Alice jumped onto the bed and embraced me. "I will miss you, but I will come and see you when I can."

"Thank you," I felt like I should cry, but my tears were all used up. It was all happening so fast; I still had questions. "Am I to leave on my own? Where should I go?"

Ezra smiled kindly, "You should know better. Spooky will be taking you. They don't know about her. She will watch over you with the help of an old friend. You will be in good hands while you grow up, and, when you are ready, we'll be waiting. We all look forward to serving you."

"Serving me?" That was a strange way of putting it.

Alice cleared her throat, "Yes, yes, we all want to be like the great and mighty Melabeth. Get going already."

I laughed, "Aye, aye, Captain Alice."

Ezra left while I got out of bed and dressed. It wasn't long before I was waving goodbye, and Spooky sped off. We were riding in a 1965 Chevy Impala, black as night. I still had no idea where we were going, but I was sure I would hate it.

We left close to morning, and I was not in the mood to stay awake during the day if I didn't have to. We stopped at a little hotel so I could sleep. I might have healed quickly, but I was not healed all the way. Still tired and weak, I ate breakfast or dinner depending on how I looked at it. I really wanted some blood, but I could do without it.

I went to sleep and traveled to the land of the dead. Bow was waiting for me, "Are you ready to learn?"

"I don't mean to be rude Bow, but I really don't care to learn the violin. And, yes, I know that's not the point. The point is to use a spirit's talent; I just wish you had a different talent that's all."

Bow smiled, "You and I will be good friends. I can see it already. Through you, I will be able to do the one thing I couldn't do before I died. Hopefully, after that, I will find rest. For both of us to get what we want, first you must learn to play my violin. Learning to do what you wish *not* to do will help you master the skill. Then I will let you use some of my other skills, the ones you will enjoy."

"What other skills? How will helping me, help you? I hate it when people don't explain themselves."

Bow handed me a violin and bow. The bow was in my right hand, in my left hand, was my violin. They morphed, turning into two blades. One was a Katana; the other was a wakizashi, the weapons of a Samurai. Green lines traveled through the black blades; it looked as if rivers flowed through the blades. I said, "I know this magic. These are spiritual weapons; David turned Carrie into one of these."

Bow answered, "Yes, but these are stronger. My spirit is much stronger than your friend's and much harder to break. In the world of the living, you will be able to change my violin into weapons. Not only will they kill the living, but the dead has well."

"Why would I use you for a spirit weapon? Do you have some skill that I can use? Won't you feel the pain of my enemies?"

A wicked grin washed over Bow's face. It was the first time I had seen her smile. "You are right; you do need the whole story so that you can understand. I will sum up my life the best that I can. Then you will know what I offer... and what you offer me. As far as the pain, it will be worth it."

"I hope it's a good story. I could use a good story."

Chapter 8 Bow

In the library I had found that you could walk into a book and see the world that was in it. Also, when spirits shared their memories it was like watching a movie as you scrolled through their memories. Bow opened up her story and the library changed to San Francisco in 1905. Bow stood next to me and narrated her story.

The year was 1905 - my real name is Sonja Winters. I was the daughter of Fredrick and Annie Winters. We had traveled to San Francisco as musicians from Europe. I turned 16 that summer. My mother was an accomplished violinist, and my father played the bass. That was a bass violin that is, but back then it was just a bass. San Francisco is where I met Masi Oka.

I recall my first time in San Francisco like it was yesterday. We took a trolley ride right through the center of town. It was much different then; the people walked freely across the street. Most of the traffic was carts pulled by horse and men on bikes. There were cars, but not many and even fewer traffic laws. The cars passed where they could; still they did not travel much faster than jogging. Teenagers and men alike would jump on the back of a moving car to catch a ride. The wide street was brick and full of potholes; two sets of tracks for the trolleys ran down the center. Trolleys passed each other as travelers jumped off and on at will. On both sides of the street the buildings rose up, mostly made of stone and brick. I loved it.

I was studying under my mother to play the violin, and San Francisco was the first place I played publicly. It was my passion. In fact, it was my family's passion. We loved music, and playing for the audience was just a way to pay the bills. Still, my first show I played solo was in San Francisco, at a little theater close to the main street. Having no name I didn't really draw a big crowd, but still I played my heart out as if the whole city had come to see me.

It was after that show that I met my future husband, Masi Oka. I didn't know it then, but this man was about to turn my world upside down. He was Japanese, visiting from Tokyo. I am not tall 5' 6'', but Masi was an inch shorter, and not wearing heels. He met me after the show to congratulate me and give praise. He seemed very nice, small, but nice. For the next few months my family and I played one theater to the next. Masi greeted me after every show, and our talks deepened. I really enjoyed Masi's company, but had no feelings for him... that it is until April 18th 1906, the day that changed everything.

An earthquake struck San Francisco at 5:12 a.m. on Wednesday, April 18, 1906. Devastating fires broke out in the city; the fires lasted for several days. As a result of the quake and fires, about 3,000 people died and over 80% of San Francisco was destroyed. This is where my next life began. Demons of all types including vampires, wizards and witches were no longer just legends. After that earthquake my world was turned upside down.

Let me first tell you about my Masi Oka. Masi was born south of Tokyo. His family was well known samurai and beloved by the people. Love is the wrong word. When I speak about the Japanese, it is with respect, which is what the locals would have had for their family. They were not only respected, but they were different. The family was specially chosen by the Emperor, for this Samurai family was given the task of destroying demons. The family practiced not only the way of the sword, but special skills passed from one generation to the next.

They did not refer to themselves as wizards or witches, but they used many of the same techniques. Much of the magic known to the western wizards was unknown to them. It could also be said, that they had magic unknown to the western wizards. One of them was making a sword unlike any before or after. This sword could slash through ghosts; its cut was devastating to vampires. Unlike a normal sword you would find it hard to heal from such a wound. These Samurai warriors kept Japan safe from the dark for a thousand years. This weapon was made by spirits. Even though you have seen and used spirit weapons, these were special in their own right.

Japan was a proud country that had kept itself cut off from the outside world for hundreds of years. Thanks to the Industrial Revolution, it could no longer keep the outside world at bay. In 1877 the last Samurai fought during the Satsuma Rebellion. Few true Samurai remained as the Japanese modernized. Most who carried the title had no true training, and the sword was nothing more than a showpiece. Samurai didn't even have the right to carry swords in public. In many ways Samurai became a title, like a lord or a duke. The Samurai were land owners and their families would rule over large areas.

Masi and his family were some of the last true Samurai who remembered and practiced the ancient art. Masi still did what his family swore an oath to do, hunt demons. It is why he was in San Francisco in the first place. He and his uncle had been on the hunt for a murderous vampire. The vampire had a great love for music and for the taste of young violinists.

I was in a deep sleep, in an apartment that I shared with my parents. The apartment my father rented was located on the top floor, four stories high. Officially the earthquake hit at 5:12 a.m.; all I remember was a deafening roar... than I was falling into darkness.

My mind raced as it tried to figure out what had happened. I was wrapped in darkness trapped under some unknown object. My ears rang from some long past noise, and I fought for every breath. Not only was the weight upon me making it hard to breath, but the air was full of dust that stuck in my throat. One arm was free, and my hand covered my mouth to try to filter the air. I could feel the heat and the roar of a fire, how close, I couldn't tell.

My mind went in and out of consciousness. Soon I could see light streaming through cracks; voices soon followed. I couldn't tell how much time passed before an aftershock hit, rocking my world once again. The rubble that had me buried shifted, exposing me to the morning light. Half my body still lay within the wreckage. The air was full of gray dust, and the sky was filling with black smoke. I could hear women weeping and men yelling; the world was coming to an end.

I blacked out again, but when I awoke, I was being rescued. Masi was pulling me out of the wreckage. His clothes were ripped and dirty, his face was covered with soot. On his back was strapped a sword and, even in my condition, I wondered why. My mouth was, so dry I could not speak, for I had been breathing dust for hours. Masi brought a jug of water to my lips. It was the best water I could ever recall drinking, before and after. He lifted me up into his strong arms and began to carry me through the destruction. San Francisco was utterly destroyed; the only thing standing was the poles that held the wire for the trolleys. Fire rose into the air; it was truly hell on earth.

I asked Masi, "My parents? We have to find them."

He simply said, "I did... and I am truly sorry."

I said no more. I simply laid my face on his chest and cried, but no tears came to my eyes were too dry from the dust.

He must have carried me all day, the sun was falling into the ocean. Setting me next to an overturned tree; it must have fallen because of the earthquake. The tree roots lay exposed still covered with fresh dark soil; the tree itself was large and even on its side the trunk stood tall as a man. The branches made for a natural shelter where Masi gently put me down. He quietly sat Indian style across from me. Dirty and sweaty, he still looked ready to go. It truly amazed me on how strong this man was. It was the first time I looked at him like a man.

He offered me an apple; at first I did not want to eat, but my stomach disagreed with my mind. I ate the apple, but I did not enjoy it. We sat quietly as the sky darkened. When I finished my apple, Masi said, "I know you will not believe me; you must ready your mind for the coming dangers."

My mind was still numb with the loss of my family. My body was still in shock from the earthquake; every time another aftershock came I was sure that I would die. I could not even imagine sleeping. I could already feel myself falling into the darkness. What truth could this man want to tell me? From the sound of it, I didn't want to know. He handed me some more water and after drinking I asked, "What truth?"

He spoke with deep conviction, "This world is more than you might imagine. There are dark creatures, demons, monsters that haunt the shadows of the night. I have been hunting one such monster of the dark. He hunts young musicians, young female musicians that is. I have been watching over you, for I am sure he hunts you. Your gifts with the violin are very special; he craves that - talent and the blood of the talented. I believe, with the recent destruction, he will wait no more. He will strike… tonight. In the destruction, my uncle and apprentice were killed. Without their aid, this demon will have the advantage. I will make this place sacred. The tree was strong and healthy, but the earthquake brought it down. Together we will be an earthquake to this demon; you must find your strength if you wish to survive tonight."

I don't recall if I answered him that evening. I do recall thinking he was out of his mind, and I had been taken out into the middle of nowhere with a mad man. No one would be looking for me. A new fear washed through me, but I was soon to learn what fear was.

We sat quietly as the darkness wrapped around us. Masi had busied himself making a fire and then proceeded to dump powder on the ground encircling us. He chanted something in what I assumed was Japanese. The fear of what would happen had turned to exhaustion; this day of fear seemed endless.

The April night was cool, and the wind made me close the space between me and the fire. The air reminded me that all I was wearing were undergarments. I realize in your time today, that our style of undergarment is like being fully dressed, but, in my day, it was considered scandalous. I felt naked and ashamed that I was with a man and not properly dressed, even if the situation was far removed from me. Masi added some more wood to the fire. He then took a seat directly across from me laying his sword across his lap. He closed his eyes and sat perfectly still. All I could think was that the loss of his family had driven him mad. The only monster I was afraid of... was Masi.

It didn't take long before my mind was set straight. Night fell, and, out of the darkness, three persons approached us... two men and one girl, the shadows hid their features. Their clothes were modern for the time, but, like ours, were ripped and dirty. This of course would be expected, for who would look neat after such a tragedy. I could still see the glow from all the fires still burning. I was overwhelmed with joy, for I had been afraid to be alone with Masi. Seeing other folks, with a woman no less, puts me at ease.

What happened next haunted my dreams for many years to come. I began to stand to welcome the new guests, but Masi commanded me to sit. More out of surprise than fear, I obeyed. The three newcomers came to a stop right before the powder that Masi had laid around the fire. They were only fifteen feet away from the fire; I invited them closer, but they did not move or respond. Standing there with blank expressions on their faces, I began to worry. I felt they must have been through a great tragedy, like us and in shock.

I stood to make them feel welcome; I ignored Masi's second command to sit. Starting to cross over to the strangers, Masi came to my side and warned me to keep my distance. The fire illuminated the strangers' faces, not brightly, but enough to make out who they were. I recognized the one in the middle and the female that stood beside him. I didn't recall seeing his friend before. I meet so many people before and after a show, that I seldom remember one face from another, but this man I remembered.

During some of my first shows in San Francisco I became aware of some regulars like Mrs. Burnside, who seldom missed any of our shows, shortly followed by this man whose name I forget to this very day. I only remember him introducing himself and his sister, who looked nothing like him. Well, that is until you looked at their eyes; they were large and piercing. They both looked a little sick, too white and malnourished. He gave me the creeps and the way he spoke to me scared me. He was intense, not only his eyes, but his tongue had me sweating with nervousness. He spoke to me as if we were old friends, or even lovers. The very next show was the first time that I met Masi.

Masi never gave me the creeps, but I found it strange he always hung near when the crowds came to meet and greet. I came to notice the un-named man and his sister always kept their distance with Masi standing near. I had not realized that is why they left me alone, not until the moment in the forest. That was my first experience with demons, or as you know them, vampires.

I froze when I became aware of who had come and the look on my face brought a smile to his face. The girl laughed; his friend hissed. It was then that I noticed the teeth and the long fingernails. The lead man spoke first; he beckoned me to him. That is when I realized the mistake I had made. This was not the man that made me uneasy. It was my father, and he had survived, he was here for me.

I yelled for my father, but before I could get to him Masi tossed some powder in my face. It burned my eyes, and I fell to my knees as I tried to rub the burning dust from my face. It didn't take long before the dust stopped burning even though it still covered my face. I looked up at the vampire, who was no longer my father. He spoke to me strangely telling me that I needed to come to him. Masi said fear not, it was only a mind trick. The dust was magic and would protect me from the demon's trickery.

It happened very quickly, the other male vampire launched across the powder, his arms reaching for me. The next thing I could recall was the vampire falling to the ground. His head fell separate from his body. Masi was standing with his sword unsheathed. Blood dripped from the blade. Masi gently took one hand and slowly pushed me toward the fire. There I stood close to the flames, standing in the center of the ring.

Both vampires crossed over the dust and into the circle. The female asked what the dust did; she was asking the other vampire, but Masi answered. The dust would take away their ability to use their powers. In the circle it would be a fair fight. The male vampire smiled wickedly at this, but the female was apprehensive.

The powder keeps the vampires from what you know as flashing. Also, they couldn't fly, nor did their mind powers work. This was one of the ways that the Oka family had fought toe to toe with the demons of the night.

I wish I could tell you about that fight, but I was filled with fear, and my body shook. I swear I closed my eyes, but for a minute. When I opened them, I witnessed Masi moving between the monsters with great skill. His sword moved through the air so quickly it was a blur of motion. The sound of the swishing of his sword and hissing from the vampires filled my ears. I closed my eyes and covered my face as I fell to my knees.

I was close to a complete panic attack when I felt something touch my arm. I jumped back, startled… it was only Masi. Two more bodies littered the ground, both without heads. I noticed the woman had lost her arms as well. He whispered, "Fear not, you are safe, it is over."

With that I watched him take a stick from the fire and then set the bodies aflame. They burned unnaturally. I had watched a body burn before. In Europe my family played for many funerals. At one such funeral they burned the departed. It took hours for the body to burn up, but these bodies burned like old dry wood. I knew it would not take hours for them to finish burning and from that moment on my world was forever changed.

Masi took care of me. Lost without my parents, he was my savior in so many ways. The whole city was living out of tents as many hurried to try to rebuild San Francisco. Many left; Masi and I stayed. Masi had to find the bodies of his lost comrades so that he might take them home to Japan to bury them with their ancestors. In this time of searching, he helped the men put out fires and clear rubble. He also kept the demons of the night in check. I helped to take care of the sick and injured. He brought me the most incredible find, my violin. He found it while searching for my parents' bodies. I was forever thankful. I played many a tune to help cheer up the people.

At this time Masi and I fell in love. He asked me if I might join him taking his kin back to Japan and of course I agreed. I not only fell in love with Masi, but I fell in love with Japan and Masi's family. I cannot say that the family was completely happy with Masi and me getting married, but it did not take long before I became one of the family members. I became best friends with his two sisters.

It did however take me a few years to become fluent in Japanese. He not only taught me to speak Japanese, but to write it. He also taught me something else, something he was not suppose to. He taught me the ways of the sword. We trained every night; we trained as lovers and warriors. Most of all, we were happy.

We never had children, but we tried every chance we could. The fact that I did not have children, hurt my standing within the family. Already a foreigner, now I was barren. Even though I could hear the whispers, I could endure, for Masi is all I ever needed. The years went by. We stayed in Japan, living with his family. The Oka family stayed on one large estate; the family was large.

We were happily married for over ten years. In those ten years, Masi and I did many things. First, you must understand the time and place. Women didn't have the rights as they do with your time; furthermore, we had a place and a duty. Then again so did the men. In Japan the roles were even more defined. The fact that I was a foreigner and I played the violin, second to none meant that things were different for me than the average

Japanese woman. For that reason more than a few of the family members disliked me.

I played my violin for guests that came to the house. Visitors from the west would come to the Oka family home just to hear my music. The elder men of the house adored me, which even brought more jealousy from the other females. The only women that would even talk to me were Masi's sisters. Even Masi's mother hated me, but it did not bother me; I was happy.

The big secret to a lot of my happiness would cause a lot of problems for Masi. After that night, the night when the vampires came for me, he had decided to train me. He didn't want me to be afraid and, at first, I think he thought that practicing with a sword would just help me sleep better. Soon he realized it was more to me, and I was good with the sword. After ten years I became great, truly an accomplished Samurai.

Night after night I trained, honing my skills. After a while something new began to grow in my heart; I wanted to use my skill. Masi left regularly with his family members to hunt down and destroy the demons. Many nights I sat with him attending to his wounds and nursing him back to health.

One night while Masi laid upon his bed, healing from a bad fight. I asked, "Do you think that I might go?"

"Go?" Masi asked, confused.

"Go with you. Just think about it, with both our skills we would make a wonderful team."

"No, Sonja… you are my wife. You will bring me great dishonor; let the men fight."

I am sure there was more said, but that is all I remember. At the time we had been married for eight years, but I know that is the day the bitterness started. The next two years were happy, but that shadow in my heart grew, and my happiness dimmed. Shortly after our tenth year anniversary, I turned thirty. I wanted so badly to use my skills before I became too old.

A couple of things happened that lead to my demise. One, I turned thirty and two I invented a new sword move. My skills at the blade had more than matched my husband's. The fact is I was better and I knew that. I wanted to be recognized for my skill. Still, I swallowed my pride and life went on, that is until one spring day.

Masi's sisters' husbands practiced with many of the men at the Dojo, including Masi. It was a beautiful day, and we had decided to bring the boys lunch. The men were outside practicing. We took a bench to watch the men and wait for them to take a break. My husband was standing with his father as many of the men sat watching. Masi was teaching them; he had not noticed my arrival for his back was to us. It took me a few minutes to realize he was showing them my move. Pride ran through me, for how long had it been before anyone had entered something new into their ancient fighting scrolls.

It wasn't long before Masi's father was singing his praise. That is when it hit me; he hadn't told them I had come up with it… in fact, he had taken the idea as if it were his. I should have known, because he shouldn't have ever trained me to begin with. I was full of rage, an all consuming rage.

Laying the food to one side, I stood, and then headed inside the Dojo building. My sisters' eyes followed, confused, but they had no idea what would follow next. In the Dojo I found what I was looking for, a sword. I came outside carrying the weapon by its wooden sheath in my left hand. One of my sisters gasped when her eyes found me. I had moved into the semi circle when Masi turned and faced me… the look on his face was of horror.

I announced how I would demonstrate the move correctly being that I was the one who came up with it. He started to yell at me, but I had already unsheathed the sword. With movement and grace I executed the move with unparalleled skill. Not one of the warriors who watched me would have doubted my skill and in turn where I learned it.

My husband's face was bright red when I finished. He held the tip of the sword towards me, "Put it down… go home."

I pointed mine at him, "No."

The battle that ensued was amazing; we were both skilled, full of anger and pride. No one tried to stop it; in fact, they just stood there making sure they were not in the way. We fought like never before and never before had we used real blades when sparring.

The truth is, when you have two masters, the fight never lasts very long. We wore no armor; our blades were sharp as razors. In moments we both had long red slashes; we would not last long even if someone didn't get a fatal blow.

I will never know who was truly better… I will never even care who was better. That day Masi moved his sword to the side; he stood still when I knew he would move. My sword slid through his chest as a needle through silk. What haunts me the most was my husband's final words, "Better to die by your sword… than to be dishonored by it… my love."

His body hit the ground dead, I dropped my sword. Masi's father grabbed me and led me to a room; he never said a word. Locking the door behind him, I found myself in a windowless room. There was nothing but a mat on the ground. It looked like a cell; I hadn't even known that Oka family had cells, but what did I know?

I sat in the cell waiting for tears that did not come. I had killed my love, my life and reason for living. Why had I done it? For pride, I did not know and still am not completely sure. I know why he did it; he lived by a code. My acts had shown that he had broken that code, an act punishable by death. It was the way of the Japanese; if their honor was taken, so were their lives. I had taken his honor; therefore I had killed him before my sword had entered his chest. I tried to prepare myself for the morning. I was sure I would be facing a trial.

It happened quickly; men in black burst into the room. They quickly tied me and carried me out. They brought me to the center of the Oka home where a garden stood between many homes and the Dojo. In the middle stood a large tree, I don't even remember what kind of tree it was.

They gagged me and strung me up by the neck. I fought, but to no avail. I looked up and there stood Masi's mother with a look of anguish. For some reason the thought passed through my head that she was here to save me. The old woman bent down and said, "A real Japanese woman would kill herself if she had brought this much shame upon the family name. Seeing you are not Japanese, I thought I might help."

I tried to respond, but I was gagged. The ninjas pulled me into the air, and there I hung until dead. From that day forth I was forever cursed to haunt my violin, for I could never forgive myself. I live as a ghost trying to do the thing I most regretted in life, to use my skill with a sword to slay demons.

It was Nicks who came and retrieved my violin from Japan. He found my gift with the sword valuable and promised that I could pay my debt by serving him. Now I will serve you.

I looked at Bow for a minute in silence. Without another word I picked up the violin and bow. "I suppose we should get practicing."

Chapter 9 Dr. Camp

I leaned back on the couch; I was not sure this was helping. How many of these sessions had I been to? Dr. Camp spoke first, "Where did we leave off? I believe in our last session you told me that you had been forced to leave your family. Why don't we go on from there?"

I was disclosing my life to this Doctor, who was supposed to help? Here I am in the library again, I could be spending time with Nicks, or training with Bow, but instead I am rehashing my life story with this therapist. I asked, "Are you sure this shit, will help?"

With the same pleasant face, she always had, she gently reminded me, "The more I understand, the better I can help you. You have had a very... different life. Just pick up where you left off. It gets easier, I promise."

I gave her a big fake smile, "Ok, I think I left off right when Spooky took me to my new home. If my memory serves me that was the same night that Bow told me her life story. That's not important; I'll tell you about that another time.

"I remember traveling down a highway. It swerved to the right as we climbed higher and then to the left as we went back down. Right, left, up and down, I was so sick. We had left in Spooky's classic Impala, and the car swayed like a boat. It still sits in my garage, but it doesn't run. Spooky talks about fixing it up, I don't believe she will. We left North Carolina and traveled north straight through Roanoke, Virginia. North of Roanoke up in the Smoky Mountains, not too far from the West Virginia border, we arrived at a small town.

"Spooky told me how Alice had worked things out for me. Apparently Alice was worried this might happen and prepared a plan just for this kind of emergency. Dan Caster was not only one of the members of the Council of Twelve, but he was also one of America's greatest wizards. Just so happens, he has been Alice's ex-husband from some years back. Once again, that is another story for a different time. Still, Dan and Alice were good friends, and she had made a place for me in his town, Queen Anne.

"This town is nestled in a small valley in the mountains and, unless you've been invited, you've never been there. Not long before the Civil War, Dan established this town in the hills. He spent many years laying down the magic to hide his town from others and protect the people within. It wasn't long before he was inviting other wizards and witches to come and live with him. Part of the defense of this town is that you would be unable to find it if you were not invited.

"We passed by the sign welcoming us to the town of Queen Anne, established in 1851. The sign was bright white with black letters and looked like it might have just been painted. We first drove through the main part of town. City Hall was as white as snow and positioned next to a large church that resembled a castle. One main road ran from these buildings and was crisscrossed with several intersections. Of course, this was Main Street and it was lined with old brick buildings crammed wall to wall. Apartments and housing would be found on the upper floors. The ground floors were filled with many different shops. I spied a coffee house - The Wild Bean. I loved coffee!"

"Spooky turned down the radio so she could hear the voice on the GPS. According to the GPS, we were driving through the forest; Queen Anne wasn't even on the map. That really didn't surprise me. Then Spooky turned off the GPS and handed me some written directions. I knew Alice's handwriting so it was no surprise what happened next. I should have read ahead because the directions took us down some little side road, then pointed out a small doll shop. In the directions it mentioned that one might find gifts there. The directions then told me to turn around and go back from where we came. We ended up all the way back to the center of town. Alice was *such* a pain in the ass.

"From there it took about eight minutes to arrive at the house. It was set back from the road, deep in the woods. I hadn't seen a house for at least five minutes, which means no neighbors and that was a good thing. We pulled up the driveway to the sound of breaking wood. The driveway was cluttered with old broken limbs. The house was surrounded by large oaks, and it looked as if more than one storm had come through, and debris from the trees lay everywhere. The entire house was surrounded by overgrown trees and bushes. Vines worked their way up the side of the trees and parts of the house. The house itself was a large two story house. It had brick siding; at one time someone had painted it white. The white paint had dried, cracked and mostly fallen off, leaving the house looking worse off than it might have been.

"On the trip Spooky explained a lot of things such as how my new living arrangements would work. Spooky planned on visiting every other week, not only to check up on me, but to bring me supplies I might need. Looking like a child, it would be hard for me to grocery shop by myself.

"I had a monthly allowance for personal use. I could order what I needed from the internet. Every month Alice would call to me. I would meet her in the woods and together we would hunt. I still needed blood and a friend every once in awhile, which was nice, too. My Kindle was soon to be my best friend, for I was home alone much of the time.

"We stopped the car and headed down, what I believed, was the walkway to the front door. A large bush with thorns had taken over the front porch and made the front door unusable. I asked Spooky if she had the right address. She responded that it seemed kind of nice for the likes of me. We had both been moody.

"I told you earlier about Spooky's and my relationship. No matter how much we tried, it was hard for us to get along. We knew how one another felt about everything, so there was very little reason to talk. Even if she had forgiven me for killing her parents and enslaving her, she was still a slave, and it was equally hard for me to not boss her around from time to time. It didn't help that I was so miserable about being taken from my family. I remembered commanding her to clear the thorny bush away from the front door. She did it, and, because of her super strength, it wasn't much of a chore. She did get cut a few times, I made her do it because I was being moody, and, to this day, we still fight about everything. I love Spooky, and I know she feels the same, but I find no companionship with her. I really miss having a friend like Carrie."

The Dr. asked, "Do you have any regular companionship?"

"No, but there is a reason for that, and the older I've become the more apparent the reason is. For the last nine years I lived in this house, I've grown up. You need to understand that I didn't become what I was; I became something new. Nicks has been helping me through this; if it weren't for him and Bow, I would have been lost long ago."

"I have become three things, separate and together all at the same time. I hope I can explain this... sometimes I don't believe I understand myself. First, I am human; my heart beats, I breathe and eat human food. Second, I am a vampire; I need blood, and I have their powers. Well, except for bending people's minds that is. Thirdly, I am the Daughter of Death, a grim reaper. I feed on the spirits, taking the last of their life energy and sending them on to the final death.

"The vampire and reaper side of me hate the day, so I sleep all day long. The sun is bright and hurts my eyes and skin, and that is another reason I meet few people, but far from the only reason. Three months ago I had my second fifteenth birthday, and, for me, it was nothing to celebrate. I stood before a mirror naked, my hair down to my waist, looking exactly like I did at fifteen almost twenty years ago, when I was ten years old, the first time living with my parents in a small apartment in Buffalo, I had fallen off a swing set. I cut my knee pretty bad; I remember it well. My mother bandaged me up and sang to me while I cried. This all happened before my mother became so hooked on heroin that I did not know who she was. As you remember, she died from a drug overdose when I was twelve. The scar on my knee was a reminder of the end of the happy days with my parents. As a vampire I would wear it for all time. When I was reborn, there was no scar, but, when I turned fifteen, the scar came back. One of the curses of being a vampire is that you will always be what you were from the day you died. The fact the scar came back let me know that I will never change from this form. Once again, I am Melabeth the Vampire.

"When the reaper side of me comes to life, you'll know it. My eyes glow; my fingers become elongated with black claws. The shadows around me move unnaturally, and I, myself, cast no shadow. When I become like this, my second vision is unaffected, but a new vision comes to life as the world of the dead overlaps the world of the living. Ghosts and humans are almost impossible to tell apart; even Bow becomes solid. I can make her violin into two swords. One is a Katana; the other is a Wakizashi. The Katana is a long sword while the Wakizashi is short. Depending on the situation and the terrain, I can use both or one. I am able to fight with skill far beyond my own. I hunt the spirits in this form when the spirits become aware of me. Most of them are afraid, for they know Death is among them.

"Any one of these things on their own would be tolerable, but that's not what happens. When either I choose vampire or Reaper, I take the chance that they merge and become one. When that happens, all hell breaks loose and I have no control... maybe some, but it feels like I am watching rather than driving. I need blood; I need to kill spirits… hell, I need coffee. The three worlds merge as one - death, life and un-death. Nicks has been trying to help me control it; he's at a loss. I don't blame him. I am one of a kind. How could he know what I would become or what to do about it?"

I don't know if this counselor could help, but I was definitely keeping her entertained. She hung on every word, and her response like many times before made me wonder if I was wasting my time. "This being out of control... do you feel you might hurt others?"

I shrugged my shoulders, "Maybe."

"This must make it hard to find new friends, if you are afraid you might hurt them."

"Duh," I responded.

My response did not irritate her, "Well, tell me more about the last few years living alone. What do you do? What have you done? What ways have you tried to control this power of yours?"

I huffed, and then went into detail, "I guess I can sum up all my days in the same way. The house that I now live in is big, bigger than it looks on the outside. Between the overgrowth and trees I would have never guessed the size. Not only was it large, with a great room and eight bedrooms and baths in almost every one. It also had a very large basement that used to be a wine cellar. Now it was full of empty wine racks and spider webs. I found a room in the far back of the cellar that someone used as a kind of utility room, no windows and large enough for what I needed. It had a giant worktable someone had crafted out of two by fours. It didn't take me long to make it into a room. I built a secret door with the help of Spooky. Hell, Spooky and I tore out a lot of these wine racks and turned them into nice racks to hang our clothes on. That's, of course, after we fumigated."

"It wasn't so bad at first. I visited my parents all the time through the eyes of Spooky. When she visited I was able to send them messages. Alice came once a month; we would meet outside of Queen Anne and go hunting. As I aged, my powers increased, so I could fly, flash and kill anything that got in my way. As my powers started to merge, I lost control and things started to get difficult. I was now hunting evil men, ghosts, other vampires, werewolves, shape shifters... hell anything humanoid. My lack of control coupled with my new diet, even had Alice a little worried. She thought it best that we meet and catch up, but let me hunt without her. She soon started to visit less. She tells me there are other reasons, but I do not believe her. Well, I really do believe her, but I'm mad about it.

"When hunger doesn't drive me to feed and go crazy, I have two hobbies. One is computers: I play games, tear them apart, and order parts. It truly is a great time-waster and time I have. The other is practice with Bow. Of course, this is yet another thing that has driven fear into the hearts of everyone who has met me in a dark alley. I am devastatingly fast with swords as I slice my enemies down.

"Oh, and you asked what I have done to control my power. I found that if I keep my eyes closed and only use my second sight, the madness of seeing life and death is less. I went online and ordered some costume supplies, a robe and mask. The mask is for a masquerade; it only covers right below the nose and lower around my checks. This leaves my mouth able to bite. I covered the eyes with black tape so I could not see out. My power of death stretches out and makes ghosts solid so my second sight still can see them, but I do not have to look at their faces. It's not that I am unhappy, just lonely. What do you think I should do? I mean, is there anything?"

The counselor tapped her finger against the bottom of her chin. After what felt like an hour, she said. "You should get a job."

"What?"

Chapter 10 Application

That counselor, what an idiot, what a hack! I was staring at the bare rafters as I lay on my workbench/ bed. I tried to toss up a queen-sized mattress, but it was too large and overhung. So with some two by four and nails, I made it bigger. I am sure if anyone saw my handy work, laughter would follow. I crawled out of bed, because I had to. The room wasn't much larger than the mattress so I had to crawl off one end.

It took some doing to open the door; it was made of stone the same as the wall. Spooky and I did a good job, but, if I were honest, someone who knew what to look for would find it pretty fast. Still, I felt it gave me time to wake up, or prepare myself. Then again the whole thing could just be a waste of time. It most likely was a waste of time, because I had fallen asleep upstairs more times rather than bothering to come down here to sleep. What use is a secret room to sleep in, if you're not in it?

I went upstairs and straight to the kitchen for some coffee. This was a large house, but I only used four rooms. I stayed in the basement to sleep while using the kitchen and breakfast area for eating. I used the large bathroom in the master bedroom which wasn't far off from the kitchen. The master bedroom had been transformed into storage for clothes that almost touched the roof. Between me and Spooky buying and stealing clothes, we never had much laundry, because I seldom wore the same outfit twice. The main room was where I truly lived. Once this great room was the pride of this house, but now it was a wreck.

There were computer parts and computers piled against one wall. Right next to that was a large screen TV hooked up to a very impressive surround sound system. The wires were draped off the walls leading to each speaker. Of course the TV itself was nothing but a giant monitor for one of my computers. The room had couches of different colors and patterns. All of them were couches from victims of mine. Not that I stole a couch from every man I killed, but some of them had nice furniture, and they wouldn't need it. Hell, some of the paintings I had taken weren't so bad either. I had chairs and tables as well. Stuff lay everywhere along with some trash. I shook my head… I am such a slob. I need to get myself together, I thought, as I took up residency in front of my TV. With remote in one hand and coffee in the other, I soon found myself nicely distracted.

I felt the need to hunt as the sun fell below the horizon. It had been quite a week. I wasn't expecting Spooky for a few more weeks. I loved popping into her mind to visit my family, but, of late, she had been spending a lot of time with Ezra. One time I popped in to see what she was up to… big mistake! I not only knew what she felt, but I could feel it too. I was so surprised that it took me more than a minute to pull my mind out and back to my own body. I suppose if I thought about it, Ezra and Spooky had always been so close, but lovers? Well, it wasn't any of my business, and I didn't need the visual either. Since then, I tried to make sure I knew where she was going to be and when.

The worst thing about her love for Ezra wasn't the weird fact that he just about raised her. No, the worst thing was that Spooky visited me even less. Even though we didn't get along well, I still enjoyed her company. It also reminded me of how much I missed Ezra.

I was thinking about what outfit I would put together tonight. Along with the masks, my costumes were becoming more elaborate. What can I say? Too much time alone and hanging out online with geeks. I was about to get up and dress for the evening out when I felt Alice. She was calling to me with excitement as I got ready. I did grab my violin and packed my mask and a scarf. Never knew when I might need that.

Bow didn't bother to materialize much like Carrie, and, when she did, it was for training. Now the training is done, so now she only pops up when I make her. Bow is one hell of a loner and way too depressed about her existence to really hang out with anyways. Still, she could move around at night and watch out for me, and she liked to walk through the real world quietly among the trees.

I flashed across the yard and into the woods. I was running between the trees. I flew over valleys, but I was careful not to take flight until I was out of the town of Queen Anne. I didn't like anyone to take notice of me there. Dan Caster, the wizard, who ran the town, had stopped by a couple of times when I first arrived. Alice did not tell him anything about me, so I was sure he had questions, like why would she allow a little girl to live mostly alone? The war between the Council and Necromancers was intensifying. He soon was too busy leading men to war. Also, Queen Anne had become a refuge for many hiding from the war. Dan was too busy to keep tabs on me and that's the way I liked it.

I ran in between trees at a high rate of speed, practicing a new technique that Bow had come up with. I swear it was one of the few times I had seen the girl smile when she witnessed me do it for the first time. When she learned about my power of flashing, she thought I could do more with that movement. The movement was too quick to use my eyes, or even my second sight. The only way I knew to do it was to concentrate on one place where I wanted to be, and, before I knew it, I was there. Bow noticed through watching me that I still moved my feet when I flashed.

The idea occurred to her that I could incorporate more than one move before I flashed. After a lot of failed attempts, it worked. After lots of practice, I could move and slash at blinding speed. One night I had been attacked by some hunters; three had surrounded me. They all had assault rifles loaded with tracer bullets. In three moves I slashed them all down. If they would have been standing next to me, it would have looked like some kung fu movie. Three well-choreographed moves, turning from one attacker to the next slicing them down. This time was different because my attackers stood yards away from me, all in different directions.

I flashed to the first, and in mid-swing, brought him down. I started my next swing as if the next gunman stood right next to me. Simultaneously, I flashed as my swing fell through the air. My target materialized right in front of me, or at least that is how it appeared to my eyes. My third backhanded swing, I did it in the same manner. The gunmen had been trained to stay apart so they could cover each other. With my new style of fighting, I killed them so fast that their friends didn't have time to shoot me. By the time they trained their guns on me, I was in front of them slicing through them. I may be losing control, but I am becoming one hell of a warrior.

I was in a hurry to see Alice; as soon as I was far enough away, I took to the sky. Flying was still my favorite thing, and sometimes, while floating through the air, it all seemed worth it. I knew where she was. I could feel her. I came to love the sound of the violin and played it eagerly, even without Bow's prodding. I played a gentle tune as I moved through the sky, bouncing from tree top to tree top.

Alice had found a nice view on the top of a hill overlooking a small dark valley. One road stretched out at the bottom of the valley as a seemingly unbroken stream of lights snaked its way around the valley floor.

I approached her as she sat upon an overturned tree. The tree sat at an angle, held up by a group of smaller trees. Alice jumped down; I flashed and hugged all at the same time. "I missed you. Like my new trick?"

Still holding me, Alice replied, "New? I have been doing that for over a hundred years."

We separated, and I clarified, "I mean that I moved in a flash."

"I understood."

"Oh well, Bow will be disappointed... she thought she came up with it."

Alice laughed, "No, but once again it is a talent that should be far out of your league. Ezra has been practicing for as long as I can remember, but can't do it half that well. If it weren't for that skill and my mind power, I am not sure that I could defeat Ezra in a fight. Then again, without Ezra's gift of perception, I don't know how good he is. Speaking of perception how does that fit in the magical classes?"

I groaned, "Come on, ALICE."

She retrieved her doll that was still sitting on the log. "Dolly, do *you* know? What's that? Dolly said she doesn't believe you've been studying. She thinks you've been lying around on your ass, not doing the one thing Alice asked of you. Well, that's what Dolly thinks."

I pleaded, "We have to go over this right now?"

Alice was looking at the stars now. If I hadn't known her so well, I would have believed she had tuned me out. It took her a second longer to answer than it should have, "What's wrong with tonight?"

"Hungry for one, let's just go over it another time." I tried to change the subject. "I thought you should know that I have been having better luck in controlling my power."

Her eyes narrowed, "You're trying to change the subject. It will need to be tonight. I will be leaving. I will tell you why, after you have proven to me you know. So, does this new found control mean I can hunt with you?"

I shrugged, "Not really. I most likely would just remember I ate you, but not be able to stop myself. It's like watching TV. I see everything but have no control of the outcome. Still, I feel like it's getting better because, before I was blacking out and couldn't even remember what happened. Why must we go over it tonight? Can't it wait until after I have fed? One night, what's the hurry?"

Alice was firm, "NO... tonight, it has to be tonight. I have a lot to tell you, and I need to know you have been taking things seriously. I know that I act childish, but I also know how not to. The war is getting worse; the last time it was this bad, the Great War broke out. I feel like I will live to see World War III, and I *don't* want to see that.

"We cannot join The Council and we're not about to join the necromancers. The necromancers have vampires working for them. In turn The Council now sees all vampires as their enemies. It only gets better for you. Your nights of insanity have had their price. The necromancers are sure that you are a weapon created by The Council to stop them. On the other hand, The Council is sure that you are a weapon created by the necromancers to stop them."

I closed my eyes, "Oh, fantastic, and we still have no idea who has that book."

Alice went on, "Yep, so you see I need to leave for awhile, but first I need to know you have studied. I feel that you will need to understand this in the days to come."

"Yes, I have been studying, but where are you going?"

She moved her finger back in forth, "Uh, uh, uh, none of that. I'll tell you when you have told me what I need to hear and not before then."

"Dolly, do me a favor and bite her in her sleep."

Alice's face was full of mock shock, "She would never."

I floated up and gently came to rest on the log. Alice took a seat next to me as I lay my violin and bow down. "Ok, the five schools of magic: Elemental, Summoning, Charming, Enchanting, and Conjuring. Really, there are six, but magic users don't like to admit that Necromancy is a school of magic, but yet most all wizards have practiced it. Wizards are nothing more than a title for a magic-user who, has mastered all five schools of magic. In doing , so they practice and learn Necromancy, so that they might know how to deal with it better.

"Not all magic users bother to become wizards, a lot become sorcerers or specialists. A sorcerer is normally someone who masters the art of elemental magic. Other specialists are normally just called whatever class they mastered, like, an enchanter, or a charmer and so on. An example of the first specialist I ran into was the creepy Devon. I still have fond memories of his death and the film to prove it. He was a conjurer and when I fought him, he had conjured up some sort of giant shadow hands."

Alice added, "Very good so far. I remember that man, too, and you're right, that was a good movie. Go on."

"I'll explain each class to you. First, the art of Necromancy, because of my experience it is the easiest."

Alice interrupted, "First, explain manna."

"Oh, yes, right, manna. Well, it is what all magic users draw their power from. Where it comes from, no one really knows. Some say it is the sun or life itself, but, so far, it is a mystery. It is the ability to control, hold, and gain this power that determines how strong the magic user is. With that being said, this is one reason that it is argued whether or not Necromancy is a magic class at all. Manna is used to cast spells to control the spirits or raise the dead, but, once the cast is done, the power comes from death itself which is a different power source than manna. There is a great advantage to this, like a summoner uses his own magic to raise a creature and maintain it, but necromancer's only need to summon. That is why they can raise a whole cemetery at once and control them. In short, they use a limited amount of manna to manage and control the energy of spirits...."

Alice looked at her doll, and then announced, "WOW, that was boring. Damn, I thought I was going to die if she said one more word Dolly."

I yelled, "What the hell? You're the one who wanted me to tell you all this crap!"

Alice shook her head, "I only made you because I was sure you hadn't done as I asked. Therefore, not only is it surprising, but dull as all get out."

I narrowed my eyes, "You are such a pain. Now that I told you all that boring shit, where are you going?"

"I can't tell you that... it's a secret."

I shook my head in disbelieve, "Of course you can't." I followed that up with an eye roll. "I don't even really want to know."

Alice giggled, "Bad liar... of course you want to know. Being serious, I really can't tell you."

Alice's tone had changed, and I knew she was not goofing around, "Why can't you tell me? Will you be back soon?"

She shifted her weight; she was nervous about something. "I can't tell you where I am going, but I hope to be back quickly. I won't lie to you, it's dangerous. I need to find this book, or, better yet, come to understand it. I need to know what power it holds... no, that's not it. I need to understand who made you and why. We both need this and believe me there is only one place I can get answers to all my questions."

I demanded, "Take me with you. If it's so dangerous, don't you want someone to watch your back?"

She smirked, "Don't take this wrong, but I really can't trust you in that regard right now." Alice read the hurt that crossed my face. She reached up and took my hand, "Don't worry about it. It won't be long before you get control of your power. For now it's just as well that you remain the Dark Fiddler."

"The Dark what? Fiddler...?"

"Oh, I forgot, that's your nickname. What did you expect? You roam around at night on top of buildings playing that violin and then when you're approached, you kill them. Well, at least that is the way other people are putting it, but I think the concern you're causing both sides is a good thing for now."

I wondered, "If you say so. What do I do if you don't come back?"

Alice paused for a minute. She looked at me and tried to hide the worry in her eyes, "Come and get me, silly. That is when the time is right."

Confused, I asked, "How will I come and get you if I don't know where you are? How will I know when the time is right?"

Alice grinned, "When the time is right, you will know. Change of subject... how are you holding up alone?"

I couldn't even keep eye contact when I answered, "Fine."

"That bad, huh? Maybe you should try to make a friend."

I tried not to sound too grumpy, "Now you sound like my counselor."

That was a mistake; I shouldn't have said that. Alice's eyes lit up, "You have a counselor? No way... how crazy are you, and is there any hope? Wait, wait, I know it's all your parents' fault... except that's kind of true."

"Shut up, troll. She told me that I needed new friends because my current ones are selfish psychopaths."

Alice laughed, "Where did you find this counselor, and I hope you didn't tell her too much. Dolly won't like that; she might want to pay her a visit."

"No worries, she is a ghost trapped in the library. She won't be telling my secrets to anyone. She thinks I should get a job, that way I'll meet people."

Alice stood and twirled around. She never stayed still for too long. As she spun, she about sang, "I agree with her. That would be a great way to meet new people. Plus, I get sick of paying all your bills." She stopped spinning and looked at me with a strange look. Her tone went serious, "I just thought of something. Why didn't your counselor go on? I mean, don't spirits get trapped in our world and the library because something in their lives holds them here… right?"

I never asked, "I don't know."

"I do," Alice had an evil grin, "It's because she was a horrible counselor. All the nut jobs that came to her for help never found any. They all took their own lives, and some killed others, but now, if she could help you, she could move on. Which means… *she will be trapped in purgatory forever*!" Alice burst into tears of laughter, "How awful."

I burst into laughter! Between fits of laughing, I said, "There is no way I am coming for you."

Between giggles it almost sounded as if she might have snorted. Alice added, "Just ask yourself. What would my counselor do?"

Before she could say another word, I froze. I could feel a presence, "Shh… we're not alone."

Alice's laughter stopped cold as she looked around, "Who?"

"Spirits, and lots of them." I picked up my violin and bow, and, with a swish of my wrist, I held two swords with black blades. I slid the shorter sword into the sheath that appeared at my side. There was plenty of space to wield the Katana with both hands. I could feel the spirits approaching, and I let my power out. Now the world around me was life and death, and I knew my eyes glowed with power. With this power the world changed and now that spirits could not travel through objects such as the trees. "Time to say our goodbyes."

"I hate that our time together is so short, but this only enforces my belief that I must help solve this book mystery. So, which would be the best way out?"

"Follow me. I'll cut a path, and, when I have their attention, head south. And Alice?"

"Yes"

I smiled, "I love you and come back to me."

Alice smiled and then embraced me, "I love you. Before you lose control, see me off… and don't forget about me."

"Forget about who?" I teased.

Alice teased back, "Don't forget to put me down as a reference for your application. I will give a glowing lie about your ability to work."

Before we could go back and forth anymore, we could hear the spirits as they took form. As they entered my radius of power, they were forced into their human forms. The spirits gathered about a hundred yards away in the woods. There were hundreds of them, and they were spirits from the long ago past. Most of them were some kind of Celtic warriors. They were all wearing kilts and held all types of weapons, most with axes and round shields; they began to bang them together.

Alice gasped, "Wow, can you handle all of them?"

Bow had materialized. Unlike Carrie I always forgot she traveled with me at night. She had no reason to speak to me and seldom interacted unless it was in regard to fighting. Her whole demeanor changed when the battle was upon us, she went from school teacher to intense warrior. It was just not her skill that I now fought with, for Ezra had taught me plenty. We had learned in practice to mix our skills, sword, hand to hand and even claws. My black claws could rip apart spirits. Bow looked over at Alice with distain; she never cared for her. "I will watch over Alice as she slips away."

"No, I will need your skill. Alice can handle herself. Alice, once you leave my sphere of influence, the ghosts will be invisible again, but I can draw them to me. Stay with me, and I will cut you a path through them, once through, you can get away."

Alice nodded, "Dolly, I sure hope Melabeth will be around to rescue me later."

I tried not to laugh as I yelled at her, "Shut the hell up and follow me."

Chapter 11 Attacked

Alice followed close behind as I charged at an army of ghosts.

With my powers the rules had changed; the ghosts became solid. Their swords were real, and so was their bite. When they sliced against my skin, it cuts as if it were metal. The warriors used their round shields to block me... locking them together to form a wall. With a quick slice, I cut a shield in half along with a man's arm. This followed with another quick slash and stabbing... I killed the two closest men.

The spirits did not bleed; instead, blackish smoke rose from their wounds. When I killed them, they turned into clouds of dust, but the dust itself, disappeared before it found a place to settle. Using the large Katana with both hands gave me large powerful swings. With my second sight, I moved into the men slashing, parrying and dodging.

It didn't take long before I was too crowded to use the powerful two handed moves, so I quickly pulled out the smaller sword with my left hand. With two swords I was faster and could stab and slash in different directions and distances... less power, more speed.

With my second sight, I could see from all directions, and, strangely, it was like watching a movie. Alice moved up behind me. I was such a warrior that somewhere in my mind, I had surpassed Alice, and she was no longer in my league. What a fool my pride made me. Alice moved through the ghosts as if she was strolling through a garden doing a strange but elegant dance. I had been sliced and stabbed several times already, but I healed quickly. Alice, on the other hand, did not have a scratch on her as we passed through the group of warriors.

I turned around fighting as Alice passed by. I felt my mind slipping into that madness as all my powers came to be. Alice said, "I hope to see you soon, sister. I will be on my way now before you kill me accidently... have fun!" With that, she sped away through the trees. I was too busy to respond.

As I fought, I realized this was not madness, for I was not crazy. I fought with skill outside my own as Bow merged with me. My vampire powers came to life, and I craved blood as the hunger ran through my body. It had been awhile since I last fed. When I was a vampire, this would have been starving. I still was not sure of my reaper powers. Did it give me strength, speed, healing or was that coming from my vampire side? I knew the fact that I could kill the ghosts, and that was part of that power.

The more I fought, the harder I fought, the saner I felt. So, with this new found control, I thrust forward into battle, just in time to see more spirits charging through the forest to reinforce their friends. Moving into the trees helped as now they were shooting arrows. I flashed between trees trying to engage the smaller groups of men. I would quickly kill two or three and then move away before they could surround me, but this plan didn't work for very long. It didn't take them, but a few minutes before I felt like a donut hole the donut had come back for.

Only one thing was left to do, straight up. I flew into the air, but I quickly found that the spirits could follow. I flew to a large tree; standing on its trunk, the world took on a new reality. It now appeared that the tree was flat, as the world hung attached to the base of the trunk. As I ran around the tree fighting the spirits, it now appeared that the world spun like a giant apple on a stick. The warriors ran up the tree as some flew higher and landed at the top of the tree. I fought them slashing them down as fast as I could.

I could feel a gateway, a gateway to the land of death. It opened not too far away from where I fought. I needed to get to that place; once there, I could destroy this gateway. I didn't know how I knew this, but I did. I also knew that necromancers must have opened this gateway. They had followed Alice, and it looked as if this was an attempt on her life, or mine. I had to fight my way to the source of these spirits' power.

I stabbed a ghost with my left hand and left my short sword stuck in him. With both hands, I swung with all my skill slicing through the trunk of the tree. Then I pulled out my short sword, and the ghost turned to dust. The top of the tree fell to the ground, it took spirits with it, crushing them below. I flew through the gap, landing on another tree. I bounced from tree to tree fighting off the ghosts as I went.

Finally, I worked my way back to the forest floor where I flew between the trees toward the gateway. I took out the ghost who tried to block my path. The necromancers must have known I was coming for them, because they collapsed the gateway. There would be no more reinforcements.

There were plenty of ghosts chasing me, and, when I got to where the gateway had been, spirits awaited me as even more chased me. On the other side of the group of spirits, I could see four necromancers jumping into a Jeep Liberty and making a run for it. My mouth watered with the thought of fresh blood, but it would have to wait. Once again, I was surrounded.

I had a lot of free time during the last nine years, and, at that time, I watched way too many movies. I looked upon the warrior ghosts and said in my best Chinese accent, "You are no match for the green destiny."

These spirits were from a time long ago… so much for getting a laugh. Oh well, I attacked; if I didn't get any blood, I was sure to dine on the energy of the dead. The next ten minutes belonged in a Jet Lee movie as I fought the large crowd. I would dodge, block and spin through the hundreds of attacks of my enemy. At one point I went into a vertical spin to move through all the swords… even with that spin my two blades found their marks.

It didn't take long before I was just using my one sword, and, shortly after that, the spirits ran away. The sun would finish off the last of them. They were not attached to any item, and the gateway was closed; they would not be coming back. The necromancers had at least a ten minute head start, but I would still give chase, for no other reason than the fact that I still wanted some blood.

I felt alive as I bounced from treetop to treetop. My swords were both sheathed on my left side. It was the coolest thing as the sheaths reappeared only when I needed them. Ever since I read the Harry Potter books, I compared things to that world. Couldn't help but think about when Harry pulled the sword out of a hat.

I landed upon a large tree and hung from its highest limb, looking down into the darkness of the forest where nothing moved. The sound of a light breeze rustling through the leaves filled my ears. I could not hear the sound of the motor nor see the light from the headlights. It was too quiet and too dark; it was a spell. The necromancers had cast a spell of some sort to cover their escape.

I thought about it for a little bit. The first thing they would want is a road; a dirt path would be too slow. The nearest highway lay west of me… I should be able to hear it. That confirmed my belief that there was a spell. Once on the highway, they could go north or south. North would lead them higher into the mountains, but south would take them into Roanoke. I could fly over the hill in front of me traveling south. This would accomplish two things: one, I would leave the effect of this spell and two, I could hope to catch them coming into town.

If they traveled north, I would miss them completely, but, believing the odds were greater, they headed towards the city. I knew of the perfect overpass to spot them coming into town, but I must hurry. With that thought, I took to the sky. I flew high and fast; time was short. Wait... I am in my right mind. Of course I know I really lose control when the blood starts flowing, but still I felt in control. This was positive, and the night would get better when I found some blood.

I landed softly in a tall oak just overlooking the overpass. It had taken about twenty minutes to arrive here as the vampire flies. The area was littered with housing developments. This was the first exit off the highway outside of the mountains. They could have gotten off somewhere else, but I was gambling they were heading to the city. Of course they could have traveled north. I watched the cars pass by, hoping I would get lucky.

It was a cool May night and there was a stiff breeze in the air with heavier gusts every few minutes. Hard to believe it was 2012 already, and I was the last American not to own a cell phone. The thought crossed my mind as I watched at least four close calls on the highway below, almost all of the drivers with their hands against their heads. I wondered if I should get a cell phone, but then who would I call?

I didn't need to call Spooky, and it would be too dangerous if I did. She has been hanging with Ezra, and I assume he's being watched. When she went to my parents, she went as a cat only changing to her human self inside the house. I couldn't do anything that could be so easily traced. Then there was Ezra and Alice and there was no way to contact them without drawing attention. Nicks was beyond a cell phone, no signal in death. Bow had nothing to say. I needed to get a job, and then I could meet people.

I was thinking about my resume and what I might put on it: expert swordswoman, good at killing, and never held a job of any kind. Yeah, that sounds good... just where am I applying anyway? My thoughts were interrupted; the jeep finally passed by. I took to the sky once again, but this time I had lights to follow.

The SUV pulled onto a dirt road that led to the back entrance to a parking lot. Landing gently on a large tree, I could see the SUV parking next to some other vehicles. The parking lot surrounded what was obviously an abandoned hotel. The dirt road came in from the back so none of the houses from the front of the building could see it. The parking lot was full of cracks with tall weeds bursting out everywhere. Most of the windows of this four story building were boarded up. I watched the four necromancers get out of the vehicle and go inside. I doubted they were alone. It looked like I was in for a bigger meal tonight.

I was looking for the best point of entrance when I noticed some movement from below me. A group of well camouflaged men came out of the bushes. They most likely hadn't seen me land or else they would not have given away their positions as they moved toward the apartment complex. They had been watching the apartment complex and most likely waiting for the return of these four. Eight men moved in, most of them looked like the military, but one stood out among them. I could not make out his face, he was a taller, older man is the best I could tell. I could only see the back of his head, and his white hair. He wore a long trench coat and carried what looked to be a staff or a club of some sort. From a distance it was too hard to tell.

They moved quickly to the building's outer wall. There the man with the trench coat started to draw on the wall. He stood back and waved his hands; if he said something, I could not hear him. The wall vanished, and the soldiers rushed in. From the lack of noise they had yet to make contact with anyone in the building. The man with the trench coat was obviously a magic user, perhaps a wizard. He was the second to last to enter the building.

With all of them inside, the real fun would begin. I pulled out my mask and a long scarf. I used the material to wrap my hair and my eyes. I couldn't stand seeing the world of the living and the dead as one. I put the mask over my face. The mask was black and had a sinister look about it. Only my mouth showed the better to bite them with.

I took to the skies playing my violin so that my second sight came to life. I could use my whistle so no one could hear, but what would be the fun in that. I'll let them know that I am coming… let the games begin.

Soon as my feet touched the roof, my violin and bow became swords. Using my long sword, I made three quick slices into the roof. A triangular piece of roof fell inwards. I sheathed my long sword. It was much too long to use indoors; that is what the short sword was for. I dropped down into the rafters of the building and quickly moved through the attic. The attic was unfinished, and I had to walk on the beams or I would fall through the ceiling. I listened for sounds below… then I heard one.

Two men were whispering below me. I felt them and others calling for the aid of spirits. My reaper powers came to life. My vampire side was wide awake; I was ready. I dropped through the roof and into the room. If the men were surprised, they didn't have time to show it. I took the first one's head right off and quickly flashed and elbowed the second man right in the face. He flew into the wall crashing to the ground with a thud. I knew when I dropped into the room that there could be more than two men, and I was right.

The men had summoned two spirits and some kind of wolf. My right elbow that had driven the man into the wall was the same arm that held my sword. I simply spun around and followed into a natural swing slicing the first spirit in half.

The large dog lunged itself at me. I didn't have time to swing or stab; instead, I jumped and spun in the air as the dog's lunge sent him under me. I drove my sword downward landing on the dog and driving my blade through its head. I drove it so hard that my blade was buried in the floor and did not stop until the hilt was crushing the dog's skull against the floor. The dog was down, but not the last spirit.

The final spirit was a large barbarian man. He came at me swinging a large axe at my head. Not having time to pull my sword out of the floor, I let go of my blade and jumped back. I nearly missed the edge of the axe as it swung inches from my face. My body came to rest against the far wall. The large axe man didn't give me time to rest as he stepped in and went for another swing. This time I pushed off the wall toward him. I dropped to my knees and leaned back, sliding across the floor and underneath the axe swinging through the air.

The dog had disappeared being that it was some kind of summoned animal. So I slide ended when the handle of my sword went between my legs, bringing me to a sudden halt. It didn't hurt; I grabbed my sword and pulled up on it like it was Excalibur. As I came up, I turned to the side just in time to deflect a blow from the axe with my sword.

I was too quick; before the axe man could, bring his blade around for another swing, he became a pile of black ash. The man I had elbowed into the wall was now starting to recover, but I had no intention of slaying him with a sword. He was not a spirit or a summoned creature, he was a Necromancer. Therefore, he was full of blood.

I helped the man to his feet, then pushed him into the wall… he was delicious.

The blood did three things for me. One, it filled me full of life and energy; it was like a good night's sleep in ten minutes. Two, it sets off the vampire side in full, now reaper and vampire were one. I felt little control. Thirdly, it made me happy, so I wanted more.

More is what I got.

I attacked who ever got in my way and fed on everyone I could get my hands on. I was aware that in the lower levels, there was gunfire and small explosions going on. Good thing I didn't come in here all alone. There were a lot of necromancers along with some werewolves. I hadn't killed any werewolves, but I could hear them downstairs.

Even in my madness, I knew that I didn't want to fight everyone. Best to leave before the unknown attackers came upstairs. I pulled my fangs out of my latest victim. Blood was pouring from my mouth. I fed to the point where no more would go down. I felt the slime of the blood on my hands as I gripped my sword. I felt it slide down my chin and soak my shirt. It sickened me; I felt like an addict.   All I could think about was blood, but, now that I got it, I was sickened by what I had done.

Somewhere in this blood lust I felt just a little bit of sanity… time to leave. The room I was in had no windows according to my second sight. Most likely they were all boarded up; still it would be easier to leave the way I came in. It took me a second to retrace my movements through the building. I remembered what room I had dropped into.

I went to the hallway and started to head toward the way out when a man burst out of a door with a machine gun. I didn't think about it, I just reacted. I flashed the distance and attacked. The man was quick; he got a few shots off, but he missed me. He used his rifle to deflect my blade.

Two of his friends had joined him in the hallway. I grabbed the man and used him as a shield so the others couldn't get a clean shot. One of them yelled vampire, and the other pulled out a cross. I felt its effect, but it was not enough to stop me. The man I was using as a shield had pulled out a knife and shoved it into my gut. I slit his throat with my nails.

Using his dying body as a shield, I rushed the other two men, pushing the dead man into the closest soldier. As the man fell on the floor, the third man now had a clear line of sight. As he fired I moved so fast he missed. I threw my sword right into his eye. His machine gun fire went wild as his body fell. His gun and his body now lay dead.

I jumped and flashed, landing on the other side of this mess. Then I reached down and pulled my sword out of his face. The man in the middle, who had just pushed off his dead friend, came up with a fireball in hand. Unfortunately for him he was facing the wrong way. He hadn't realized I had flashed over him to retrieve my sword. As he prepared to throw his fireball down an empty hall, I stabbed him in the back. My sword found its mark; the blade slid through his ribcage and straight to his heart.

The door they came out of led to the staircase. I could hear a voice saying, "Go back."

I was full of rage and no longer in control. I burst through the door to the surprise of two more soldiers. I stabbed the first one in the chest. He did get off a few rounds, but they were not tracers and did nothing to stop me. I kicked his body off my sword.

The second soldier tried to shoot me, but he was shaking so bad I was able to move around his gunfire even though I stood five feet in front of him in a small hallway. I ducked, jumped and weaved while he shot wildly. Unlike the movies, machine guns that are shooting fully automatic run out of ammo in seconds. The soldier was now pressed against the far wall holding down the trigger of a gun that was no longer firing.

I swung my blade cutting the strap of his rifle, I disarmed him. He stood there with so much fear; I could hear his heart trying to jump out of his ribcage. His breathing was labored. At first I was going to rip his throat out and feed, not that I needed any more blood. Something about him gave me pause. I approached him and slowly reached toward him.

He tried to move away from my claw-like hands, but he had nowhere to go. I could not see him since I was still wearing my makeshift mask. Still, I wanted to touch him... I felt in control. My hands covered in blood slid across his face; the boy whimpered at my touch. My voice was harsh and sounded like a snake, "You smell good. Don't fearrr me... I am going to let you livvve."

The boy was brave as he pulled himself together. "Humph, ok... thanks... I guess."

This boy smelled so good. Then I felt something... pain, pain in my side. I looked down and remembered the soldier who had stabbed me. I even felt the gunshot wounds; they hurt. I pushed the bullets out and healed my wounds by will alone. Reaching down, I yanked the knife out and let it fall to the floor with a clatter. Weird, the vampire side of me seemed to be gone.

I moved away from the boy and back into the hallway. By the time I reached the room with the hole in the ceiling I felt the vampire return. Strange, how did the boy do that? I wasn't sure if I liked it or not.

Not long after that I was flying through the air again. I needed to get home before the sunrise. Once the sun came up, it would be a long tiring walk home.

My vampire side had returned, but being so well fed I was able to keep control. What had that soldier done to me? Why did I regain such control around him? Why did it feel like the vampire side left in his presence? Who was this man?

Returning home with a thousand questions bouncing around in my head, I stripped off my clothes and started a hot tub. Laying there in the pink water, waiting for the rest of the blood to come off, I fell into thought. Had I made a mistake? Should I have figured out who he was, or what he was?

I had to know!

Chapter 12 Coffee

What time is it?

The noise was pounding in my head. The alarm clock sounded like a herd of elephants with accordions for legs. It seemed like a good idea to put that damn device outside of my sleeping hideaway. Apparently I don't have good ideas.

After dragging my ass out of bed, I moaned and walked like a zombie straight to the kitchen. There I worshiped the coffee pot as it slowly spit forth the nectar of the Gods. I poured some hot coffee, then fell into a comfortable love seat. The chances I would fall back to sleep were high, so I started to sip my coffee right away. It was ten in the morning and it had been at least five years since I got out of bed before four in the afternoon. If I wanted to find a job, braving the daylight world would be a must.

I put on some brown pants followed by a green sleeveless shirt. I topped it off with a pair of brown shoes with just a little bit of heel. After I finished my makeup and put my hair up in a braid, I looked into the mirror. Well, at least I looked alive. I grabbed the keys and the sunglasses and went to the garage.

In the garage, sat only two items. One was Spooky's broken down Impala, the other was a motorcycle. Alice was pissed when I bought this on ebay, but I needed something to get around with. Of course I only rode it a half a dozen times. I told Alice that I couldn't very well run through town picking up groceries and then run back. Of course I had my groceries delivered because I couldn't fit them on the bike.

I bought it two years ago; it is a 2005 Suzuki gsxr-750. It has been modified, in what ways, I couldn't tell you, but you could see most of the changes. The bike is what they call naked, with no plastic on the side. The whole bike was solid black and looked cool as hell.

I never registered the bike, but then again, I didn't have a license, so what did that matter? Hitting the garage door, and then jumping on the bike, I started out. That's when I remembered I had forgotten my helmet. I got it free with the bike; it was black with a full face. The best part about the helmet was that it had red spikes across the top like a Mohawk. I put on the helmet and then took off like a bat out of hell.

Pushing over a hundred miles per hour, it only took a few minutes to reach the town. At which point thirty-five felt like I had stopped moving. It was a beautiful spring Tuesday morning. Lots of people were out and about. It was getting close to lunch; better get going and see if I can find a job. A lot of the stores were antique or clothing shops. Most sold some kind of furniture. One place after another simply said, "Sorry we're not hiring right now. You can always check back later."

Sadly, I just wanted a job to mingle. I didn't really need the money, stealing from the dead was easy enough. Still, earning money without killing might do the soul some good. I would like to think that I feel bad for living off of Alice, but I don't. I came up to the coolest shop, something different. The sign said, "The Wicked Broom." The whole store had a dark look about it. Wow, these witches weren't even going to try to hide what they were doing, but then again why should they? I mean this whole town is full of supernaturals. Where is Diagon Alley anyways?

I really wanted to go inside this strange store. Soon as I opened the door, I felt it, this place was protected big time. I could feel the protection on every building. If I were a full vampire, I would need to be invited in. I could push through it easily enough in my new body, but this protection took some doing. I was almost ready to turn and leave the store, but, once I got a few steps inside, I felt better.

Once in the door, I walked slowly taking in my surroundings. The ceiling was open and you could see the air ducts which were painted black. The beams and roof were all large pieces of lumber, darkened with age. The floor was wood, dark brown and worn out. It was uneven and creaked whenever someone stepped on it. Not me, I was light on my feet. The store was so full of stuff it was hard to concentrate on any one thing. I walked from shelf to shelf taking in all the strange merchandise.

As I took in my surroundings I became aware of other people. The lady behind the counter was older with thick hair. It had been pinned up so the long black and white curls didn't hang in her face. She was heavyset but had a friendly look about her. She wore a black apron with the store name embroidered on the left side. Another worker was wearing the same apron and looked about the same age, but she was thin, and her curly hair was jet black and cut short. The look on her face was not happy, and it only deepened when her eyes made contact with me. I also noticed a young girl. I would guess her to be under twenty. She had long black hair. Along with her, a young man, who was watching me out of the corner of his eye, was wearing all black, but his messy untrimmed hair was brown. Soon two more customers came in, one with black hair, the other with fire red hair.

It wasn't the fact that they all colored their hair... well, except for the brown haired boy. It was the way they dressed, wore their makeup and the jewelry they all wore. It reminded me of the time I hung out with the Goths. I was dressed like a yuppie, and the looks I was getting were saying, "Your kind is not welcome here." When the two customers came in, both ladies perked right up; they knew each other by name. So far, not even a "Hi," had been uttered at me. I really didn't care. I was too interested in the merchandise. How many witches' stores had I been in?

There were jars full of all kinds of things. Most of the labels I couldn't even pronounce, but they appeared to be a kind of plant. Some of them were small pieces of animals, like the eye of bat or snake bones. What one would do with this stuff was beyond me. The store even had books; most of them were about witchcraft, but, stuck in-between some of them, was a *Twilight* book. I had read them and enjoyed the series, but I really felt it would have been better if there would have been real vampires in them.

I caught sight of the *City of Bones*; I hadn't read it. I was about to reach for it when a very unfriendly voice asked, "Can I help you?"

I turned to find the skinny older lady sneering at me. I said pleasantly, "No, just looking... thank you." I moved on down the aisle forgetting about the book. The end of the aisle brought me to a set of refrigerators with big glass doors, the same kind you would find at any gas station, but I didn't see the normal sodas and energy drinks. Instead, it was filled with glass jars marked with tape; on the tape they had written the contents in black marker. One of the jars caught my eye; it simply was marked, "Human Blood Type O". It was a quart size bottle with a bright orange price tag... $14.99.

Having an out of body experience, I watched myself open the fridge and take out the bottle. I stare at the blood, knowing that if I opened, it the shit would really hit the fan. I swear I used to have more control than this. The young girl with the long black hair brought me back to the here and now, "Thinking of a spell?"

I quickly put the bottle back, "No, just looking."

The older skinny lady, who had just asked if I needed help, now joined us. Her voice was full of venom, "This isn't a freak show. This is a place to buy things."

"If this isn't a freak show, then why are you working here?" I inquired.

Her face tightened, and I could see the anger in her eyes. Before she could speak, the heaviest set woman said in a loud, but friendly voice, "Darlene, can you go in the back and check on the potions table?"

Darlene started to argue, "But, Betty..."

Before she finished, Betty said in a very quiet but stern voice, "Now!"

"Fine," Darlene responded, but not before turning and giving me a death stare.

The young girl spoke again, "Mom, she was being pretty nasty to Darlene."

Betty smiled, "Sweetie, why don't you go check on her."

She tossed her hands up, "I got things to do... I know when I'm not wanted." She left but didn't travel far. She joined the now staring boy, who both pretended to be busy and not paying attention to me.

"Thank you, Veronica," After Betty thanked her daughter, her eyes turned to me. "How can I help you?"

"Just looking," I responded.

Her face was nice and so was her tone, but what she said didn't match either. "What would your kind want in my store?"

I asked, "My kind?"

She looked as if she was trying to remain calm, "Little white witches will find nothing in my store."

I burst into laughter, "You think I'm a witch?"

Betty's face was no longer kind and nor were her words. "I don't care if you're a witch, a shifter, or whatever. You are one of them and have no business in my store. I don't think you know who you are messing with."

Her threat was akin to hitting me. I filled with rage and knew that I would kill her. Betty jumped back and moved several steps back with a look of horror upon her face. I had no idea what she saw in me, but it saved her life. Her reaction stopped my own, and now that I was in control again, it was time to leave. I moved to the front door with inhuman speed. Slamming the door behind me with enough force to crack a window, this has been enough job shopping, slash, friend making for one day.

I was flying out of town on my motorcycle before I knew it. I needed to get control of that anger of mine. If I planned on getting a job and hanging out with people, I would need to learn some people skills. Just because someone threatens me doesn't mean I need to kill them, or eat them.

I was lost in thought when a new sound found its way to my ears, the sound of sirens. I looked into my mirror and could see the blue lights of the cop behind me. Glancing over at my speedometer, I noticed I was close to one hundred miles per hour. I thought about running, but then thought better of it and pulled over, the whole time chanting, "Keep my temper, keep my temper".

I was still in the town of Queen Anne, so I had no idea what to expect from this cop. Once I stopped, two police officers stepped out of the vehicle. One was black, and the other looked to be Hispanic. As they approached, the wind blew their scent to me. Hanging out with Spooky, I learned that this hint of smell that I would describe as gamey, most likely meant that they were shifters.

The officers took up positions on both sides of my bike. The Hispanic asked, "License and registration?"

Taking off my helmet they both looked me over. I answered, "I don't have either."

"Do you know why we stopped you?"

I knew, but I was a smart ass by nature, "Because you wanted to talk to a pretty girl?"

The officer chuckled, "No, because Betty called. She said you came into her shop today. Sounds like you really scared her."

I asked confused, "You didn't stop me because I was doing a hundred miles per hour?"

The black officer laughed, "*Hell no girl*, no one cares about that. You know the rules."

I didn't really know the rules, but wasn't about to point that out. Both officers were smiling and being really friendly. I wasn't sure why until the Hispanic officer said, "My name is Rocky, and this is my partner Justin. From the bottom of our hearts, thanks."

"Thanks for what?" I asked.

Justin informed me, "We can't stand the dark witches. About time someone scared them. God knows that's all they do to everyone else."

Rocky added, "I don't even know why we let them stay in town. Dan says we're helping them hide from the necromancers, but I bet they're in league with them. Hey, girl, what did you do to her anyways?"

"Names Mel, and really I didn't do much."

"Come on Mel," Justin pushed.

"I just threatened to eat her… with my eyes." I said this with a shoulder shrug, like I had no idea why it bothered her. Both the officers just laughed.

Rocky then asked me, "Ok, you had some fun with her. I understand why you did it, but don't do it again. We don't want any problems, ok."

I agreed, "Ok".

Justin gave me a wink, "Ride safe."

Rocky nodded, "Nice to meet you Mel and welcome to Queen Anne's."

With that, I said, "Later," put my helmet back on and took off like a bat out of hell. Seconds later I roared into my garage. It hit me; it must be like high school. It must be the way you are dressed. I thought about all the people I saw that day. They were dressed in two different fashions, old and young alike. One group was clean shaven and dressed almost like they were going to church or a golf club. The other wore mostly black with leather and silver jewelry. My outfit is why the witch was so pissed off. Everyone just thought I was with one group. It must have been understood that her store was for dark witches. No matter, I was glad I didn't kill her, she just thought I was making fun of her.

I came into the house and instantly knew… I had a guest.

Chapter 13 Understanding

Spooky was sprawled across the couch with a beer in one hand and the remote controllers in the other. She stopped flipping through the channels to say, "I was almost worried, but then I remembered I don't care."

I came back with, "I can honestly say, that I was not worried about how you might feel."

"Where were you this morning? Don't misunderstand me; I don't care; just curious as to what gets a bloodsucker out of bed before noon."

"Job hunting," I said with defeat.

Spooky muted the TV, "Really... any luck?"

She was grinning; I knew she was loading up for a smart-ass remark. I sat down as she pulled her legs out just in time. I announced, "It appears that I am overqualified for most jobs in town."

Spooky about spit out the swig of beer she just took. Still laughing with a mouth full, it was leaking through her lips and onto her chest. Wiping her face with the back of her hand, she said, "Yep, that would be the problem. Have you put in an app at the Red Cross?"

"Hardy, har, har... I didn't see the Red Cross building or I would have." We both laughed when I asked, "Wasn't expecting you. What's the special occasion... you and Ezra fighting?"

"Nope, more like two's company, but three's a crowd. Michael came by with his woes, and my problem is that I don't care. Ezra's problem is that he does."

Michael... it had taken a long time before I could hear his name and not get mad. The man was as deep as a puddle, but prettier than a sunset. After my death, it took him a whole week or two before he and Lea got married. I asked, "What's his problem? Did he wake up next to Lea and realize what he had married?"

Spooky chuckled, "Damn girl... bitter? You don't get the news, livin' in isolation."

"What news?"

Spooky was dead serious, "Lea's dead. She was killed like three months ago."

Now I felt bad for dogging on Lea, "Did hunters get her?"

Spooky answered in giggles, "No... I shouldn't laugh, but I can't help it. Of course I couldn't stand the girl. She was killed in an automobile accident. Texting and driving is what I heard."

I burst into laughter, "What, you're kidding? How the hell does a car accident kill a vampire? I can't believe Charlotte didn't live to see this."

Spooky ignored the Charlotte comment. No one likes to hear about their lover's dead lover. She went on with her story. "She was driving a little compact and moved into the oncoming lane where a large truck smacked her head on. The car burst into flames and she was trapped inside the wreckage. Now Michael is crying on Ezra's shoulder, it's so bad I'd rather hang out with you."

"Wow, that's bad," I said this as I pinched her leg.

She yelled, "Owww, don't do that, you evil monster... that hurt."

I mimicked her, "Don't worry. It's better than listening to Michael cry."

Spooky finished her beer, "No argument there, any boyfriends yet?"

"Get lost," with that I got my own beer. It didn't take long before me and Spooky were watching a movie and, shortly after, a nap. One thing about cats and vampires, we love to sleep during the day. One of the great things about having Spooky over, she would awake if anyone were to come by.

The next few days Spooky helped me fill out applications. We also worked on the Impala. It would run now, but it needed a new alternator. By the third night, she joined me for a hunt. Unlike Alice, Spooky was not afraid of my losing control when I turned. For some reason I would not pay the giant cat any attention. I suggested that she should turn back from a tiger to a human to see if that's why I am not killing her. I think telling me to go to hell was her way of saying no. One thing about me and Spooky, we were always ready to take cheap verbal shots at each other's expense.

We awoke late the next afternoon, feeling lazy from full tummies. Spooky asked about Alice, who she never much cared for, but had wondered where she had gone off to. I explained what had happened. We sat in quiet for a while when Spooky broke the quiet with, "I don't understand."

I rolled my eyes, "I don't understand what you don't understand."

"Alice... I don't understand why you trust her. I would have to know where she was going."

I shook my head, "Not that it is any of your business, but I don't trust her. Still, she is my friend until she proves otherwise."

Spooky stared at me confused, "Explain… she controls your life and Ezra's. Everyone acts like she's something special, but I don't trust the little monster. I tease you, but I trust you."

I knew Spooky never understood my relationship with Alice, but I never thought about how it affected her with Ezra. He was so loyal to Alice. In fact, if it came down to it, he would choose Alice over Spooky. I don't know how much of this was because of the fact that Alice was his master. I bet Spooky must lay awake at night thinking about this, poor girl. "Well, let me try to explain. I know you know that I was raped and murdered when they turned me into… this, vampire, or whatever I am."

"I do," Spooky nodded.

"What you don't know is what happened the first four days of my new life. On the first day of my new life, I awoke in the dark. My life came back to me in pieces, followed by digging my way out of my own grave. From there I made my way to a town where I killed my first man. On the same night I discovered that over fifteen years had passed since my death. I died in 1975 only to be resurrected in 1990.

"What you really need to understand is, not only was I confused, scared and angry, but I was lost, lost in a way that tested my sanity. My father sold me to men, who planned on killing me. What had been lost to me, had been fifteen years, my purity and my life. Where do I begin in this new life? My father raised me alone and cut me off from the rest of the world. Where should I go? Nowhere to begin; I chose to go home.

"On my second night I was picked up by men, who wanted to rape and kill me. I guess it's tattooed on my forehead, *rape and kill me, please*. At any rate, they took me to a cabin. That night I fought my first fight and killed two more men. I also met a ghost. I have told you in the past how good a friend Carrie was to me, but the first night I met her I wasn't sure of her. I mean she was a ghost, all this supernatural stuff, all at once. To me one day I was a girl, the next day I was a vampire dealing with a ghost."

"The third night I met a boy, David. When I figured out he was in the same boat I was, well, I fell for him right there and then. He was like me, lost in a world of magic that he didn't understand. He had a power he never even heard of. I look back, and the whole thing was pretty damned amazing. Meeting the right person at the right time, someone who was cute, and we could figure out this new world together.

"I killed three more people at a mall, before we even made it back to his house. Once we were there I was given knowledge of where I could find more vampires. By the fifth night, not even a week, I was being cut open by a child vampire, not any vampire, but one of the most powerful vampires in the world.

"Then, with luck on my side, I came to find out one of the men I needed revenge on was working in the same town. Hell, he was a teacher at the school my new Necromancer boyfriend was at. Michael made me feel lust while I crushed over David. Still, I found time to train and plan the death of Devon. In the end we killed Devon, and, before I knew it, I was in Vegas. There I worried about David because of the loss of his family. I filled my heart with hate, and David and I set out to right the wrongs. Now stuck in this house for a little over six years, I've had time to think. Was it all too convenient, David leading me straight to Alice. I mean, was I a fool because of my need for companionship and help."

Spooky stared at me with wide eyes, "If you believe this, then why don't… you know… get out of here, get away from her."

I smiled, "Relax Spooky, I don't know if Alice had anything to do with it. That really wasn't my point."

"Ok, what was your point?"

I narrowed my eyes, "My point is, trust no one on this side of death. Nicks is the only one I trust… Oh, and there's you."

Spooky looked honored, "You trust me?"

"Oh yes, you weren't even around when all this began. Also, I can do this… I now commanded you never to speak any of these words to another soul on this planet."

Spooky's face darkened, "Thanks a lot you nasty tampon sucking blood whore. You know I would have kept your secret without you pulling the… I control you, power trip."

I hated that I hurt her feelings, "You know I can't. It's not personal; what would you do in my shoes?" Spooky's eyes softened just a little bit. "I need you to know, but I need to guarantee that no one tricks this information out of you. The way I see it, Alex was not working alone when he cast that spell. In fact, from the film of my murder, he looked as if he believed that the effects would happen to him. I think someone else is behind all of this. If I am correct in my assumption, then I have no idea who my enemy is. Furthermore, they know everything about me. If it's Alice, she not only has control of my life, but my family's life."

Spooky's voice had lost its earlier rage, "Is there no hope? I mean it sounds like we are nothing more than dolls on strings."

I thought about it for a minute or two, "No, there is hope. No one knows that I survived that fire. If I can trust Alice, then she is really trying to help me out, but I can't put all my faith in that. If Alice is behind this, well, then God help me. I must figure out why they would want to make me in the first place. I cannot even do that until I learn to control my power. The way I see it, I must find out the truth for myself."

"Not true, I'll help. Ezra knows a lot, but I don't really listen. Maybe I should be paying attention; we both can't afford to follow the Whites blindly. We both will die for your family, for your brother."

I hoped Spooky would understand. I had my doubts because of her relationship with Ezra, but her words reminded me of the relationship with my family. "Thank you." We knew how each other felt, and it was close to impossible to lie to one another. Right this moment I had an ally, but just in case she changed her mind, I was glad to have control of her. "Let's find me a job."

Spooky shook her head, "Impossible, most people want to hire someone useful."

Chapter 14 Wild Bean

I should not be here, but it had been so long.

The night was black as the rain fell hard. Flashes of lightning and crashes of thunder filled the sky. I made it to the back porch, then took off my wet rain jacket, letting it fall to the floor. The house was dark inside, and I could not hear anything over the howl of wind and the rumbling thunder.

I was about to see my parents and my baby brother, yet I knew I shouldn't be here. I quietly slipped inside coming in through the backdoor. Standing in the kitchen, it was covered in darkness. Flashes of lightning illuminated the empty kitchen. The power must be off, for there was no light, not even the clock on the microwave.

I moved through the house, and, as I did, a strange feeling came over me. The air was thick and without smell. It was so still and the lack of sound was deafening. A sudden loud crack of thunder made me jump.

I was being silly. I really could not wait to see John and Mindy. When I last saw my brother, he was less than a year old. He would be twelve now. It's not like he would be a stranger; Mindy has shown him pictures of me, and I have seen him hundreds of times through the eyes of Spooky. Still, I could not wait to see him with my own eyes. It was going to be fine, and I picked a good night to come. No one could have seen me coming through the storm. If I didn't stay too long, I could use the storm to cover my escape.

I moved upstairs and went into my parents' room. It was so dark I had to feel my way around with my hands. I found the edge of their bed. A flash of lightning illuminated the room for a second. There were two body shapes lying with each other. "Hey, don't want to scare you guys, but it's me, Molly."

I pulled back the sheets, and, as I did, another flash of lightning lit up the room. This time a new picture… John and Mindy lay on their backs with their eyes wide open, swimming in a pool of their own blood.

My hands shot to my mouth to stifle the scream.

I left the room as the panic set in. That's when I noticed the light coming from my brother's room. I trembled as I went down the hall. His door was ajar with light streaming out… I opened the door to behold what was in it.

They're suspended in midair in the middle of the room, was my brother. Chains hung from his ankles and held him up by his wrists. His head hung to one side. I could not see his face. Someone had cut his chest wide open. His heart pounded as his lungs moved up and down, exposed to the open air.

That's when I noticed a man standing to one side. He was dressed as a doctor and covered in blood. The man held a scalpel in one hand. He spoke matter of fact, "He is a lot like you... hard to kill."

I was in shock with horror; my feet were frozen to the floor. My brother's head slowly rose. When I could see his face, he looked just like me.

He screamed in pain, *"You have killed us all."*

I jumped slamming my head into the wall.

"Ow," I yelped. My body was covered with sweat. "What a horrible dream," I mumbled to no one.

My head dropped back onto my mattress. Spooky had left yesterday, and I watched her go into my parents' house through her mind. I knew my family was fine. Normally I didn't sweat, but that nightmare had me going. I looked over at the clock, ten am. So much for going back to sleep; may as well go job hunting.

After a quick shower, I jumped on my bike and went to town. I was sitting in a downtown coffee house, The Wild Bean. Spooky had left to go see my parents, and then she planned to go to Ezra's. She had stayed for a little over a week, which was a record for her. At this time we found some new companionship, but no luck with a job.

This place was pretty neat, brightly lit with lots of couches and at least eight fireplaces. The place kind of reminded me of the library. Full of books and tables, it has been just so comfortable. I snuggled into my soft seat, awaiting my hot coffee. I was sitting in a small loveseat next to one of the smallest fireplaces. None of the fireplaces were burning, but that was probably because it was late spring. The place had a full menu and deli.

There was one more thing about this place that stood out; both dark witches and white witches were eating or drinking here. They seemed to have drawn an imaginary line right down the middle of the store and just pretended the other side wasn't there. Interesting, I had to wonder why. Only one girl was waiting tables and her name was Summer. I knew this because I heard it called out thirty-three times in the last thirty-three minutes. Using the same deductive skills, I figured out the one behind the counter preparing the drinks, running the register, was her mother.

At least one person was in the kitchen, but I could not see back there. Still, someone was handing the orders through the small window. Business was hopping, and poor Summer looked like she was dizzy from running back and forth. She was a pretty girl with auburn hair that fell in waves past her shoulders. She wore glasses, and that always brought a smile to my face. The Harry Potter books have it right, all the magic in the world, but no corrective vision spells.

It took twenty minutes for me to get my coffee, and the groups of people just kept coming in. I could see the impatience in the customers' eyes as the woman behind the counter was starting to have a small panic attack. There was a small line at the register, but if she rang them out she wasn't making the sandwiches or the special coffee orders. The cook was dinging the bell as I watched at least four orders sit upon the window ledge awaiting pickup.

I couldn't stand it anymore; it was like watching people drown. I had finished my coffee anyway, so I jumped up and decided to help. I grabbed the orders and took them to the tables. The people had stopped talking and now we're staring at the counter, so when I brought them their order, it was easy to find the proper table. The girl, a little shocked, mumbled, "Oh, you don't have to do that."

I said with confidence, "Help your mother behind the counter. I'll run the orders."

Confused Summer countered, "We have this."

I gave her a look, like yeah right, but, before I could argue, her mother, with a rushed voice, added, "Summer, help me. Grab the register." Looking over at me she said, "Thank you…"

"Mel," answering her unspoken question.

The mother responded, "Mel, I'm Katharine, but you can call me Kathy."

We didn't have time to utter another word as I sped from table to table. I filled orders and delivered orders as the mother and daughter ran the counter. The invisible cook would yell, "Order up!" The time flew by, and I really enjoyed what I was doing.

I gave a big fake smiles as I took and dropped off orders and moved through the crowd swiftly. I could balance dozens of drinks and orders on my tray and move in between the tightly laid out coffee house and never drop a thing. Finally, a use for my vampire powers that didn't end up with someone dying. I sure do hope no one gets food poisoning and dies tonight or I'll be proven wrong.

The crowds died off, and, before I knew it, I was cleaning off the last of the tables when Summer closed the door and flipped the sign to closed. "Mel, you're a real life saver." Turning to her mother, "We should hire her."

Her mother looked uncomfortable being put on the spot. "Well, we don't even know if she is looking for a job."

"Yes, I am, I've been looking for weeks."

That was not the answer she had hoped for. Summer chimed in while loading dishes, "Come on, Cindy calls in sick at least three times a week, and when my summer classes start, how can I cover for her all the time?"

Kathy answered, "She has a new child. I can't afford to pay two employees. Do you want me to let a new mother go? What about Bob?"

"What about Bob?" Summer and I asked at the same time. We then gave each other a knowing look and burst out laughing.

Kathy was confused and didn't get the movie references and asked, "What's so funny?"

Summer didn't explain, but instead said, "I know Bob is our cook, but look at what a good job Adam did tonight."

The young man in the kitchen yelled out, "HEY, you're not making me full time cook!"

Summer answered my unspoken question, "That is my little brother in the back, cooking. Cindy and Bob are off tonight. Most of the time Bob cooks, and Cindy runs the counter. Normally we don't need two people out here, but lately it's been getting so busy that mom needs help. Tonight we needed three people out here. In short, the whole Shepherd family was called in."

The voice from the kitchen chimed in again, "And more help in the kitchen. I'll be doing dishes all night long."

I decided to make an offer that Kathy couldn't refuse, "Kathy, you misunderstand. I said I was looking for a job, but I never said I needed to get paid. I'll work for tips."

Kathy smiled at me, "I couldn't ask you to do that."

"Yes, you can. I don't need the money. I need work experience... for school." The last part I made up.

She looked at me like she knew I had lied about the school, "I don't know."

Summer jumped in, "Now what's the problem? First, you didn't want to pay her, but now you just don't want her help."

Kathy gave Summer a warning look, "It's not that... how do I put this? You worked hard, Mel, but you were a little fast."

Summer elaborated, "Oh yeah, she was like flaassssh, and then she was like fssssh over there." Summer's hands were all over the place as she told the story. "She was going so fast and with a tray full of food. Over customers' heads, the tray was like... whoa, and then it was like... waaaaoooo. It was fabulish."

Kathy corrected, "Fabulish is not a word."

"It's in the book of Summer," she said, and, when her mom looked away, she made faces at her.

I laughed, but stopped when Kathy went on, "My daughter is right; you did move... fast. You know the rules; we're not supposed to show our power. If you work here, you need to control whatever that was. I don't need any trouble. All the customers were staring at you."

Summer put her arm around her mother, "Oh mom, that's not why they were staring. Look at that body, she's curvy. When she moved like woossssh, her body moved like hmmmph hmmmph, boing boing. If you know what I mean? I couldn't keep my eyes off this lushish girl."

Kathy looked at her and shook her head, "Sure, you want the job?"

I was laughing, and at the same time, I couldn't remember when a female made me feel so uncomfortable. It wasn't just what she said, but the way she looked at me, like I was a piece of meat. I had a feeling we would get along just fine. "I can't wait to start."

Summer ran over and gave me a hug, "You already have dinglhopperlish."

I chuckled, "Not a word."

"Book of Summer, read it," then she pinched my ass hard, turned and went back to work.

Her mom yelled, "None of that."

I started back to work and thought to myself. What have I gotten myself into? Before long, we finished up, and it was close to midnight.

Summer thanked me again. She was one strange girl. She headed back to help her brother. I finally caught sight of him, and he was good looking with shaggy brown hair. He seemed really nice, but I really didn't get a chance to talk with him.

It was amazing how quickly life fell into a pattern. For the next two weeks I worked at the coffee house for three days straight and then on my day off went hunting. I met Bob and Cindy, and they were really nice, but the nights Cindy worked Summer didn't. Bob has worked every night since the first night I started. Adam would come by some nights and join a small group in the corner of the coffee house.

At first I didn't pay much attention to this, until about the third night when Dan Caster joined them. Dan hadn't seen me for many years and did not recognize me. Dan reminded me of Ian McKellen, so I really wanted to call him, Gandalf, but I didn't. Every time I brought them drinks, their conversation would stop. Every once in a while they would start cutting up, but most of the time they seemed really serious. With my hearing I should have been able to hear every word, but I couldn't make out what they said. It sounded all mumbled; it must have been a spell.

What I came to look forward to was my time with Summer. She was a nut and liked to make up words. One night I asked her, "Summer, are you... never mind."

Summer laughed, "Spit it out, or it will leave a bad taste in your mouth."

I blurted out, "Are you gay?"

She looked as if she was thinking about it. "Not sure, let's go to your place and make girl love. In the morning, if I didn't like it, we'll assume that I am not gay."

"Girl love? You're stupid."

"Why did you ask? Can't you tell?" She was challenging me.

I didn't think she was, but I couldn't be sure. She was always making remarks about other girl's bodies, especially mine. "I really don't know. I would think you were straight if it weren't for how you talk about me. Then again, you could be doing it just to make me uncomfortable."

She laughed, but never really answered my question. By week two, I found out that her need to make others uncomfortable was a passion of hers. We went shopping, and she made it look like I was trying to shoplift.

She pulled me out of the store saying, "I can't take you anywhere. You think your sexiness will get you out of jail?"

Time passed by, and the more my life became separated. In my sleep I visited Nicks, who had less time for me lately because of all the dead escaping. Most of the time we sat around and planned on what we could do to stop them. I still hadn't figured out how the necromancers were blocking Nicks' power in the cities. Nicks felt I needed to spend more time in Roanoke to figure this out. It didn't help that I wasn't one hundred percent in control.

The second part of my life, I spent at my home alone, with small visits from Spooky, missing my family and worrying about Alice, who I hadn't heard from or felt anything for over two months. Ezra was worried, and Spooky was annoyed by this. In between all this, I needed to sneak out and hunt whenever I could.

The job and my time with Summer's craziness was a nice distraction from all my worries. With all these different people, I was never whole. Not one shared my life.

Chapter 15 Holding Hands

Summer and I were closing The Wild Bean when she asked, "What're you up to tomorrow?"

I was off the next day and planned on going to Richmond to hunt. I couldn't very well tell her that, "Nothing, really."

"Cooleo, I want to show you something frostyloshy cool." She went behind the counter and pulled out a baseball bat. "I don't think I've told you, but I am a fourth generation enchanter. That little fact makes me really popular with everyone around here. When I'm not working here, I am making magical items for everyone. This bat is for me. I am part of a softball team, *The Enchanters*. We are playing against Black Magic, and, when I say Black Magic, that's the name of their evil team. Everyone cheats, but wait until they see me hit a homerun with *this* bat. It will knock the ball out of the universe and beyond."

"You enchanted it?"

Summer smiled, "Oh yeah, I've enchanted almost all our equipment. Our team would suck supercycles if it weren't for my enchantments. I was wondering if you would play with us? The way you move around here tells me you would be good even without my added benefit. Before you say no... Adam will be there."

I gave her a funny look, "So, why would I care about that?"

"Don't you think he is fropalushs?"

"I do, but I don't have any interest in him. Plus, I thought witches played Quidditch on broomsticks."

Summer laughed, "We tried that... right after the books came out. My friend, Jennifer and I enchanted some brooms. Two broken arms later, our parents were ready to kill us. Man, you should have been there. The only thing that didn't work was the golden snitch. I enchanted a golden ball, but it just floated there and slowly moved. Worst of all, the bludgers attacked everyone, even in the audience. They flew away and attacked people in town until Dan dispelled them. Grounded for six months over that."

I was laughing while envisioning her game of Quidditch. I've never played softball before, but I had a feeling this was less about me playing ball and more about me meeting her brother. "So, does your brother talk about me?"

"Absolutely, non stop. He thinks you're so hot… and smart. I think he is falling head over heels for you, and he's completely smichened with you."

She was lying, "I don't know what smichened means, but you're laying it on a little thick, girl. What's up?"

"You've met my brother." She put her hand on my shoulder. "It's about time you started dating." I gave her a sharp look. "Ok, ok… you have met Veronica, that evil little witch that works at the Wicked Broom. She's been hitting on my brother, and he's been responding. You're the best looking friend I have. I need you to woo him away from the dark princess."

I knew there was more to this, "You mean Betty's daughter?"

"Yep, that's the one," she confirmed.

I told Summer about my run in with Betty. It also didn't take long before I heard that Betty had gone around telling everyone that I was some kind of monster. She may be right, but no one likes to be talked about. "What time?" Summer beamed with excitement.

I rode up to Summer's house the next day. She didn't live far from The Wild Bean. The house she shared with her mother and brother was in the historical district of town. All the homes were from the early 1900s or the late 1800s. The houses were big and sat very close to one another. I pulled my bike into the small driveway as it led down the side of the house to a small parking area in back. There sat a Malibu and Volkswagen Fox that looked like it had seen better days.

Summer came out the back door dressed in her uniform. Bright green and black were the colors of her team. She was carrying a large bag with the baseball bat coming out the side of it. I helped her load it into the trunk of the Fox. We jumped in the car and took off, well, kind of. The car was a manual drive and Summer almost hit the house, then the mailbox, and then someone on a bike, finishing it off by pulling out in front of someone. She then stalled the car in the middle of the road.

The car she pulled out in front of honked then drove around and took off. Summer looked in front of her and almost looked as if she might cry. I asked, "Drive much?"

She shook her head, "I enchanted this car… damn Adam, he always screws… never mind. I can do this."

She had said too much. Something she said she had not wanted me to know. I offered, "Would you like me to drive?"

Relieved, she said, "If you don't mind?"

"Not at all," is what I said, but I was thinking it's the only way we will make it there alive. I drove and it didn't take us long since the ball field was down the street. I couldn't help but wonder what she had told me that I shouldn't know. Something about her brother breaking the car, I was probably just reading into things.

I had met Adam before, but only for a minute. Adam was already there with their mother, my boss, she was the coach. It wasn't long before I sat right next to Adam as the other team arrived, and the game was about to begin.

It wasn't really surprising that the other team's colors were black and white. Adam and I engaged in some small talk, but, other than that, we sat in silence. Summer ran up and whispered into my ear, "Remember, that witch Veronica is here. Flirt, girl, flirt." She gave me an encouraging smile and rejoined her team.

The game started, and boy, oh boy, was it interesting. For a game that was not supposed to have magic, there sure was a lot of it. Dan Caster had shown up, and he was the umpire. He spent most of the game calling for illegal use of magic items. Summer went up to bat; the pitcher threw a ball so fast that a sonic boom went off so that it sounded like a gunshot. I was sure Dan would have called that, but before he could, he would have to find the ball, because Summer's bat swung so fast that my eyes could not follow it. The smashing noise blended with the gunshot noise and erupted as the ball launched toward outer space.

One of the outfielders was being dragged across the field and into the woods by her glove. She let the glove go and it flew into the air to catch the ball. Summer ran all the bases, but Dan was calling fouls on everyone. The bat was taken and Dan announced that if either ball or glove were found that they, too, were out of the game.

I turned to Adam and asked, "I don't get it. Why is magic against the rules when everyone is using it?"

Adam smiled, "Really, that's the point. They encourage the use of magic. Dan likes everyone to practice, so really the idea is to use magic, but not to be caught using it. Basically, you need to blend it. This is just over the top."

I shook my head, "I see, well it does make for a good game."

Adam added, "It's not a good game until someone gets hurt. That's the part I'm here for."

"I didn't realize you are a healer."

Adam gave me a wicked grin, "No, I'm not here to heal. I'm here to laugh at them."

I chuckled, "Good, I won't be laughing alone. So what's your magical talent?"

Adam's face tightened, "I don't have magic, and the only talent I have is playing the guitar."

I liked that, "I would love to hear you sometime."

Adam was now staring at me and the game had lost focus. "What about you? Do you have magic? Where are you from?"

Avoiding answering, "My life is boring."

His voice was passionate, "Really, I would like to know about you."

I tried to tell him something about me, "Ok, here it is. I am twenty-two."

He interrupted, "You're twenty-two?"

"That's what I said."

He smiled, "Sorry, you don't look that old. Go on."

I told him a much watered down version of my life. He told me about himself as well. He was twenty-three and still lived with his sister and mother. They all ran The Wild Bean. His sister spent a lot of time enchanting things for other people. Then he told me he was in a kind of school. When I asked for clarification, he said it was kind of a secret. I understood secrets, so I left it at that.

The game suddenly grabbed our attention as one of the girls created a fire monster to eat another player. Dan cast a small tornado and sucked up the fire. Shortly after putting it out, there was a lot of screaming and yelling. It looked as though both teams might burst into a fight... along with the parents on both sides. I could see Betty, who had jumped out of the bleachers to join the girls. It took Dan a minute or two, but, to my surprise, they resumed the game.

It was starting to become evening, and I was feeling hungry, not for the food of man, but for blood. I was doing the math in my head. It had been over four days since I last fed on blood. I was so hungry, and I could smell the sweat of the players. I could feel their heartbeats and see their veins carrying the blood right below the surface of their skin.

I shook my head and thought, need to keep it together. Adam laid his hand on mine and gently asked, "Are you ok?"

That's when the weirdest thing happened. The hunger vanished, and the vampire in me went away, and I felt like a human. The pressure backed off, and I could breathe again. I shook my head, "Yeah, fine." I hadn't said it very nicely. I hadn't meant to sound like a bitch, but I was still catching my breath. He took it as if I was annoyed and slid his hand away. I could see the rejection in his eyes as he pretended to be involved in the game again.

I was about to say something when the hunger hit me like a tidal wave washing over me, and I could feel my teeth, long and sharp in my mouth. If I spoke now, it would be through hisses right before I fed on him. In fact, I was now staring at his neck as he was busy watching the game. Somewhere in my blood hunger, I found my control again, just long enough to think. I reached up and took Adam's hand, and, as I wrapped my cool hand into his warm grip, calmness found me once more. Once again, the vampire in me was gone, and, as I sat there thinking, the puzzle pieces in my head clicked together.

I remembered when I was full of rage just a few months ago, the same night that Alice had left me. I chased a couple of necromancers down after their failed attack upon Alice and me. I chased the necromancers back to their lair, the same night soldiers attacked. One of the soldiers made me feel this way; he made me feel human. He didn't stop the power of death, but it did stop the vampire in me.

I remember thinking that I would like to find that man, so I could find out what he had done, but now I knew. His power, it was the same, or perhaps he could do the same thing. I leaned my head toward him, and he stiffened. I wanted to smell him, to see if he was that man. His scent was familiar, and it took me a minute, but I was sure it was him. The smell filled my head, and I remembered the first night I met him.

It would have been the first time I'd met Summer as well. They were younger. They had been kidnapped and forced to help some men kill Alice. I saved Adam's life. I made sure that Alice did not kill them. Alice told me that she had given the children to Dan. I was sitting next to the purple eyed demon that Alice had so feared.

I've been doing lots of studying about the world of the supernatural. I have read plenty about the purple eyed demon. I understood why Alice feared him and why he was hated by all. In fact, I knew that right this minute, he was wearing contacts made by man, and, if someone could have invented them hundreds of years ago, there would be a lot more purple eyed demons alive today.

It amazed me. Their power was so great and, yet, it was not. It was simply the power to destroy magic. Anything he touched or even looked at too long would be wiped clear of magic. Vampires were living creatures. The living part was the blood, but it used magic to animate the body. One touch, or a long enough look, and a vampire would become a corpse. Of course, once he let go or stopped concentrating all his power upon the vampire, shortly, the vampire would reanimate the body again.

I read that all sides used purple eyed demons. If vampires had a demon working for them, they could destroy the magic that restrained them. Crosses would have no power, and no longer would they have to be invited into a home. Wizards could use them as well, since they were the perfect offensive weapon. These demons were only randomly born by wizards and witches so they didn't happen very often, kind of like a birth defect. The offspring of two magic users, should result in a more powerful magic user, but every once in a while you would get a backfire.

Being a purple eyed demon meant that everyone wanted to use your power. Of course, that also meant that everyone wanted to kill you. After a while, it became a practice just to kill them at birth. Even if you made it to adulthood, your life wasn't going to last long. Even with all the power to destroy magic, in the end, they were just human. Because they destroyed magic, they couldn't use any magic item such as healing magic. In short, one nice sword thrust to the heart, and they died just like a human.

I suddenly really felt bad for Adam. His life has been one of fear. His family most likely has been on the run since his birth in order to keep him safe. I also realized why Summer got so upset with the car. He must have un-enchanted it by touching something. My mind tried to wrap itself around the fact that Summer the enchanter, had to live with someone who could destroy her work by looking at it for too long. In my mind, I could imagine some pretty funny fights between them.

I was lost in thought and then realized that Adam, the purple eyed demon had held the vampire part of me at bay. I looked over and noticed that Summer was staring at me with a shit eating grin that wrapped all the way around her fat head. It occurred to me that Victoria hadn't even tried to talk to Adam and hardly took notice of the fact that I was sitting next to him. So here I sat, hand in hand with Summer's brother. Summer was sure she had made some kind of love connection by tricking me. If she only knew that I was holding his hand so that I would not *eat* him.

I heard them yell, "Watch out!" but in my human state my senses were not that quick. I felt something hit my head and it all went black.

Chapter 16 Cold Water

Dazed and confused, I could feel Adam carrying me in his arms. His soft voice asking, "You ok?"

I heard myself respond, "I think so."

"Is she ok?" I heard a female voice ask, followed by similar questions by other voices. I made out one of the voices to be Summer's, "The ball hit her in the head. She didn't move."

Adam answered curtly, "Yeah, she didn't move. I guess she was trying to catch it with her head. I'm taking her home; she might need some ice."

"I'm coming. The game is about over anyways." She then yelled off in the distance, "Mom? Adam and I are taking Mel home, ok?"

From the distance I heard a reply, but couldn't make it out as my world spun. My body was in motion as Adam carried me to the car. I felt him putting me into the backseat when he asked, "Maybe we should see a doctor? She doesn't look good."

Summer's voice was low and frustrated, "Maybe you should stop touching her."

Adam was really defensive, "This is my fault?"

Summer responded with, "No, that's not what I meant." Her voice became real quiet, as if she didn't want me to hear her. "She isn't a witch, but I don't know what she is. You've seen her at the Bean, and there is no way the ball could have hit her. She was holding your hand."

I felt Adam move away, leaving me lying on the backseat of the car. His voice sounded heartbroken, "Oh, I affect her, too."

Summer responded indifferent, "You drive and by the way, thanks for letting me know that my car is no longer enchanted."

Adam retorted, "It was an accident. Maybe you should learn to drive."

Summer sound upset now, "I wouldn't have to if you would *stop touching my shit*."

I could hear the front door of the car slam shut followed by another. The car started, and my head cleared. The bump healed, and I felt fine. Well, except for a hunger building in my stomach. I sat up and Summer turned to me, "You ok? Maybe you should lie back down."

I smiled, "No, I feel fine now, thanks."

Adam stiffened at this remark for now he knew that his touch had kept me from healing. I would have healed quickly if not for his touch. My reaper side would be able to come to life soon. The sun was close to gone for the day. I still had control, and, while I maintained that control, I needed to get away from Adam and Summer Sheppard.

It only took ten minutes to arrive back at their house. "Well guys, thanks for the good time, but I need to get going."

Summer looked mortified, "Oh no, you don't. I'm not about to let you leave on that zippish wipe rocket after being banged in the head. Come inside for a minute until we know that you're ok." She had wrapped her arm around me and started dragging me toward the front door. I pulled free.

Adam spoke for the first time since we got in the car, "Mel."

I looked at him, and the pain in his eyes broke my heart. The boy was in pain, not physical pain but pain nonetheless. "Yes, Adam?"

"Are you sure you'll be ok?" He gently touched the top of my head where the ball had hit me. Moving my hair to one side, he looked for a bruise, "It was swollen before we left the park. Did you take a healing potion?"

His touch made the hunger leave, but I still needed to leave before it came back. "No, I heal really fast. I really need to go, don't worry, I'll be fine."

Adam looked sadly, "What are you?"

"Jerk," Summer said loudly. In the city of Queen Anne, it was considered rude to ask that. Everyone knew that everyone else was in hiding. The whole community tried to pretend that we were just some normal town. I suppose this did make it easier for the hundreds of humans that did live here.

Adam defended himself, "I didn't mean it like that. You don't have to tell me; I was just... curious."

I challenged him, "What are you?"

His face tightened, "Just a human."

"And I'm just a girl," I turned to his sister. "I'll see you tomorrow, Summer," I turned and walked over to my motorcycle.

Summer was still trying to talk me into staying as I put my helmet on. Adam went into the house. Summer stood in front of my bike, "No way, you cannot leave. That ball must have given you brain damage if you think you're leaving before we talk. So, what do you think about my brother?"

I should have known this was why Summer didn't want me to leave. "He's fine… nice."

"Oh, hell no, you were holding hands. You sat next to him and quicker than a flying moose and did I mention you were both holding hands." Summer was all excited and talking with her hands, "Isn't he hot, or perhaps tublishish?"

I laughed, "Flying moose, tub-whatever you just said. Ok, ok… he's handsome. I kind of like him, but don't want to get involved with a man right now."

Summer smiled like she'd won something. "Oh, ok. Well then you wouldn't be interested in a double date this Friday."

I rolled my eyes, "Got to go. See you at work tomorrow."

As I took off on my bike, I could hear Summer yelling, "Get a phone!"

That's right; I had forgotten to pick one up. Summer had been bugging me for weeks now to get a phone. Maybe I would get one after I got something to eat. With that in mind, I pushed my speedometer over a hundred. I would be out of Queen Anne in a few minutes, and my plan was to stop at the first bar I came across.

*   *   *

A few hours later I was enjoying a beer somewhere in the Smoky Mountains. I had run across a small tavern. When I came in, there were only four men in the bar. Two played pool while the bartender served one at the bar. The first words out of the mouth of the bartender were, "Little girl, do you have an ID?"

Those were his last words. I was too hungry for games. I was proud of myself as I washed the blood down with the last of my beer. Four men lay upon the floor of the tavern, but they all lived. I hated killing when I didn't have to. Having no evidence that this was evil men, I was glad I could spare them. Being so hungry, my control was not great, but being there were four men meant that I could satisfy my hunger without having to finish one.

My reaper side stayed at bay. I felt I could call upon it, but no need for all that. In fact, I just realized that I had left without my violin. Bow was going to chew me out when I got home. I left the tavern and headed back toward my house.

Riding slowly through the night, it was cool, and the wind felt refreshing as it slid over my body. I took in the scene and watched the beauty of the night scroll by. My mind wandered, and, before I knew it, I was thinking about Adam. Not good, I don't need that kind of distraction.

The week flew by. Nicks looked tired when I went to the library. My worry for Alice increased along with Ezra's and Michael's. I could feel Spooky's irritation with it all. She couldn't stand Alice, and now her lover was worried sick with her disappearance. The last time I looked through her eyes, she was running through the forest as a giant cat, filled with anger and looking for prey to take it out on.

I ended up working Friday night, but that didn't stop Summer from trying to hound me about a double date. She finally admitted the truth - she didn't even have a date. She then thought it would be fun for us to go watch a movie. A new movie was in the theater, and she really wanted to go see it. I agreed, so we planned to meet at a little Italian restaurant and eat before the movie.

Saturday night came quick enough. My mind was still slipping into that moment with Adam on the bench, holding his hand. I really needed to be fair; I could not drag him into my life. My interactions with Summer we're taking enough of a chance. Maybe it would be best to stay home and be a shut-in.

Summer came in the nick of time and pulled my mind away from the depressing thoughts. She was dressed in jeans and a shirt. It kind of looked like she was going to work, "Are you hungry?"

She smiled, "Let's get a seat."

She led the way, and, as we passed the hostess, she quickly added, "I already got us a seat."

My mind puzzled over this; I didn't arrive before her? It didn't take me long to realize what was happening as I was led to a table. There sat an equally surprised Adam. He was dressed nicely with a tight- fitting colored shirt. He looked good as he got out of his seat to offer me a place at the table. "You didn't tell me that Mel was coming."

"Oh about that, I've got to fill in for Cindy again. Can you please see Mel to the movie? I promised I would take her, and now I can't make it."

Adam answered her, but he looked at me, "I would love to."

"Great," Summer said, slapping her hands together. "Well, sit down Mel, and enjoy your scrpishish meal."

I gave Summer my best angry face, but it was useless against her. I sat down in defeat. The worst part was I wanted this. I wanted to sit across from this handsome man and go on my first real date. At the same time, I needed some distance before I had too many real emotions for him. I put on a smile, "I guess this is just you and me then." Summer took off without another word.

"Just to let you know, I didn't have anything to do with this. If you want to go home… it's not a big deal or anything." Wow, he couldn't lie. The look on his face said if I left, he would be heartbroken.

I picked up the menu, "No way, I'm starving." Adam smiled and relief fell over him as he picked up his menu.

The waitress took our drink orders. "I was wondering, what's your whole name? Everyone just calls you Mel."

"Sorry, I'm not ready for that level of commitment yet." My face was hidden behind the menu. I wasn't trying to be rude, but I needed a minute to think about that. I could never give out my name as Mindy Brook. No link could be made to my old life, and on the other hand, giving out the name Melabeth might not be good either. Alice told me that, in my short life as a vampire, I had left quite a statement.

I lowered my menu with a smirk on my face. Adam was in the middle of saying, "You don't have to tell me…" when he could see my face and its smirk, relief washed over his face.

I laughed, "This town is weird. Everyone is hiding from someone or something and no one gives their real name. My name is Melanie Elizabeth Dare."

"Is that your real name?"

"I will come to that name, when you call it. Maybe someday I can tell you my real name. Is Adam Sheppard your real name?"

He paused, looking at me. I couldn't tell what he was thinking, but he finally said, "Yes and no. Adam are my real first name, but maybe someday I will be able to tell you my last."

"Maybe," I agreed. Before he could speak, the waitress asked if we were ready to order. Adam asked for another minute, and we both got busy deciding on what to eat. After ordering, we chatted about movies, TV, and a variety of other common topics. His manner was easy, and he was easy on the eyes. Under the single lamp that hung over our table, my world closed and it was just us.

I really wanted to ask him about being a purple-eyed demon, but I wasn't supposed to know. The food finally arrived when he announced, "About time. I don't think we will make the movie."

"What movie were we going to watch?"

"Summer didn't tell you?" I shook my head. "We were going to 'Abraham Lincoln, the Vampire Hunter'."

"Is that a joke?" I laughed.

"No, really," He showed me his phone to prove it.

"Wow, the whole vampire thing is out of control. I bet the real vampires don't care much for that kind of attention."

"I doubt vampires care; they're just a bunch of monsters anyway. I was looking forward to watching a couple of hours of Lincoln carving them up with his axe." Anger washed through me, for I felt deeply for some vampires. Adam noticed, but misread my feelings, "Too much for you? Maybe something with unicorns in it?"

He was trying to joke, but I was already upset so it felt like he was making fun of me. I took a bit of food to keep my mouth busy. I needed a second before I spoke. After swallowing I said with venom, "What do you know about vampires or unicorns?" My anger caught him off guard.

He answered carefully, "Didn't mean to upset you, sorry. I wasn't trying to make fun of you, and, if it helps, unicorns can be as dangerous as vampires." He added this part with a big smile.

I narrowed my eyes, "How's that... gas perhaps?"

We ate in silence for the next few minutes. As time passed, the air thickened, and the more uncomfortable I became. I really wasn't any good for this man, and I shouldn't have gotten angry over killing vampires. I knew better than most that finding a good vampire was as likely as finding an honest politician. Alice was a prime example of why you should fear vampires. Yet, I loved her like a sister. What did this say about me?

I looked up, and Adam had a huge grin. He sat up, and his face became serious. "How would you know when a unicorn passed gas?"

"The noise," I responded irritated, yet I felt the child in me begin to chuckle.

Spoken with great authority he said, "No, in fact, when a unicorn passes gas, it is ALWAYS silent....SBD; silent but decorative....that is, they create little rainbow gas clouds which eventually rise up through the atmosphere and waft along on the jet streams seeking rain clouds in which to imbed themselves. Then when the rains come, they help create the lovely rainbows we all love so much. WARNING: DO NOT try to capture unicorn toot in a bag and huff it. The vivid hallucinations caused by uni-toots are similar to ones caused by LSD. This often leaves victims singing and dancing and frolicking in the enchanted forest for the rest of their lives."

I looked at him dead serious... I couldn't take it; I broke. I laughed so hard tears came out. "There is something wrong with you. Uni-toots? Think you can get it on the black market?"

We were both laughing when the waitress came by and asked if we needed refills. "Oh yes, you can get anything on the black market."

The waitress hadn't understood what Adam was talking about. Plus, it was hard to understand us between all our laughing. She tried to clarify, "Is that, yes, to some refills?"

"Sorry," I said between giggles. "We were talking about uni-toots... but we could use some refills." The waitress gave me one of those looks that said I was high. I snorted, which made us both laugh louder. Even the waitress chuckled as she hurried off, "Ok, you are forgiven."

"Do I dare ask what I did wrong in the first place?"

"Careful," I pointed my fork at him and narrowed my eyes, but I was still grinning ear to ear.

"Yes, mama," and with that we ate and talked.

Long after we finished our food, we sat there talking. I found out that Adam played the guitar and was starting a band. He was also going to college in the fall. I told him I loved to sing and could play the violin. He was very interested in this and wondered if I ever thought about joining a band. I told him I didn't think I could, and I was busy.

Adam asked, "Let me make sure I understand this. You live alone, but you don't have a clean house. You work part-time for my mom at The Wild Bean, but only for tips. You love to run, read, play violin and sing. Still, you have no time for a band?"

"Look dad... I mean Adam." I paused then laughed. "I need a lot of beauty sleep. Do you believe all this," I waved my hands over my whole body, "Comes from overworking myself. I'll think about your band."

"Really? We could use someone like you," Adam claimed with excitement.

"Hold on there, you never heard me play or sing. How do you know you will want me in your band?"

Adam smiled slyly, "Just look at you... with you on stage, we will only need half the talent of any other band."

"Yeah, right," Is what I said, but I was thinking, wow, he's good.

Not long afterwards the waitress informed us that it was getting close to closing. We had been sitting for hours, and, after paying the bill, I needed help getting to my feet for my legs had fallen asleep. Being a little after midnight, I thought it was best to call it a night. I needed a little space, but I didn't want any.

Adam walked me to my motorcycle, "You sure you need to go home?"

"Oh yes," I said, unable to stop staring into his eyes.

He closed the space between us and slowly put his arms around me. I knew he was going to kiss me, and my mind raced on as to whether I should let him. Before I could make up my mind, our lips came together as my eyes closed... decision made.

It started slow but progressed as our body's came together. His arms around me, the heat spread through me as pleasure washed through my body. The taste, the feel, it was all so intoxicating. I pulled away slowly as if my body was a sticker, and I didn't want to rip it.

Head spinning, breathlessly I said, "I really need to go."

"I would rather you stayed," his voice deep and with need. I wanted to give in to that need, but the other half of my mind was screaming at me.

I used the rest of my will power to turn from him and mount my motorcycle. I started to put my helmet on, but as the fully enclosed part covered my eyes, Adam pulled me to him and once again our lips came together. His hands slid the length of my body sending shivers throughout. I pulled the helmet down, forcing him to pull his head away.

Starting my bike, I took off without another word. I couldn't stay or I would regret it, because my body no longer could say no. I rushed home on the motorcycle, at home I had a cold shower that couldn't wait.

The entrance from the garage led to the kitchen. I barely entered into the kitchen when I became aware that someone was in my house. My mind had been... distracted. I went from horny to ready for a fight so quickly, that it physically felt as if I had pushed the round peg through the square hole.

I came to realize this intruder was crying quietly in my living room. I came in slowly ready for anything, and what I found was Spooky. "Why are you closing yourself off to me? Especially when you're in my home."

Spooky's makeup was smeared from tears. With a shaky voice, "Sorry… I didn't want you to," sniff, sniff, "Feel my pain." She returned her head to the pillow that now was ruined with makeup and tears.

"Well, no need for the cold shower now," I mumbled to myself.

Face still in the pillow, I thought what I heard was a, what or why. I shook my head as I sat next to her. Looking over at her crying into the pillow, all I could think was… killjoy.

The next four hours I spent on the couch listening to Spooky's woes. Ezra and Michael had become so concerned with Alice's whereabouts that they decided to go looking for her. This, of course, prompted Spooky to give Ezra an ultimatum. "If you leave me to go find Alice, then you need never to come back." Ezra still left. Of course, that is the problem with ultimatums; it's either going to go your way… or not.

During this time listening to Spooky's troubles was sobering. Half-listening to her go on about Ezra, my mind drifted to Adam. Crushing hard on that boy is what came to mind, but if I put my hormones on hold, there were other things to consider. Like the fact I knew that Adam was running around with Dan and a machine gun, doing God knows what. That brings up other things. When I first moved to this town, Dan had come by and visited and when he did, he asked lots of questions. He received a few answers, and he eventually didn't come around.

Now I know Adam is working with him directly, and I can assume that Summer is enchanting weapons for Dan. There is a chance that they… including their mother Kathy… could be under orders from Dan. The thought broke my heart. I would need to keep my feelings in check. It was imperative I understood exactly who the Sheppard's were… and what they really thought of me.

Chapter 17 Baby Huey

I took off early from The Wild Bean. Business had been slow, and I was in a hurry to leave. Tonight I was going with Summer and Adam to a party. One of Summer's friends had just turned nineteen. I really didn't care about that. I just wanted to hang with Adam. I tried my hardest to tell myself it was for research reasons, but I knew better than that.

Over the last couple of days I had come across more information about the Sheppard family. In 1991, Adam's father was murdered. He was a part of The Order and was killed by a vampire. When Summer told me this, my heart hurts, because I understood their hatred towards vampires. It also made me wonder if they would hate me once they knew the truth. Would Adam want nothing more to do with me? The thought made me shudder. After his father's death, the whole family was moved to the town of Queen Anne.

Without Adam's dad around, his mom didn't feel that she could protect her purple-eyed son. After a few years living in the town, mom didn't feel like Dan was keeping her son's best interests in mind. She took her kids and left, and for many years stayed hidden. Summer told me something awful happened and forced them to come back and live here. I knew what that awful thing was. They were kidnapped and used to help try to destroy Alice. That was the night I stopped Alice from killing them.

Alice later told me that she had sent them to Dan, and he would take care of them. They were reunited with their mother, but now she was too afraid to leave. The reason she left was to protect Adam, to keep Dan from using him. Of course, now Dan was using him and Summer both, and Kathy appeared powerless. Summer did not tell me all this directly; I figured it out by asking questions of different family members at different times. They didn't know that I knew about Adam, and, of course, they had no idea how deep I was involved with everything.

The only thing left for me to clarify was: what was the exact relationship between Adam and Dan? Of course I wasn't a hundred percent sure of what Dan was up to.

I rode with Summer and Adam to the party. It wasn't a wild party with people drinking and dancing. It was a dozen young teens with some adults. The girls were very nice and all wanted me to join their softball team. After seeing me serve drinks, they thought I would be great. About an hour into the party Adam whispered into my ear, "Want to blow this joint?" I nodded my head, and we snuck in the front door.

We weren't quick enough because a chorus of, "Oooooo, hanky, panky!" The sound rang up from behind us. We laughed as we quickened our escape.

I asked, "Where are we going?"

"I thought you might like to go for a walk... you know, and talk. We don't have to if you want to stay, and party?"

"Not a chance," and he took my hand as he led me into the night. The air was cool with a nice breeze as we made our way to the street for there was no sidewalk. We just walked down the road. I couldn't even hear a car, let alone seen one, and I enjoyed the quiet with his hand in mine. I broke the silence, "I hate to ruin the mood, but I need to know something."

"Uh - oh," he said with a smile.

"I don't want to make you mad, but what is your relationship with Dan?"

"Why would that make me mad?" I could hear the defensive tone, "He is a family friend and an ally. If it weren't for him... well, my family may not be here."

I knew I was treading on dangerous territory, but I needed to know. Of course that meant I would have to tell him about me sooner than later, but the thought alone brought a knot in my stomach. "I want to know what you're doing with, his... not sure what to call them other than, his warriors."

He stopped walking and gave me a glare, "Summer talks too much."

I quickly defended Summer, "She didn't tell me. Don't assume that I get all my information from your sister... or your mother."

His face tightened as he turned and started walking again, this time without my hand. "Then you really shouldn't know. Dan doesn't trust you, and he thinks that I shouldn't hang out with you. Why does he think that? I wonder."

I was calm and took his hand, "Long story, but involves his ex-wife. Maybe you should ask him sometime. Look, I don't want details. I just want to know how much I should be worrying about you. No one has said anything directly, but I kind of overheard your last mission went bad. You almost got killed. Don't you think if I start... caring about you that I might want to know what you're up to. No, scratch that, I don't want to know what, I want to know when. When might I worry about you and for how long?"

He was grumpy, "You don't need to worry."

I let go of his hand and turned away from him. He stopped and turned back as I hid my face. I tried to hide my hurt, but my voice betrayed me, "Excuse me for caring."

He came up behind me slowly and put his arms around me. "I like that you care. I just can't stop what I am doing, not for you, not for anyone."

"I didn't ask you. I just wanted to be a part of it in some way, in any way you'll let me."

"I can't tell you what's going on; it's too dangerous."

"Because," I pushed?

His voice was pleading, "I didn't want to drag you into this. I have to help, and we can't lose to the necromancers. Look at this town, the more and more people come every day. They're hiding from the evil that is spreading across the land. I know you work with my sister and mom, and they let things slip, but believe me when I say, that I am well protected in my role."

"Then why are *they* so scared? If you're *so* protected," I challenged.

He sighed and looked as if he was internally debating on whether to tell me. Finally, he said, "Because of the FUBAR mission a few weeks ago. I have been on a lot of missions with Dan, and I always thought my life was on the line, but I never came close to getting hurt before. Dan teamed me with some of his best men; seldom do I even engage the enemy, even with support.

"One night we were attacking a Necromancer stronghold. They had taken up residence in an abandoned hotel. They had a pack of werewolves with them, but we were ready for that. We even thought there could be some vampires. Even if there were, we would be ready for that as well. What we weren't ready for was the Dark Fiddler."

A lump formed in my throat, "I've heard of her."

"So had we, but we thought it to be a legend. Dan thought it was an excuse for failure. He believed the last few groups to report about it had taken huge losses. In fact, on more than one mission, we had heard the sound of a violin playing. The legend has scared some so bad that the mere fact, you hear a violin causes fear. We were not afraid, and on the night we attacked, we heard a violin. Before that night the music had just been someone playing it on a stereo trying to scare us. Something about live music not being played on a set of speakers, but that wasn't it completely. The song, the song was... eerie and wonderful all at the same time.

"My team worked their way up to the upper floors of the building. We hit the third floor, and that is when we met it. It killed... it killed everyone on my team. It happened so fast. Before I knew it, the monster stood before me. I opened fire... point blank, in a hallway... and yet I missed. Thirty rounds gone in a moment, and, at that moment, I couldn't follow the Dark Fiddler. It moved *so* fast, like a shadow. It was on me before I could even think about reloading.

"That's when the monster paused. With no eyes, it approached me. It was clad in black with long arms and even longer fingers with sharp black nails. The creature wore a mask, like you would see at a ball from long ago, only there were no eyes, just black.

"It touched me and my body was frozen in fear. I truly thought I would die that night, but for a reason I could not tell you, it let me live. It left and now I am the one of two surviving members of my unit."

It was hell listening to someone else describe me. I asked, "What about Dan?"

"He was downstairs dealing with a Necromancer. By the time he came up he found me huddled in a corner surrounded by my dead comrades. The monster didn't just kill us; it had killed dozens of necromancers on the third floor. The funny thing is that if it hadn't been there we would have been in trouble anyway because we had greatly underestimated the strength of their forces."

I told him, "Next time... if there is a next time. When you meet this Dark Fiddler, do not attack it. It will protect you and your friends. Just don't attack it."

He gave me an odd look, "How would you know that?"

My voice was small, "Just trust me."

He laughed, "How can I trust a statement like that? If you would have seen it, you wouldn't be saying that."

I shook my head, "Just take my word... or not, but it will help you if you wanted it to."

Adam smiled, "Ok, if you say so. I know better than to argue."

"Smart boy, of course you will be even smarter if ever the opportunity arises for you to listen. I doubt you will." I decided on a gamble, for I needed him to open up to me. I needed to end the game between us. I loved the way he was holding me and never wanted it to end, but, we were living a lie. "I know what you are."

I felt his body tense and his pulse speed up. "What do you mean?"

I spoke softly, "I don't need to see your purple eyes to feel their effect on me."

He stepped away so fast it was as though he pushed me. I looked into his face, and there were rage and fear. His voice trembled, "How did you find out? How long have you known?"

I held my hands out to him "Don't fear me. I would never do anything to bring harm to you."

At that he turned and walked away. Well, that didn't go as planned. He hadn't walked far, when he turned and with anger, he demanded, "Now you know about me. What are *you*?"

I moved with speed so fast the world blurred. I ran in-between some house and into the woods. Tears rolled off my cheeks as my emotions boiled. He was right to ask, and he had a right to know, but the way he asked. The hate in his eyes… what would the eyes hold when he found out what I was? When he knew that I was the same kind of monster which had killed his father. Even if he could understand that I was not evil, I would still have to tell him about the evil things I've done. Vampires are never the good guy, not in any story.

It seemed like mere moments before I reached the house. There Spooky awaited my return and treated me to a big hug. She felt my pain, and tonight we would both suffer together and comfort each other in our misery.

The next morning, Spooky presented me with a gift. Last night with all our cries and whining she had forgotten to tell me that she bought me a phone. It was an Android smart phone. I loved it! With all my free time, sitting around playing with computers, it wouldn't take me long to figure it out. I would be playing with this new toy for days. I had to get ready for work. That reminded me, would I have any names or numbers in my contact list?

I already knew that Adam was mad or afraid... maybe both, but I wasn't sure how Summer or Kathy would react to me knowing the family secret. I didn't have long to wait. I was scheduled to work tonight between five and closing. It was raining, and, with no other transportation other than my bike, I was going to get soaked. I arrived early so I could dry off and put some dry clothes on.

There was a small office in back that I was using to change in. A knock on the door startled me. My mind was lost in thought. I yelled, "Changing. Who is it?"

"It's me..." sounded like Summer's voice. "May I come in?"

Didn't she hear the part that I was changing? Oh well, I thought as she barged in. I didn't open the door far because I was still in my undergarments. Summer eyed me, and I waited for a remark, but she remained quiet while I dressed. "I see you just wanted to come in to see me naked."

Summer smiled, but it did not reach her eyes; this was worse than I thought. She asked flat out, "How long have you known about my brother?"

"Honestly... the first time we met." Of course she didn't remember me being the little girl who saved them from Alice.

Her eyes were pleading for some unasked question. "We have been hiding for so long. You don't understand the danger it brings my family every time someone knows about Adam. We left this town... so that Dan wouldn't use him. We were kidnapped and forced to help these wizards." She paused as if she might not be able to go on. "They wanted us to fight vampires. Vampires killed my father, I wasn't sure if you knew that. It's a long story, but the short of it is that we ended up back in this town. Now Dan is using him for the same reason we left. I don't want Dan to mess with you because you know, but honestly, I am glad you know. I could use someone to talk to. I hate all the secrets in this roduckulis town."

"I'm guessing I'll find roduckulis in the book of Summer," I laughed.

Nodding, "You sure will. It means something greater than ridiculous."

I asked, "Friends?"

"Friends," she said as she embraced me. Then she grabbed my ass, "You are way hot. So, glad to catch a glimpse of the goods. Oh, and hurry up... it's going to be busy tonight."

I laughed as I finished pulling on my shirt. "What about your mother? Is she good?"

Summer held her hand out flat and wiggled it back and forth. "Kind of, she is having a nervous breakdown about everything right now. Her biggest problem is... well, she doesn't know you. She feels like you are hiding too much, who you really are, what you really are and why you are really here.

"It didn't help that Dan said you have lived in this town since you were about seven, living alone in a house, growing up by yourself, no friends, parents, kind of weird. Just be aware now that you know our family's secret, my mother will want to know all about you."

She said it in a friendly way, as if we will all be one big family. I smiled and said with the nicest tone I could, "Just because I know your brother's secret, does not grant you access to mine."

The hurt was on her face, but she tried to play it off. "Oh, I know that. Well, I'll let you finish getting ready. Mom's probably wondering where I'm at." She hurried out of the office, leaving me wondering if I had been too blunt. She had been hoping I would open up to her.

I knew that by telling them that I knew about Adam that three things could happen. One, they could accept me, and I would learn more about them and if I could trust them. Of course, in my head, I would learn all this before letting them know what kind of monster I was. Second, they would be highly suspicious of me knowing and want to find out everything about me before trusting me. This was the most likely event and the one that made my stomach hurt just thinking about it. I had no illusion of their reaction when they found out that I'm a vampire. Thirdly, they'd distrust me and decide the best thing to keep Adam's secret is to kill me.

I pushed the thought to the back of my brain as I hurried out to go to work. Of course it would be hard to stop thinking about it, because as soon as I got to the dining area, Dan and Adam were seated together. Their eyes found me. They both turned and went back to talking to each other like it was nothing. I inwardly growled at them. This was going to be a long night.

As promised, it was nice and busy. Kathy was pleasant and did not seem mad at me, but there was worry behind her eyes. Dan was openly curious about me. Dan and Adam sat on a couch near a fireplace; they had books piled between them on both adjacent coffee tables. I asked, "And what would you two like?"

"Mocha Cappuccino," Adam said with an emotionless tone and little eye contact.

Dan gave me a warm smile, "Mel. It's been too long. I've been so busy I haven't had a chance to come and visit you. Still living alone up there?"

"Yes," I simply answered, adding no more information.

He held his smile, "You and I need to talk sometime. You know, catch up. I can see you're busy right now, but maybe soon. Can I have coffee… black? Thank you."

"No problem, I'll be right back with your orders," and, without another word, I left. Dan had confirmed what I had hoped would not happen. Now that I let Adam know that I knew about him, they would want to know everything about me.

It didn't take long before a new problem helped me forget this one. Mrs. Thornburg had just come in with her son. This was good and bad. Bad that she was here, but good because she would thin the crowd. Mrs. Thornburg was in her fifties, dressed like she was twenty and did her hair and makeup like she had been in a tornado while applying it. Her colored hair was platinum blonde, while her dark eyebrow's said otherwise. Fake tan, fake nails and loud mouth to boot, but she wasn't much of a problem.

Mrs. Thornburg wasn't a problem, but her son little Timmy was. Little Timmy stood almost seven feet tall with wide shoulders and no neck. His face had never seen a razor, but there had never been a hair to shave. His whole body and face from a distance would have reminded you of a baby. He appeared to be a fat little baby with big fluffy cheeks that moved like a toddler, running into people and things. Looking as if he might fall over at any time, he worked his way over to sit with his mother. Everyone called him Baby Huey… behind his back that is.

If you wonder if that big childlike monster was strong, I could answer that. Little Timmy broke stuff all the time, cups, bowls, tables, chairs, books and even a concrete pillar once. Kathy hated his visits with a passion. She felt bad for the mother who had this large man with a mind of a child. Kathy told me that Timmy was a half Rock Giant. Not all giants are stupid; come to find out most of them are very intelligent. Rock Giants were in a class of their own, for their I.Q. Was never very high. How Mrs. Thornburg got pregnant with such a child was a constant conversation in the rumor mill.

As normal, I would be dealing with Little Timmy. I sighed as I went over to check on our new guest. "How are we today?"

Mrs. Thornburg looked worn out, "Fine, dear. I'll have my usual, dear."

Half interrupting his mother, Timmy cut in, "I want, I want hot *chocolate*. With marshmallows and whip cream, sprinkles, and M&M's."

"What else do we say?" His mother prompted.

Timmy was straining to figure out the social cue, "In a cup?"

"Please," she said like it was the most exhausting word of the day.

"*Please*," Timmy yelled happily.

"I'll be right back with your order," I replied with a smile.

The only positive thing about Timmy being here was that I had forgotten about Dan. Well, mostly, but my eyes always found their way back to Timmy. I was always worried about what he might break. "Order up," yelled Summer.

I loaded the tray and headed over to the first table to drop off their coffee and salads. I also had Mrs. Thornburg and Timmy's order as well. Tonight had been busy, and, with Dan here and Adam treats me like I was the plague, my nerves were stretched.

I dropped off their orders with my plastic smile, "Here you guys are."

Timmy looked at his hot chocolate, "M&M's?"

Summer had told me that we didn't have any, but I had forgotten to come back and tell Mrs. Thornburg. "I'm sorry, Timmy, but we didn't have any M&M's, but we added extra chocolate."

"I wanted M&M's," Timmy whined while he squeezed his fist.

Mrs. Thornburg sounded worried, "Are you sure you don't have any?"

"Yes, I'm sure, sorry about that. Timmy, what can I get you to make up for not having M&M's?"

His face had gone red, "I want M&M'S... *now*!"

"Don't worry, pumpkin; they'll get you M&M's." Mrs. Thornburg promised her son, that *I would do it*.

If anyone really knew me, they would know that I have a switch. On and off, are the only two settings. I am either calm or killing someone, but I was well aware of how close the switch was from being flipped on. Wisely, I decided to retreat from the situation and let someone else handle it. I was still in a bad mood and this event had me even more irritated, so my mouth opened and this is what came out, "Let me go to the back and see if I can't find you some M&M's, you big baby."

I turned around and started to head back to the counter when I heard the violent shoving of a chair. Mrs. Thornburg commands, "No, Timmy." I knew what was happening behind me through the use of my second sight. Timmy was jumping to his feet and in the act, throwing his seat behind him.

Somewhere in my mind a small memory came back. Mrs. Thornburg had pulled me aside the very first time she had come in with Timmy. "Dear, I don't mean to be a bother, but I need to speak to you for a minute."

"Of course, what do you need?"

"Well, dear, you've met my son Timmy?" I nodded, "He's a special boy. He doesn't get out much, and few establishments will even let him in because he breaks stuff. Kathy's a dear friend and one of the few places where Timmy gets to go.

"I just need you to understand that, even though Timmy is big, he is still a little boy. Unlike most little boys, Timmy is really strong and, if he throws a fit, it is hard to stop him. I can control him, unless you really upset him. Just talk to him real sweet, and I'll handle the rest… one more thing. Please do not call him names, especially the baby. That always sets him off and he can become dangerous, ok, sweetie?"

In a moment I realized I couldn't hurt this boy. With that in mind, I ducked. His fist went over my head, destroying my serving tray which hadn't had enough time to fall. I stepped away and turned to face him all in one motion. I needed to keep this fun for me, or I might lose control. With a smile, I teased, "Missed me, missed me, now you have to kiss me."

With rage Timmy came at me like a bull. Fist is swinging, he could not make contact. I moved around his swings as if they were stationary. His fist went toward my face, only an inch from contact I leaned back. With ease I pulled my head away as fast as his fist was moving. I knew that I had become faster, but there was more to it than that. I could think faster, and the world appeared to move slowly.

He swung, and I laughed. I stepped to one side, then the next. Eventually I moved right around to his back. Timmy had gotten confused on which way I had gone and had lost track of me. As he turned to find me, I moved with him, staying glued to his back as he was spinning around the room looking for me. I laughed from behind him, "What's wrong, big boy?"

He spun around, but I remained behind him. Timmy was grunting and cursing me. I also became aware that everyone was standing around us, some in fear, and some just looking on in wonder. Mrs. Thornburg was yelling, but everyone had tuned her out.

Timmy was frustrated and now was going wild. He threw his whole body backwards trying to land on me. I was too fast for that and decided to go up since he was going down. I flipped gravity's pull and landed on the ceiling. I looked up to see Timmy land on his back against the floor. He landed hard enough to knock some of the air out of him.

Timmy pulled his legs up, about to make an effort to stand. I flipped gravity again, spun in the air and landed upon his knees. I was now looking down upon his stunned face. With a smile I whispered,
"Have you had enough? Do you want to hurt me? I don't want to hurt you."

He was breathing hard, "You called me a babbby. You're mean... I don't like to be called names."

He was right, and sincerely, "Neither do I... I'm sorry. Will you accept my apology?"

He was still angry, "You laughed at me and made fun of me." He had hardly finished his last sentence when he came up swinging.

I had jumped into a back flip landing gently on the ground as Timmy rose to his feet. His mother pleaded, but Timmy had only eyes for me. I remained calm, but I could not laugh at him. It only enraged him further.

Needing to stay calm and keep Timmy from destroying the place, I began to sing. I was a pretty good singer, and I had lots of practice. It wasn't uncommon for me to play the violin and sing a song at the same time. I picked what I felt to be an appropriate song for the moment. I sang "Gutter Glitter" by Switchblade Symphony.

"Iridescent eyes of the seahorse rise,
Treasure she loves others despise.
A shooting star shan't fall very far.
Dim fireflies held in glass jars,
April showers brings May flowers
Dazzling dust tossed in wind gusts
The trapdoor is open, the window half closed,
The tapestry curtain vivaciously blows.
London Bridge did fall down;
My fair lady did nearly drown.
What is the reason to lock her up?

When already she had such rotten luck.
Bracelets of silver adorn my wrists
Candy kisses from sugar lips.

The music was eerie, and I sang with strong, intense sounds as I effortlessly moved around Timmy's punches. After a few lines, Timmy's punches kind of petered out. I swayed my body as I sang, my body moved seductively to the rhythm. A few more lines in the song and Timmy was now standing and staring in awe. I lightly laid my hand on his chest and, with a small bit of pressure, he walked backwards.

Everyone, even his mother was now quiet and as still as corpses. I pushed Timmy all the way back to his seat where he sat without hesitation. I ended the song and purred into his ear, "Now sit. Enjoy your hot chocolate and relax. Ok?"

He nodded wordlessly and, as I walked away, I could hear Mrs. Thornburg saying, "What did she do? My poor boy… Timmy, are you ok?"

"Yes, mommy," Timmy responded, but sounded far away. His mother didn't buy it. I had retreated to the back rooms before Mrs. Thornburg could get Timmy to get up and leave with her. She hadn't been gone long; the crowd had begun whispering to each other. Mrs. Thornburg burst back in the door and walked straight up to Kathy. "As long as that, that… girl works here, you will never see me come in here again." She yelled loudly, I suppose so I could hear her, "If you hurt my Timmy, you'll be sorry. You hear me?"

Kathy said with no uncertainty in her voice, "Get out. We'll talk later when you've calmed down."

"I most seriously doubt it," she hissed as she stormed out the front door.

She had just slammed the door when the whole place erupted into a roar of conversations. Summer had joined me in the back, "Holy crap, white rabbit. What Ninja/siren shit was that? You thought Dan was going to bother you before. He'll never leave you alone, and he'll want you for his band for sure."

Confused, I simply said, "Band?"

"Oh, you've never heard? Only one thing Dan cares about and that's the band. He will wrangle anyone with musical talent he can. After that debut, you're a shoe in."

I shook my head, "You're all crazy. Band or no band, I showed him a little bit too much."

Summer's look was unreadable. Her voice lowered an octave, "I know this isn't the time. Someday I hope you trust me enough to tell me what you are. The curiosity is killing me."

Before I could respond, Kathy burst in, "I need you two. There are a hundred customers, and you two leave me alone. Mel…"

"Yes."

"No more musicals tonight," she said with a strange kind of smile.

I still didn't know what Kathy really thought of me. Summer was still my friend. Dan and Adam were now giving me even stranger looks. Two customers were calling for me at the same time. Most of all, was this night ever going to end?

Chapter 18 Late Nights

No one bothered me at the end of my shift. Maybe it's because I announced that I was tired and ready to kill someone. It was the truth.

It was still raining, so by the time I got home I was soaked again. I didn't even bother drying off. I parked my bike and grabbed the violin. I would hunt tonight. Spooky joined me as a giant black tiger with red stripes.

After our hunting trip, Spooky and I washed up and decided to watch movies past sunrise. I wasn't on the schedule at The Wild Bean and in no mood to be interrogated by anyone. I couldn't remember what time I fell asleep, ten o'clock maybe. My new phone started to ring. I sat up wiping the slobber off my face and looked at the screen. It was Adam; I hadn't exchanged numbers with him. I wondered who might have programmed in his name.

My mind cleared a little as the phone finally stopped ringing. I let Summer enter some numbers into the phone last night. She was really happy that she could now text me. Looking at the phone, I had twenty-six missed text messages. They were all from Summer... I hated the future. I dropped my head back down on my pillow.

My new couch was wonderful for sleeping on; in fact, now that Spooky was here, I seldom left the living room. My phone rang again, again it was Adam. "Hello," but my voice was still not fully functional. I tried again, "Hello, what's up?"

Adam sounded careful, "Didn't mean to wake you."

I tried to sound more cheerful, "Well, what's done is done."

He spoke quickly, "Sure glad you got this phone. I need your help. I know I haven't been a very good friend, but it would mean a lot."

If it meant peace with Adam, I would do it. "What do you need?"

"No one can make it in tonight. I can't run this place alone. Do you think you can come and work for a few hours? I'll pay you extra... supposed to be slow tonight."

Out of all the things he could have wanted. Oh well, what did I expect? "I'll be there," I moaned. "Give me a couple hours to get up and have some coffee."

"Thanks Mel! You're a lifesaver... owe you one."

"Later," I hung up and moaned as I forced myself not to fall back to sleep. Looking at the time it was four in the afternoon. The stronger my powers became, the more nocturnal I became. The daylight bothered me more and more. Not that I cared, I loved the night and I loved to sleep.

I was applying my brakes on my motorcycle. I had been traveling at close to a hundred miles per hour, but I always slowed down when I came into town. As I passed through town, something started to bother me, but I couldn't put my finger on it.

At least it wasn't raining, and I didn't have to dry off before work. I parked my bike in the lot behind the Bean. Wow, there are no cars. Maybe this will be a nice slow night. That would be a good thing because I was still a little tired. I walked up between the buildings and onto Main Street, turning to go into The Wild Bean.

It hit me, today was Monday. Everything in Uptown was closed on Monday. That's why there weren't any cars, and the feeling I got when I came into town was because of how still it all was. I approached the door slowly. The open light was off. Maybe Adam wasn't over it, and this could be a trap.

I took a step back. I had no idea what Dan was capable of, and I really didn't want to have to hurt anyone. Plus the sun was up and my powers fell dormant. The door opened, and Adam's head popped out, "Good, you're here. Come on in."

"Yeah, right," I mocked. "Is this some kind of trap?"

Adam laughed, but quickly stopped when he saw the look I gave him. He looked hurt, "No, no, nothing like that. Damn this was a half baked idea." His tone changed, and he sounded a little angry, "Hadn't thought of you looking at this... like that." He paused for a minute. Before I could respond, he said so sincerely, "Sorry, I didn't mean to scare you. Kind of hurts my feelings that you would think I would hurt you, but what else would you think after the way I acted last night."

I still was not sure of the situation, "So why am I here? And who's inside?"

"Just me," then I realized he was nervous. "Look, this may seem silly or something, but I thought maybe I could make up for being such a jerk. Would you let me try?"

The fact he wanted to make up made my heart jump, but this could still be a trap. I needed to keep my wits about me, "You can try, but I don't promise nothin'."

He smiled, stepped forward, and took my hand. He then led me into The Wild Bean. Inside, the lights were mostly off, and the ones that were on being dim. In the center of the room all the other tables had been pushed away. One table sat alone with a white cloth covering the top. The top was set up with a candle, plates, silverware, and a bottle of wine with two glasses. The lights had been dimmed by the use of what looked like shirts tossed over lamps. The shirts were of different colors, so the room had a soft feel to it.

My body was shaking as he sat me down. I could see how nervous and excited he was, all rolled up in one. "Ok, sit... no, I didn't mean like that." I laughed and he tried again. "What I meant was. You make yourself comfortable, and I'll be right back with my apology." His grin was so cute, as he hurried off to the kitchen.

Tears slipped down my cheek. Never had anyone ever done something romantic for me. Not David, not Michael, not like this. It wasn't that it was that great, but I could see, feel and even taste Adam's feelings. He was doing everything in his power to impress me, and it was working. I dried my eyes as I heard Adam's yelp from the kitchen, followed by the sound of dishes crashing, "Everything all right in there?"

"Fine," he yelled from the kitchen.

I went ahead and poured the wine that had been sitting on the table. A few minutes later, Adam came out with two plates. He laid mine before me and then his. It smelled wonderful, some kind of pasta dish. There was freshly cooked asparagus and some garlic bread on the side. Before I could ask he said, "My own dish. I made this up some time ago and couldn't come up with a name for it. I finally have one."

"And that is?"

"Apology dish," he said with a smile. "Of course, after eating this, if you still don't forgive me, I might need to find a new name."

"All up to me then," I picked up my fork and took a small bite. "Wow, that's good. You should be a chef... why don't you make something this good for The Wild Bean?"

Adam beamed, "Thanks, I couldn't really make it for the Bean. It takes too long to prepare, and besides this really isn't a four star restaurant."

I took another bite, "Too bad. You would put this place on the map."

"You haven't told me if I get to keep my dish's new name."

I tried a sip of the wine. "That's good, too." I paused to gather my thoughts. "Let us get it all out in the open. I easily forgive you, but now you would like to know more about me. You don't trust me and, most likely, are befriending me so that you can get information for Dan." The last part I didn't truly believe to be true, but I'm having a hard time trusting anyone.

Adam was hurt, "This isn't a trick. How I feel isn't a trick… I think I understand you better than you might guess. I know what you are."

I didn't do a very good job hiding the surprise on my face, "You do?"

"Yeah, Dan figured it out last night."

"He did?"

Adam explained, "He sure did. It was the way you dealt with little Timmy that gave it away. The way you moved was a big clue, but there are lots of fast supernaturals. It was your singing that gave it away. He knew by the way everyone felt and the control you had over Timmy. It all made sense - how you knew what I was. Everything now makes sense, and I want you to know that I still care about you regardless."

It was too good to be true, and my heart fluttered as he took my hand. "Truly, it doesn't matter?"

"No, I don't care that you're a Siren. No wonder you live alone. You've probably been afraid to touch anyone, to drain them of their life energy. Then you touched me, and nothing happened. You're so beautiful, and your voice is magic. You knew when you couldn't drain me because of what I am. Dan had told me that I was the only creature that could withstand a Siren's touch. Hell, he was amazed to think the only purple-eyed demon and the only Siren, here together."

Dan was a fool, and my voice held no power. I was a good singer, and it was one hell of a scene as I calmed Timmy. I believed my eyes were blinking more than necessary. "Wow… you guys nailed it."

Adam smiled and went on clueless to the fact he had still no idea what I was. "Have to warn you, Dan's pretty excited. He can't believe that you're a Siren. With you in the band, we could be a big deal. Of course, the drummer was killed in that apartment raid by the Dark Fiddler, but we will find another."

I smiled, "I am sure you will. We should probably eat this before it gets cold."

He nodded, and we dug in. I needed a minute for a mental reboot. After a few more bites and some more wine, I came up with the idea of not correcting him about me being a Siren. Later, I would do some research and learn more about this creature, but for now it was better than a vampire. Plus, I was really enjoying my date; no reason to mess up a good thing. "Take off your contacts," I asked sweetly.

"What," He looked a little shaken, "Why?"

My voice purred; "Take off your contacts. I want to see you as God intended."

He stared at me for a minute. He smirked, "Ok, give me one minute." He got up and headed toward the restroom.

When he came back, I watched him cross the room. The way he walked and moved, it all was so beautiful to me. His blue button-up shirt and tight fitting jeans, he was looking good. He took his seat, and his purple eyes seemed so bright that you might think that they were illuminated. He looked at me awaiting my response, but it didn't come. I stared at him, taking him in.

After a few moments he misread my stare, and a look of hurt fell over his face. Of course, I found his puppy-dog face to be cute. He asked timidly, "So, what do you think? I look like a freak?"

I said nothing, stood up and slowly walked around the table. He looked at me bewildered. I sat down in his lap and took his face in my hands. Inches from his face, I whispered, "My favorite color was red, but now it's purple. Your eyes make me hot..." Before he could respond, I kissed him deeply.

In my mind he will never feel like a freak again. With my reaction, he will know that I accept him for all he is. I readjusted so that I straddled him on the seat. We kissed as our bodies melted together. His mouth moved to my neck and then my ear. I moaned in pleasure as his mouth and hands moved across my body.

In one fluent pull, I slipped my dress right over my head. The look on his face was priceless. "Hold up," he said between gasps of breath.

I tried not to sound put off, "Hold up for what?"

His eyes full of need, "I didn't think... you know that we would... do this."

"Surprise, surprise," I teased as I unbuttoned his shirt.

"I didn't bring anything," he looked broken hearted. It took me a second to figure out what he was saying. He hadn't brought a condom. As this thought registered, he added, "Sorry."

"Aren't you?" and I gave him a kiss. Then I moaned as I retreated from his lap. "I guess you were never a Boy Scout."

"You know this one time; you need not... rub it in."

"You wish I would rub it," I teased as I slid my dress back on.

We didn't need a condom, but I'm glad that it stopped us. I wasn't sure if I should sleep with him, not until he knew what I was. I was already starting to have way too many feelings for the boy, and a broken heart was right around the corner. I'm sure sleeping with him would make it worse.

The rest of the date was truly magical. We eventually took our conversation to the rooftop. There we talked about all kinds of things, a little more kissing too. In fact, I might have said too much as I spoke of my fathers. I never told him when I was talking about Nicks, John, or my birth father, Jack. I just told stories of growing up from three different perspectives. At one point, we just held each other watching the stars.

It felt like the date was going well, when I realized it had been going on for a long time. The light started to fill the sky, and I realized we had been together, talking, all night long. I faked a big yawn, "I hate to do this, but I better call this a night... I mean morning."

"Yeah, that's probably a good idea. You working, tonight?"

I laughed, "Yes, but there will be no secret date... what a disappointment."

"No secret date and I won't be in tonight. Dan and I got some shit to do for the band. I'll see you tomorrow, ok?"

I gave him a hug and kiss, and he walked me to my bike where we said goodbye all over again. By the time I got home the sun was threatening to pop up over the trees. I came inside, and it all hit me at once. The excitement of being with Adam kept me wired, but now I felt exhausted.

I crashed onto the couch. I was about to fall to sleep when I heard, "Details... there is no way you're going to sleep without telling me details. Left home alone, bored out of my mind, all night long. Come on, spit it out."

"Go away, Spooky," I said as I threw a pillow at her, but I knew that I wouldn't get any rest until I talked to her.

The next evening I awoke late. Between Spooky needing a play-by-play and dreaming of Adam, I didn't want to get up. I lay in bed realizing I would be late for work, but not caring at all. The days were becoming harder and harder; something about that bothered me.

I didn't want to admit that I might still be changing. I had enough stress without knowing what I was or would become. If I were to be honest with myself, even when I hunt and fight, I also held back my power. I'm afraid that if I let go I'll become something else and no longer be myself.

I couldn't lay around feeling sorry for myself, so I forced my body to rise and head to the shower. In a blur of routine, I found myself running to the back room of The Wild Bean. I grabbed my apron and pen as I prepared for work. As I came out, Kathy was working behind the bar as usual. "Sorry I'm late."

She answered like a bored professor, "It's ok, dear. Really, I don't pay you anyway."

That's strange, Kathy is normally so friendly. She didn't even make eye contact, I hope everything is ok. That's when I saw Summer, and I knew that everything was not ok. She looked like she had been crying, and she looked very sleep deprived. The Bean was dead tonight, only three customers. One was working on his laptop while the others were in deep conversation. I grabbed Summer's hand and pulled her into the back room. "Ok, spill the beans? What's happened?"

Her head was downcast; she fiddled with the strings of her apron. "Nothing really, probably just getting worked up over nothing... Dan and Adam took off."

"Explain 'took off'." I did not ask nicely.

She looked up at me, eyes pleading. "You heard about the night, Dan's team got killed. Adam told me he told you. Now there are only three members left - Dan, Adam, Rick or Richard can't remember his name. Dan left for Charleston to investigate some kind of necromancer's activity. Mom and I are worrying to death."

My blood boiled, "Dan can handle it. Don't you think Dan can handle it?"

"Sure, sure he can. You're right. I'm working myself up for nothing." I hadn't really been trying to reassure her, I was trying to see if I should freak out.

Kathy stepped through the door. She had heard us talking, "No, he can't. Dan's no battle wizard. He has great power and is clever enough, but in a fight… well that's just not his calling. Why he drags my boy into it? Damn him!" She was on the edge of tears.

Summer was now crying, "Adam's not defenseless. He has great power; with his help… they will be fine."

If I hadn't been so upset, I would have laughed. Who was she trying to convince? I asked now in a panic, "Do you know where in Charleston he is going?"

Summer just shook her head. Her mother added, "Too bad you couldn't have charmed something of his so we would know where he is."

Summer's face changed, "Oh yeah. I thought of that before, so I programmed an app on his phone." She took out her phone and pressed some buttons. "I can track his phone, almost as well as magic. Not that it matters. We can't help him, but at least we'll know his phone is ok."

With hurt and anger Kathy announced, "I can't stand around looking at that screen. I need to take my mind off it," she turned and left.

"I've got to go. Sorry I can't help tonight." I snatched Summer's phone and headed toward the front door.

Behind me I heard, "Hey, what's the big idea?" She chased me out of the store and down the sidewalk grabbing my shoulder, "What are you doing? Give me back my phone."

I lost my control. Anger, fear, I wanted Adam safe and every moment that passed, I built pressure like a pot of steam. When I turned to face her, I knew what she would see, long teeth, big eyes that most likely were slightly illuminated. "I need to go save him. I'll need your phone to find him."

Her face shifted from one look to the next. It wasn't really fear, but wonder. She stared for a moment, taking it all in, "What are you? I thought they said you were a Siren."

I smirked, "Dampier, half human, half… vampire."

A long pause fell between us. It felt like hours waiting for her response, but I was sure it was only seconds. Finally, she said, "What are you waiting for? Go save him."

I simply nodded, then flashed across the parking lot to my bike. My ride home had to be some kind of record as I rushed into the living room to get ready. I didn't care who knew about me; all I cared about was Adam. Still, it would be better to go as the Dark Fiddler.

My outfit was black from top to bottom, mostly leather except for the mask and the black cloth I used to cover my hair and eyes. My mask had large black feathers that jutted out on both sides of the eyes. I picked up my violin, and I was ready to go in record time.

I heard Spooky ask, "Where are we going?"

With haste I said, "To save Adam, no time to waste."

Chapter 19 Rescue

Spooky squealed as she squeezed me tighter. My motorcycle approached a hundred and eighty miles per hour as we tore down the interstate. Spooky yelled into my ear, "How can we help him, if we're dead?"

I laughed, because I loved the speed. The bike would not go much faster as I gave it all the gas I could. Teasing I yelled, "Would you rather fly?"

"I hate you," was what I believed the response was. It was hard to hear her with all the wind rushing in my ears. I knew that Spooky was afraid of heights, but I never realized what a problem that was until tonight.

Even if I took to the air, I doubt I could fly this fast. Spooky could turn into a small cat, but it would be hard to keep myself from dropping as fast as I jumped from one location to the next. I weaved through the cars at breakneck speed almost hitting a bus.

A bright yellow light popped on signaling I was almost out of gas. At these speeds I was burning gas fast and would have to make a quick pit stop. Flying off the interstate and into a gas station, I informed Spooky, "I didn't bring a credit card."

Spooky's hair was windblown, and neither of us had bothered with helmets. My feathers from my mask were now bent around my head. Spooky gave me a dirty look, "No pockets in your Lady Gaga outfit? I guess you think I should buy gas?"

I hissed at her, "Damn it. I guess were robbing the place."

The holdup didn't take long. I bet the video of me holding a sword to the cashier's neck was fantastic. At first he thought it was a joke, but my teeth and the fact I cut him, made him think otherwise. Spooky pumped gas while I made sure he didn't call the police. When Spooky gave me thumbs up, I put my sword away and grabbed a SunDrop. Spooky was thirsty.

Maybe he had a panic button. I had almost made it back to the bike when two squad cars squealed into the gas station. The police jumped out with guns drawn. I tossed Spooky the SunDrop. Before the drink hit her hand, I flashed to the first officer. With movements too quick for him to react, I took his gun apart while he still held the bottom half.

By the time the other cop noticed that I was attacking his buddy, I had already disarmed him and threw him on top of the hood of his squad car. As the other officer turned his gun towards me, I flashed to his side. I quickly disarmed him too. Then I broke his arm as I swung him face first into his car. The other officer got to his feet, recovering quickly.

He pulled out his taser gun. The laser found my chest, and he fired. The two pins attached to wires came at me, but my mind quickened, and it appeared they were moving slowly through the air. I grabbed them in mid-flight, then flashed right up to the officer and shoved them in his neck.

He fell to the ground his body shaking violently as his own taser gun shocked him. I then kicked him hard enough that I heard a rib break.

Pulling my sword, I quickly flattened one tire on each car and flashed back to my bike. There Spooky was polishing off her drink. "Little rough, aren't you?"

I didn't respond. I just started the bike and roared out of the gas station. Seconds later, I was back on the interstate with one thought on my mind… I hope I make it in time.

I hadn't traveled long before I noticed a cop sitting on an overpass as I flew under it. I looked back and noticed a helicopter was following me. I didn't have time for all this! I yelled at Spooky, "Time to shift into a kitty cat! I will hold you to my chest!"

I heard her yell back, "I hate you!"

Shortly afterwards a gray cat slid itself around my body and quickly latched itself to my chest. I pushed my bike to go as fast as it could. I turned the bike ever so slightly and then jumped straight up. The bike went straight into a cement column that held up an overpass. The motorcycle was moving at least a hundred and seventy when it hit. The bike exploded into a million pieces.

I had been betting that a black streak flying straight off the bike right before it exploded, would be missed by the men in the helicopter. I was right. As my body moved upwards, I looked down at the helicopter. The helicopter started to circle the accident. Well, they would be looking for bodies, and I would have to fly the rest of the way.

I started to let all my power out, for my need was great. Running power through me like a river, maybe then I could get there faster. It scared me; what if I lost complete control? What if I never regained my mind? I would find out, and I would find out to save Adam. I needed to become whatever it was I was meant to be. I stopped holding back, letting the power pour through me until it felt like my fingers and toes would pop.

The palms of my hands became as big as my face. My fingers were longer, and three inches of them were claws. My hands became as black as night along with the nails. I was not sure if my skin turned black or that no light would reflect off my skin. I felt like I was surrounded in shadows. I wished to move faster through the air... my spine felt like it was growing as something ripped out of my back.

It felt as if giant hands had grown out of my back. I could feel the air with them. It felt like I was swimming as I sped through the air faster. I used one of my fingers to cut the material over my eyes. I needed to see what had come out of my back. When I looked, I gasped. Huge black bat wings were flapping.

As I took in the wings, my eyes showed me the world in a new light. Before it was awful, because the land of the dead merged with the living, because of this, I used my second sight to see. Something had changed, and it was... beautiful. I saw the world in multicolored layers. As the land passed below, I witnessed spirits moving about. They were white and bright and easy to see. Humans were different now, and it was like seeing ghosts only inside a shell. The dimming from the body made it easy to tell them apart. I realized with a start that my mind was crystal clear. During the change, I felt the madness, but now that I let it all go, I felt fine. I flapped my wings with my need to arrive in time.

With time to think, I wondered... I wondered if this was love. I cared for him. I couldn't afford to lose people I cared about. I also cared about Summer, and the loss of her brother would be awful. Love or not, I would do this for him. I would do it for Ezra, Alice or any member of my family. Still, there was something more. The worst part was, the more I cared about him the closer I would come to having to tell him the truth. Then what?

It hit me like a brick. I had vamp vamp out, right in front of his sister. Summer now knew what I was, and there was no way of taking that back. Oh boy, even if I save him, I will have to face him about what I am. I reached down and pulled out the phone to see where he was. The little dot looks like they had left the hotel where they were earlier. They were on the move. I needed to get there.

I felt his presence before I saw him. Nicks was walking next to me. Well, walking wasn't really it. He floated to my left. He turned and smiled at me, "Hello, Melabeth."

I smiled, "Like the wings?"

"Love them, and it is good to see you have accepted your role. It is time now."

I really was nervous, I wasn't ready, "Time for what exactly?"

"Time for you to take your place at my side, for a great enemy has arisen. Who he is, I don't know. He has barred me in the library and stopped spirits from moving through the library for their final rest. I do believe this man is set to destroy the world."

I didn't really understand, "But why?"

"To rule, maybe... who knows? It might help to know why, but it might not. My power on this side has been greatly diminished. I have given all I can and will not be any more assistance to you."

Now I was worried, "What do I do?"

Nicks thought for a second and with kind eyes said, "Perhaps find the book, but first find out what these necromancers keep doing from one city to the next. This will take time, but I'm sure you will figure it out."

I had a mission, of course, right after I saved Adam. I wondered, "Nicks, do you think I can trust Alice?"

Nicks smiled, "If you have to ask me, then there's your answer."

"Thanks," I said half-heartedly. Nicks laughed and I added, "First, I need to save Adam."

Nicks gave me a strange look, "Are you sure this boy is worth it?"

"No, but do you know any men that are?"

Nicks smirked, "Not for you, not for you my dearest. The best of luck, I must return now. My love will always be with you, come see me soon. By the way, I will need to meet this Adam."

"I love you, too," the words had barely left my lips when his image disappeared. His visit and words always made me feel whole. How do people do it, people who don't know or have unconditional love?

Even at the amazing speed I traveled, it would still be a little while before I reached Charleston. I felt some pinching from Spooky's claws as they dug in. I laughed as the thought crossed my mind... Spooky is spooked.

Hours later, I landed softly upon an old building. Spooky jumped off me without a second to spare. She took her human form. She was naked as she walked to the edge to look around. "I hate flying. That was the worst." She turned and looked at me and jumped with a start. "Oh shit? What the hell? You look like the... angel of death. Wow, glowing eyes, huge claws, and now wings." Her face, filled with concern, "Hey, you still in control?"

"Yes," I said with a wicked grin. I flashed over to her and had her in my arms before she could even react. "If not, you would be dead."

She pushed free, "You're not funny. Where's your boyfriend?"

I pulled out the phone with some trouble because of the size of my hands. I couldn't work the phone so I tossed it to Spooky who quickly went to work. A minute later she announced, "Three blocks in that direction were his last location. Well, his phone is in that direction. Doesn't look like he's moved for twenty minutes," My mind filled with images of his dead body. Spooky quickly added, "His *phone* hasn't moved. Don't freak out before we even find him."

I pulled out my swords and let them become violins. As long as they were spirit weapons, Bow was trapped inside of them. A few seconds later, she reappeared in a mist form. I commanded, "Scout ahead."

Bow simply bowed, "Right away." I never felt bad bossing her. I knew she loved these outings and any chance to unleash her skills.

"I'll take the ground," Spooky announced. She jumped off the side of the building. Landing on a power cable that hung off the side of the building two stories down, she slid down the cable to a pole. She was on the ground like lightning. She turned into what appeared to be a cheetah and ran into the shadows. We had done this so many nights we moved together like clockwork.

I took to the air, and my wings had barely flapped. I flew up like a rocket. Leveling out my flight, I scanned the ground. While I looked for Adam I couldn't help but think. My wings were black and looked very similar to my sword. It was not so much that they flapped, but it was more like they pushed the air away moving me like a jet. Of course I can make myself weightless, so one flap moved me quickly.

As I circled in the air thinking about my new developments; my attention was quickly diverted. Flashes of light came from the second floor of a parking lot. As I flew above it, three figures emerged on the uppermost parking deck.

It was Adam, Dan, and the drummer in Dan's band. I could not remember his name, if I ever knew it to begin with. They were all dressed in black. Adam and the other man looked military in their style of gear, but Dan wore a cape and looked a little like Magneto without his helmet.

They moved quickly across the parking lot. Four new people emerged where they had just come from, three men and a female. Dan stopped and said some words, and a bright blue circle filled with strange symbols appeared on the ground around him. The drummer and Adam took cover behind a parked car.

The three men headed toward Dan while the girl stopped running and turned in Adam's direction. She pulled out what appeared to be a wand. Who did this girl think she was? Hermione? The drummer had taken aim with his M4 and fired at her. She walked forward with her wand out in front of her, and the bullets just fell to the ground with no effect.

She then fired what looked to be a cheap sparkler out of her wand. The effect might have looked lame, but the end result was not. Everything the sparks hit burst into flames. Adam pulled the drummer under cover just before the sparks reached him. I gasped in horror as Adam stood between the sparks and the drummer.

The next thing I saw was nothing short of amazing. The sparks hit Adam as if they really were nothing more than a sparkler. Adam pushed his hand out before him and stared at the witch intensely. All the flames caused by the sparks went out, and soon she was standing there with nothing but a wand and a stupid look on her face.

The drummer took aim. I was sure that the bullets would kill her now; there was no magic protecting her as long as Adam's power was upon her. Still, Adam's power had limits, and he could not stare at everyone.

Dan had been engaged in some kind of magical duel with the other three men. One of the men just stood outside of Dan's protective circle, pacing back and forth, while the other man looked to be preparing his own circle. One of the attackers stood back watching. The man that had been pacing back and forth had noticed that the drummer was now shooting at the girl. He flashed up on the drummer, obviously a vampire.

The vampire grabbed him and tossed the drummer against the car, ripping the rifle from his hands.

The drummer fought him as the vampire struggled to get the rifle. It was looped over his shoulder by a strap. Adam couldn't help himself and turned and grabbed the vampire. The vampire was still struggling, but becoming weaker by the second. Still, turning his power away from the witch, he had let her access her power again. She began to cast again, when she realized that her power had returned.

I wasn't sure how I should attack, but I thought it best to get close to Adam. I pulled out my violin. Adam once again turned his power back upon the witch because she was starting to shoot sparks again. The vampire almost became lifeless. The drummer was now back in control of his rifle pointing it down upon the vampire's head, ready to finish him. He fired his weapon point blank range and the vamp's head exploded.

The vampire was not dead, but it would take hours or longer to repair that kind of damage. Afterwards he would need blood. It looked as if they might be winning as the witch now ran for cover. Realizing her powers were gone, she slid behind a car as the bullets impacted around her.

I held back attacking, not sure if I should enter the fray if they were winning. It would be better if they never saw me. I would float up here and help only if I felt Adam's life was endangered. I called Bow's spirit to me, and my violin and bow once again became swords. I wished to be ready.

Chapter 20 Old Friends

As I watched the drummer spray bullets at the witch, Adam turned his power towards the wizard who was fighting Dan.

Spell fighting would not make a good Michael Bay movie. No explosions or sparks, just two men, standing inside glowing circles, mumbling strange things. I understood that both of these wizards could cause some serious collateral damage, but for every big attack spell there was a counter spell. With their shields up, they both cast spells trying to destroy each other's defenses. The winner would be allowed to devastate whoever was left standing.

It was a third man, who had stood there watching it all from some distance. I failed to notice him create a green circle and now was being surrounded in darkness. I felt it, the gateway to death. Spirits began to arise around the man. He was a Necromancer. He was summoning spirits to fight for him. Adam was concentrating his power on him, but his power had no effect. The spell had been cast and now the Necromancer was controlling the dead. Adam's power destroyed manna, but not the dead. That was *my* job. The spirits poured forth from the gateway and took the forms of pirates. I guess being in Charleston, that should have not surprised me. I tightened my grip on my Kanata and headed straight toward the Necromancer.

I dropped from the sky, the Necromancer must have felt my power, and his eyes cast upwards. I must have been quite the sight. The spirits looked upon me with fear. A glowing-eyed creature with large black wings, wielding a Kanata, falling from the sky… I suppose that would get anyone's attention.

The next thing that happened surprised me. The ghosts fired upon me with their muskets. Some had rifles but most with pistols. The bullets ripped through my skin and shredded my wings. The sudden hit made me spin off course. I was forced to land far to the right of the Necromancer or risk being shot more. My wounds healed fast, but still I had lost blood. I could not afford to lose blood in battle.

Now ghosts wielding blades stood between me and this Necromancer. Naturally, a battle ensued.

My second sight could now see the ghosts as they became solid. There were at least fifty and more coming out. I needed to destroy the gateway, or

I would be fighting ghosts all night. I came to realize that, during the fight toward the gateway, some of the spirits had headed toward Adam and the drummer.

My mind raced as to how to save them when I felt her. Spooky came flying across the deck; she had come in the form of a tiger. She was massive, black with red stripes. The ghosts were up on the drummer and stabbed him to death as he tried in vain to shoot them.

Adam jumped over a car and made a run for it, but hadn't gone far. Some pirates shot at him making him take cover. They were almost upon Adam when Spooky flew through the air. She clawed, bit and ripped the pirates apart. Their black smoke filled the air. Spooky had my blood in her, and the dead stood no chance.

With Spooky taking care of Adam, I could return to the task at hand. I drew my smaller sword, and, with two swords I could fight multiple enemies easier. I flashed and moved, killed, then moved again. Within a few well planned moves, I was standing at the gateway. I stabbed my sword down into the gateway.

With a loud popping noise, the gateway shut. The Necromancer had tried to cast some spells on me, but none of them had any effect. Now he pulled his own sword with fear in his eyes.

I fought, killing the spirits and deflecting the Necromancer's blows. He swung with all his power. I sidestepped and, in one move, removed his arm. He screamed as I turned to kill a few more pirates. The Necromancer had fallen to his knees and hunched over, screaming in pain. At last I drove my blade through the back of his head.

The few pirates who had remained ran away with the death of the Necromancer. Without their master they lost their will to fight.

I turned as I heard a new and terrible noise. Behind me with her back to me, the witch stood over Spooky. She stood there like the Emperor in Star Wars with streams of electric arcing from her fingers. Spooky jerked back and forth. I could feel her pain.

Adam lay upon the ground; he was moving, but holding his head in pain. He looked as if he had taken a serious hit to the head. I flashed up behind the witch. I grabbed her hair and pulled it back until she was looking at me. She had a look of surprise on her face as I growled, "That's my kitten, bitch." Then, with my right hand, I brought my sword down removing her head.

With my second sight I noticed another man running up behind me. He had what appeared to be a shotgun. He raised the shotgun to my head. I had the witch's head in my hand, and, with one quick movement, I swung it underhanded straight at the man with the gun. He fired, but he had not seen the head. The head was only inches from the front of his shotgun when it exploded into what amounted to a blood bomb.

While he wiped the blood out of his eyes, I flashed past him. Then I ran my sword through his chest and into his heart.

I took stock of the situation. Spooky had recovered, and Adam appeared to be ok as he got to his feet. He was a little shaky, but ok. The two wizards were still battling it out. The ground was now cracked between them as they both fought on. I hadn't even seen where the man with the shotgun had come from, but I had a feeling that there were more enemies, and time was short.

I approached the wizard Dan fought, but found that I could not pass the circle of protection. Under great strain Dan yelled at Adam, "Run. Get out of here before it kills you."

Adam, still rubbing his head, walked carefully past Spooky, eyeing her warily. He calmly pointed out, "If the fiddler wanted me dead, all she had to do was stay out of it." Pride ran through me as I realized he was taking my advice.

Adam stared at the opposing wizard. I felt the barrier that had kept me out fail. I had used so much energy I needed blood. I flashed upon the wizard before Dan could even react. I reached one hand under his left arm, digging my fingers in right below the neck and above the rib cage. My right hand reached over the top and grabbed his chin. I then pulled him back, and, as he moaned in pain, I bit into his neck.

The blood rushed into me along with his life's energy. Wizards had always had a lot of kick to them, but I had never fed on a wizard this powerful before. He was like eating ten men… it was amazing! I couldn't get enough as I drained him greedily.

I was feeding when I opened my eyes and there in front of me, both Dan and Adam stood. They were about fifteen feet away. Dan looked at me with curiosity, but it was Adam's face that brought my pleasure to a halt. He had a look of fear, disgust and hatred. I stopped feeding, and the wizard's body crumpled dead at my feet. Tears threatened to fall from my eyes, for the way Adam looked at me broke my heart. I could feel the blood running down my chin, staining my black outfit. My wings healed along with the rest of my wounds. Even healed, my wings looked to be solid and of smoke all at the same time.

A new sound brought my attention elsewhere. There was a staircase twenty feet from us that is where the man with the shotgun must have come from. I heard the sounds of footsteps shortly followed by people running out.

I turned to see the new threat with my eyes. That is when I realized what they were… zombies. They moved with only the speed of a human, but they would never stop. Humans don't seem fast until they run at you full speed with no fear or dwindling of strength. My sword quickly took off the first few heads. From behind me, I heard Dan yell, *"run."*

With both blades in hand, I would cover their escape. I moved backwards staying near Dan's and Adam's rear, killing one undead after another. More corpses came up from the lower levels, and, before long, hundreds were chasing all of us to the other side of the parking garage. There were no stairwells close by, and we were four stories up. I was wondering how I would get Adam out of here safely when Dan cast a spell. A bridge formed out of thin air, and it looked like it was made of crystal. It extended from the top of the parking garage to the nearby hotel roof.

Adam closed his eyes and held the back of Dan's shirt so that he could be led across. If Adam looked at or touched the bridge, the magic would be destroyed. Dan, Adam and Spooky wasted no time running across the bridge. No matter how fast I killed the dead, I could not keep them at bay. Some of the dead got around me and started to chase them across the bridge. As soon as Spooky made it across, Dan waved his arm and the bridge popped. Little sparkles filled the air for a split second, and then the bridge was gone. The zombies that had been crossing fell to the ground.

I jumped free from the zombies and took to the air. I followed right behind Dan and company as I landed on the roof. Adam looked back at me with a blank face, and then he turned and followed Dan into a doorway that led off the roof and into the hotel. Spooky followed, then me. We all moved swiftly and quietly to the ground floor as we headed out of the front of the hotel.

We ran out through the lobby getting very startled looks from a few people as we passed by. A woman with black hair was behind the counter and she asked, "Can I help..." followed by a stifled scream when she noticed the giant tiger.

As we went out the front entrance, we came out, and enter into a square. There, in the center of the square, sat a large water fountain spraying water upwards. Pretty as the fountain was with its many levels of water each pouring upon the lower levels and eventually pooling at the bottom, the fountain was not what we all stopped to watch and wonder about. Standing to the left of the fountain was a man.

The man standing next to the fountain was over six feet tall with large shoulders. He stood there, wearing boots and black pants, no shirt, but he wore a cape with a hood. His muscular build reminded me of the men from the movie "300". In the hood there was a mask that was so black you knew there was magic in it.

The only thing you could see was his eyes. They were dark and green. His eyes seemed to glow like a rich, deep emerald, burning with power. On his left side, he had two large chrome hilts. He pulled one hilt with his right hand across his body, revealing a sword rapier. With his left hand he pulled a long dagger. Both weapons had large hilts that protected his hands.

I stepped out in front of my friends and said, "Spooky, I'm leaving them to you. I will deal with him."

Adam started to say, "I can help..." but Dan interrupted him, "Let's go. I cannot transport you, and the undead will be here soon. She can fly."

Dan grabbed his arm and, grudgingly, Adam followed with Spooky taking up the rear. I readied myself in case this man made a move on them, but he did not. He just took a few steps closer to me, stopped and then gave me a slight head nod. He then raised his swords in a fighting position, and I did the same.

I could feel Bow's excitement… finally someone that would truly test her skills.

Within a heartbeat our body and swords moved like water. As our swords deflected one another, I came to notice that this Necromancer was using spirit swords. No doubt he also used some skill from a spirit who spent a lifetime mastering these weapons. He moved like a vampire as we encircled each other, testing each other's defenses.

The man could flash, and he felt just as strong as me. It didn't take long before my blade slashed his stomach. Shortly afterwards his sword stabbed my shoulder. I quickly healed, but so did he. No verbal words passed between us as we continued our deadly dance.

I could feel Bow, and she was strong and moved my hands with indescribable accuracy. My opponent was just as good, but with a completely different style. We fought, and, at the same time, we were studying each other.

As we squared off, a loud noise erupted from my right. From inside the hotel where we had just exited, I could hear screaming quickly followed by silence. The silence was broken by the sound of shuffling feet. The undead poured out of the lobby and into the courtyard.

My sword quickly sliced off the heads of two of them. My opponent moved forward, trying to take advantage of me while I was fending off the zombies. I flashed behind two of the undead while engaging more zombies behind them. The Necromancer sliced down the two zombies who stood between us, but this move gave me time to counter his next attack.

The zombies didn't seem interested in my Necromancer friend. Their attacks were clumsy as they all piled after me at the same time. This might have been to his advantage, expect the zombies kept getting in his way. In his frustration, he kept slaying the zombies to get to me. It was not long before our feet were sliding around on blood. Bodies and parts of bodies made movement difficult as we battled on.

I finally had had enough and took to the air. I landed on the wall of the building overlooking the crowd of undead. The zombies piled against the wall with their hands raised in the air, trying to reach me. The Necromancer followed my move landing on the wall, ten feet away. The perspective of the world changed, and the wall seemed like the ground. Next to me it looked as if there was a pile of bodies as the undead stacked against the wall. They began to crawl over one another, and soon they would be able to reach me. No more messing around, I thought. I flashed forward and attacked with all my skill and strength.

The Necromancer was fast and skilled. I was wondering if this might ever end. In his left hand, he was using a large dagger with a large guard. The blade itself had notches in it. I slashed at him with my sword. He blocked it with his dagger at the same time and he caught the blade in one of those notches. He twisted his wrist, wrenching the sword from my hand. My sword fell into the mass of zombies below.

He came at me with his sword, which I quickly deflected with my short sword. Grasping the short sword with two hands, I pushed his sword aside. I had meant to close the distance between us and then slash him, but I missed. He countered, and his dagger stabbed into my chest. The blade was over a foot long and easily went right through me. His spirit blade had found my slow beating heart, and I felt a sharp pain in my chest. The sudden pain made me lose concentration for a second, but I realized in time that his sword blade was heading toward my neck.

I raised my short sword blocking the blow. I was losing strength and could feel myself being pulled back to the earth and the zombies. The only thing that kept me from falling was the fact that I was impaled on his dagger. The Necromancer let out a dark chuckle, but he had laughed too soon.

My right hand was free, because he had disarmed my katana. My hand grew with long black claws and struck forward. Like a wild beast, I slashed him, tearing his arm and chest up before he had time to react. We both fell towards the outreached arms of the zombies.

We crashed into the center mass of zombies. He had to let go of his dagger, and I kicked him away from me. I found myself being grabbed by hands from all directions. The monsters were biting me as I fought for all I was worth.

Pinned in against the wall with a dagger in my chest and cuts and bites all over my body, things were looking bleak, but I wasn't done.

Fighting them off enough that I was able to use my short sword again and the fact I was against the wall, meant that only four or five at a time could attack me. The more I killed the more I was protected by a wall of bodies.

I didn't know how much longer I could hold on, when I realized there weren't that many undead left. I pulled the dagger out of my chest and then threw it into a zombie's head. Breaking free from my position against the wall, I fought the zombies by flashing and killing them before they could encircle me again.

I pulled my katana out from under a pile of bodies. The Necromancer was leaning against the fountain still healing from his wounds. He still had his sword, but had lost his dagger. He hadn't bothered to stop me as I finished off the rest of the zombies. Instead, he had used this time to heal himself.

He slowly stood up, still breathing heavily. I raised my swords at the ready. His left arm had healed, but it was still full of red scabbed-over wounds. His chest was no better, and some even looked to still be bleeding. His mask had been hit by one of my strikes. I had cut through the left side of his cheek. Four claw marks had ruined his mask, and it looked as if it was now sitting sideways on his face.

Reaching with his free hand, he pulled back his hood; wavy brown hair fell free and dangled almost to his neck. He then removed his mask. There stood a striking man, dark green eyes with a strong face. He was in his mid thirties, built like a tank and devilishly handsome. My voice shook as I said his name, "David."

His eyes narrowed as his head slowly cocked to one side. He asked, "Do I know you? How is it that the Dark Fiddler knows my name?"

I removed my mask and watched David's face go from curious to jaw-dropping surprise. I smiled, "Remember me now?"

David laughed a deep laugh. "They told me you had been killed. I should have known better."

I wondered, "*They*?"

"Does not matter, what matters is, they were wrong. You being alive will change everything."

I didn't trust David, it had been too long, "What does it change David?"

He had a devilish smirk, "You still hanging out with Alice? Or have you learned the truth?"

Sick of his game, my tone was less than friendly, "What truth might that be?"

"Oh, I don't know. Wait, yes I do, I just have no reason to tell you. I'll tell you what... I'll let you know what I know if you tell me who has the book. What do you think of that?"

The question caught me off guard. "It's been a long time David, straight to business huh?"

He put his sword away, "Afraid so. Look Melabeth, it's not that I wouldn't like to get a cup of coffee, then take you back to my place and crush that ass, but too much time and too much stuff has happened. I don't know who you're working for, or what side you're on. In fact, I dare say I've never really known you at all. At one time I thought you had my back and together we would bring an end to the Fascist Rule of the wizards. Look at us now, fighting to the death and for what... to protect a wizard. Your life is worth those two?"

His words hurt and the look on his face was full of pain. I cast my eyes away and what I saw reminded me of what he was and who I've become. On the ground before me, lying in a puddle of blood was the severed head; it belonged to a woman with black hair. Bodies lay everywhere, and the whole courtyard was stained in red. The smell of the dead filled my nose, and the face of the head came into my mind. I had seen it moments earlier as we rushed through the hotel lobby. She had been behind the counter just moments before, trying to make a living.

I finally found my voice as my eyes stared into his, "I remember you. A man so selfish, that no life had value if it stood in his way... full of hate, with no love, and killing with no regard. At one time I did have your back, but thank God that I have freed myself from your evil. To answer your questions, yes is the answer. Both of their lives are worth mine, for it is noble and pure to protect life from a monster like you."

"Monster?" David's voice rang with indignity. "Oh, so now I'm the enemy. Let me guess... you're the good guy?"

"Yes," I answered directly with no pause in my voice.

This brought a condescending laugh, "Vampires are the good guys... yeah right. Do you know that Luna knows that Alice has the book? It won't take long before she brings you all down. You're either on my side or you're alone. They will never see you as anything but an enemy. Join with me and together we can take down the wizards and save the world."

He had truly lost his mind, "I don't think so. By the way, Alice does not have the book."

He smirked, "So sure are we? Well, if you don't join with me, will you need to kill me or will you let me go?"

I paused; I had no answer for him. Do I kill him? What if he doesn't want to fight? After a few seconds I asked him, "Are you going to leave without trying to kill me?"

David tossed his sword at my feet. He then held his hands out wide, "I will now cast a teleporting spell. I will be unable to stop you if you want to kill me. The choice is yours… good guy." He smiled and then chuckled. He followed it up with a spell.

I watched him cast the spell as I stood there unable to move. I didn't want to kill him. Without him attacking me, I would not attack him. Seconds later, his body disappeared along with his sword. I released Bow, and my swords turned back into a violin and bow. Bow's spirit reappeared in front of me, "Find Spooky." Bow nodded and without a word disappeared.

I felt weak from my fight and could really use some blood. My chest still hurt, which was strange. I put my hand to my heart and felt nothing. I stopped breathing… it didn't bother me. What was going on? I knew from my other senses that Bow and Spooky would soon be here. I decided that I had seen enough of the dead and would meet them halfway, so I took off in a flash.

In a small alley, I met up with a giant tiger that turned into Spooky. I asked, "Adam, Dan?"

"Took off in a car, I followed them as long as I could." She looked at me strangely, "How did you fare? You look like shit."

Trying to hide my worry, "Fine," I answered flatly.

Spooky shook her head, "You don't look fine… Oh shit, I can feel it."

Panic flared up in me, "Feel what?"

"You're dead."

I shook my head, "Damn, you scared me. Stop screwing around."

She shook her head, "Not screwing around. I thought this would happen, but didn't know when. Did you get injured tonight?"

I was confused, "Yes, but what are you talking about? You knew what would happen?"

Spooky paused for a moment. "I'm sorry, I thought you knew. Your human side was dying. Your heart has been slowing, you've got paler and daytime sensitivity has become worse. Alice, Ezra and I used to talk about this. Alice wasn't sure, but Ezra believed your human side would not survive long."

I could feel the tears forming, "He stabbed me in the heart."

Spooky looked lost as she tried to come up with something to say to me. She simply said, "Oh sweetie, it'll be ok," and she wrapped her arms around me.

I kept the tears at bay. I pulled away from Spooky's embrace. "I need to return home."

With a small voice, Spooky pointed out, "You will not be able to go out during the day for too long, and you probably shouldn't go into town; those eyes, everyone will know. Your eyes are huge. I know you like working…"

I interrupted, not needing to hear the many different ways my life would end, "I know, I know, already. I'll figure it out, later. For now… I just want to go home."

"Ok," Spooky answered.

"Go see my parents. It's on the way back, and you don't like to fly."

Spooky started to say, "But, " I interrupted her again, "I need time alone and I would like to see my family."

She nodded; looking reluctant, she finally agreed, "Ok… take it easy then."

"Bye," is all I said. She turned into a cat and took off into the night. I took to the air.

After a short while I landed upon a tree overlooking a small road. I had traveled quickly, but I wasn't sure how much longer I had. My mind was torn up as I thought about everything. Summer knew, so of course Adam would know. Then there was the fact that my heart does not beat, and my eyes are large, and I am a vampire once again. I let my sword become a violin and could feel Bow's presence. She was angry about tonight. As Bow reappeared, she gave me a hard look. I was not in a good mood, "What's your problem?"

With a venomous voice, "Well, we saved your love. So, glad we made it in time. Well worth risking all our lives. Then you let David leave; do your feelings rule you?"

I reached over and slapped her hard. Bow's look was a cross between pain and surprise. With great authority, "I know that I'm crushing on Adam… in love, we'll see. I don't even know his birthday. In fact, I know very little about him. Loneliness and the fact he is one of my few friends has helped fan the fires of desire. I also know that the true tests have not happened. What will he say when he finds out what I am?" I made a high pitched voice and acted all ridiculous, "I'm so in love. I'll do anything; I'll die for him because he's hunky." With my normal voice, "There will be no hiding what I am now."

Bow nodded, "Sorry, if I offended."

"*You did*… on more than one level. First, that I would have put my life or others in danger just because I have feelings for a guy. I would put your life in danger just because. I believe Dan and Adam are important and therefore worth saving. Furthermore, their lives were at risk, a risk I didn't mind risking you on. Would it be wrong just to save them just because they needed saving? In the end, I will risk your life when and where I like..." I changed my tone, "What is my name?"

A little confused, Bow answered, "Melabeth."

"Again," I commanded.

She looked me in the eyes and with a clear and solid voice, "Melabeth, my master."

"Remember that, and the last time I checked, you came along just so you could re-live some old dream. I'm not your friend, and you will never question my decisions again. Now do that trick… where you disappear."

She gave me a head bow, but quickly added, "I was wrong, and Nicks was right. You will lead." Then she disappeared.

I really hadn't meant to go all general dickhead on her, but I needed to make sure she never questions me again. Deep down I'm not that little girl anymore. I know I play a game of truth and dare, life and death. I can't trust Alice, Dan… David, no way could I trust David. I will not be led around by the nose again. So, wrong or right, I will forge my own destiny.

My hunger was upon me; I unfolded my wings and took flight. If lucky, I would make it home before the morning light.

Chapter 21 Haunted

I was close to home when I about fell from the sky.

I was too weak, and my wings had started to come apart like old paper. As I coasted through the air, I witnessed a couple making out in a convertible. The car was parked far from the road overlooking the city below. "Make out Lane" and silly names like that came to mind. Landing in their back seat, I grabbed both their necks. I fed on the boy first while the girl screamed.

My wings had healed, and my power returned. Two young teenagers lay passed out, breathing shallowly. I came close to killing them. I knew better than to wait until I was so weak and hungry. It was much harder to control myself when the hunger took over.

My eyes closed as I took long, deep, calming breaths. My heart still lay dormant. I still felt no life in me. I didn't want to eat. I didn't want to feel the let down when my heart did not heal. I had hoped when I took off from Charleston, that I hadn't used too much of my energy to properly heal. Now that hope was gone.

Once again I took to the air. Long before I could sort out my worries or emotions, I had to return home. Landing in front of the old house, my wings turned to black dust and disappeared. I let go of my reaper self and felt… just like my old vampire self. The light had filled the sky, and soon the sun would rise. I had flown to Charleston, fought, and made it back in one night. Not bad, I thought.

I stood on my porch and awaited the sun. When it broke the tree line, it also broke my heart. The sun burned my eyes, and my skin felt like it was on fire. I hated this feeling. I went inside to escape the sun's merciless rays.

I tossed my mask and violin onto the coffee table. Pushing a pile of crap out of my way, I fell face first onto the couch. I lay there with one arm dropped down, fingers in the carpet. I had fed, but I hadn't slept in a long time. I was tired. Being upset and feeling a little lost didn't help me sleep. I really wanted to talk to Alice or Summer. I had sent Spooky away. That part made me happy, for, when I fell asleep, I could visit my family.

As my world became hazy, I was aware that subconsciously I was fighting sleep. Something was on the edge of my mind… something important. I was forgetting something and could not concentrate on what it was. The sleep was taking over, and my last thought was, I'll remember in the morning.

*   *   *

I felt better, spending the day while I slept inside Spooky. She had talked to my mom and father for hours that morning. She then hung out with my eleven-year-old brother. He was becoming a fine man, and I was missing it. Spooky generally slept during the day and seldom did I get that much time with my family. She must still feel bad for me, and she was going the extra mile. Not sure if I deserve her pity and that thought reminded me of my heart. It still lay dead within my ribs.

I felt my mind awakening. The floor was hard and cold. Had I fallen off the couch while I slept? I already knew what I would look like in the mirror, big eyes, pale skin and rings around the eyes. The makeup would hide most of it, but I would need contacts to hide the eyes. I would have to give Kathy a story of why I couldn't make it to work. Also, she'll need to know that I will only be available at night.

The laundry list of activities was growing in my mind. With my newfound hope, I would find a way to make it all work out. Plus, I needed to check on Adam and make sure he was ok, so I sat up and opened my eyes... and what I saw floored me.

I hadn't fallen off my couch, and, if I did, I had fallen into another world. I was sitting on a concrete floor surrounded by bare concrete walls. Steel bars, an inch thick, formed two walls enclosing me in the corner of the room. I could not make out a door, and all the bars looked permanent. I noticed that I was wearing two steel cuffs that were chained to the wall. On the far wall next to a steel door, a camera was mounted. Underneath the camera sat one small stool with wheels. Other than that, the room was empty.

I remembered what I had forgotten last night. I had vamped out in front of Summer and then told her I was going to go and save Adam. Then Adam and Dan would have returned today. Wow, how stupid am I? I was still wearing the clothes I had worn as the Dark Fiddler. I had laid my bow and mask down right beside me.

There was no clock in the room, but I knew the sun was still up. I would not have the strength to break these chains until sundown. On closer examination, there were strange markings on the cuffs and chains. If they were enchanted, I might not be able to break them at all. I wondered if I could ever bend those bars, even if they *weren't* enchanted. Escape did not look good.

As the minutes passed, I was able to make out more details of the room in the faint light, such as the fact that the floor on which I sat was full of markings. They were very strange and did not seem carved. It was like the concrete was glass, and the symbols laid within. How much magic did they use to hold me here? All I could do now was wait.

A few hours passed, and I had begun to nod off. The sound of footsteps filled my ears. They sounded like hard soles, perhaps a female. The footsteps stopped, and I could hear the latch of the steel door being undone. Shortly afterwards it opened, and Summer stepped into the room. Her hair was a mess, and her eyes looked puffy as if she had been up all night crying.

She shut the steel door behind her. Then she walked slowly toward me, staring. Her face was blank, and I could only guess what she might be thinking. I was betting she would be telling me what was on her mind shortly.

Summer's voice was flat, "You look like a vampire today. How is that we never noticed? How did you trick us?" When I did not answer, she went on talking. "I suppose you could be something other than a vampire. I mean my brother's power... it really doesn't seem to work on you." She rested her hands upon the bars and stared at me. A few awkward minutes passed by, but I said nothing. What could I say? She finally tired of the silent treatment. Anger and hurt now registered on her face as well as in her voice, "You lied to me."

I felt empty inside. I missed Alice and wished I hadn't sent Spooky away. I wasn't ready to deal with her hurt. I've never had many friends, and now it felt like I had none. I answered her, knowing she would not like what I had to say. "I didn't lie to you. It was my secret, not yours. Just because we became friends does not entitle you to know everything about me."

Her eyes were searching me, "You're right. This city is a place to hide, and you didn't have to tell me. Of course, you're full of *shit*. *Yes*, you had to tell me; we were best friends. *Yes*, you had to tell me because you knew all of our secrets and we let you into our home like you were family. I told you how fablishish you are... we danced." She stopped in tears.

"Sorry," was the only word I could find.

She wiped her face off and sniffled a few times. After regaining control, she said, "Thanks. I guess you saved Adam and Dan last night. Of course now we know you murdered our friends."

I tried not to get mad, but the murder remark got me worked up. "You're welcome; I told you I was going to save him. What friends did I murder? Are you talking about the apartment complex?"

"Yes," she responded, sounding angry as well. "You know, the one where you nearly killed Adam. Right after that, you made an appearance at the Bean. You came looking for work. Once you found out about him, you got close and made sure nothing happened to him. I bet you're waiting for the right time… AND BANG, you'll trap him. Then you'll sell him to some shithead or something. Sound about right?"

I was stunned, "That's not what happened." I stuttered out my defense, "I-I wasn't looking for him. I was hunting the necromancers. Dan and his team just happened to hit the same place that I followed the necromancers to. Then it was; it was self defense. They attacked me!"

"So they attacked you. After killing all of them, Adam fired his rifle at you, but you didn't kill him, why?"

I heard defeat in my own voice. She would never believe me. "His power does affect me. It slowed me down, I smelled him, and then I remembered him."

Summer shook her head, "Liar, liar, pants on fire. You hadn't met him yet, so how could you have remembered him? Dan was right; I shouldn't have come down here. You're just a monster."

I was trying to think up a response when she turned her back and slammed the door on her way out. Well, that went better than I thought. I slammed my head against the wall and closed my eyes. This day was becoming really shitty.

I was in the middle of feeling nothing. My emotions were lost to me, or perhaps I was in shock. Either way, I needed to get out of here. It's one thing that they found out, but it's another to get captured. I couldn't be sure that they wouldn't have found my secret sleeping place, but the fact that I crashed out in the living room proved that my mindset was all wrong. I really needed to get my head out of the clouds, go find Alice, and perhaps save the world. The last thought brought a small smile to my face. If the world was waiting for me to be a savior, then it was in big trouble.

I was trying to think up an escape plan when my second guest arrived. The metal door squeaked open, this time Dan came in. Shutting the door behind him, he came to the bars, stopping a few steps from them. In a pleasant voice he said, "It's been awhile since we talked, too long perhaps. Who do you work for?"

"The Wild Bean, but they don't pay me."

Dan's eyes narrowed, "I was hoping you would be more accommodating."

"And I was hoping you would be tall, dark and handsome. Apparently we are both disappointed."

"Truly…" Dan put his finger to his chin as he slowly paced the room. "The true disappointment is that I am down a drummer and singer."

I was confused, "What?"

"You were going to be my singer in my band, and my drummer was killed. My band is destroyed."

He was crazy, "Well… ok then. Maybe I should ask the questions."

He looked surprised, "You?"

I asked him my first question, "Do you know where I might find Alice?"

He looked amused, "The one person who might clear all this up. Unfortunately for you, I have not heard from her in some time. She dropped a little girl off in my town and asked me to keep an eye on you. Then I came to find out that you're some kind of monster I've yet to identify. Not even sure who's side you're on. You've killed a lot of members of my group, and I realize that might have been a mistake on your part. Still, there are questions that need answers. How did you know what Adam was? Why did you spare him the first time? What are your true motives for being here? Really none of these questions matter, for I can't believe a word you say."

What he said was true, "So why are you even talking to me?" He shrugged his shoulders for an answer. His eyes were studying me. It might not be a good idea, but I decided to be honest with him. If Alice trusted him, maybe I could. At any rate, my situation was looking grim. I asked, "Do you remember the first time we met?"

He nodded, "I do. It was almost ten years ago; you were five or six. I thought it strange for Alice to leave someone so young alone in that large house, but she was insistent that there was a reason. She had said that she would explain. I do believe I have an explanation."

"Don't be assuming you know. It's a long story; I'll give you the quick version. First of all, that was not the first time we met."

This interested Dan. He swirled his hand and the seat across the room slid over and he sat on it saying, "Really?"

"Yes, the first time we met was in 1991 in Las Vegas."

He chuckled, "How did we manage that?"

"It was the night you came for the book." Dan's eyes widened, and his smile faded. I went on, "The book ended up being a fake. I was in the room with Alice, wearing a towel... wait, Alice had made you see me in a beautiful dress."

Dan was in shock, "The vampire who stood in that room. I remember her well... you do look like her. In fact you could be her twin." He stood up so fast the chair fell over with a clatter. He sounded almost angry, "That vampire had a name."

I finished his sentence, "Melabeth."

"You died, or that's what I heard." Dan looked lost in thought, "You are the little girl I met ten years ago?"

"Yes," I answered, but he wasn't really listening. Instead, he paced back and forth, quicker this time.

I sat quietly while the wizard thought. "How did this come to pass?"

"The short answer is I was reborn. I am the daughter of death."

He stopped walking and yelled his question with anger in his eyes, *"How did you become this?"*

I said his name slowly, "Richard... Alexander... Longaeva. He did this to me."

His voice was but a whisper, "I should have known. He meddled in magic that he could not begin to understand. You killed him. Did Luna know he created you? Alice should have told me."

Before I could ask him what he was talking about, the steel door burst open, and Adam came into the room. His sister was pulling at his shirt, but it was not enough to stop him. Dan started to say something when Adam spoke first, "I must talk to her." His voice carried an authority I had never heard. At the same time I felt like hiding my face. I did not want him to see me like this.

Summer explained loudly, "I tried to stop him. He'll ruin the magic that holds her."

Before Dan or anyone could stop him, he turned toward me and walked my way. The bars burst into dust, and he walked up to me bending down to one knee. I suddenly felt fear, for my heart no longer beat; what would happen when his power touched me now? It would not be long before my unspoken question was answered because I could feel his power upon me.

Adam's voice was kind, but I could not meet his eyes, "Mel, or should I call you Melabeth?" I did not answer him. "That doesn't matter; what matters is this… were you the little girl that my sister and I met so many years ago?"

His power was upon me, and, at first, I felt like it was draining me, but then it changed. I responded to his question, "Yes, if you are referring to the night you were forced to help those men kill Alice, the night I was shot in the heart." He grabbed my face and forced my eyes to his.

My heart banged against my chest, beating like a drum, and I gasped for air. I heard Summer gasp and Dan asked, "What magic is this?"

Adam smiled at me, "You are my savior. Three times you've saved my life. You may not remember this, but the next morning after you were shot, I came to visit you. You lay there with no heart beat, dead to the world. Alice had said you may not survive, and, if you didn't, neither would I. I held your hand, and you came back to life. I don't understand why, but I do know you saved us, and I was able to pay you back in some strange way."

Tears were now falling from my face, "No one ever told me that."

Before I could ask another question, I found my mouth was busy, busy kissing Adam. I had never felt as happy, as I did in this moment. In dirty rags, lying on a concrete floor, chained to a wall, all that didn't matter; he accepted me, and he wanted me.

I could die happy in this moment. Then a miracle happened. Adam's lips parted, and, at first, I felt sorrow for the loss of them, but was happily reimbursed by a giant hug from Summer. She whispered in my ear, "Sorry."

Chapter 22 New Life

I lay in a bedroom at Dan's house, or should I call it a mansion. The sun had risen an hour ago, and I was dead tired, but my mind would not allow me to sleep. It kept replaying the night before and all the new information I had acquired.

After my kiss with Adam, I shed some tears on Summer's and Adam's shoulders. They undid the chains, and we journeyed upstairs. There we engaged in an all night conversation about everything. I gave them a summary of my life and what I was. Dan had lots of questions, but I did not answer all of them. I wasn't ready to share everything with my new found friends, so I kept the library and Nicks to myself.

I found out lots of information from Dan. Things were starting to come together, and I could now see a much bigger picture of my death. At first I thought that Alex and his friends had simply made a snuff film. Simple, yes, cruel and inhuman also comes to mind. When Alice and I watched the film of my murder, I became aware that I was a human sacrifice for a spell. Of course, at that time, I didn't care what the spell was for, or why. I just wanted revenge on the men who murdered me.

With the war, Alice has gone missing, the fact that someone still wanted me dead, I had been stuck in a mystery with no clues and no idea where to turn, but Dan gave me an entirely different point of view. After I finished the telling of my life story and stopped Dan from asking anymore questions, Dan had a story for me. His story began in the late eighteen hundreds, deep in the heart of Imperial Russia, about a wizard named the Red Adder. Where he was from or who he really was, is lost to history. What's important about this man was that he was a genius.

He lived and worked in Moscow, where he was considered by many to be one of the greatest wizards of all time, but he had a secret. He was a great wizard, but he was also a great Necromancer and did more than a little dabbling in the forbidden arts. In fact, he was obsessed with how to defeat death itself. Believing vampires held part of the secret, he delved ever deeper into the art of Necromancy. All the while he worked he kept a book. In this book he recorded his findings and his secrets.

In his search for power, he found something; what it was Dan did not know. Whatever it was, it drove Adder to destroy his magical book, but he could not do it. The book could not be undone, and the knowledge in it was a curse to the world. Shortly after his failed attempts at destroying his book, he was attacked and killed.

Dan believed that the killers had come to destroy the book and the author. They did not succeed in either; both the book and Adder survived to this day. When I asked him how that was possible, he explained that Adder had become a powerful Lich. Red Adder was aging, and he knew that his life was coming to an end, but, rather than die, he chose a half-life, a cursed life.

I found out that a Lich was an undead Necromancer or a wizard. They cast their soul into a phylactery. Upon death, they would be able to reanimate their corpse and live on. It was, in short, a form of immortality, but it sounded like it was a high price to pay to live forever. A Lich maintained its power by draining life from the living, like a vampire. They still could cast magic, and their minds were intact. One sign of a Lich was that it would cast no image upon a mirror, most likely where the legend came from for vampires.

Red Adder had done something no one had ever thought of; he created a circus. In this circus people came to have a good time and all the time he drained just a little bit from all his guests, but that wasn't all. The whole circus was a supernatural trap; if a vampire or magic user went in, they never came out. He would force his *guests* to work as carneys, forever feeding off them. The name of the circus was known as the Dark Circus. He didn't always call it that, and the name changed from time to time and place to place.

The book was used in World War One. During the Russians great retreat from Warsaw, the Germans captured the book. A young, angry wizard got a hold of the book. He was angry about how the war turned out for the Germans. He used the book's power to bewitch crowds and control others. His name was Adolf Hitler, and World War Two had begun. Hitler had evil necromancers who used the book during the war. Millions died through their use of its power.

After the war, the book was captured. Twelve wizards came together to deal with the problem. It was determined that the book could not be destroyed, so they must lock it away instead. Dan was one of the twelve wizards, standing for America. Luna Longaeva was the head and stood for the united European Union. Richard Alexander Longaeva, her son, was one of the twelve. Together they locked the book up and cast it into a vault deep within Paris. Without all twelve, no one could get the book, or so they thought.

It was 1990 when Dan got wind of the fact that Alex was running around with the book. It took Dan a long time to track him down. When he did, he had a problem, how to get the book from him. If he openly accused Alex of having it, Luna might come after him. Luna had to have known that her son had the book all this time. Furthermore, she was helping the creep, and she called upon her other son, Peter the Lionheart.

That's when Dan told me something that my mind could not understand. He said the only thing he could think of was to ask for help from the same person who told him the book had been stolen. This means that Alice knew about the book before Dan. All Dan knew was that one night Alice came to him and told him that she had been bad. She then informed him about the book. The rest is history.

The mystery was giving me a headache. I was still missing too many pieces of the puzzle. Alice was still holding back information. Why? I could not be sure. I was starting to think it was time to pay a visit to Ezra and Michael. If Alice expects me to save her, she would have left clues, hopefully big ones, because I'm no detective. Shortly after that I turned in for the day.

I felt the arrival of Spooky. I could almost hear her knocking. I had told them last night who she was and that she would be here. They can make their own introductions, I thought. Sleep had finally found me.

I awoke to snoring. There, sleeping next to me was Adam, snoring away. It wasn't very loud, and I liked the sound. I rolled over to him and put my arm around him. As I pulled him into my body, he stopped snoring, but did not wake up. I lay there holding him; I was in my happy place.

The evil cat opened the door, "Hey, you two getting it on? Don't sleep the day away Mel... we're going to be in a band!"

She slammed the door shut as she rushed off, but I was still yelling, "What in the Sam Hill? Stupid... I'll kill her."

I wonder what she was talking about?

Adam's voice sounded dry; I responded to his unasked question, "Trust me, you don't want to know."

I tighten my grip as if somehow I could get our bodies even closer. "I trust you."

"How much longer do you think they'll leave us alone?"

My voice was dark, "If I kill them…"

Adam laughed, "That would buy us some peace and quiet, but then their spirits would haunt us."

"You forgot, I kill spirits, I'll kill them too."

Adam spun his body around so that we were now facing each other. "How are you doing?"

"Amazing," and I wasn't lying.

He smiled, "Whenever you're ready, we can go have breakfast, I mean dinner. I'm sure Dan is dying to tell you about the band."

"In a minute," I said. He nodded and we lay there in silence, staring at each other.

I was falling hard, and I knew it. With David, I needed him, but Adam, I wanted him. Adam is every bit as sexy as David was. Still, my eyes were for the man who was lying next to me. I never really had any feelings toward Michael, other than friendship and lust. The lust for Michael never went away. All I ever had to do was think about him, and naughty thoughts would come to mind, but not now. When I was with David I found lust for Michael, but now I can see the difference between love and lust. I couldn't even think of another man like that.

What was it about Adam? I thought about it for a minute. He had lost his father and has been hunted all of his life. His life was kind of similar to mine, but that wasn't it. It was the way he looked at me; no matter what he found out about me, he still looked at me the same. Last night when we were all talking, he sat next to me with his arm around me. It felt almost protective. I said to everyone, "You don't know what evil I've done. I'll leave if you need me to."

Adam asked, "Are you still doing evil?"

"No, maybe," I replied.

"I am not your judge for your past sins. Try to be good," He smiled at me and I could see he meant it.

Dan added, "But, one's past sins can complicate things."

Adam snapped back, "Yes, they do, but we will let you stay anyway, Dan."

Dan narrowed his eyes, "I wasn't saying she couldn't stay. We wouldn't have a band without her."

Summer moaned, "Shut the hell up about the band. What about mom?"

Adam answered, "She'll need to deal with it."

*   *   *

He was ready to defend me against his friends, his mother, everyone. I never felt so accepted in all my life. That's what made me love him… it was effortless and natural. My peaceful thoughts were once again interrupted by Spooky. She yelled through the door, "Get your clothes on, and come downstairs already."

Murder was what I felt; Spooky felt that. She said much quieter, "Sorry to interrupt. Take your time." She left quickly and quietly.

Adam gave me a quizzical face, "Did you do something to her?"

"Kind of," I said with a devious smile.

I was able to get in a few kisses before Adam and I headed downstairs to join everyone. Downstairs led to a large living space. The room was longer than it was wide, and the walls were at least twenty feet tall before the ceiling began. The ceiling itself looked to be a piece of art, with its large beams and painted designs. Nothing modern was in this room, phones, computers or TV's. Couches and large chairs all faced a huge fireplace that dominated one wall.

Dan was sitting in a chair playing with an electric bass without an amp. Summer and Spooky were immersed in a conversation. It looked as if Spooky was getting along just fine. Dan looked up and smiled at my arrival, "Finally, she's awake. Now we can discuss the band."

I took a seat across from him, and Adam joined me. Adam explained, "First, let me tell you what the band is. First of all its Dan trying to live out some kind of rock and roll fantasy."

Dan grumbled, "Not at all."

Adam went on, "The real idea of the band was to move from city to city without drawing attention to ourselves. A lot of the goings on in any city can be found in pubs and bars. By getting gigs, we can go into a city and play different events, and when we're not playing, we can explore the city. The idea is to get a jump on some of the necromancers and help support our friends. The problem so far is that we don't have enough members to form a band."

Summer added, "That's not the only problem. The other problem is our band sucks. No one's hiring us, because we sound like crap. We need to get gigs, and to get gigs, we need to be able to play music."

Dan was excited, "And that's where you come in; we need talent, and you sing and play the violin. With that, we've got something. I play the bass, and your Adam is one hell of a guitar player. Summer plays synthesizer and works the sound board. What she lacks in musical talent, she makes up in her ability to enchant the equipment." Summer beamed at the compliment. "Of course, we seem to be short a drummer."

Summer clarified, "Really, we don't need a drummer. I can enchant some drum sticks, plus some ankle and wrist bands. No musical talented needed. What Dan should be saying is: I enchant, Dan's a hell of a wizard, and my brother can destroy the others' magic, but when the shit hits the fan, we need people with skills with hand to hand. In fact, what we really need is someone who can kick ass and take on ghosts."

I shrugged, "Don't even need to ask."

Adam smiled, "See, I told you she would join us."

Summer smarted back, "Right as always, back to what I was saying. I can see you guarding Dan or Adam, but both would be hard."

I asked Summer, "What about you?"

Adam laughed, "She stays in the van or a hotel. Summer's not hands on, but her power to prepare items is second to none."

Dan, sounding like a proud father, added, "Have you seen her last creation?" Without waiting for a response, he said, "She has created guns that don't run out of ammo. I call them movie guns."

Summer quickly explained further, "That's not precisely true. They run out, but not for a long time. I created a bag that can hold ten times the stuff in it than the size of the bag. Of course I'm not the first to make a bag like this, but I added something else to it. I created a teleporting symbol in the bottom of the bag, so, when you fill it with bullets, they will teleport. I put the other side of the gateway symbol, into the magazines of two guns. When the magazines begin to run out of bullets, it just teleports the ammo from a bag to the gun."

I clapped, "Brilliant!"

Spooky asked, "Can you make me something?"

"Maybe," Summer then asked the question she really wanted to ask. "Would you like to be our drummer?"

Spooky grinned, "Thought you would never ask. I would love to kick ass with you guys… and playing the drums sounds fun too."

Dan jumped to his feet, "We need to practice."

Adam shook his head, "Dan? Don't you think it would be more important to practice on how to fight as a team?"

Dan looked at Adam as if he told him that Christmas was canceled, "Well, we can't suck as a band either. Maybe we can work on both."

Summer moaned, "At any rate, we better get at it. Who's calling mom? There is no way we will have time to work the Bean."

For the next twenty minutes, Summer and Adam argued over whose turn it was to call Kathy. After a while Adam lost the argument and left the room to make the dreaded phone call. He returned and said all was well, or as well as could be expected. We began working out how we might fight as a team.

It didn't take long to pair Adam and me and then Spooky and Dan. Dan used magic, which Adam screwed up. I didn't use magic, and Adam didn't really affect me. Spooky could guard Dan so that he would have time to cast his spells. Summer would hang back, not only because she had no fighting skills, but because she was good at managing.

I found out that in the past, she had made all kinds of magical items for whatever task was laid before the team. Summer was also very technically savvy and could help work on keeping the team connected. She could bring up the schematics of buildings and tap into local security cameras. She also enchanted four robotic owls that could fly around and spy for her. I could see how useful she would be. I always relied on my ghost Bow to do these things for me.

We worked on this most of the night. Dan was upset that we wouldn't try any band practice until tomorrow night, even though Summer had explained that she wasn't ready with drum sticks and that it would take some time to teach Spooky how to use them. Dan had acted like it would be quicker to teach her how to play for real. He was such a goof! I could see how he was married to Alice; he was crazy too.

I said my goodbyes to Adam. I wanted to go to my own bed. As I kissed him goodnight, it took all I had not to invite him to stay with me. I wanted to make sure this was going to work before sleeping with him, but my willpower was never that great to begin with. In the future we would be traveling together, and, in my mind, we would have time to slip away and have romantic adventures. Then I thought about how it would really be. A group of people all piled in together crushed for time and space… I really didn't want to be in a rock band.

Spooky was with me as we walked back to our home. She was strangely quiet, and, against my better judgment, I asked, "What are you thinking?"

"The band thing sounds fun," she paused for a minute. "Just not sure about us teaming up and fighting the necromancers. They seem like good people, but I think you and I kick ass on our own."

"I wouldn't underestimate them," I objected.

"It's not that their powers won't help us in battle. What are the right words? Not sure of the dynamics of the team. We really don't know Dan, and you're too close to Adam and Summer for that matter. For example, Dan and I are both in peril and you only have time to save one of us."

I threw up my hand, "I know, I know. I would make a club sandwich."

Spooky moaned, "Great we both die. What about if it were Summer and me?" I almost formed a word when Spooky yelled out, "I KNOW, I'm dead."

I laughed, "You're worrying too much. We need to get out and do what we can. Also, I need to find out any information on Alice that I can. I am really worried about her now."

Spooky mumbled, "First Ezra, now you… All I hear you talk about is, Alice *this* and Alice *that*. I wouldn't trust that monster for anything, let alone worry about her well being."

I didn't respond to her. I kind of understood how she felt; Alice toyed with her a lot when she was young. Ezra's relationship with her ended because he was more worried about Alice than her. I hadn't really thought it out when I mentioned Alice. She didn't care if I ever found Alice.

It would have only taken us a few minutes to run to our house, but, instead, we walked. Still ten minutes away Spooky's voice was muffled, "Summer seems real nice."

I answered, "She is."

"She thought I was pretty; she is too."

"Sorry," I said sarcastically. "Did you want to know if she was single or something?"

Spooky's face went red as she barked, "No."

I had always wondered if Summer was gay; she never really gave me a straight answer. I never really thought Spooky played both sides, but what did I know? We were frienemies, and the bond made our relationship difficult at best. We only recently were even getting along.

Chapter 23 P.T.F.

I moved to the next room in a flash. My attempt was to take the witch by surprise, but I was the one surprised by her.

The old witch was haggard and thin. She would fit nicely into any witch story I had ever read as a child. Her face looked like dried up prunes. She smiled wickedly with her face stretched in an unfamiliar shape. This old hag hadn't smiled in a long time.

Six undead zombies flanked her as she threw me against the far wall with some unseen force. With only her hand outstretched before her, I was pinned against the wall twenty feet away from her. My feet dangled below me as the zombies started to come for me. What an *easy* victim I appeared to be.

When her power failed and my feet found the floor, the witch's smile fell as well. Before she could even fathom what had happened, I flashed upon her. My sword cut, in a downward motion. It started at her left shoulder and came out her right hip. The witch's body parts fell to the ground.

I wasted no time as that one swing fluidly turned into three more. The sound of gunshots filled the air and, what zombies heads I didn't cut off, exploded. Adam stood there searching the room for more targets, his gun at the ready.

"Nice shooting," I declared.

Adam complained, "I can't move as fast; wait up for me. If we came into this room at the same time, I could have dispelled that witch before she threw you against the wall."

I shook my head back and forth, "My hero. I like to draw the attention on me first."

Adam mumbled a response, but I ignored him as I left the room to clear the next area. This warehouse was pretty large, and I cleared four rooms before I popped in on that witch. I wasn't about to argue again with Adam, but I couldn't have him getting hurt.

Dan came out of a hallway that intersected ours. Spooky followed behind him as a giant tiger. He informed us, "All clear on that side of the warehouse. A few booby traps, nothing more."

Summer spoke over our earpieces. We all could hear her, and she could hear us. She also had small cameras on each of us so she could see what was going on. "Ok, guys. According to the building's blueprints, you've cleared most of the office space. If you keep going straight, there are a few more rooms left on the second floor. On the north side of the building, there is a large open area. Be careful, we have disarmed a dozen magical traps and a few normal ones. One more thing, Adam, let Melabeth go in the rooms first."

Adam hissed at his sister, "Mind your own business."

Dan in a stern voice said, "Both of you, stop. This is serious work! Let's work together. Melabeth lead the way. Spooky, take the far hallway. Watch yourselves. Adam, you're with me."

With orders from Dan, we all moved out. Dan and Adam were behind me as I moved into the final room. The room was long with two windows against the far wall. There was a long table running down the center of the room with chairs all around it. On the walls, there were dry erase boards. At first glance it appeared to be an empty meeting room, but I learned long ago that's when you should be the most afraid. Magic users liked to hide the worst things in plain sight.

Dan blurted out, "Stop!" I came to a halt just a few feet into the room. Dan was poking his head in through the doorway, "I sense a trap; give me a minute, and I can disarm it."

Adam pushed his way past Dan, "I only need a second."

He moved into the room and past me before we could react. Adam disarmed traps so fast you never even knew they were there, well unless they weren't magical. Time slowed down as I heard the mechanical movement of something in the room.

In no time, I flashed at Adam slamming into him. The door was behind me, but the window was where I was aiming. I didn't have time to turn around. We smashed through the glass and sailed out. We were two stories up, so I formed my wings. As I flapped to pull Adam and me into the air, a huge explosion burst out of the room.

The fireball that came out of the window, hit us for a split second as I rose to safety. I heard Adam cry out in pain. I quickly landed on the roof of the building. Adam was holding his shoulder where I had smashed into him. His lower legs had been burnt right below the knee. His pants looked half melted from the fire. His feet had been protected by his shoes.

Summer yelled over the mic, "Is he okay?"

I answered, "Yes, but stop yelling! That hurts!"

"Sorry," Summer responded.

Adam spoke, but obviously in pain, "Just dislocated my shoulder. Melabeth hit me pretty hard. Few burns, but I've had worse."

"Sorry," I said to him. I felt bad for hurting him.

He quickly added through his clenched jaw, "You saved my life; I was being stupid." He even tried to smile at me.

I reached down and gently rubbed his shoulder, then, without warning, I grabbed him. With one firm push I shoved his shoulder back in. He screamed in pain, and Summer screamed at me over the mic. I yelled, "For heaven's sake, I'll be deaf before this night is over!"

Dan spoke next, "So will I... Oh, by the way, I'm ok. Used a spell to encase myself in a stone shield. That's how I survived... I mean, if anyone was wondering?"

Summer started to apologize, but I just said, "Dan, Dan who? We have a Dan in our group?"

Dan chuckled, "I can feel the love, Mel. How's the dumb ass... I mean Adam?"

"Okay, Dan," Adam answered. "Of course, you could have mentioned it wasn't a magical trap."

"And you could have asked," Dan responded tartly.

"How's the shoulder?" I asked, interrupting their back and forth. "Can you go on?"

"Yes, help me to my feet." Adam grabbed my hand as I pulled him up.

Summer was complaining over the mic, "If he's hurt, he should sit it out."

We all ignored her and went on. Dan put out the fire with magic. A few traps later and we had made our goal. We worked our way through the rest of the building and into the large storage area. A few more traps, but no more people. My heart sank, and we were too late, again.

We all four stood around the ring of power. It was in the middle of the warehouse, where the necromancers had made it. Around the ring in eight spots, lay the bodies of their sacrifices. Some were magic users, one vampire and a werewolf. Four were humans, one old woman and man, one young woman and man. It made me sick.

My voice sounded defeated, "Once again we are too late."

Spooky hadn't bothered to turn human just growled. She turned and left; she couldn't stand it. Just as well, we would be here for a little while, and it was good to have her comb around the building.

Adam asked, "Fifth circle of death now?"

I could hear the van; Summer was pulling up outside. She would be here soon with all the cameras and magical and non magical equipment that she and Dan would need. They collected a lot of evidence at each death circle we found. I couldn't tell if it helped or not.

Dan finally answered Adam, "Yep, the fifth one. How long have we been on the road?" Answering his own question, "Little over two months. How many have they made, that we don't know about? What do they do?"

Adam continued on with the questions that we had been debating. "Better yet, how do we stop them or figure out where and when they will strike before they commit these horrible crimes?"

Summer yelled out as she came in carrying two large boxes. "Enough! Get over here." She was yelling at Adam; in one arm was her med kit.

Standing over the horrible scene of death, Dan and I stared while Summer worked on Adam. Dan broke the silence, "We have no idea where they'll strike next, but it won't help us get in front of them if we have another performance like last night."

I moaned, "Just stuff it, Dan. I think you're more worried about how well your rock and roll dream goes than stopping these monsters."

Dan seldom got mad, but he was livid now. "Don't be a bitch! You do not need to imply that the death of innocents is less important than our band. We all deal with stress in different ways. I prefer to concentrate on things that make me happy, like music. Adam prefers quiet time, and you like to kill someone... we all handle it differently!"

He was right, but I really was not in the mood to talk about it any further. "Whatever." And with that response, I turned to leave. I asked Adam, "You going to be ok?" He just nodded, following with a wince as his sister poured some rubbing alcohol over one of his cuts. I hadn't even noticed the cuts on his hands. Most likely happened when we broke through the window.

Flashing outside, I felt the need to clear my head. The last two months had my head spinning. I walked up to our van that Summer had just parked. It was an older Chevy Express Van with no windows. The van was white and every time I looked at it, I thought there should be a free candy sign on the side. We used the van and the bus to move our group from place to place. Adam stayed in the van while the rest of us lived in the bus. Summer could use the van for surveillance in our operations.

It was becoming a big problem in our group, and we needed Summer to make magical items, but hanging with her brother ended up destroying her work. Dan had had it. The last show was a disaster because of Adam. Summer had been trying to work on Spooky's magical drumsticks. Adam looked over for a minute too long and poof the magic was gone.

With no time to fix them, we had to go on stage. Spooky sounded like she was at Chucky Cheese trying to hit the head of the moles. We had to play without drums. It wasn't horrible, really. We played well, and my voice has an eerie effect upon people, but this was a rock and roll crowd. In the end, we were booed off the stage. It was bad timing and the wrong audience not to have drums.

Spooky strolled up behind me. She had taken her human form, but hadn't bothered to get dressed. She was now staring at the van, because that is what I was doing. She asked, "What are we looking at?" I shrugged my shoulders. Spooky went on talking, "I still think we should put our band's name on the side of the van. I know it's supposed to be undercover, but I think they should know they're about to be purified."

My voice was empty, "No, we can't put Summer in danger."

"I'm going to loop around the building," then she shifted into a large alley cat and took off.

A smile came to my face as a funny memory came to me. Right before we hit the road Dan had asked us what we should name our band. We went back and forth, but nothing stuck. The next night we were practicing and still trying to think up a name.

*   *   *

Spooky jumped up and down, "I know a good band name, 'Vampires Suck'."

I snapped back, "I have a better one, 'Killing Kittens'."

Adam piped in, "What about 'Killing, Kittens and Kangaroos'. In short, we'll be called the KKK."

Summer moaned, "*Really guys.*"

Then it hit me, "I know… we should name our band after our true mission."

Dan was quick to add, "We can't name it 'Necromancer Exterminators'. We need to stay undercover."

"I know," I explained further. "I was thinking of purification. That's what we'll do to our enemies. We'll purify them."

"Purify?" Adam asked.

"Yes," I said through an evil grin, "We will purify them through fire, 'Purification Through Fire', or PTF for short."

*   *   *

The smile faded as I recalled the scene of death that lay a few yards away inside the building. Eight people died in every city where they created one of these circles, the horror of it all. I headed back inside to check on their progress.

Summer slowly walked around the death circle, taking photos and looking for evidence. Summer asked aloud, "I wonder what this ring of power does?"

I should have kept my mouth shut, but I had come to trust my band. "It keeps the dead trapped on earth."

Dan responded as if I were guessing, "It could be that; it could be anything."

Adam and Summer knew at once that I was not theorizing. Summer stopped what she was doing and stared at me, while Adam asked. "How do you know?"

When I had told them my life history, I had left the library and Nicks out. "I have always known. You all know that I'm much more than a vampire, but what you don't know is what that other thing might be."

Summer walked closer, "We all assumed you didn't know yourself. Why would you hold back information?"

Dan furthered that, "Information that could help us."

I shrugged, "I had my reasons, but for the life of me, I can't remember what they were."

Adam put his arm around me. Being with Adam, I learned that he was the most understanding man alive. He wasn't perfect, and he was not beyond getting mad at me, but, in the end, he always made me feel safe. His eyes never judged me, not even when he watched me drain someone to their death. These were but a few reasons that telling him the truth seemed like an easy proposal.

I started by telling them about Nicks. They were all pretty speechless when they learned that I was the daughter of Death. I then went on explaining what the necromancers were doing. "Ok, so, these sacrificing rings are creating some kind of spell that blocks Nicks from coming to the land of the living. Furthermore, I can't go to the land of the dead until I get far enough away from the spell. The area's effect is huge, and the necromancers are going from one city to another."

Dan looked almost in shock as he asked, "So these spells are just to stop the angel of Death?"

I went on, "No, Nicks told me they're doing something much worse. They are stopping spirits from entering the land of the dead. The fact the spell blocks Nicks and I, just makes everything harder. I had been expecting that the cities that were hit would be full of spirits. Only a few stick around after death, but I can't find the spirits of the dead. They're not in the library, and I haven't seen a single spirit within the affected area. Last I spoke with Nicks, he had no idea what this means, but I'm sure it's not good."

Dan shook his head, "Not good at all."

Summer added, "Well. Things just keep on looking better all the time."

Adam picked up a gas can, "Let's purify this area; it's getting late."

We all agreed, and it wasn't long before I was watching the glow of the fire from the window of the van. It was only a ten minute ride back to the parking lot where the tour bus was. The tour bus was really cool, and Dan had done a great job. The outside of the bus was covered in flames and in big print the band's name ran across the side. The inside of the bus was full of magic, so poor Adam was not allowed in.

I had been sleeping in the bus for several reasons. One, if I were sleeping with Adam, I would be sleeping with Adam. I was trying to take our relationship slow, but I knew that I was losing that battle. The other reason was, that the first time Adam and I were to make love, I was really hoping it wouldn't be in a van. I wanted to wait in our relationship before taking it any further, but Adam's recklessness tonight had me thinking.

We pulled up and Dan, Summer and Spooky raced to the bus. They were all trying to take a shower first. Adam was sitting in the back of the van putting on medication and wrapping one of his burnt legs.

Sliding up behind him, I whispered in his ear, "That's going to scar."

He leaned back into me, "Do you find me hideously deformed?"

Rubbing his shoulder I teased, "Yes, but I have always thought that."

"HEY, easy on the ego… By the way?"

I simply respond, "Yes?"

"We're driving into Flagstaff tomorrow, and we'll have a few nights before the first gig. I was wondering if you would like to go out on a date with me?"

I pretended to think about it, "Let's see… kinda busy doing nothing. Okay, fine, I'll take one for the team."

Adam smiled, "Gee, don't get too excited." I kissed him passionately, and he declared, "That's more like it!"

Chapter 24 Flagstaff

"Thank you," I said as Adam held the door for me.

I was dressed in a pretty emerald green dress with matching high heels. The heels made me almost as tall as Adam. My hair was pulled up in a series of buns and braids, courtesy of Summer. I wasn't sure about the hair, but she had worked so hard on it. Adam was wearing slacks, with a dress shirt and jacket. What really made the outfit was the color. His pants and jacket were a purple that I would expect the Joker would feel right at home in. The shirt was yet another shade of purple and, to top it all off, was a neon green bow tie.

The night before, Adam tried to dye his hair red. It was green. He wasn't wearing his contacts, and his purple eyes shown like jewels. When I asked him why, he told me that with all the aftermarket contacts, the best disguise would be no disguise. I laughed; it would most likely work but, if not I would protect him. I don't know if I would call Adam's look handsome, but it was certainly cute.

We entered the club, the Ringtail Martini. Who knew the Arizona state animal would make such a great martini? The college was right down the street, and, even though it was a Thursday night, the place was still hopping. We made our way through the crowd to claim a small table with two chairs. The place had tons of dark brown woodwork, and the chairs and table matched. Our location was near a corner overlooking the street.

We would have talked, but it was just too loud. After ordering a drink or two, we decided to go dancing. After a few dances, we went upstairs where it was quieter, and we could order some food. Everyone stared at us, and we really didn't dress right for this club. None of that really mattered because the moment we walked through that door, my world was just big enough to see Adam.

We talked, we laughed and I made up my mind. I wanted Adam in every way you could want a man. Looking across the street stood a nice looking hotel. That would be better than a van. Adam had been saying something, but I had tuned him out.

Adam chuckled, "Am I boring you?" I smiled, and then I rolled my eyes while nodding toward the window. He was looking out the window and back at me. He asked, confused, "What?"

I pointed out the window and said, "Just thought I saw something across the street."

"All I see is a couple walking into that hotel."

I tightened my eyes and in a serious tone said, "What kind of girl do you think I am?"

"What?" Now he was really confused, but quickly thought I misunderstood him. "No, no, I had watched a couple go into the hotel. I didn't say we should."

"So you think we should go? Right now? I don't know; will you respect me in the morning?"

His face went from confused too… well, I hadn't seen that face yet. "Oh, I think we should follow those people. They looked awful suspicious." He then flagged the waiter down like the table was on fire. "We'll need our check." The waiter hurried off to get the tab.

His eagerness and the way he took my hand and the world slow down. It also made it feel like the waitress was taking her sweet ass time, just because her life had no future bliss. The waitress made minutes turn to hours, and before I got up and killed her, she dropped off the check. Hand in hand, Adam and I went across the street, and I would be lying to myself if I wasn't as nervous as I was excited.

I barely recalled the check-in process, or what floor the room was on. He held the door as he ushered me in, "After you, my lady."

"Thanks," I said, adding a smile.

The room was amazing, and I became worried about how much he had paid for all this. The dinner, the drinks and now a suite in a much fancier hotel then I realized. The room had a large open space with a couch and TV sitting upon a fireplace mantle. The room was painted a nice green and accented with dark wood. The fireplace matched, and so did the bedroom with a king size four poster bed. "Wow, this place is something else. You have to let me help pay for this."

"Oh, you'll pay alright," he spun me around and pulled me into his arms. We kissed, and his touches became gentle as he explored my body.

I pulled away playfully as I backed toward the bed. I was slowly undressing while I asked, "What kind of girl do you think I am? You want me to pay?"

He smiled as he removed his shirt. I hadn't realized how built he was, until this moment. I had seen him once or twice without a shirt, but I hadn't allowed myself to think about it. I was thinking about it now. My dress fell to the floor and then his pants. I slid out of his reach, and on to the bed, as I pulled off my bra.

Wearing nothing but his boxers, he followed me onto the bed, crawling on all fours. Removing my panties, I lay naked before him. His eyes roamed all over my body, and they approved. He came to rest in my arms as we fell into a passionate embrace. He removed his boxers; I took the sight in, "Oh, my, " came out of my mouth. "How do you walk around with that thing?"

He laughed and turned red in the face. Then his facial expression changed, "Your eyes... they're glowing."

"I know," and I pushed upwards. We flew straight up until we hit the ceiling. I kissed him and started to make love to him while holding him against the roof as if it were the ground.

He was entrenched in passion and looked as if he might need to speak, but just couldn't get around to it. I rolled over and landed against the far wall. After that I wasn't really that interested in what wall I was against.

All I could recall was bliss.

*   *   *

I lay next to him, basking in my afterglow. He breathed deeply, but he wasn't sleeping. I was trying to wrap my mind around how good sex makes me want to have a conversation afterwards. "Do you need to sleep?"

He shook his head, "No, not really. Want to talk?" I laughed, and he sounded defensive, "What's so funny?"

"Nothing really, I just thought of how lucky I was. I would have never guessed I would fall for the only guy who would want to talk after sex." Adam started to pretend he was snoring. I slapped him on his chest, "None of that, I want to talk now."

"Ouch," he said, "You don't know your strength. Bad enough that I'm going to be covered in bruises."

"Don't be a baby."

He gently slid his fingers down the side of my face and through my hair. He looked at me like I was the most valuable thing in the world. "So, what's on your mind?"

"I'm just glad that hotel security wasn't called."

Adam burst into a belly laugh, "I was thinking that too."

"Liar," I teased. "That's not really what I was thinking."

"I know what you're thinking about," Adam said with confidence.

"Oh yeah," I challenged. "What am I thinking about?"

"You wish I'd be more careful, not to get myself killed."

I laughed, "Wow, you missed it by a mile, dude. I know you're going to get yourself killed and, truthfully, I'm not really worried about it."

Shocked, he said, "What?"

I explained myself, "What I mean is I'm not really worried about you dying. I'm not worried about Summer, Dan, Spooky or even myself dying. Life is like that. It's this happy bliss that I'm in now followed by pain and suffering, I know this. It's not something we can control, and I've given up trying. I know you want to prove yourself for whatever reasons you might have.

"It is the reason I made love to you now. I had just come to realize these things. I would have liked to wait until we had dated longer… and perhaps you could have asked me to marry you. We could have waited like they used to do. How special it could have been? Don't misunderstand me; it was special, but it should have been more so."

Adam did not mock me; in fact, he sounded very concerned. "Perhaps we should have waited to get married?"

I asked, "What is marriage anyway? An institution by man or a covenant in front of God? Nowadays I think it is more an institution of man. I mean I need a court paper to get married in a church, but I don't need a church to get married. Marriage is so much more than a piece of paper. It is a declaration of commitment to all of your loved ones and to each other, a declaration for all to see, so the community knows you belong to each other and no one else.

"Who would I invite? My family who can't be around because I would get them killed. Alice is MIA, and Nicks is trapped in the library. Let's face it, the chance of surviving all this so we could even have a wedding, is a slim chance in hell."

Adam shook his head, "Wow, your positive attitude is really uplifting."

I defended myself, "I've been fighting this fight a lot longer than you. I watched my first boyfriend's family killed right before my eyes. I have lost my best friend Carrie… even though she was technically dead. Other friends have died fighting for me. Charlotte was like a mother to me, but she was killed in a battle against Alex. You may know him as Luna's son, Richard Alexander Longaeva, but I knew him as a murdering rapist named Alex."

"Well, maybe I should be calling you my wife?"

I smiled my heart flutter at the thought, "Haa, no… you could just call me your everything."

He smiled at me, "I love you, my everything."

"I love you too," and I really meant it. In fact, it was kind of scary saying it, because it made it so real.

He kissed me with such passion. Then he huffed, "You're such a pain."

"What?" I asked, confused.

"You're a pain… I'll go in the room second."

I laughed, "You don't have to. I told you, you can kill yourself if you want."

Adam looked deep into my eyes, "You know that all I wanted was to be your hero."

"Adam," I almost cried, "There's all kinds of heroes."

"It's hard on a guy's ego when you're always saving me, not that I want you to stop."

I had never understood his recklessness until this moment. I decided that he needed to understand what he had done for me. "Love, there are all kinds of heroes. You can save people in so many different ways. You have no idea how lonely I've been or how empty. The night you accepted me for what I was, the night you walked through bars with no fear. You have no idea how much you saved me. I've only saved, your body; you've given me hope and, more importantly, love. *You* are my hero."

Adam reached down and wiped the tear from my cheek. "Know this… I will always love you."

Chapter 25 Joker's Wild

The crowd was dancing, and the music was incredible tonight. We were playing our hearts out, and the crowd responded to every note.

I loved LA. The crowds were electrifying. It was hard to believe that Flagstaff had been less than a month ago. Flagstaff, Phoenix, Barstow and now LA, our gigs were getting bigger, but my mind was on my lover. We hadn't run into any trouble for a while, and I wasn't in a hurry to find any. I was too busy enjoying my rock-and-roll lifestyle.

The crowd cheered as I broke free from the mic and started into my violin solo. Of course, this was Bow's favorite part. She never imagined what her instruments might sound like pushing through electricity. I danced and played, and the crowd went wild. I spun, and my red dress flew through the air as my hair made a golden umbrella. The crowd danced and swayed with the music. What a night!

We played our last set and gave our bows as the crowd whistled and cheered for more. Dan yelled in my ear, "You really have talent. We may all become famous at this rate."

I added, "Or at least sell enough shirts and CDs to pay for the gas."

Summer and Spooky did all the clean up and break down of the equipment, not because we were too lazy to help. Summer had to have everything packed just the right way, and Spooky did what she asked; I did not. Also, Spooky didn't mind helping, she is strong enough to pick up a small car. Adam was not allowed to help; in fact, he wasn't even allowed to look at the equipment. He stood as far to one side of the stage as he could. When he was done, he put his guitar down and left.

Dan was a whole different story. He couldn't help because he was too busy trying to be famous. When we arrived, he would have to go hang with the owners and put up flyers everywhere. Of course, he cheated with the flyers, because it only took him ten minutes to put up hundreds around town. After the set, it was even worse. This is when he would push merchandise and sign autographs. After all, he was the songwriter.

Dan hated that I got all the attention. I never really thought of myself as pretty, but if you dress in the outfits that Dan picked out for me, and danced in front of a bunch of drunk guys... well, they were all over me after the show. Adam would point out that I was extremely hot and sold myself short. I did sell tons of shirts and CD's.

Adam would just sit next to me and play it cool. I hadn't realized how cool he was. He didn't talk a lot, but when he did it was very witty. The girls would hang on him. It made me laugh because I could tell just how uncomfortable this made him, especially with me standing right next to him. Funny thing was, I wasn't jealous. I knew deep down that he had chosen me. He didn't need me, but he wanted me, and that gave me all the confidence I needed. So let the hoe's fall over him; he was mine.

The crowd was thinning, and there were enough people that Dan stayed engaged with fans all night. He was all smiles. Spooky and Summer had announced that they had enough and were turning in for the evening. Spooky wasn't ready to go in, but she and Summer had really bonded. We wouldn't allow Summer to leave on her own, so Spooky volunteered to see her back. In fact, she did this so often she just acted as if it were her bedtime too.

A young man came up to the table. He was well built and drunk. He gave me a huge smile, "Hey sexy... you were so hot. On stage, you were hot on stage."

I answered, "Yeah? It was from all the dancing. Maybe I should get a fan?"

Adam chuckled, but the drunk didn't understand I was making fun of him. He proceeded to explain himself, "No, man... you're not a man. I mean chick, lady, I didn't mean hot like hot. What I meant was you were sexy. You gave me a hard on. Do you have a boyfriend? Maybe you would like to go hang with me?"

"I would love to," I smiled wickedly. "Can we go somewhere fancy, like the back seat of your car?"

"Oh yeah, that would be cool," he proclaimed with a smile.

Adam said, "Mel, really?"

I gave him a big bottom lip, "Sorry Adam, but I need a real man."

I went around the table and locked arms with the drunk. He was proclaiming what kind of real man he was. Adam mouthed, "Don't kill him."

I smiled, "I'll be right back."

Adam was such a gem. He understood my need for blood and seldom got in my way. He also understood that, if men tried to rape me during this process, I would kill them. It only happened one time in our little band trip, but Adam gave me such a guilt trip about it that I was really hoping that this guy would not turn out to be some kind of rapist. Dan didn't really care how many rapists or pedophiles I killed, just as long as he didn't have to cover it up for me.

It's hard sometimes to make sure that I was on the right side of the killing. I killed necromancers and other vampires, or whatever got in our way. So if some evil man gets caught in my trap, it is almost impossible for me *not* to kill him. Still, I wanted Adam to think well of me. Deep down I felt lucky. I found a man that not only loves me, but understands enough to let me go off with strange men so that I might feed.

I was lucky because the drunk ended up being a nice guy. He was drunk, so he was stupid, but he wasn't trying to hurt me. In fact, he asked me twice on the way out to his car, "Now I'm not pushing you into anything you don't want to do? To be honest… I'm a little drunk."

I even got a good laugh. After a few minutes looking for his car, he came to realize that he had come here with friends. That was a good thing because he was too drunk to drive. I lead him over to a dimly lit part of the parking lot, and there I fed. Afterwards, I helped him back over to the club where I deposited him by the side door. That's when I heard a noise coming from the adjacent alleyway.

Curiosity killed the cat. Spooky wasn't with me, so I decided it would be safe to check it out. It was an overcast moonless night. The alley lay between two buildings. They were both three stories and made of brick, so even if there had been starlight, none of it would have been in the alley. I moved into the dark alley and as my eyes adjusted, it appeared empty. It would have been even darker, if not for some light from an intersecting alley.

I walked and whistled quietly, just enough that my second sight was alive in my head. More noise was coming up ahead; it was coming from the other alley. I was close enough to realize it sounded like fighting. I flashed to the opening of the adjoining alley and slowly peered down the connecting alleyway. Beside the trash lying on the ground, I could see three things, one, a big trash bin and close to that, a man and a woman fighting.

At first, it appeared that a well-built man was holding down a girl. I almost flashed in to save her, but the girl kicked him off. She jumped to her feet and flew at him. The man punched her, but it barely fazed her. She clawed his arm, drawing blood. He yelled out, "Ow! You bitch!" Then he tossed her into the brick wall that lined the alley. That's when I could make out her teeth as she hissed at him.

Pushing off the wall, she flew right at him. He sidestepped past her. She just kept going then ran up the other wall. She went straight up for almost twenty feet before kicking off and doing some impressive flips. She landed behind him and, before he could react, she jumped onto his back.

As they fought, I slowly walked closer, not making a sound. The man was a good size and well built. His hair could be brown or black; it was hard to tell from the lighting. The girl was very tiny with black curly hair. The girl had dark skin. She was a young vampire, and, even though she was super strong, I didn't believe she was stronger than her intended prey. Of course, pound for pound, she was stronger. She made up the difference in speed and agility.

She had finally managed to bite his neck while riding on his back. He slammed her between his back and the wall, yelling and cursing all the while. He couldn't pull her mouth away due to the pain of her teeth that were sunk in his neck. It seemed to take awhile before the man fell to his knees. Loss of blood and panting from exhaustion, he was close to passing out.

As the man's breathing slowed and his eyes started to fade, I wondered if I should save him from the vampire. This line of thinking was interrupted by the fact that she had now quit feeding. The man lay below her, covered in blood and dead. Probably should have figured out if I was going to save him earlier.

I was still standing in, a shadow, not far from the vampire. She was looking upward with her eyes closed, moving back and forth to some invisible music. She was enjoying the pleasure of feeding. I knew this feeling. It made me hungry just to watch her, even though I had just fed.

She lowered her head and looked back and forth to ensure the coast was clear. She looked toward me and froze. I smiled at her, but she turned and ran. She was fast as she sprang over a gate and down another alleyway.

I don't know why, but I was interested in her. I hadn't had a normal vampire experience, if there was such a thing. I had been taken in by very powerful vampires, and I was no mere vampire. I wondered what it was like to be her. She needed to feed, but this one man was a challenge. I was born stronger and faster than her, and it would take her years to get as strong and as fast as I was on my first day.

I flew straight up forming my black wings and rising quickly above the buildings. I pulled the blackness around me, becoming a dark shadow in the sky. I hardly needed to worry about it on this dark night. It didn't take long before I caught a person moving too fast to be human. I followed her. She was jumping and swinging like an acrobat around and through objects throughout the city. She was impressive; her fighting skills were poor, but she could move.

She had stopped and watched behind her a few times, but, most of the time, she zipped through the city. I hadn't caught her smile, and I wondered if she was wearing garlic. She started to slow down and check behind herself more often. When she was sure that she had not been followed, she quickly scaled a wall and crossed over a few roofs. She was in an apartment when she dropped off the roof and into a window. I landed without making any noise right above the window she entered. I lay upon the roof and listened.

I could hear a man speaking, "About time."

What I assumed was the vampire replied, "Had a visitor, so I took the long way home."

"Hunters?" his voice was full of concern.

"No, another vampire, I've never seen her before. She snuck up on me while I was feeding. She was only ten feet away before I even noticed her."

Another woman spoke, and her voice was older and very concerned. "How did she do that? You need to be more careful. Did you get rid of the body?"

"I didn't have time. Like I said, she was ten feet away from me when I noticed her."

The boy asked, "What did this weird bitch look like?"

"Like a blonde bombshell. Long hair and extremely beautiful, I've never seen her before."

The man's voice was louder as he teased, "Take me to her at once. I'll deal with this foul creature of the night."

The older woman scolded him, "You'll do no such thing."

The girl vampire added, "She was more than a bombshell, Tyler; she was weird. Her eyes… they almost looked as if they were glowing. I plan on staying away from her."

The older lady added, "We'll need to move tonight. We can't take a chance that she is tracking you."

The vampire girl sounded like this was a nightly thing. "Just as well, the bodies are starting to stink."

The man agreed, "Yep, it is starting to smell. It won't be long before someone comes to check up on the old hag. Let's find a nicer place to stay this time."

I had heard enough and took to the sky. Looking down I could see that this apartment complex was a retirement area for the elderly. The vampires killed whoever lived in that apartment, and they planned to do it again. It was close to three in the morning and I had a feeling these vampires wouldn't move until tomorrow night. We would be waiting.

Adam would get worried if I stayed away much longer. I checked my pockets, and, once again, had forgotten my cell phone. They were going to give me such hell when I got back. I was supposed to go nowhere without it. They could track the phone in case something happened, and they needed to find me. I touched Adam every chance I could, so there was no way to charm me. Dan would be mad about the phone, but he would be happy that I made first contact.

I landed in the same alley, I flew out of. Pulling the shadows back into myself, burying my reaper power within me, I hurried along back to the club where we had been playing. I've been to so many clubs I couldn't even remember its name until I saw the neon light saying, "The Joker's Wild".

I was walking up to the entrance. I stood to one side to let a crowd out the front door. That's when I noticed a poster. There were paper signs and posters all over the wall, but one that hung in the window, right next to the front door caught my eye. I wasn't sure why. I walked up closer and examined the poster trying to decipher the nagging thought in my head.

The poster was an advertisement for a circus that was coming to town. The Wild Circus was in big black print across the top of the poster. The body of the poster was a collage of images; a big top was in the background. There were photos of a strong man, the bearded lady and a man with a top hat in front of a lion. There were statements all over the poster: "Come and See the Wheel of Death" and "The Wild, Wild West Show". At the bottom right hand corner, my eyes froze. There was a picture of a very wicked-looking doll and below it said "New Attraction: Be the First to Explore the Haunted Doll House".

Any thought of a doll reminded me of Alice, but this was different. I knew that old tattered doll. The doll itself was an antique, but no collector would want it. The doll was worn and most of the hair had fallen out. The dress was filthy and in horrible condition. I knew this doll... Alice carried it *everywhere* she went.

Chapter 26 I, Devil

We finally cleared out of the Joker's Wild and headed back toward the bus. Spooky and Summer had most likely fallen asleep. I was waiting until we got out of earshot of anyone we didn't know to ask Dan about the Wild Circus.

I told Dan about my find. He went back to the club to check out the poster. He was sure that I was mistaken. So, Adam and I waited next to the van for his return. Adam spoke, "Been meaning to tell you something."

"Oh no, that doesn't sound good."

Adam gave me a weak smile, "It's not that bad, just thought you should know that Kathy is coming to visit."

I was thrown off by the use of her name, "You mean your mother?"

Adam had a strange look, "I thought you knew."

"Knew what?"

"Kathy isn't our mother. She's our aunt, but when we lived in Queen Anne, we always called her mother. It was best, just in case someone came looking for us; they would probably look for our mother first."

I never knew this and was surprised. "Where's your mom?"

Adam kicked at the ground, "She's dead… murdered."

I gasped in surprise, "Sorry, I had no idea."

Dan was walking back and was almost upon us. Adam added, "I'll tell you about it later. For now I just wanted you to know that my aunt was coming to visit. She doesn't think highly of you, and it would probably be best if I keep her away from you."

"If that's what's best," I tried to sound supportive and not bitter about Kathy's feelings for me.

"It's her alright," Dan announced. "But why? Why would she be there?"

I inquired, "Now the Wild Circus, is it the Dark Circus you told me about? Red Adder the Lich, the circus he controls?"

"The same," Dan answered. He held his face down and began to pace, lost in thought.

Adam asked me, "This is the writer of the *Book of the Dead*?"

"Yes," I answered. "There is only one reason Alice could be there. She went there for me, to find out more information. She knew she might not be able to escape, but she went anyway. That Circus is a trap for anyone magical."

"Don't be a fool," Dan said. He stopped pacing, and now he was looking at me. His eyes were full of pain, "She could have gone there to return his book."

I tried not to sound angry, "What? No, she doesn't have the book."

Dan held his hands up like "don't shoot me". Then he proceeded to say something that made me want to shoot him. "I'm just saying that a lot of people believe she has the book. She is a vampire... and not a good one. Alice has always... how do I put this? Looks out for herself first and foremost."

"But... I know Alice," I stated defensively.

Adam put his arm around me protectively, or perhaps he was making sure I didn't hit Dan. He spoke calmly, "Dan, perhaps we should call it a night?"

Dan went on like Adam hadn't spoken, "I know Alice too. I was married to her for fifty plus years and served her for many years before that. My father was taking me to the New World, but our ship was attacked by pirates. My father was a very capable wizard, but the pirate ship that came was hosted with a crew of cutthroats and vampires. They attacked, and my father died that night and, at the age of fifteen, I was taken prisoner.

Alice was the captain of the ship and quickly named me her cabin boy. She knew I had a talent with magic. I know her heart, and if someone told me that she killed a child, I would not believe it. Alice has shown heart where few vampires have, but that does not make her good. Her need for power and wealth has fueled her for centuries.

"I have stayed friends with her, but sadly it has been for my own benefit as well. I will not stand in front of you and tell you what an angel I've been, so why don't you stop pretending that Alice might not betray you if it served her."

I spoke slowly, keeping calm. "I understand that she is not an angel, but neither am I. What I'm saying is, just because she is with this Adder, does not mean she betrayed me. She kind of told me where she was going, but, at the time, I didn't understand. Trust me, you're jumping to conclusions."

Dan nodded, "Perhaps I am. It's just that... well, never mind."

Adam sounded put out, "Dan, you can't say something like that and leave it. Spit it out."

I took a calming breath and stated, "Go ahead. I won't get mad; let's hear it."

Dan thought for a second, "Ok, ok. Understand that maybe I am jumping to conclusions, but nowadays I'm having a hard time trusting anyone. It all began, good God, it was over thirty years ago. Early eighties perhaps, that's when she came, for one of her visits; she comes by every decade or so.

"She was very upset and it took me hours to get her to tell me what was bothering her. She finally let it spill. She told me that she had indirectly caused the death of a young woman, but not any woman - a woman from her family line. Four hundred years of protecting her line, and all was lost for her greed and need of power. She never told me what she hoped to receive, but the visit showed me how lost she had become through the years."

I interrupted, "I don't understand. What do you mean her family line?"

"Oh, I should have told you that first. Her family line was from her mortal life. She followed her sister and her sister's children, following some kind of family magic that was only passed from one female to the next in the family. She watched over these girls and insured her line remained unbroken. I remember very little about it; she really never told me much. You know how private Alice can be."

"I do; I've never heard any of this in all the time I've been with her."

Adam asked, "So are there any Whites left in her family that still might have this power?"

Dan shook his head, "No, and the family name wasn't White. It was Dare; she followed the Dare family."

I froze in shock. I never told Adam or Dan my true name. Never could they have known that my name was Melanie Elizabeth Dare. My face must have had, holy crap written all over it. Adam asked concerned, "Are you ok?"

I shook my head, "Fine... wow, I'm tired. Let's call it a night. We'll figure this out later. At least I know where Alice is. We'll figure out how to save her later."

Dan didn't buy it for a minute, "What aren't you telling us?"

"Goodnight, Dan," I pulled Adam along as I headed for the van.

Dan yelled back, "Goodnight, we'll finish this conversation later."

Adam and I crawled into the van and shut the door. Adam asked, "Do I get to know what that was about?"

"You get sex," I said with a big smile.

"Ok," he said instantly distracted.

*   *   *

My eyes opened. An arm was wrapped around my naked body with only a light blanket laying over us. Adam was snoring softly while he spooned me from behind. My mind was full of troubles, but as I thought about last night, a smile crossed over my face. If I could do that every night forever, then I truly had something to look forward to.

It was hard to hold that happy thought. I just couldn't believe that Alice had betrayed me, not just betrayed me, but just possibly had something to do with what I was. She very well could have been in league with Alex. Holy crap! That thought hurt. I couldn't believe it. I just *won't* believe it. I will rescue Alice, and she will be able to explain it, and I would believe it because she has been known for her honesty. Oh, this sucks, I don't even want to know if anyone else I've come to love has secretly betrayed me.

I had other things to worry about, like the ominous visit by Kathy. After making love to Adam, he still had energy to question me about why I acted so unusual when I heard the name Dare. I quickly turned the conversation to what happened to his mother.

The whole story left me with mixed emotions and wondering how Adam could love me. The night he and his sister were kidnapped, his mother was killed. She was killed by a vampire, no less. The vampire was traveling with magic users. Once the vampire killed his mother, the group took the children and drove away in a van. It was the last night they ever saw that vampire. They were locked in a basement for several days. Finally, one of the captors came down offering food. He told them if they wanted to be free, they had to help them kill an evil vampire. They were going to help them kill Alice.

Adam's father was killed by an unknown vampire when Adam was just a baby. Summer was thirteen, and Adam was eleven when they found their mother dead on the floor and surrounded by enemies, forced to go to some unknown place and watch yet another murder. Of course they were there to help kill Alice, but, instead, they watched me kill three of their kidnappers, and then witnessed me being shot in the chest and the man who shot me killed by a giant tiger.

I was truly thankful for Adam's love. How could he be betraying me? I started to think of all the reasons he might want to use me. I closed my eyes and whispered to myself, "Stop it... just stop it." If I didn't trust him, I would be truly alone. I wiggled to get even closer to him in my moment of doubt. If ever there was a reason for positive thinking, this was it. I needed to see Nicks because I needed help. Too many questions and clues were rolling around my mind. If only I were smart enough to understand them.

The door of our van was being forcibly opened. It was followed by the blinding light of the sun. This brought my internal debate to an abrupt end. My mind was on full alert as Adam yelled, "What the hell?"

The sun was behind the person who opened the door, but I knew who it was. Summer was somewhere in the distance saying, "I tried to stop her."

She was cut off by a booming voice, "Both your mom and dad were murdered by a vampire. Won't they be proud?"

I defended myself, "Glad they weren't murdered by blacks. Then he would be a racist."

She sneered at me, "Listen to the lies that come so easily from her mouth. She tries to equate people with monsters. I'm sure you wouldn't have to look hard to find a person of any color, who hasn't murdered anyone. Answer me this, queen of lies, have you murdered anyone?"

Adam spoke up before I could answer, "That's enough. We need to get dressed."

"I'll be waiting," she then slammed the door shut.

Adam touched me gently, "I'll deal with her, okay?"

"Yeah," I said with a nod. My mind was lost in thought while Adam moved around looking for clean clothes. My voice was small, "I couldn't answer her question by saying 'no'."

"What?" he asked, but then it must have registered. "Don't worry about, I... we don't think you're a monster. Don't let my aunt upset you; she doesn't know shit."

"Maybe she does." I quickly changed my tone, "I'm too stressed. I'm not helping. This will be a handful for you." I was doing my best to be supportive.

"Don't worry about me," he said this with a smile, and it was accompanied by a kiss.

Adam left, leaving me another kiss on his way out. It took me a few minutes to motivate myself to dress. I slipped on my jeans and then put on a red shirt that hung like a skirt. I was brushing my hair when the door opened, and Spooky hopped in. She shut the door behind her. She was dressed like a punk rocker, and every time I saw her I swore her hair was shorter. She informed me, "It's World War Three out there! Dan just remembered things we needed at the store. Damn, his mom is going off."

I rubbed my temples, "Oh, this has been a rough twenty-four hours."

Spooky's voice was full of venom, "So Alice knew who you were. I told you that bat-shit crazy bitch was no good. I know how much the betrayal hurts you…"

"*Do you?*" I shouted.

"*Yes,*" she shouted back. "I feel your feelings, remember." Her tone became friendly again. "I also know you don't hate her like me. I have my reasons, and you have yours, but I can't help but celebrate that she is gone."

"We'll find her," I informed her.

"Maybe, but after all this we won't be hanging out with the little creep." She said this about Alice with a deep satisfaction.

"Enough, I need a walk. Why don't you, guard the van." I gave her a big fake smile, then slid the door open and left. Slamming the door behind me, I took a small walk across the parking lot and toward the club. The Joker's Wild just now opened, and a great idea came to mind. I needed a drink.

It wasn't long before I found myself nursing a glass of wine. "Just waiting for someone," I said to the approaching man before he could even speak. He had been the third one in the last two hours. I could feel the sun fall below the horizon… night was at hand.

I paid my tab and decided to check up on everyone. I had a small buzz that would not last long. I quickly made my way out of the club. I hadn't made it very far when Adam came jogging up to me. He smiled, but he couldn't hide the worry on his face, "Hey, I was wondering where you were off to."

"Just having a drink, how's it going with you?"

He laughed, "Little drunk," he said while holding his thumb and pointer finger a few inches apart. "I know my aunt hurt your feelings, but she was just mad. I don't want to make excuses for her, but I don't want you to hate her."

I waved my hand through the air dismissively, "I don't hate her. In fact, I understand what she is saying. I mean, I'm a killer. What vampire isn't?"

He countered, "She also knows that you have saved me more times than I can count. She's sorry… even though she isn't ready to tell you that. In time, she will come around."

I laughed and hugged him. Whispering in his ear, "Ever the optimist."

"Hey, I just believe that, with love, all things are possible. She made me so mad tonight; I wanted to change my name back."

Confused, I asked, "Back?"

"See, when my sister and I came to live with my aunt, we took her last name. She had been married years ago and never bothered to change her name back from Sheppard. My mom's maiden name was Thomas, I always wanted to go by that name."

"What about your father's name?"

Adam thought about it for a second, "Too dangerous. Everyone knew us by his name, and it didn't help that he was a pretty well known enchanter. I bet Summer could give him a run for his money. He would be proud. Still, it will be a long time before I can call myself a Reite."

I said it like a curse word, "Reite?"

Thinking I didn't understand, he clarified, "Yeah, after my father, Aaron Reite."

My eyes closed as old memories flooded my mind, the night I killed Aaron Reite and the memories I stole from him in his death. Adam picked up on my panic attack. His voice was full of concern, "What, what is it? Did I say something?"

"Yes," I answered while my body shook. With my eyes closed and my mind swimming in wine, my mouth betrayed me, "I killed him."

The pause, it felt like a thousand years. He said in a very confused voice, "Killed who?" I didn't answer him. Silence passed between us as he absorbed what I had said. While he accepted it, my heart broke. I opened my eyes, and his facial expression was pure hell.

"You… you… I," he just couldn't find the words. "Are you kidding?"

My voice shook, "Long ago, I had no idea he was your father." My voice had left me.

"*I hate you.*" Burst forth from Adam; his face was full of rage and betrayal.

All I could say was, "Sorry."

He started to yell something about how could I, but I had already taken to the air. My mind turned off as my wings spread and I flew ever higher. I was the devil.

Chapter 27 Ace of Hearts

I was walking... walking where?

Some place in L.A., in a giant concrete storm drain. The night was coming to an end. I couldn't even recall what I did with the time. I walked deeper into the tunnel, and the white creamy concrete surrounded me like a tomb. My feet splashed in the few inches of water that was flowing across the floor and down the storm drain. The sound of cars came from the distance as the morning traffic started to build.

This place was empty except for some trash and an old shopping cart lying on its side. I headed deeper into the ground and came to an area that looked as if an earthquake had broken up the walls and ground. The concrete was cracked, and, in some places, the rebar came out of the wall like black worms.

While walking, I was thinking about him, and, in my mind, I could hear us talking. All the things I wished I could have said just echoed around in my head.

I'm so sad; I could feel tears falling freely on my chest. I reached for Adam, but I reached in vain. It's just not fair... when one loves and the other hates. I would have done anything for him, for I adore him. How will I keep from falling apart? It all needs to stop haunting me. It should be easy, easy as when he stopped wanting me, but I wanted him. The pain was so great - great enough to break out of my chest. It would overtake the world and crush it, destroying everything. I had to bury this pain, bury it so deep... bury until I felt nothing.

My world went quiet, and a strange sense of calm fell over me. My heart beats evenly. I would feel nothing. If my feelings were to surface, I would surely drown the world in tears. The planet would split in half, and the world would die. I couldn't be sure this would not happen, but it's best to take no chances. It would be best for everyone if I just stopped... stopped hurting.

My heart quickened, betraying my promise to stop feeling. I ran... I ran toward the wall. Impaling myself upon a piece of rebar; my body came to rest. I hung lifeless from the steel bar. Hands at my side, head hung, my aim had been true. The cold steel had pierced straight through my heart.

As my human life faded, all I had was the monster inside. The reaper side did not care if I lived or not. The sun had risen, and, with no reason to live, or breathe again, I cursed myself to the night. Falling into a deep vampire sleep… a sleep where I would feel nothing.

*   *   *

I came to in another state of mind. I was in the library, sitting upon the floor. So much for a break from my distress, and, for some reason, I felt more confused than I usually did when I arrived here. Something was wrong. My eyes started to scan around me, and the more I saw, the more worried I became. The library was dimmer. The fire that normally lit the fireplace smoldered in hot coals. The wooden floor was usually clean and well polished, but it now appeared to be worn out. The polish was gone. It appeared that, instead of sliding across the floor, you might end up with splinters.

Everything looked older and dirtier. The books appeared to be ancient and falling apart. I stood and walked slowly through the room. Picking up a book from a shelf the pages fell out and scattered across the floor. Some of the pages turned to dust. I lay what was left of the book back onto the shelf. I walked further into the library hoping that this was just a place I had never been. Perhaps it was an older part of the library.

It did not take me long to find out I was wrong. I moved into a great room, and it was old and worn down. Dust covered everything; it looked like the rest of the place. I had been in this room a hundred times before. If I hadn't known better, I would have thought I had traveled through time and a thousand years had passed. Finally, I spied Nicks sitting on his chair; he had not noticed me yet.

Nicks face was cast downward with a book in his lap. He appeared to have fallen asleep. He always had the most beautiful brown hair that parted from the middle and hung down past his shoulders. His hair was twice as long and full of white and gray. His face was covered with a gray beard, and he looked to be an old man if not for his face, for it was still strong and young. His eyes rose to meet mine. I expected to see those brightly lit eyes, but instead his eyes almost seemed brown.

He smiled with a little bit of effort, "Come to me, my dear. It has been too long."

I ran over and took him into my arms, "What has happened here? What has happened to you?"

Nicks chuckled, "No worries, and do not get upset. Nothing here is what I would like it to be, but this allows me to save on the use of power. It's all rather complicated, but the spells these necromancers are casting keeps me under constant attack."

"Attack?" I asked with worry.

"Yes, but nothing I can't handle, you can trust me. What these attacks have really accomplished is to keep me trapped here. This means I have been unable to do my job, or help you for that matter."

"You don't need to worry about me. I can handle myself. If you need me to help you, I can do it."

Nicks gave me a strange look, "Handle yourself, yes, but, not sure if you can help me."

I didn't understand at first, "Why can't I?" Then it hit me, "I see; I haven't been much help."

"It's not your fault," His eyes were full of kindness. "We all have talents, and you are full of them, but being a detective has not been your strong point. I had hopes that Dan might lead you to some success, but alas, he has not."

I could not hide my bitterness, "Just as well. They'll have nothing more to do with me now."

Nicks put an arm around me, "Walk with me." We walked slowly through the great room, and Nicks did not speak for some time. Finally, he said, "I do believe he loves you. I hope it works out. I'm struggling to give you some tidbit of wisdom about this, but I'm afraid that some things just need time. For good or bad... they need time."

"I have time... maybe," my heart hurts just to think about what an awful person I was. My mind had been asking the same question over and over again. I asked Nicks this very question, "How can I make it up to him?"

He answered slowly, "You can't."

"I see," I replied as he wiped a tear off my cheek.

He did not tell me not to cry. Instead, he changed the subject, "You need help. Not with Adam, but with more pressing matters. You need a detective, and I have just the one."

I liked talking about something else, "Who?"

"His name is Alex McDonald. I do believe you know him."

"Wait... he's the man that helped David and me. You do know I tortured him for information about my father and sister. It was the same information I used to try to kill both of them." Nicks nodded his head. My voice was louder and I spoke faster, "So, you want me to ask him for help... must I enslave, love or need something from everyone I hurt?"

Nicks gave me a sideways smile, "I do believe I have wisdom in this situation. Karma is a real bitch."

As snotty as I could, I piped back, "Thanks, maybe I better write that down so I don't forget it."

Nicks laughed, "Trust me, you'll remember."

Nicks then gave me information on where I might find the detective. We had a good visit and time flew by. I wanted to stay in the library forever. I didn't want to deal with the real world. The library was in rough shape; in turn, that reminded me of my responsibilities... reminded me of what kind of failure I had been. Now I'm thinking of Adam again.

I awoke in my body that was still impaled on a steel rebar. The sun was setting outside and, once again, I was truly a vampire. Without my second sight or even smelling the air, I knew that I was not alone. "I hadn't expected you."

Spooky's voice was kinder than I had expected, "Why not?"

I shrugged my shoulders. I pulled myself off the rebar. My chest healed, but my dress was ruined with dry blood. Spooky was leaning against the far wall dressed like a punk rocker, blue jeans, a black shirt with some rock band's logo I wasn't sure of and an oversized army jacket with patches and buttons covering it. Next to her sat a black case;, and I realized at once that she had brought Bow.

She saw me looking at the case, "I figured you might need this at the very least... maybe you might even need a friend."

I asked, "Is that what we are?" This time she shrugged. I asked yet another question, "How? How did we become friends? Don't get me wrong; I want this, I need this... I just don't understand it."

She gave me a weak smile, "Must you understand it?"

I closed the distance and hugged her, "No, no I don't, just glad to have a friend."

Spooky and I talked for a while. She had explained that after watching Adam and Summer trash me for about four hours straight, Dan started to complain about the band. She had enough. She grabbed a bag and Bow and, without a word, took off. It hadn't been hard to find me; she could feel me from a mile away.

It took a little while, but I eventually figured out why Spooky's feelings had changed. She finally explained, "You've suffered enough. If I had to suffer through all my past sins, I doubt I would have been able to handle it. I just can't hate you for what you have done."

After that I was hungry, so we decided to do something together that we hadn't done in awhile. We went hunting. We were strolling through a bad neighborhood awaiting our meal to come and introduce itself. It kept my mind busy waiting for a pervert to come looking for us. Spooky asked, "So, what are you going to do now?"

"Nicks told me that I suck at being a detective. Really couldn't argue with that, so I guess, since I am paying for all my sins of my past, he thought I should deal with one more. A great detective once helped me, and then I tortured him for information to hurt innocent people. Nicks thinks he can help me solve what's going on."

Spooky whistled, "Damn girl! Time to clean all the bones out of that closet. How do we find this detective?"

"Short of hiring one, I was thinking Ezra might be able to help."

I could feel her hurt, before she could even speak, "I really don't want to see him, but... you can."

"You can go to my parents; it's been too long."

She calmed down when I mentioned going to my family. She had been missing them as much as me, "When the time comes, because, in case you forgot... we don't know where Ezra is?"

I was surprised, "Really. I was hoping this part of it might be easy."

A moment later Spooky interrupted my worrying, "We will need to go through some of the vampire clans to find Ezra. This means you can't be the Dark Fiddler. You don't know shit about the vampire world."

I chuckled, "And you do?"

She huffed at me, "Yes, yes I do. I've been hanging with Ezra for almost ten years. Been in every cracked out bar and back alley you can think of. You don't even know how the covens organize themselves or what the rules are."

I shrugged, "Okay, I might have missed all that. Tell me what I need to know and I'll learn on the way. After tonight, you will need to go to my parents."

"Let me help you for a few days," she sounded a little rejected. "What's the hurry?"

I didn't answer her; instead I asked, "Who do you trust?"

"Well, I trust you..." she stopped answering and thought for a second. "I need to move your family. Alice put them there, and when you seek the truth... if you find out that Alice is a part of it. Oh, I hadn't thought about that."

I nodded, "You recall our little run in with David. It's all so messed up in my head, I can't help but wonder if we're on the wrong side of this. Maybe David's the good guy, and we're the arch villains. My head is spinning, and this thing between me and Adam has made me an emotional wreck."

Spooky suggested, "Can you skip a meal tonight?"

I nodded, "Yes."

We headed to a park. It was empty, and we found a quiet spot in a wooden ship in the middle of the playground. I commented, "Our playgrounds were never so nice."

"Before you want to play a game of underwater mermaids, I need to tell you some information. It won't be enough, but it will get you a head start. First, the vampire world in the United States is wild. There is order between the covens, unlike the European clans. There are very few rules, and most covens monitor themselves.

"Still, there are some rules, and Alice rules them all. She has always been childish, so there is no wonder her system of rule is very childish. Alice and three other powerful vampires rule America. I'm not going to go on like Ezra did. If he were to tell it, you would have to hear about the whole damn history and who ruled what part in what year.

"All you need to know is that the U.S. is broken into four parts. If you lived in the Northeast, you would be part of the Diamonds. The Southeast is the Spades; the Clubs rule the Northwest."

I finished her sentence, "Southwest is ruled by the Hearts. She has the country broken up like a deck of cards; go figure."

She proceeded, "Like I said, childish. One rule to keep fighting down between vampires is that you are given a card. This gives you status, and it also helps keep the number of vampires up. Let's say you are a two of hearts, and you meet an eight. The number eight would destroy you. Because vampires don't appear to age and can be anyone from burly men to little old ladies, it is hard to find the right level of respect. The cards tell you who you're dealing with, get it? ... *dealing with*." I gave a big fake chuckle. "Moving right along, then, the face cards like Queen and King are easy. There is only one King and one Queen to any suit. There can be thousands of the number cards. Alice is the Queen of Spades and, therefore, rules the southeast. She has a king, but I've never met him."

Surprised, "It's not Ezra?"

"No, I'll get to his card in a minute. Her King is powerful and does most of the real work of running the south. Alice really runs the whole thing, but appears to be an equal when the royalty meets. The next card is the Jack. Jack is the one card everyone wants to be. Sometimes vampires are very important, but not very powerful. The King or Queen of any region can name anyone a Jack and they can even be human.

"Jacks are under the protection of any vampire who meets them. Failure to protect a Jack is a death sentence. Your sexy Michael is a Jack, his ability to control animals... and pleasure women had found him a very nice position."

"He's the Jack of Spades... the one eyed Jack," I burst into laughter.

Spooky was laughing, "I hadn't thought of that before." When we both calmed down, she cautioned, "Where were we? Aces - this is how Alice keeps control. She has four Aces; they are the number one and eleven. This means that they have no say over any other vampire when it comes to local coven business, but they are also an eleven, so no one can tell them what to do. They are the enforcers and they're supposed to be loyal to the four Kings, but really they just obey Alice. Ezra is the Ace of Spades and you, my dear, are the Ace of Hearts."

"Wait, I'm an Ace? Also are the kings more powerful than the queens?"

Spooky yawned, "Sorry, let me answer the Queen/King question first. The most powerful vampire of the most powerful coven is made King, or Queen. Then they name their second, and they have to be the opposite sex. Not sure why, because they are not necessarily lovers, except that Alice likes it that way. To let you know, the four other decks are all lead by Kings, and only the Spades are lead by a Queen.

"To answer your first question - yes, you are an Ace. The reason is simple. Back when you and David started killing everyone, she had to name you or it would look like you were an out-of-control vampire. This, in turn, would force Alice to stop you, but, as an Ace, it looked as if you were just enforcing Alice's law. And since she's nuts, no one really knows what that law is anyway. You were killed just a year and a half into the job and strangely she has never filled the empty position."

I let out a puff of air, "That explains why all the vampires in Vegas were scared of me. She had already labeled me as some kind of badass killing machine. It's strange, but going into this vampire world will feel like traveling to another planet."

"It's only a few hours before the sunrise. Let us find you a place to sleep. I will guard you today. I'm tired anyway. Tomorrow evening we'll say our goodbyes."

"Sounds like a plan, but now I'm hungry."

Chapter 28 Visiting Old friends

We found an empty house in which we took refuge. After sleeping the day away, we awoke late that evening. The sun was about to set when Spooky and I said our goodbyes.

A weight lifted off me knowing that my family would be safe. It was only after talking to Nicks that I thought of the fact that my family might be in danger from Alice. Was it because I was stupid? Or perhaps I thought with my heart? I still instinctively felt that I could trust Alice, but there was enough evidence that I should be careful in doing so.

It didn't take long before I forgot about Alice only to start pining over Adam. I looked out the window, and the sun felt like hot pokers in my eyes. It would still be a little while before the sun went down. I was so hungry… I never liked being hungry, but it did give me something else to think about.

After the sun fell below the trees, I headed out. The sky was still full of light with a red horizon. I walked aimlessly until I spied a park. By the time I entered, it was dark. I attracted the attention of two Hispanic boys and one white guy. I moved away from them and further into the darkness. They followed, quickening their steps.

I heard from behind me, "Hey, chica, what's the hurry? Sweet thing like you, all alone, don't you know it's dangerous?"

I turned around and watched the three men encircle me. "Let me guess, you'll protect me."

One of the Hispanic men spoke up, "Oh yeah, we'll protect you, but it won't be for free."

He said, while his buddies stood around laughing like morons. The other men were parroting him with comments like, "We'll protect you, baby. Won't cost much…"

"Speak for yourself," one boy said as he grabbed his package. They all laughed at his crude joke.

I was hungry, and game time was over early. The laughs were about to be turned into screams. Kicking the white boy's knee, it buckled backwards. Before his body hit the ground, my leg spun around in a kick, landing square in the chest of the second boy.

The third one stood there confused as his friend lay on the ground screaming and holding his broken leg. The other boy was lying on the ground trying to breathe. He looked at me with hatred, "Bitch!" He yelled this as he stepped forward swinging his fist.

I grabbed his wrist and brought his arm to a sudden stop. My grip was like iron as I twisted his arm. He screamed as he went down to one knee. I yanked him towards me, biting into his neck.

Lost in the pleasure of eating, I lost track of time. I wiped my mouth as the third empty body fell to my feet. I burped loudly and said to no one, "Better out than in." I decided Shrek really knew what he was talking about as I chuckled to myself.

Taking to the sky, it felt good to feel the air rushing over me. My wings formed as I traveled ever higher into the night sky. My belly sloshed around as the blood of three men gave me a high. It didn't take long before I arrived at my destination. I hadn't really thought about it, but I knew from the beginning where I would start my search.

I landed softly in front of the large house, the house I was taken to when I first met Alice. It sat high on a hill overlooking a valley of lights. The city of Beaumont lay at the valley's bottom. I knew that this was a dead end, from the moment I landed. A "For Sale" sign hung at a strange angle in the front yard. There were no lights on, and the yard hasn't been taken care of for a long time. The smell that came from the house, let me know that no one had been here for a long time, years perhaps.

I didn't wait long before taking flight and coming to land at my next destination. I landed on the Fox Theater in uptown Banning. Someone had put some real money into the renovation of the building. I dropped softly into the alley and walked out onto Main Street. The place was empty, the shops having already closed for the night. The movie theater sat quietly bathed in lights. At any time people would come to buy tickets as the crowd from the last movie was let out, but, for now, even the ticket seller had retreated inside.

I could feel the wards. All the shops and even the theater were protected from me. Before my heart stopped, I could have passed through a magical barrier or walked through the power of a cross or an amulet. I was a walking talking corpse again. I would need to be invited to enter any of these shops or businesses. Arriving at this new destination, in gold letters, the window said, McDonald's Detective Agency. It had been awhile, I do hope he has forgiven me.

I walked up to the door feeling for the protection. It was not there, but then I remembered how I forced him to invite me in all those years ago. Wait. Does that work? Wouldn't he have revoked my invitation? I stood there holding the door handle; there was no sign of protection. The door was unlocked, so I hesitantly entered.

Inside was completely different than what I remembered. The whole place had been redecorated. It was much more retro with bright colors that centered on different shades of blue. The chairs were round and different colored lights gave the place a nice feel. A young secretary sat tapping away at her computer. Without looking at me and with a very pleasant voice she said, "If you would give me one minute, I'll be right with you."

"No problem," I assured her.

She was wearing slacks and a nice brown blouse. Her strawberry blonde hair was pulled up in a sloppy ponytail. Slightly overweight, she was still very pretty. Finally, she finished her task and turned her whole body to show me she was now giving me her full attention. Her smile was comfortable and natural, "How can I help you this evening?"

"Well, I'm looking to speak with Alex McDonald."

Her eyes narrowed, but her smile stayed, "Alex has retired. His nephew Cory runs the place now. He's in his office, but I'm afraid he's really busy."

"I'll wait," I offered.

Her smile was now forced, "It might be awhile."

"Don't make this difficult. Just let him know that he has a client waiting." I tried my hardest to not make it sound like a threat, but, at the same time, let her know that I was not about to put up with any of her shit.

Her smile was now tight, "I'm not afraid of vampires. You need to make an appointment... I have some openings early next week if you like."

The fact that she knew what I was and that this place was not warded made me hesitate. I was at a disadvantage here, having no idea what magic tricks or even non-magical defenses they may have prepared. I really wanted to kill her, but that's when it hit me. I killed three men earlier and was ready to kill an innocent girl. The men had it coming, but that wasn't it. I had forgotten what it was like to be a vampire. Being a vampire was like having all your emotions turned up: pleasure, hate, anger, love or loneliness.

I relaxed, "Sorry, I'm being rude. Let Cory know that a Melabeth is here to speak with him. If he does not have time, I will come back at another date."

The young girl calmed a little bit, "I can't promise anything... go sit down while I message him."

I took a seat in a small egg shaped chair. It looked uncomfortable, but surprisingly it was not. The secretary looked up at me surprised, "He'll see you now."

"Oh," half surprised, I got up and headed toward the door behind her. She hit a button, and a buzzing noise went off as the door unlocked. I entered the room. It was unlike the waiting area, the walls were a dull white and in need of painting. Overloaded filing cabinets and loose papers filled every inch of the empty wall. In the middle of the mess sat a desk with a young man behind it.

He reminded me of Alex, only younger. He looked as if he had missed his hair appointment. He wiped the shaggy brown hair away from his very large brown eyes. Those eyes, with his pale skin and no protective wards, could only mean one thing... this detective was a vampire. He motioned toward one of the two chairs that sat before his desk, "Have a seat."

"Thank you for seeing me," I said as I made myself comfortable. I laid my violin case on my lap.

"Melabeth," he said my name drawling it out. "The stories I've heard. Not to mention the fact that you're dead... and yet here you are, sitting before me."

I smiled, "The reports of my death have been greatly exaggerated."

"I noticed," he responded with a grin.

I shouldn't have used my real name. I bluntly got to the point, "I'm looking for Alex McDonald."

"My uncle," he gave me a wary look. "He's not a big fan of vampires. It's been awhile since you've seen him. He's in rough shape. Maybe I can help you?"

This guy was off... not sure what it was, but I didn't trust him. "Afraid I need to speak to him. I realize he might not be a fan. Where might I find him?"

"Sorry, I'm doing a poor job explaining. My uncle was attacked five years ago, and he found out something he shouldn't have. They killed his wife and his son. Now he's dying from cancer. He used to visit Weaver Cemetery to visit his family, but now he is unable to leave the hospital. I'm afraid that he doesn't have much time left. Before you rush off to visit him, you should know he is under a curse, some sort of spell, and no one has been able to break it. He has been unable to speak about anything relating to his cases."

"I see, I'm truly sorry to hear that," I still felt as if this vampire was hiding something.

"I have a lot of information on his past work," he said this as he waved around at all the paperwork. "I'm sure I could help you if you just told me what you wanted."

Waving around the room made me realize something. The room looked less worked in, than ramshackle. The feeling that something was wrong was growing, "Thank you for all your help." I got up to leave. Carrying my violin case in my left hand, I loosened the latch just in case.

He stood and asked again, "Are you sure you don't need anything else?"

"Afraid not," I turned and headed out.

He followed me to the front door saying, "Well, it has been a pleasure meeting with you, Ms. Melabeth. If there is anything, anything at all, do not hesitate to ask."

Pushing the front door open, "Thank you once again for seeing me, Cory."

"Cory," the vampire repeated, appearing confused.

The secretary interrupted, "Cory, you have another call."

He looked a little puzzled, but then said, "Oh yes, need to go. Duty calls."

"Of course," I replied. I walked out the door.

I had barely taken a few steps when I took to the sky. I needed to get out of there, those two were up to something and his name was not Cory. The phone had not rung, and the secretary had only said that to let him know that was the fake name he was using. It was not a total loss. I learned where I might find poor Alex.

It didn't take long to find Weaver Cemetery. I wished to pay my respects to his family. I had been here before. This was the place where that boy, Eric, had seen me come down from the sky. He then took me to his house to use his phone. I walked the gravestones, looking for Alex's family. I found the markers and the dying flowers set before them.

Bow materialized next to me. She seldom did, and I regularly forgot she was with me. She spoke; "I've informed Nicks of your progress. He and I agree that perhaps you should hang around the gravesite until he comes to visit."

That didn't make sense, "Why?"

"He will bring this Alex to you; give it some time. After the scene at his office, they'll know you're coming for him, and Nicks wishes to handle this."

I simply answered, "Okay." I trusted Nicks and felt no need to argue. The worst thing was that now I had to wait. What would I do with all that idle time, because I sure as hell knew what I would be thinking about. I needed distractions.

Chapter 29 Cursed

My hand shook violently, and it wasn't because I just had my eighty-second birthday. All I could manage was to write my name, Alex McDonald, across the top of my paper. I tried and tried, but no matter what, my hand would not obey. I was a cursed man.

I spent my life being an investigator, bringing criminals to justice. In the end, what is my reward? I lay in this hospital bed dying. Friends come by to visit and talk, but, no matter how hard I try, I cannot speak about Luna or anything to do with the murder of my family. I am beginning to believe that some of my friends are starting to wonder if I might have had something to do with it.

Every night it is the same nightmare. My son is driving down the highway with my wife sitting in the passenger seat. I sit in the back; we are conversing and laughing about the movie we just left. It is a dark night, and the rain is coming down in sheets. My old eyes can't see, and I trust in my son to get us there. Strange thing, flying down the road with no idea what is happening outside of the box we are in.

I barely listened to my wife and son converse. My mind was lost in a case I'd been working, an itch I couldn't scratch, just one piece of the puzzle away from seeing a clear picture. In the middle of it all was Luna Longaeva, the most powerful wizard in the world. She was the last full-blooded elf and loved by many. My son's voice rose in volume as he spoke passionately about the movie. I had just tuned into his conversation, "The movie had so much potential... *oh shit!*"

I awoke a week later in a hospital. Shortly after I awoke, they informed me that my wife and son did not survive the crash. At first I believed this to be an accident, but once out of the hospital I discovered something. I was unable to talk or write about anything to do with the case I was working on. People followed me wherever I went and shortly after that I went to a witch I had known for years.

She confirmed that I was under a spell, but shortly after I visited her, she was killed by yet another car accident. I became sick and the doctors found that my body was full of cancer. Now I lie here dying and whoever killed my family got away with it. The thought alone was worse than dying itself. I could die in peace if only I knew that justice was served for my family. Hell, the cancer that killed me could be magical by design. I was no match for whoever was behind the murder of my family.

The pencil slipped from my weak hand. I watched it helplessly fall to the floor - such a small thing, still, another reminder of how weak I've become. A nurse with strawberry-blond hair walked into the room. The nurse was full of smiles, "And how's our patient doing today?"

I did not respond, not because I couldn't but because I didn't care. A doctor followed the nurse in, but, even with my old failing eyes, I knew he was no doctor. First, he was too young to be a doctor unless I had fallen into an episode of Doogie Howser. He had shaggy brown hair that hung in his face and reminded me of myself when I was younger. Those eyes said it all… vampire. He spoke in a kind tone, "Time for some medication."

The woman slipped a needle out of her lab coat pocket. I finally asked, "Why bother? I'll be dead soon enough."

The man grinned, "They weren't kidding; you are a great detective. It's nothing personal, but someone has been looking for you and we can't have her finding you. I will take over as your nephew, Cory, so don't worry about your detective agency. Soon your secrets will remain secret." Just like a B-movie villain, he laughed.

The nurse was preparing to inject the syringe into my IV when I notice another man. I hadn't seen him come in. He walked slowly toward the end of my bed. I realized that the vampire doctor and the nurse had frozen, not in fear but in time. The world had simply stopped moving except for the man at the end of my bed. He wore a black suit and smiled kindly.

"Fear not, for I am Death, and you may call me Nicks."

I could not tell you why, but I had no fear, and my heart filled with joy seeing him. "Are you the Angel of Death? Can I see my family?"

Nicks looked thoughtful, "Yes, yes I am. To answer your other question, I'm afraid not." My heart hurt, but before I could panic Nicks held his hand up. "Be calm, my friend." And I was, "You are a restless spirit. I fear that if you pass that you will haunt these halls looking for justice you will never find. I offer you a deal."

"What? What must I do?" I asked eagerly.

Nicks smiled, "You will serve my daughter. When you have helped her, you will find peace. For my daughter's tormenters will lead you to the ones who killed your family."

My mind filled with the possibilities and questions. "How can I serve her in this dying body? Who is your daughter?"

"You will not need that body for you will serve her as a spirit. You should remember my daughter, Melabeth." He paused for a few seconds, "Are you willing to serve her?"

"Yes, I can help her… I see it now."

"Then you must not die for now," Nicks was now holding a scythe. Where it came from, I could not tell you, but it was huge - standing taller than him, the blade hung over his head. He stepped back and swung the mighty scythe through the air, and the blade passed right through the nurse and then through the vampire.

Nothing happened, no blood. It was as if the blade was nothing more than a hologram. Nicks faded away into the shadows of the room. Then it was like someone hit the play button and time resumed. The nurse was just about to squeeze the syringe when she grabbed her chest.

The vampire snapped, "Hurry up. What's wrong with you?"

Her eyes rolled back as she fell to the ground in a spasm. The vampire bitched as he moved around to check on her. "We don't have time for this. What is… ahhh!" He hadn't made it around the bed when he pulled his arms around his chest in pain. Seconds later he fell to the ground.

I suddenly felt good, not great, but good. I heard a voice fill the room and knew at once that Nicks was speaking. "Visit your family. There you will find my daughter, and you will offer your life to her."

I pulled out my IV and got out of bed. Stepping over the dead vampire, I went to the restroom to go pee. It was a wonderful thing, not having to use a bedpan. I had some clothes tucked away in the closet. I hurried as fast as an old man could. I knew this would be my last night in this dying body.

The walk was refreshing, and I hadn't left the hospital for weeks. It was well past ten at night as I passed under one streetlight after another. I didn't understand it, but I knew that Nicks was with me. When I left the hospital, no one stopped me. I walked like a ghost, but the ache in my knees and shoulders reminded me that I was very much alive.

It was a long walk from the hospital to the cemetery where my family rested. Somehow I made it, without even taking a break. My body hurt, but it was manageable and unimportant. I arrived at the cemetery. A large stone wall encircled the cemetery, and black steel gates denoted entrances. Normally at this hour they were closed and locked. I wondered how I might scale the wall. I didn't have to, as the gates opened before me. I passed under the black steel arch where the words "Weaver Cemetery" were written in black steel bars.

Standing before the graves of my wife and son brought me to my knees. "I'll soon be with you my love. I'm so sorry... for everything." I stood up. My mind was muddled due to age and the fact I had walked across the entire city. I found my way over to a concrete bench, knees killing me.

I sat there half asleep when I noticed her. I did not hear her approach. She stood ten feet away and looked beautiful. It took me a moment to recognize her without the Goth makeup and black hair. "I have to say, you're much prettier as a blonde."

"Huh? Oh, that's right, last you saw me I had it dyed black." She paused as her fingers absentmindedly combed her hair. I thought she might not speak again, "I am so sorry for what I did to you."

"I'm dying, old, and very tired. I don't see a reason to worry about the past. I tried to protect your father, but in the end you didn't kill him or me. No harm, no foul. I don't mean to rush, but I feel like..."

"... Shit," she finished my sentence with a smile. "I just need information, whatever you can tell me."

Nicks came forth from the shadows, and she seemed a little surprised, "Father, it is good to see you. How did you leave the library?"

Nicks smiled, "As it is with you. I am short on time here, take this man's blood. I have used the last of resource to help you my daughter. All my hope is in you."

Melabeth looked surprised, "I certainly hope I can do what needs to be done. I will do my best, but if I feed from Alex, he'll die."

"I know," Nicks confirmed. "He will be a spirit, and he will serve you. By taking his blood, you will bind him. Your power works differently than mine. Bow has been bonded to her violin in death. Alex will bind his spirit to whatever object he found most valuable in life. It could be his home, and that would be hard to travel with. By taking his blood and his life, he will be bound to you until his spirit finds peace."

She had begun to say, "But..."

I interjected, "I am ready."

Nicks added, "And I must go. I love you, dear, and come to the library soon. I am sure Alex will lead you where I could not."

"Bye Father, love you. I will see you soon." With that Nicks shrunk back into the shadows and disappeared. She turned to me, "I suppose we will have plenty of time to talk when you die."

I chuckled, "And here I thought I would get some rest in death."

She sat next to me and took me gently into her arms. Her face dropped to my neck. It was like falling asleep.

Chapter 30 Preparing

I watched Alex's spirit jumping, running and acting like a fool. His real body lay dead on the graves of his family. His spirit was not that of an old man, but rather a young one. I never knew the young Alex and he wasn't bad looking, brown hair that matched his eyes, a nice cleft chin went well on his boxy face.

He ran up to me, "Not even out of breath. I've forgotten what it feels like to run, hell, to move without pain."

"That's fine and all, but we have work," Bow said annoyed.

He smiled at her, "We do. It's hard to work, or even think when you're old - you're always tired. Not old anymore, that's for sure. Give me a minute."

He then proceeded to run through the graveyard. Bow informed me, "You have control over him."

"I don't care," I said flatly. She huffed back, but said no more about it.

Alex came back running at me at full force; he slid to a stop right before my feet. His antics brought a smile to my face. He smiled back, "I love that look on your face. As happy as I am to put it there, I'm afraid I must remove it."

"I know," I have been dreading this. He was a great detective, and I was sure he understood more about what was going on than I did. I really feared knowing who my friends actually were. "Ok, tell me what you know."

He looked thoughtful, "First, let us talk about the facts. These are the things that we believe are true. One, the magic book is the cause of all this and we must find it. Two, the last person we know to have it was Richard Alexander Longaeva. Three, Alice White and Luna Longaeva are in the center of this mystery. What their part is we shall discover."He picked himself off the ground and began to walk as he talked, "What do you know of Alice?"

I gave him a run down. She was a four-hundred-year-old vampire that manipulated everyone. She was controlling and childlike, but smart and always seemed to be a step ahead of everyone else. I also told him about what Dan had told me, that perhaps I was some great-great-great niece. He stood quiet and still as I tried to explain how that might make her somehow involved in my murder.

I explained how it made me feel, and yet, somehow, I still wanted to believe that she hadn't betrayed me. My next move was to find Ezra and see if he could help me with rescuing Alice from the circus, or maybe she didn't need to be rescued? Perhaps she was in league with this Adder who ran the circus.

Finally, I stopped rambling. He gave me a second to make sure I was done. "You've given me some pieces of the puzzle, but not enough. I've heard of the circus and a wizard named Adder who runs it. You know what I think? I think Alice does not have the book... I mean, why take it to Adder? Alice isn't the kind of person who shares. Can you see her sharing power? Let alone be under someone else's power, and she would be under this Adder's power if she were to give him the book.

"No, she doesn't have it, and I dare say she might really be in trouble, but before we can rescue her, we must find someone who knows more about The Dark Circus. Also, it might be wise to try to obtain the book first. I think we need to take this back, back to the beginning, and, between the two of us, maybe, we can figure out where the book really is."

"The beginning of this story clearly starts with my rape in 1975," I said bitterly.

Alex nodded, "Yes, that's where it begins. If, what you told me about Alice is accurate, then it could mean that she offered you up for the spell."

It hurt so bad to hear that, "You think so?"

Alex's face was full of sympathy, "It's a possibility, but not a fact. Understand that we are dealing with possibilities and facts. Let's work out the story and see if the pieces of the puzzle stay together. If she offered you up, maybe she didn't know the particulars of the spell. I've read Alice's history. In her history I can only point out two things that show she might have a heart. One, she adores children and kills anyone who hurts them. Two, she has been a protector of women in the same manner."

What he said made me feel better, but only a little bit. "Yeah, this is true."

"Let us say that Alex stole the book. He could not have done this without Luna knowing about it. Maybe she didn't know until after he stole it, but she knew soon enough. I know that, while I was investigating several murders in the supernatural world, that she was, and is, committing murder to cover up her part in the use of that book.

"The chances are that she had my family and me killed, to silence us for the same reasons. This leads me to believe that she was well aware of the spell he cast and the use of you as a sacrifice. From everything I remember of you rising in 1990, I do believe they had no idea *you* would happen."

I agreed, "I don't think they knew about Nicks. I watched the video of my rape and murder. I watched them cast the spell and drink my blood. I'm not sure what they were expecting, but it was clear they didn't believe the spell worked."

Alex nodded, "Then that's confirmed. The next part is how you came to know Alice."

"By chance I would say. I mean I traveled with David to his parents' house. I was looking for someone to help guide me, and I had no idea of how to be a vampire."

Alex held up a finger, "I don't believe in chance. When I was helping you and David, I did a little background check on Alice. You would be interested to know that Alice bought that house, the day before you arrived in Beaumont with David."

"How would she have known?" I was dismayed at where this conversion was going. "I met David, and he had no idea about vampires or magic for that matter. So who could have told her?"

Alex eyed me funny, "What did you say about David? He had no idea about magic?"

"Yes," I remembered it like it was yesterday. "I remember meeting him on a bus. I was trying to get to California. I had been thrust into a crazy world, and it had only been my third day. Two days prior I killed three men and made a new friend who happened to be a ghost. It was all so much to take in... and then there was David.

"He made me feel safe, and he was going through the same thing. He had just discovered his powers, and his father was a normal human. He was heading to his mother's house because she was a witch and would be able to help him. We were able to help each other."

Alex's face looked more than a little concerned. "I see now."

"See what?" I demanded.

"See David," Alex said with a gleam in his eye. "Just listen for a minute."

Now I was worried, "Ok."

"Tony, David's stepdad was my friend for many years. In fact, I was his best man at his wedding. David was little then, maybe two. Mab didn't argue with his biological father about who would raise him not because she didn't want to. It was because his father is a terrible wizard and involved with the mob. There is no way that David had just discovered his powers, and I have a sneaky suspicion that I wouldn't have to dig too deep to find a connection to Richard Longaeva and David's father.

"I remember when Tony called me to tell me that David had suddenly moved in. At the time they didn't know he was a necromancer, but they sure as hell knew he had magic. Why lie? My guess would be... yes, that's why."

His realization of something made my stomach tighten even harder, "Not following you, why would he lie to me?"

Alex was pacing, and his eyes were closed. His mind was putting together the pieces of the puzzle that I had never seen. "It's the way you described your first time when you met him. He was in the same boat; you both discovered things together. He most likely told you he was your age, but he was much older." I nodded, confirming his hunch about what age David had told me. "You trusted him, because he had the same problems. Let me ask you one question; how did you find Alice?"

A tear slipped down my cheek, "Can I trust no one? He sent me; he told me about some vampires that lived on Mile High Road. In fact, once I got to the place, I had no idea where to look. Alice found me. You could say... that she had been waiting."

Alex shook his head, "I'm so sorry, Melabeth. No matter the pain, we must find out the truth, ok?" I nodded, "Good. I helped you and David with destroying The Order. I realized how out of control you both had become, so I stopped feeding you information. In the beginning, I really wanted to help you get your revenge on the men who killed you, but it just became a bloodbath. After you broke free of David, you came to see me. We both recall that little visit, and that's when you talked me out of the information on your biological father."

"Sorry about that," I truly felt bad.

Bow hadn't said anything until now, "You'll have to tell me about that later. I'm sure it will be entertaining."

Alex ignored her, "Water under the bridge. Where was I? Oh yes, after you visited me, then you went to seek vengeance on your father. We both know how that went. Fill me in on how you came back and what you have been up to."

"First we find a place to sleep. It will not be long before the sun rises."

Bow added, "Better yet, while you sleep, I'll show young Alex here around the library. Let me fill him in; ghosts don't sleep."

"The library?" Alex inquired.

Bow clarified, "It is where ghosts go during the day. The place between life and death, you'll like it. There are lots of books. Most spirits can't remember being there when they were on this plane, but you're special. Or rather, Melabeth is."

Alex responded, "Sounds like fun. Melabeth; tomorrow when you're not sleeping, start thinking about how to enter into vampire society. I think I have a plan. We'll talk more tomorrow when I'm all caught up."

"Sounds good," I agreed. I took to the air with both spirits in tow, forced to follow me. Bow always disappeared and never made a noise. Alex was hoping and a hollering about how cool it was to be flying. Normally I would be very unhappy about such a tagalong, but, in truth, any distraction was a good distraction.

The next few days I spent wandering around LA hiding in abandoned buildings talking about my life with Alex. He was very intense when he found out how I met David recently and how powerful he had become. He also questioned me about his creation of Zombies.

Alex walked around the old factory where I was staying. He looked like he was lost. Finally, he said, "You look like shit, Melabeth."

"*Excuse me?*" He caught me off guard.

"I've been with you for three nights. In those three nights, you haven't bothered to bathe or get a clean pair of clothes. Look at that top; there's a big hole in the chest. It looks as if someone tried to stake you. Is that dry blood all over your clothes?"

"Yes…" I was almost crying as I looked down at myself.

"Melabeth, I know it's a lot to ask you for your trust, so I won't. Instead, I want you to realize that I'm attached to you, and my peace will come when we bring these people to justice. It also might mean that we save the world while we're at it.

"I think I understand some things that you don't. You don't need to worry about that, because your ignorance is a part of my plan. You need to stop moping around because you lost your boyfriend. Get up, get dressed, and most of all, do what I say."

I thought about what he said for a second or two, "Ok. Why not? I suck at understanding the big picture and apparently I'm no good at judging others. So what would you like me to do?"

Alex smiled and looked very surprised, "Well, that went much better than Bow said it would. Ok, great, here's what I need you to do. I need you to find some clean clothes and a little bit of money. Then, you need to go to some local clubs and find other vampires. Use your real name, and, if anyone attacks you or gets in your way, fight them."

He stopped speaking as I sat there waiting for him to go on. "Wait, is that it? What else do I need to do?"

"Nothing, just do what I told you and our enemies will come to us. I should warn you some serious shit will happen to you. If I'm half as smart as I think I am, they won't kill you, but if I'm wrong… well, you get the point."

I was confused, "What enemies am I looking to provoke?"

Alex smiled, "All of them. Luna will come for you first, but trust when I say, she will not kill you. We need to know what she knows and this is the only way I know about finding out. If I give you too much information she might be able to get it out of you. For now you're on your own, I will return to you when you need me."

"Where are you going?" I asked.

"To the library, I'll be able to watch you from there. Nicks has shown me that everyone that passes through, leaves their knowledge behind in the form of books. While you get captured, I'll be researching."

Unbelievable, "You *want* me to get captured?"

Alex shook his head, "See, no more talk. What I want you to do is fight anyone who gets in your way. If they capture you, so be it, but don't you dare let them. Fight them with everything you got… understand?"

I put my hands on my hips, "No, not really. Just go; I can handle it, clean up and go to some parties. If anyone gets in my way, it's *go* time, that's not a problem. Just do me one favor super detective."

His eyes were a little wary of my request, "What would that be?"

"Find out, or come up with a plan to help me write my wrongs with Adam."

Alex's face filled with pity, "That would be my pleasure. He's a fool if he doesn't forgive you."

"Thanks," and with that he floated off and disappeared. I looked down at my ratty clothes, it's time to go shopping.

Chapter 31 Hearts Pub

I felt good as I twirled around in front of the mirror. I was wearing long stockings with large vertical red and black stripes. The shoes were red with large heels and matched the skirt. The skirt wasn't skin tight and flowed nicely. To top it all off, a black, long sleeved shirt that didn't cover my belly. A silver skull was on the front of the shirt; some cheap silver jewelry finished the outfit nicely. My hair was braided, and I was ready to go.

I looked like half the girls in LA with my outfit and blonde hair. The only thing that stood out was the fact that a violin hung off my shoulder resting against my back. The bow was slid through a cheap black belt. I laughed when I realized I was carrying it like a sword.

I was in a little punk shop I found and, fortunately, I happened across a few men who didn't mind giving me some money. I tossed my old clothes in a waste basket and proceeded to the cash register where a very bored girl awaited me. She was dressed in more colors than the rainbow; tattoos and piercings were everywhere. She stared dreamily at me, "Find everything?"

I tossed the tags on the counter, "Yeah, ring those up… please." I was looking at all the knickknacks on the shelf and around the register when I noticed a pack of cards. I picked it up and tossed it in front of the girl, "This too."

She gave me a look as if to say, "You want me to ring up more. Do you think I'm your slave?"

I tossed her a wad of cash. She looked at the bloody money, and her eyes tightened, "What? Can't afford tampons?"

I had given her more than enough, "Keep the change." I left without another word.

The poor girl had no idea that she was playing with fire. I was moody, lonely and just plain mean right now. I was proud of myself for not taking that money and shoving it up her... I realized I was squeezing my fist. I needed anger management… bad.

There weren't a lot of trees in Southern California, but I found a large oak tree overlooking a small neighborhood. I took refuge on a high branch, straddling it; I enjoyed the night's cool air. I lay my violin out before me resting on the branch. I then pulled out the deck of cards and found the Ace of Hearts. Bow materialized above me, floating like a cloud of mist.

She watched me with a sour face, as I laid the ace upon the violin. I asked, "Can you make this a part of the violin?" Somehow I knew she could.

"It will be ugly," she complained. She closed her eyes as her face tightened in disgust. I watched in awe as the card melted into the violin.

The violin had been already a dark brown that in dim lighting appeared to be black. Now the Ace of Hearts with white backing and red letters showed brightly in the corner of the instrument. It looked like it had been painted on and then many layers of gloss placed over it. The whole instrument looked so shiny it appeared to be wet. "Thanks," I said happy with how it turned out.

"Don't thank me," she sneered. "Why did you want that anyway?"

I explained, "I have a plan. The guys who so graciously donated money for my outfit also donated a smart phone. I searched some information about some local clubs. It wasn't hard to find the one I was looking for. I found a club called the Fly Trap, and it had good reviews. In the basement of the same building there is another club called The Hearts Pub. It has bad reviews, mainly because no one can get in. I read a reviewer whining about how the bouncer will ask you to declare yourself, but then he doesn't let anyone in.

"I noticed another comment saying that they noticed that the members would show a playing card, and then the bouncer would let them in. He hadn't been able to figure out what card to show; he figured it would take no more than fifty-one tries to get in, but he is wrong. The bouncer is really just asking you to declare yourself, and the vampires are showing their status."

Bow laughed, "Oh, I get why the club upstairs is called the Fly Trap. They come up from The Hearts Pub and feed on the guest at the Fly Trap, clever. Still, how can they be so obvious? What about vampire hunters?"

"Vampires are powerful, especially older ones. Don't you think that the vampires have powerful wizards and witches of their own? I mean the blood of a vampire can keep you young and alive for hundreds of years… and not to mention being under the spell of the vampire. There are spells of protection for vampires as well. I doubt any cross or magical item that would hurt a vampire will work within the halls of that club. Hell, fire might not even burn. Alice told me about all kinds of tricks, trust me, the hunters are fighting a losing battle if they step foot anywhere near that club."

Bow thought about it, "I can see why the magic users are so afraid of the vampires joining with necromancers. What about the werewolves?"

"Shifters, like Spooky, are known to help both sides. Werewolves are diseased, and neither side wants anything to do with them."

"I see," Bow looked lost in thought then finally asked. "Do you trust this Alex's idea of coming out of the shadows? Once you announce that you are Melabeth, the Ace of Hearts, there will be no going back."

"I know, that's my favorite part. I like the idea of leaving the shadows. I don't want to go back. As far as trusting him, I really can't say that I trust anyone right now, but Nicks, and Nicks trust Alex. I guess I will find out if he's better at judging people than I am."

Arriving around ten, I stood across the street from the Fly Trap. The name of the place was displayed on a giant neon sign in black light. The building and surrounding streets were well lit. The place seemed lively and inviting.

The front of the building had a large valet area before the front door. A line formed and wrapped clear around the side of the building. I was surprised considering how late it was. I crossed the street and circled around back. In the back of the building there was an alley, but this too was well lit as a steady line of cars drove in. The ally led to the parking lot.

Midway down this side of the building was a staircase headed down into the ground. I looked down to see a landing where a big bald man sat on a bar chair leaning against the wall. Next to him was a door; above the door in plain letters it said, Hearts Pub. Well, I was here.

As I came to the last step, the big man's deep voice boomed, "Are you lost?"

His voice startled me, I had been lost in thought, and he was so loud. He smirked at my reaction. I answered meeting his eyes, "No."

His grin stayed as he asked me, "Declare yourself?"

At this point I flipped my violin off my shoulder and showed it to him. This time he was startled by my quick movement and the fact that I pulled an object out from behind me. It took him just a moment to realize that I wasn't pulling a weapon on him. It was my turn to smirk.

He puzzled over my violin for a moment or two. I was beginning to think that I might have to point out the Ace of Hearts that was clearly marked on my instrument. Then he said much quieter, "Ace, huh?" Only I didn't really think he was asking, just surprised. He looked at me, and I strapped my violin on my back. He seemed worried, "Are you sure?"

I simply nodded. I was sure he was asking like this was some kind of joke. I would bet that most Aces don't arrive unannounced. I eyed the door, "Must I open it myself?"

"Oh, no ma'am," He quickly grabbed the door and held it open. He stood as if he were standing at attention.

I walked inside the door, and it quietly closed behind me. I worked my way down a short hallway that opened up into a big hall. I expected more noise, perhaps dancing. Instead, I came into a large room with pop music playing softly in the background. The dance floor was empty, but it took up most of the center of the room. Off to each side of the large wooden floor were carpeted areas that were full of comfortable-looking love seats.

Men and women filled both sides of the room. There were tables next to the love seats where glasses sat; the liquid levels in them were in various degrees of consumption. There were flat screens across the wall and some of the vampires were playing video games. Across the room, along the wall, was a huge bar with two bartenders, one on each side. They didn't look too busy, and only a couple of people sat at the bar itself. Rows of empty chairs sat in front of the bar.

I traveled across the empty dance floor and sat dead center of the bar. I could feel the eyes on me. With my second sight I could see that the bald man had come inside. He walked over to one side of the room and leaned down and spoke something into the ear of another vampire. He then hurried back outside, most likely to resume his post. They know I'm here now.

The bartender was a middle aged woman. She approached me and asked, "What can I get you?" Her... um, his over-the-top-voice brought a small smile to my face. The cross-dresser was all smiles as he awaited my response.

"Why don't you surprise me?"

"Sweetie, I'll knock your socks off." He was loud and animated. "Trust me, I'm about to blow your mind."

He went to work in a whirlwind of fury. A giggle escaped my lips, which only encouraged him to act even more outlandishly. With my second sight, I could see a man approaching me. He came to rest leaning on the bar facing me. The bartender slid the drink over to me. I caught it; I then turned to meet the man.

I was caught off guard. Before me stood the sexiest man alive and he was wearing a rust orange button up shirt that looked smart on him. He was smirking at me. I half screamed as I jumped to put my arms around him, "Michael, where have you been? It's been so long."

Michael sounded suffocated, "Too tight." I let go, and he laughed. "Wow, you're strong and I missed you too. What are you doing here?"

"I could ask the same of you. Where's Ezra?"

Michael shook his head, "I have no idea. We followed leads to some Dark Circus, and that's where Ezra believes Alice is. It's supposed to come to LA soon, but he found out information on the circus, and it appears it's like a roach hotel."

I laughed, "I know all about it and let me guess, he is off trying to figure out how one might get out?"

Michael winked, "Apparently your arrival in this city isn't that random. We should talk about this somewhere else." He said this as a young vampire woman passed down the long dance hall and to the other side. I nodded and Michael asked, "What happened to Adam? I was hoping to be able to meet this man. I mean I've heard all about him, love of your life, must be special."

I took a sip of the drink, "Wow, this is good." I could taste the blood infused with alcohol and who knows what else. I said it loud enough for the bartender to hear me. He smiled and yelled, "Thanks, gorgeous!" Then he went back to take another order.

Michael didn't miss a beat, "Uh oh, what happened?"

"Nothing," I responded quickly and then took another drink.

"Don't want to talk about it, must be your fault then. If it were his, you would be going off the deep end."

I smiled at him, "He found out that I killed his father."

"What?" he responded, surprised.

"Remember Aaron Reite?" Michael nodded. "Adam is his son."

He looked stunned, and then shook his head. "If it weren't for bad luck, you wouldn't have any luck."

"Funny, that's not how I see it. I feel very lucky, or perhaps blessed." Until now I hadn't really thought about it, but as soon as Michael said I was unlucky, I knew he was wrong.

He mocked me, "Oh, please tell. I mean I've known you a while and it always seems like there's another disaster around the corner."

I thought for a moment, "Well, let me see. Lots of bad shit has... and will happen to me, but in-between it all, good things have happened. I mean when you look at your life you can pick out the bad, or the good. I made friends, some more than others. I was able to make peace with my father and get to know my sister. Most people, who are raped and killed, stay dead.

"I found love, not the way I felt about David or the way I felt about your body, but love. Yes, I screwed it up, but I can't help but wonder if that didn't work out for the best. Once I forgive myself, I can return and see if he can forgive me. I can beg for his forgiveness and, in the end, even if he doesn't take me back, at least I got to love him."

"Beg? You mean grovel." He laughed, "You're a terrible liar. You're just glad he isn't here because, once again, it's Melabeth facing off God who knows what. If I my memory serves me, the people around you get killed."

I felt my anger rise up in me as the truth of what he said rang in my ears. "Doesn't mean I won't go back to him, when all this is done... if I survive it."

With a big smile, "And then beg?"

I shook my head and took a calming drink. This stuff is good. I need to get the recipe. "I don't think you need to worry about how I'll get him back. You're right, I'm glad he's not here. I would never have sent him away, but now he's gone. I still feel lucky that at least I loved him before I died. What about you? Did you feel that way when Lea died?"

His eyes lost contact with me, "I didn't love her, not like that. I loved her like a sister even though she was deeply in love with me. I know I'll sound like a jerk, but I'm happy I got with her before she passed. I know it was for all the wrong reasons, but she was so happy."

I wondered what had changed to make Michael finally get with her. I thought he had finally fallen in love, but now I didn't understand at all. "What made you do it? You shouldn't have taken the relationship to the next level, especially if you didn't love her."

"I've only loved two women in my life." His eyes were full of pain and fear, and it was brave of him to tell me his true emotions. "I loved Robin… she died when I tried to turn her. I also loved Lizze, but she died before her time as well." I started to say something, but he held up his hand to let him finish. "It's ok, it's not your fault, and it is. I've forgiven you for your part in Lizze's death.

"When Robin died, I became… a whore. I'm not proud of what I did and not all of it was in my control. I mean, how do you say no to someone like Alice or Charlotte? I was to serve the stronger vampires in any way they felt I should. I became ashamed of what kind of man I was. For the first time I was going to change my ways. If I were with you, Alice couldn't control me."

I teased him, "You're making me all weepy. Let's get out of here before I cry. We have other, more private matters to discuss." I was still blown away and suddenly remorseful for thinking bad about him. Ever since that cave, I lost respect for the man, but now I wondered what it was like to walk a mile in his shoes, to think that I was the hope he had for being free.

Michael nodded, and I finished off my drink. The bartender came over and asked, "Another?"

"No, thank you," I responded as I stood to leave.

The bartender cleared his throat, "Cash or credit, dearie?"

"Put it on my tab," I gave him a sharp look. "And the next time you clear your throat to speak to me, I'll cut your throat out." I changed my tone and smiled brightly, "Have a nice evening."

Michael laughed, "Tom, she's the Ace of hearts."

The bartender laughed nervously, "Oh, it's on me, of course. Come again and you can cut my throat anytime you feel like it." He then was speaking to the other bartender, "I would bleed for that girl anytime."

I ignored his remark. A young lady approached us carrying a small red cooler, "Your order." She handed it over to Michael, and he simply nodded.

We turned and left. Michael led me to his Chevy Camaro and before I knew it, we were flying down the road. Now that we were out of earshot, he asked, "So, why are you flaunting yourself? Up to now everyone thought you were dead, and, with Alice missing, this isn't a good time for you to pop up in LA."

I smiled, "Don't you worry your pretty little self about it. Where's Ezra?"

"Really don't know and furthermore don't want to get involved. You noticed the cooler." I nodded, "I have a young girl to take care of now and with the necromancers and Nosferatu on the loose I have to make sure she feeds."

"Well, I need details."

Michael nodded, "Of course you do."

Chapter 32 Zoey

Michael filled me in on his new daughter, of sorts. The way he spoke of her I knew at once he was in love. Apparently, after my death, Michael and Lea were finally allowed to live their own lives. Not long after they began their life together, Lea was killed in a car accident. Ezra was busy with Spooky or Alice. Michael had been living alone during most of this time.

Michael was lonely and just recently had been hanging with some local teenagers. One of the girls, Zoey, was dying of cancer. Being such a great guy, Michael started to give her his blood so that she might feel better, but she would die anyway. Now, according to what I've heard, most people have to be healthy to be turned, but this girl defied the fates and rose all the same.

Michael was very concerned with a newborn vampire. Enemies were everywhere, like the Nosferatu, a word I've heard a few times now. Alice calls them our unwelcome cousins. Like vampires, but not, they are monsters. And it is only too obvious that the necromancers were breeding them.

The way Alice described them to me was that they were vampires lost in the madness of blood. They got stronger with age, but seldom lived long because everyone hunted them like rats. Even vampires knew not to let these creatures roam the nights. The big difference between Nosferatu and vampires is the way we spread. They could change people easily and quickly with little failure. We, on the other hand, had to grow our numbers slowly, and only the strong lived long enough to become stronger.

I could see the deck being stacked, each side trying to get the upper hand on the other. Yet this was a war with no borders, and it was hard to determine friend from foe. I looked over at my friend as he filled me in on his life. I knew at once that I couldn't hang around him long, or else I might get him and his new daughter killed.

It wasn't long before Michael arrived at a five-story glass building. He waved a security card at the gate, and the gate slid open. The entrance, dropped down into an underground parking garage. Michael explained that this was one of the most secure apartments in LA. His apartment was on the top floor. The elevator opened into a small hallway with only two doors. He opened the door and invited me in.

I entered a large, beautiful apartment. It was huge and open with lots of plants. Fans moved the air, and it felt as if there was a breeze. The smell was that of a forest, and the apartment was decorated in earth tones, browns and dark woodwork. Somehow it felt classic, yet modern. The most amazing thing was all the green plants, trees and flowers. I could feel the moisture upon my skin. There were actual full grown trees, winding up the large ceiling.

In amazement, I remarked, "Wow, you've been suffering. This place is out of this world."

Michael laughed, "Yeah, it's been rough. A witch used to own this place and most of these plants have spells on them. It looks like crazy work to keep shit alive in here, but it just grows on its own."

I heard laughter from another room. It was just on the edge of my hearing, but I knew there was more than one person. I asked, "Zoey and friends?"

"Yes," he looked like he was lost in thought. "She really hasn't met any other vampires before." He read the shock on my face, "She's only a few weeks old. I never thought she would even rise."

"It takes days to rise. I have a hard time imagining that the family just buried the body without embalming it." Shame washed across his face. "You must have had some hope. You stole the body... right? Then you buried it, and waited?"

"I still... there's no way I would have guessed it would work. Everything they told me, they always said the healthy turn and the sick do not. Robin was healthy, but she stayed dead." He shook his head like he was trying to rid himself of a bad memory. "She's up there with her brother Tim and her best friend Rachael. I better get this to her," he held up the hand carrying the cooler. "Her friends are in danger if she becomes too hungry."

He headed up the stairs without me. I explored the apartment while he fed his child. I wandered around until I found the sliding glass door to his balcony. Walking outside I looked upon the city, taking in the noise and smells as they traveled through the wind. I was in a strange mood, ready for something to happen and hoping nothing would.

Alex stepped out of the shadows, his ghostly body forming. He smiled, "I will make this quick." A letter formed in his hand from smoke and shadow. He laid it down on a small table adjacent to a chair. "This is for your friend Michael. It is for his eyes only. Michael is on the phone now, and they are asking for you. Make him understand that he is to turn you over before reading this. Do you understand?" I knew what was about to happen. I simply nodded and turned to look over the city once more. Alex whispered in my ear, "Enjoy your evening. I do not envy you for the tests you will face." With his dire words I felt his spirit once again leave this realm of existence.

Michael stepped out onto the balcony. He made more noise than a vampire needed to; it was considered polite. He walked up next to me looking over the city. He spoke quietly, "Cream Puff called. He is of no importance, except for the fact he works for the king. He knows you're in town. Furthermore, he knows you're with me. Rumors travel fast."

I turned. His face was full of concern, "All that worry will give you wrinkles. Who the hell goes by the name Cream Puff?"

Michael smirked, "A lot of vampires take nicknames. The younger the vampire, the worse the nickname."

I could see how worried he was, "Before you get yourself all worked up, I wanted this. You are not to get involved, so, all you have to do is turn me over to them. I'll keep them busy, and you should be able to leave and take your ward with you."

"Ward?" He laughed at this. "You have been hanging with Alice too much. No one uses the word "ward" anymore." His voice went from funny to serious, "And how can I just stand aside?"

"Protect this girl and get Ezra." I gave him a serious look, "Do you trust me?"

He huffed at me, "Of course…"

I interrupted him, my voice full of force, "Do you trust me? With your life? I've been told that I'm going to save the world. Failure would be the end of my family, your family… everything."

Without a blink, "What do you require of me?"

"Turn me in and afterwards read that letter," I pointed over at the envelope. He eyed me funny, "Trust me when I say, I have no idea what's in that letter, but no more of that tonight. Tomorrow we shall face the lion in the den, but tonight we shall dance."

Michael smiled, "Let me get you a drink." He picked up the letter and escorted me inside. He opened a small wall safe behind a painting and put the envelope away. Then he went to the kitchen, returning with two glasses of bloodwine. "Here's to trust," he said as we shared a drink.

A few drinks later, I was feeling better about things. It didn't take long before Michael and I fell into a conversation about our lives. We missed each other over the years and had spoken little. I heard the sound of feet coming down the stairs. Michael heard them too and looked upset, "Dear brother, did you leave them with strict orders not to come and meet me."

"You have a temper," He was full of panic.

I giggled at this, "You're like a new father." He started to argue, but I wouldn't let him. "Come on, let me meet the girl."

Michael and I had been talking for at least an hour, but we spoke in volumes not much higher than mice squeaking. It wasn't that we were afraid someone would overhear our conversations or something; it's just that, when you hear as well we do, it becomes natural to speak quietly. His young, new creation most likely thought we had left as she moved around the lower part of the house. She was moving as quietly as she could, and I could imagine her peeking around corners. Michael was tight-lipped over the whole thing because we both could hear her as if she was standing next to us.

I can't say that it didn't hurt my feelings that Michael did not want his little monster to meet me. Of course, he did have a good point about my temperament, at least from his point of view. It had been years since he had hung out with me. I've learned to control and tried to convey it to him, "I solemnly swear, as a girl scout, that no harm shall fall upon this girl."

He spoke through clenched teeth, "If anything happens to her... I'll never forgive you." I clapped my hands together in excitement, and he quickly added, "Like hell you were a girl scout."

"Alice and I have uniforms and everything." If looks could kill, I would be dead. "Ok, no games. I will not act like Alice."

"Thanks, but no thanks. Let me send her away." He was unsure of me. It was my fault. The mere mention of Alice's name must have put thoughts of me tormenting the girl into his already-worried mind.

He stood up and left me in the room to go intercept the girl. I was trying not to pout. I poured another glassful and listened to Michael approach the girl. She about screamed, "Oh God, you scared me." She was new to let another vampire sneak up on her like that.

"What are you doing down here? I thought I asked you to remain in your room." Michael sounded like a scolding father, which brought a smile to my face. It was good to know he found something that made him so passionate.

She was full of spunk, "Why, who's here?" Her voice raised an octave when she asked this.

There was a moment of quiet, which led me to believe that Michael was in the midst of performing sign language. She responded in a much quieter, smaller voice, "I don't understand."

Michael almost growled, "This is not a private conversation."

I spoke loud and clear, "Truly it is not. Bring the girl out so I can meet her."

She finally caught onto the situation, "Who is that?" She whispered so quietly I almost didn't hear her.

Michael sounded so stressed, "You may as well go meet her. She can hear every last word we are saying. Come along now."

I stood up and moved into the center of the room. Michael came in the room first, the girl half hidden behind him. She was roughly my height and build. Her skin was olive, and her brown hair hung off her head in big brown curls. She was not overly thin, and her face was round, so it made her large brown eyes look even more alien. She was a very pretty girl and probably not much older than I was when I was turned.

Michael made the introductions. "Melabeth, may I present Zoey. Zoey, this is my sister Melabeth. Do not be rude, nor shorten her name. She likes to be called Melabeth."

Her voice was soft and nervous, "It's a pleasure to meet you. You are a vampire, right?"

"Sister," I moved to one side of her to get a better look. She jumped back almost knocking a plant over. "Relax darling, I just wanted to get a better look at you. Would you like a drink?"

She spoke to Michael, "Did you see how fast she moved?"

Michael shook his head, "Melabeth is acting very natural for a vampire of her… power. She will not hurt you." When he said those final words, he gave me his best death stare. That, of course, only made me smile.

Zoey was a great way to take my mind off things. She was so interested in everything vampire. Truly Michael never believed she would rise again, but he taught her nothing. She had lots of questions which I answered until

I became bored with them and changed the subject. It was so very interesting to see another story being played out before my own. Still, this was just a distraction, and it was not very long before I was helping Michael put the girl in bed.

When I walked upstairs to see Zoey off, I met her guest. Her brother and friend was really nice, but the whole time their hearts beat a million-miles-a-minute. It made me hungry, so I excused myself downstairs again. Shortly thereafter, Michael once again joined me. He was thankful for such a pleasant evening. That was his way of saying, thanks for not killing anyone.

I slept well that day and enjoyed my evening with both Michael and Zoey. Zoey's family had left during the day, probably a good thing. The sun barely set when Michael received a call. Zoey awoke later than us, and was just now joining us in the living room. Michael said very little and then hung up the phone. "They are ready to meet you, Melabeth. They told me where to bring you, but it's not one of our usual places to meet and greet. I smell a trap."

"I know, don't you worry about it. Just give me a ride, and remember you have this one to take care of." I gave Zoey a little smile.

Zoey's face was full of worry, "I don't want anything to happen to you, Melabeth." She truly meant this, and it warmed my heart.

"I'll be fine. Do me one favor?" She nodded in agreement. "Watch over him while I'm gone."

She surprised me when she gave me a hug. "It has truly been a privilege meeting you."

I tried not to sound too choked up, "You too, my new sister."

*　　　*　　　*

It wasn't long before I found myself standing in front of an old-looking building with Michael by my side. He whispered, "I don't like this."

I told him on the way over here that it was best if he pretended that he didn't care. I gave him a small growl; he needed to shut up. From here on in, there was no way to tell who might be listening. The building that stood before us was huge. It might have been a factory. I couldn't tell, but whatever it was, it was not anymore. You could smell the fact that nothing but rats lived here.

Two large doors stood wide open, and, next to the doors, stood guard. Two young-looking male vampires, dressed like this was some kind of ball.

They looked so out of place for the crappy dump they stood in front of. We walked forward coming to a stop in front of them.

They both gave a bow and then one of them said, "This way, they are awaiting you."

I looked over at Michael, "I will not be requiring your services."

Michael did his best to look as if this was all perfectly normal, "Of course. Goodnight and we will see each other later."

I nodded, and he left going in the other direction. No one moved to stop him, but I knew he would be stopped and questioned before he got free of this. Even if they scanned his head with some kind of spell, or used vampire trickery to get him to talk, he knew nothing. Deep down I didn't believe they would spend much time messing with him. It was me that they wanted.

I followed the two men down an old hallway. It came to an end at two huge wooden doors. I knew they were magical, and I knew this was a trap, but I would go forward. I slid my violin loose, holding the instrument in one hand and the bow in the other. The vampire gave a strange look at my violin, but said nothing. They hadn't bothered to search me for weapons.

They opened the doors; both stood to one side and ushered me inside. As I stepped from the hallway through the doors, I was momentarily blinded by the light. As my vision cleared, I heard the doors slam behind me. I now understood what kind of trouble I was in.

Chapter 33 Arena

Once my eyes adjusted to my new surroundings, it did not take me long to realize I was in an arena.

The ground was hard, packed dirt surrounded by an old stone wall. Rows of seats rose above the wall that encircled the coliseum. The heads of the onlookers looked to be growing ever higher and further away. The crowd did not cheer or scream, but rather sat in silence as I entered into the center of the arena. The wall that encircled me was not the only thing that held me. There was a giant dome-shaped net that made a roof over my head, but it allowed the crowd to look through and see me.

I didn't know for a fact, but I was sure that I could not easily break this net. I was sure it was magical. So much for flying out of this mess. The wall itself was not plain brick, but rather a dark, aged brick. Arched doorways stood every few feet, but it appeared that most of the doors were just bricked in. I glanced behind myself from where I had entered and could not make out a door of any kind.

A few rows up from the front row, was a deck. It stood higher than the seats around it. Grand chairs sat upon the deck. In the center sat a large seat that stood higher than the rest. A small woman who didn't look much bigger than a child sat still as a statue. I was sure I knew who I faced.

My eyes focused in on this woman, and she was truly alien. Her skin first appeared to be white, but when I examined it closer, there was a blue tint. Her hair was as white as snow and hung loose and straight. Her long, pointy ears stuck out with silver jewelry pierced along the edges. Her eyes were huge and gray, looking at me with slow and steady blinks. If my guess was right, this was the last full-blooded elf in the world.

"Welcome," the strange girl said. She had not spoken loudly and was quite a distance from me. Still, it was as if she spoke into a microphone, and her voice was clearly heard throughout the arena. "I am Luna Longaeva, and this is my court."

Her face was devoid of emotion, but she appeared to be pleasant. I spoke unnecessarily loud, my voice was amplified as well, "Thank you." Knowing this was the mother of Richard Alexander, a rapist and murderer, made my blood boil. Deep down I couldn't help but think she could have stopped what happened. I really wondered what her part in all this was, and just maybe I would find out. "Why have you called me here?"

With no change in facial expression, she stood, and, even though she was far above me, I could tell she was not tall. She moved toward the front of her platform and looked down at me. "I have nothing to say to the likes of you." Her words were cold but not her demeanor. "Perhaps an old friend would be more welcoming." The last part was for the crowd. They now screamed in delight.

My instrument turned into my swords that now hung to the left of me. The elf lifted an eyebrow at this, but said nothing as she returned to her seat. One of the stone arches darkened, and, even though no physical door had opened, there was now an entrance. What appeared to be a knight stepped out, and the wall closed behind him.

The man who stood before me was tall and well built. He wore chainmail covered in armor plating with a white tunic over it. A large red cross adorned the center of his tunic, and a large knight's sword hung at his side. His helmet covered his head and his face. He lifted the steel visor. I could see him clearly now as he sneered at me.

My heart dropped, Peter Lionheart stood before me. "Peter, long time, no see."

He drew his sword with a sweeping motion. He turned and faced Luna, "For you, mother." She barely even nodded as he turned to face me. His sword at the ready and anger in his eyes, "If you would have chosen me, things could have been different." He dropped his visor.

"Oh, I doubt that. Once a momma's boy, always a momma's boy."

Anger rolled through his body, "I will enjoy teaching you some manners."

Before I could get my smart-ass remark out, he launched at me. I didn't wait for him to arrive as I flashed forward to meet him.

Our swords met headlong as we battled for all it was worth. It didn't take long to realize that both our styles were completely different as were our strengths and weaknesses. I was faster, or perhaps more agile. Of course, I was not wearing armor either. It felt like he could be stronger, but, once again, his large sword and armor took this advantage away. On the other hand, I could not take a chance of being hit at all. That sword would carve me up.

He was more than a little surprised to find that I was faster, stronger and more skilled with a sword. I found out quickly enough that my blade would not slice through his armor. There was little doubt that his weapons and armor were magical in nature. There was no sword that could have taken the pounding I had given his without breaking.

He kicked me, throwing me backwards. I responded by going with it, falling into a back roll and coming up to my feet. His swing was already upon me, but I was ready. My second sight allowed me to react when most would not. I blocked his blade, stepped in and gave him a hard elbow to the side of his helmet. This of course did not hurt him, but it did throw him off balance. He tried to counter his forward motion and at the same time bring his blade down on me. This was his undoing; he had not properly found his footing, and his swing was much too high. I stepped underneath it. With a clear line of sight, I brought a powerful stroke across his neck.

His head would have been cut clean off it wasn't for the chainmail around his scrawny little neck. Still, my cut had gone deep, and the chainmail had not completely stopped it as blood poured down his chest. He was using his left hand, trying to stop the blood while making wild swings with his right.

He tried to keep me at bay while he healed, but I changed tactics and simply aimed for his sword arm. I caught the inside of his elbow. Once again, his armor saved his arm. Still, he yelped in pain, dropping his sword. He flashed backwards, his back now up against the wall.

He could not speak because of his neck wound. I mocked him, "I don't believe that I will be saving your life this time."

The thought that this was a little easier than it should have been, did cross my mind. I was preparing to finish him when my second sight caught another figure enter the arena. Being that Peter was hurt, I took my chance turning to face the new opponent.

The man that walked into the arena was cocky. The way he walked, the way he grinned at me, everything said cocky. He looked a lot like Peter but skinnier. Even though he was not any taller he looked all stretched out. He wore the same tunic with chainmail but no plate armor or helmet. His hair was long and pulled into a ponytail. He sported a long goatee that somehow made him look even cockier.

He was full of energy, "I am so very pleased to meet you." He gave a little bow. "I am Peter's brother, Luke. I have heard so much about you. In eight hundred years, I've never seen a woman turn my brother's head, but at last, here you are, so close to head in hand. So pretty, I could see what he likes about you."

"I'm about to show you why he should find someone else," I threatened.

He chuckled darkly, "I've told him, but he didn't hear my cries for sanity. Woman are like horses, they just need to be broken." He pulled two battle axes out from behind his back.

I readied my sword.

He looked like he was walking toward me, but he was moving way too fast. My reaction was almost not fast enough as he struck at me. He moved like the wind and without hesitation. Even my second sight fought to keep up with him and, as we broke away from our first entanglement, I hadn't even realized how many times he had sliced me.

Thin lines of red blood were smeared on the edge of his hatchets. I pulled my smaller sword… I must move faster.

The next few seconds were blindingly fast. I flashed while I swung, blocked or moved. The few times my swords found their target, his chainmail protected him, but I could not say the same. My shirt and skirt were in pieces.

We circled each other. He had a nasty grin. He looked confident. His victory was just around the corner. What had he given up for all that speed? He was thin, unlike his brother, but he was still bigger than me. Size has nothing to do with it in this world. I tightened my grip on my handle; I could feel Bow's mind working with mine.

We attacked. This time I didn't worry about his little blows, but instead swung through him like he was made of paper. He tried to side step me, but I wasn't that slow. As our weapons entangled, I head-butted him with all my might. His nose exploded in blood as I heard the sound of breaking bones.

He staggered; I gave him no quarter and attacked him with one blow after another. Not only was I stronger than him, I healed faster, and it wasn't long before he fell at my feet. Blood pooled around him while he moaned in pain. I kicked him in the side, and his body slid across the ground.

My victory was short lived. I turned to face what I believed was the recovered Peter. A new man stood there as fear washed through me. The last brother... he had similar looks and the same physical height. That is where their resemblance ended. He was huge in his chest, and he looked to be as wide as he was tall. He might have had chainmail, but his full plate armor covered every last inch of him. His visor was up, and his long unkempt beard hung out. His eyes almost appeared to be sunken in his face.

He held a giant war hammer in one hand and in the other, a bible with a thick leather cover. He spoke and sounded concerned, "We have not met, young miss. I am Matthew, one of The Apostles. I see you've met my brothers." He said the last part with a grin. I nodded, and he asked, "Young lady, do you know Jesus Christ as your savior?"

"I know him, just got done telling him to open the gates of Hell for three more."

He nodded his head in agreement, "True, true. We are all damned, but I am afraid we will be sending you ahead. I just hate to send someone to her Maker without a proper intervention first. Just remember, all you have to do is to ask him to forgive your sins and forever you will be in the kingdom of God. Are you ready to meet your Lord and Savior, or your damnation?"

Staring evenly at him, "I am, how about you?"

He laughed deep and loud, "I don't need forgiveness, I'm an Apostle. My word is "His." He dropped his visor and let out a battle cry.

Somehow, I doubt I was stronger.

Matthew was a stalemate. I could not cut through his armor, and he was way too slow to hit me. Of course, if he did, he might break me for good. He complained that I fought like a coward and a woman. None of this would have bothered me, but I had plenty of time to take in the scenery. Peter and Luke were just standing together watching the battle. Both of them had ample time to heal and gather their weapons.

I was wondering how much longer my battle with the human tank would go on and what I would do about the other two if I won. My question was answered when Luna spoke in a very bored voice, "I have seen enough."

I now found myself encircled by all three brothers. I was good enough to beat two of them one at a time. Maybe I would get lucky so I prepared myself for battle. I moved like lightening as I fought all three brothers and, for a split second, I thought I might just hold my own.

I managed to slit open Luke's leg and stab Peter. Matthew came in like an out-of-control dump truck, trying to hit me with his hammer. I jumped over his head and landed behind him. As he pulled backwards recovering from a massive swing, I plunged my sword in his back. With one mighty push my sword broke his armor and punched out the other side.

He screamed and fell to his knees. My victory was short lived, because I had to use my small sword to fend off an attack from Peter. My right hand was fighting to pull my sword out of the armor, but he was twisting around and going berserk.

Between the blood and being swung around, I lost grip of my sword. I didn't have time to think about this as Luke attacked me, and I found myself defending his fast blows with one short sword. They finally overwhelmed me when Peter cut my left arm off and my short sword fell to the ground.

Luke and Peter took swipes at me until I lay on the ground, with no arms from the elbows, and no legs from the knees. The pain rushed through my body quickly, and I wouldn't have to endure it long. My body was fighting to heal, to stop the bleeding. Still, I could feel my hair wet with my blood as it pooled around me.

Matthew stood over me, he smiled, "Amazing. You cut right through my armor... truly a pleasure."

The last thing I saw was Matthew's hammer heading towards my face.

*   *   *

My vision spun, unable to focus on anything. My head pounded; it kind of felt like a hangover, no, it felt like someone hit me with a giant hammer.

As I became more aware, I realized I was hanging from chains in the middle of a large dark room. My vision cleared just a little. I noticed the chains came down and attached to shackles, which were wrapped around my arms just above the elbows. The reason for this was that my forearms had not yet grown back. It was strange, because I swore I could feel my hands, even though they were not there.

I hung suspended in the air with half legs and arms. Not surprisingly, I was naked, not that there was much left of my clothes by the end of the battle. Still, a little bit of humility would have been nice. The place was large and I felt that I might be underground. The air was wet with a deep musty smell to it. With my second sight I could see I was in an oddly shaped room, partly round at one end and square on the other. Five different entrances with no doors connected to this room.

On the ground was a large circle with all kinds of symbols in it. I had no idea what kind of power it held, but I could take a wild guess. I doubt even if I were to break free of these chains, I could leave. Not that I had the power left in me to re-grow my limbs, and, without those, escape seemed impossible.

The minutes turned into hours as I hung in silence. I could hear nothing but some mice moving around in the dark. The air was cold and even though I didn't get cold, it was still uncomfortable. I nodded off a few times, but I was starting to suffer from a case of the boredoms. I sang and whistled, but the rats never spoke a word back to me.

I was just starting to think about how Alex might have been a great detective but was incompetent with plans. I was supposed to go around and let everyone know that I was in town. He told me to make sure no one got in my way. In my mind I was going to fight off hundreds of fools who thought they could stop Melabeth... so much for being an unstoppable badass. First sign of trouble and they capture me.

I was almost nodding off again when I heard the sound of footsteps. The room slowly filled with light as the quiet steps fell softly and came closer. They reminded me of Alice, close together, someone with a short stride. Alice did not come into the room; Luna did. She was wearing a bright green dress with light brown accents. It was very pretty and made her look fuller than she really was. She was tiny and now that I was up close, I could tell that Alice was even bigger than this woman.

Her hair still fell free, and her face was still soft and almost had a kind look about it, but I had no illusions that she was going to be kind to me. She came to a stop in front of me. Snapping her fingers, the vines burst forth from between the stones on the ground. They swirled and twisted behind her, becoming ever thicker until they formed a large chair. She sat down without a word on her chair of vines and stared at me.

Her staring went on for at least ten minutes. I didn't want to be the first who spoke, but she was starting to unnerve me. Finally, she noted, "Staring at one mistake does not change it."

I spit back, "Wisdom from your parents, I'd assume. Right after they stopped looking at you."

It took a second, then she cracked a smile. "Peter said you had a sharp tongue. And you are pretty, I can see that. Still, I cannot see what he saw in you."

"Good," I responded. I hung quietly waiting for her demands. She just stared at me, making me feel uncomfortable. I decided, if she didn't want to ask, I didn't want to talk to her. Plus, she was weird. We sat in silence for what felt like an hour. It was too much for me, I broke, "What the hell do you want?"

No facial changes, not even a frown, just the same relaxed look since she walked in the door. She waited a long few seconds before answering me. "I wish you to serve me. I have lots of servants, but there is always room for one more."

"I would," shaking my head in false sorrow. "Just that, well, I'm just tied up right now."

She didn't respond to my wisecrack; instead, she explained. "I have servants with all their arms and legs to retrieve things for me. I require your knowledge, and that is how you may start serving me."

"Oh, I would love to! Where would you like to begin? ABC… or perhaps you need help counting?"

She nodded, "Peter thinks it will take a lot to break you. Do you know what I think?"

I laughed, "It's hard to find grown up clothes?"

"I think it will be easy. Tomorrow, you will tell me what I want to know and be ready to serve me." Her facial expression never changed, and she spoke and acted as if this was no big deal. It made me angry; she must have noticed, "Anger won't help. No, no, no, you must realize that you were made to serve me."

I spit at her, "I realize what you have DONE. You're a monster." I shook my chains, which made me swing around a little.

Calmly she spoke, "Have you ever been tortured? Never works well on vampires. I mean vampires' systems make more sense than living creatures. Have you ever thought about it? I mean the pain that is. You hurt a human, and the pain doesn't go away… why? I mean, what's the purpose?

"Pain doesn't help you heal, and it certainly will hurt if you do it again. You break your arm and moving it should hurt, but why does it hurt when you're not moving it? It's that residual pain that makes torture work. Vampires only feel the break, or the burn, but never does the pain remain. There is no use in physically torturing you. You understand this?"

I understood what she was saying, but it scared the shit out of me. "No point anyway, cause I don't have anything to tell you. I will never bow to you." The words sounded braver than I felt.

"Let us begin," her chair rose up on feet that were made of vines. It moved back, and the room filled with a stronger light from some unknown source. I could hear steps coming down the hallway, big heavy steps. Then more steps, one set sounded if they were tripping and being dragged down the hallway.

A large bald, ugly man entered first. He wore black pants and a dirty wife-beater. He was overweight and most of it was in his belly. After him, a man was pushed in wearing jeans and no shirt. A black hood was over his head, but something seemed terribly wrong with him being here.

The man that pushed him was Hispanic with long greasy gray hair. Tattoos covered every inch of his skin that I could see. He was dressed in black leather jeans, no shirt and a leather vest with patches all over it. I noticed that he carried a whip at his side. The big man went down another hallway, but before I knew it, he was back dragging a large wooden frame. He then proceeded to untie the hooded man's hands from his back. Forcibly, he and the Hispanic hung the hooded man to the wooden rack. The hooded man's arms were stretched out tight as his chest, leaned against the rack. He was facing me, but said, nothing under his hood.

The Hispanic man nodded to Luna, "We are ready, your Highness." She said nothing, just nodded her head.

The Hispanic moved behind the hooded man and unleashed his whip. Then the big man pulled off the hood of the man strapped to the rack. His mouth was gagged tight and I knew who it was. I didn't want to believe it, but I knew the minute I saw him without his shirt... *Adam*.

Chapter 34 Torture

I cried out for the whip to stop, but no one even responded to my screams.

After the whip cracked for the third time a brief moment of hope occurred. The Hispanic stopped whipping while the big man approached Adam. Blocked by the size of his body, I could see he was undoing something. He then grabbed the wooden structure that held Adam; he pulled it so now I was viewing Adam sideways. I could now see the three deep gashes in his back. He had not untied him, but rather removed his gag. The fourth snap of the whip filled the room with his screams.

I yelled, "Stop, torture him! Stop… or I'll kill you! Do you hear me? I *will, kill, you!*"

The man whipping didn't even pause as he let another loose upon Adam's back, followed by fresh screams that were muffled by his need to breathe. Luna sat upon her throne of vines and watched with the same look on her face as when she had entered. Her eyes slowly moved from him to me, but she responded to nothing, not his screams or mine.

By the tenth lashing, Adam passed out from the pain. Blood poured down his back from the deep slashes that zigzagged across his back. I hissed with all the hatred in my soul, "I will kill you. I will… Do you hear me? What do you want? Ask your questions, damn you. Ask! I will tell you," my voice changed to a plea. "I will tell you; just don't hurt him."

None of them responded. The big man must have left. I hadn't even noticed. He was now returning with a bucket. He threw what I knew to be ice-cold water on Adam. Adam jumped, and he wheezed in pain. His teeth chattered from the cold.

The whipper once again took up his position. I screamed, I pleaded, but the whipping man just kept on whipping. Adam had urinated on himself and stopped moving by the fifteenth. My eyes had a hard time focusing through all the tears. In all this time Luna never said a word, nor asked a question.

By the eighteenth crack of the whip, he finally stopped. The big man untied Adam's limp body. I knew he was alive; I could hear his weak heartbeat. He wasn't gripping onto life with much as the large man hauled him off none too gently. The man with the whip followed and carefully walked around the pools of bloodstained water. He did not want to get his fancy boots messed up.

Luna stood, and her chair of vines shriveled away. I couldn't help but think it was akin to her soul. She spoke pleasantly as if this atrocity had not happened. "I can't just heal Adam with my magic, so he might live longer. Of course he will have to rely on human medicine. We will hope he's up for another round tomorrow. Until then, you may want to get some rest."

"No more," I begged, but she did not respond. She walked softly down the hallway, disappearing into the darkness. I screamed after her, "I WILL RIP YOUR HEART OUT!" If she even had one.

The light in the room went out, and I was left alone in the dark, with only my dark thoughts. My body hurts, and I felt weak, so sleep did come, but it was filled with nightmares. I awoke a thousand times in the darkness and my screams. Time passed slowly and painfully, and yet I did not feel bad for myself. Oh no, my mind was concentrated on Adam. What a horror I've been to him!

When my eyes opened and I realized I was truly awake, I looked at Luna standing before me. She was wearing a bright yellow dress - it was truly magnificent. It goes to show the devil does know how to dress.

She still had a pleasant look about her, "Awake? Ready to go again?"

I said nothing; I tried to bore a hole through her with my hate. Something clicked in the back of my mind, an idea. She didn't wait for my response, "The doctors say that Adam will not survive another round. His sister, Summer, volunteered to take his place."

As if on cue, the big man and the Hispanic came in. The large brute dragged poor Summer in and started to prepare to hang her on the still-bloodied rack. He ripped her shirt off and took a few seconds to feel her up. The Hispanic laughed at his partner, "She's not bad, hey?"

Luna cleared her throat, and the men became serious once again. Luna informed me, "I don't think that behavior is proper. Do you?" I did not answer, "I think whipping will cover it for the day. We could start raping the poor girl tomorrow. I wonder if Adam would be up for seeing that?"

I prayed to myself, not that I do that often, or ever. Lord, forgive me, and I'll forgive you. I don't pray, but I need your wisdom, not for me, but the innocents that I have brought great harm upon. Help me now and I will see to your justice. I would rather be raped and killed again than watch them go through it. Help me please… Amen.

I opened my eyes, and spoke calm and clear, "Don't bother. I mean, why alienate me? We both want the same thing, the book."

She held her hand up and the Hispanic paused, "You have my attention."

I buried my emotions, "Alice has the book. She has betrayed me, but we could work together. What I mean is I could work for you. I just need to understand your part in this. Can't you give me that one grace? Then I'll retrieve the book for you, for both of us."

For the first time her eyes betrayed her, just for a second, but long enough to know I have affected her. She thought for a moment. "See, twenty-four hours and you will be calling me…"

"Master," I added for her. "I will be your servant, but give me one grace, not because you owe it to me, but so I may serve you better."

She faced me, "Very well said. I will give you your one grace and explain my part. Understand this; I owe you no such explaining. What I do, is what needs to be done. It will be hard to make you fully understand for much of what I'll share is far above your understanding. We shall try for your grace."

"Thank you, Master," I gave her a little head bow. I couldn't really do much more, and this seemed to please her.

Her tone lightened up a little, "The last hundred years have been hard, for many reasons I assure you. Humans have advanced and so quickly. It has always fallen on me to see the future and save the world. Hard to always carry such responsibility, but I have. Perhaps some have become too reliant on me, leaving too much to chance. Do you know the basic history of the book? How it came to be in the possession of the Twelve?"

I nodded, "Yes, ma'am."

"Let's start where my son, Richard, stole the book. I only found out after he took it and perhaps I could have stopped him early on, but I had a vision. I saw my son cast a spell from the book, and, in this vision, a great hero rose from the flames of the spell. In my vision, the hero destroys the book and saves the world.

"Visions are hard to see fully and, even though no one matches my interpretive abilities, sometimes I read them wrong. Richard was never a good man, but I hoped that he would find a better heart. I believed that he would rise from the spell the hero. I thought this would be good for him. Up until this vision, the destruction of the book has been impossible. He would arise a hero, the book destroyed and the world's savior.

"It is beyond your understanding. I must make decisions based on what's good for all people, not just some girl. Unfortunately, Richard was not to be our hero. It appears to be you. I have my doubts, but still if I can bring you to reason, there just might be hope. That is, truly, my part in this whole affair."

She looked so innocent, as she said the last part. I knew there was a lot left out, like did she understand what he had to do with that spell? I didn't think she worried about her boy's good heart, more like his status in the world. Still, she wasn't the kind of villain I thought she might be; she was much worse. I better get as much information as I could while she was still talking. I asked, "What about Alice and David? What do you know of their betrayal?"

"Alice. She's much more of a problem than I ever thought possible. If we're not careful, she might be the cause of the end of the world. Richard sought her out; he never was a good judge of character. Still, I believe he did it because he needed her to complete the spell. He needed someone who was directly related to the Red Adder being that it was his magic that created the book.

"Alice was a direct descendent, but she's nothing but a walking corpse. Fortunately for Richard, he found that Alice had been keeping tabs on her bloodline. That's where you come in. Are you aware of your ancestry?"

I nodded, remembering the things that Alex had told me. My mind wandered back to the subject she was droning on about. I was Alice's great-great- etc. - niece. I know Alice wasn't turned until she was in the New World. Being a member of the Lost Colony must have been a hell of a story, but that was unimportant right now. I do, however, recall Alice told me, that her original people had set sail from England to get away from persecution.

The history books say that it was religious persecution, but I now think I know what it really was. They were from the same magic family as the Red Adder. In fact, the Red Adder was over a thousand years old when he died in the early nineteenth century. He had been hiding in Russia, just as other family members tried to hide in the New World. They were all killed in the fifteen hundreds, except for my family line. The first child to be born in the New World - the first English child, that is - Virginia Dare, lost with the rest of the colony.

Luna was saying, "David, on the other hand is a very loyal boy."

"Loyal to who?"

She looked at me as if the question was obvious, "Me, of course, who else matters? He is a Necromancer and that part will be his downfall. After Richard cast the spell on you, he and the others did not believe it worked. He was in search of another family member of Adder's. Of course The Apostles had hunted them all down. He had leads that led him to Brazil. The years passed by, and he had not yet been able to find a single surviving family member. The fact he had the book was becoming harder to hide."

"From my point of view, he was running out of time to save the world. Once the other members found out about the book, they would demand that I take it back. Then it happened, a vision. I saw you rise from the ground and knew where you would go. The problem was I didn't know what to think about you. A mistake that had arisen from the first spell? No matter, I would need to have you watched carefully.

"I called an old friend in New York, and it just so happened he had a son, not any son, but a Necromancer, no less. Being a creature of the dead, he would be able to manipulate you. I told him where he could intercept you and what to expect. From there, the boy was truly crafty.

"He called Alice and that was his mistake. Her need for power and control is what turned this whole thing into a bloodbath. Some days I wish my visions would stop and others I wish it would show me more. Perhaps if I would have known, we could have stopped Alice before it got this far.

"He still managed to do great things. I love how he used you to kill The Order. They were a thorn in my side for too many years, too many of my own kind supporting their right to live free in the West.

"Then what happened next was truly a shame. Somehow, Alice learned of my son's whereabouts and stole the book from him with your help, but I realized you were deceived. Then she turned you against David. Unfortunately, David has decided to embrace his Necromancer side. In the long run, he will find that he has chosen the wrong side. Alice, that trickster, even managed to use the power of the book to trick us into believing you were killed. I truly underestimated her. It will not happen again."

It amazed me how a story could vary from another's point of view. I understood now, and I could see that Alice had a lot to answer for, but, even with everything Luna told me, I knew there was still more to it. The part about David hurt the worst, but I had already figured as much. Sadly enough, my earlier life makes so much more sense now. Why did David hide my killers? How did Alice know I was special just by looking at me?

I decided to go forward with my plan. I was going to use Luna to save, or punish, Alice. I guess we'll see when I get there. "I'm glad for your grace. Without a shadow of a doubt, I now know I'm on the right path." I chose my words carefully, for I dared not lie to her. "Let me be free, and I will tell you how we might get this book from Alice."

Victory, shown in her eyes. She whispered strange words. I felt the power flow through me, and my limbs began to grow. The chains broke free, and my body fell to the floor. I stood up on my new legs, still weak and hungry. I asked, "May I feed? They know too much now."

She nodded thoughtfully, "You are correct. Summer, after Melabeth cuts you down, please show her up to your room. Have her cleaned, and dressed and ready for dinner. Please don't be late."

My fangs elongated, and I turned toward the large man and the Hispanic. The Hispanic figured out first, "Wait! My Highness!... ahhhhhhhhhhhh!"

As I fed on them, I ripped them to pieces. It was one small justice for Adam. I was also very happy they hadn't taken the hood off Summer's head. That would have been horrifying.

Chapter 35 Dinner Company

I carefully unstrapped Summer. Her eyes were squeezed shut. I didn't want her to see the carnage. I picked her up and held her in my arms, then proceeded to walk down the nearest corridor.

She looked up at me with a lost expression, and she said nothing. She simply flicked her finger each time I was to change course. This place was a maze. A few turns, a staircase, I found myself standing in a hallway with lots of doors. It appeared I had been held in a basement of a palace judging from the decorative hallway. Summer motioned toward a door, which I found to be unlocked. Inside, it did not surprise me to find a beautiful bedroom.

After laying Summer on the bed, she got up and shut herself in the bathroom. Still naked and covered in blood, I stood before a large window overlooking a huge garden. I saw no movement, but I was sure there were eyes in that garden.

Summer came out of the bathroom with wet hair and clean clothes. We said nothing as I went to clean up. I took a shower, a bath and another shower, just to feel clean again. I found clothes in a large attached closet. Nothing fit perfectly, but I put together an outfit, a green dress made of heavy cotton. When I looked in the mirror, I thought I might be at a Renaissance fair.

When I emerged from the bathroom, I found Summer sitting on the bed. She had been crying. She looked like she was about to speak. I put my pointer finger to my lips and mouthed, "Not here."

Her eyes told me that she understood this. Before the awkward silence had time to drive us mad, a knock came at the door. I said, "Come in."

Peter stepped in, dressed in a black suit. "Good, you're all cleaned up. So, mother says you're with us now."

"We have the same goals," I answered with no real emotion.

He nodded, "Friends for now. I figured the daughter of a man you murdered might not want to accompany you to dinner. Summer, why don't you check on your brother?"

She gave no pause and quickly passed by Peter, hurrying down the hall. My eyes didn't hide the fact I wanted to follow her. Peter picked up on this, "He's in the hospital wing. He'll be fine… and I really don't think he wants to see you."

It took effort to bury my emotions, "I understand."

Peter offered me his arm, "Shall we?" With a tight smile I played along letting the jerk lead me to this dinner.

It wasn't long before I was seated in a large dining hall. It looked like we were in a castle, and just might be. In fact, I had no idea where I was. The table was huge, and we were not the first to arrive. At the head of the table sat a chair that was bigger than the rest. It didn't take rocket science to know that it was Luna's seat.

Peter's brothers were already there and seated across from me. All the other faces I had never seen before. More people, most likely magic users, filtered in. They all sat down and fell into conversations. Obviously they knew one another. As far as I could tell, the only vampires were the Apostles and me.

The table looked about full when a man announced, "Luna Longaeva." With this, the room fell into silence. Everyone then stood up, and I followed. Luna swept into the room in an orange gown. As much as I loathed the woman, she knew how to look good. It was like watching some movie about a spoiled princess.

Once she sat, everyone sat too. Then the servants filled the great hall, bringing in trays of food. Some of the people started to make demands, and the servants responded quickly to fulfilling their needs. Four large golden goblets, encrusted with red jewels were set before each of the vampires. I could smell the blood wine. It was magnificent!

I quickly lifted it to my lips, it tasted even better than it smelled. A strange voice asked, "Do you like it?"

I had to lower my glass to see who had spoken to me. I realized it was Matthew, the giant brother. In his evening attire, he looked crazier than when he was wearing all that armor. His hair, now free from his helmet, was long and unkempt. I simply nodded at him.

He laughed loudly, even though I heard nothing funny. "I made that myself. Well, not that cup, but the recipe. Best blood wine you will find anywhere."

I answered with no real emotion, "I'll take your word for it."

The other brother still had a very cocky look on his face, but, unlike his crazy brother, looked very dashing. I could see him wooing a fair amount of foolish ladies. He sneered at me, "Well, I hope you enjoy our wine, now that we are all friends."

Peter sounded like he was giving his brother a warning, "Now brother, don't ruin dinner. She is on the same path as us. She follows mother's will."

"Is that so?" Luke snapped back.

His eyes bored through my skull. I knew I had to be careful; a lie could be read. "I work for a greater cause. We all do things for our own needs, wants and dreams. To truly do something great, we must strive to do it for something greater than ourselves."

Luke was trying to slip me up, "And what is greater than ourselves?"

The table went quiet, "Do you not know? God, of course, and who best to see God's plans?"

Matthew answered loudly, "Luna, our mother. See? This girl knows what's best. My God, I've waited for hundreds of years for someone to understand that we do the Lord's work. Sister, you're working with a hard-headed fool." He slapped his brother on the back. Luke looked none too happy.

What was his brother to say now? He picked up his glass and drank, all the while sneering at me. Peter was laughing, "It takes a lot to silence my brother."

"His tongue is almost as fast as his little axes," Matthew teased.

Luke rolled his eyes, "You need a new line brother. Your wit is as dull as your hammer. I said *that* three hundred years ago. YOU KNOW, the *first* time you said that damn joke."

Matthew laughed, "Oh, drink up bro. You're just pissed because that little lady kicked your ass."

Peter spoke with a menacing voice, "Knock it off! Not at the dinner table."

He hadn't finished his last word, and both brothers had already knocked back their chairs and were standing in each other's face. I started to chant, "Fight, fight, fight." All eyes turned on me, "What? Just cheering them on."

Luna cleared her throat as two servants picked up the overturned chairs. The fight died from the brothers' eyes, and, at once they both sat down. Both of them shot me a dirty look, which brought a smile to my face.

"Melabeth," sounded off in my ear. Luna sat a few seats away from me and, when she spoke, her voice did that volume-enhanced thing again. It was almost startling because I was busy making faces at the brothers, so it sounded as if she got up, walked over and started talking in my ear, "Yes, ma'am."

"This is my council; forgive me if I don't introduce you. I feel this is the time to discuss where Alice is and how you might get the book. Do you mind telling us?"

"Of course," I needed to be careful with my words. I tried not to take too long with a pause as I gathered my thoughts. "Alice is in the Dark Circus with the Red Adder."

The room exploded into conversations, "I knew it," "How can we get to her?" "It's a trap," were but a few things I made out as the voices began to sound like a beehive.

Luna raised her voice, "Enough!" Dead silence, no one even moved. Her voice was, once again, calm, "We shall keep order. Melabeth, are we sure?"

"Yes, ma'am," This was the moment I hoped that no one knew I was making stuff up. I mean making shit up, isn't lying. "I was informed that my power would allow me to leave the Dark Circus. I had planned to enter the Dark Circus and face Alice. That is why I was in LA in the first place."

Luna looked skeptical, "Informed… by whom?"

"By Alex McDonald, but he's dead now," This was true. Except he hadn't really told me how I might get out and he told me after his death. Still, I just stated that he was dead, so it sounded as if he might have told me before death. This was making my head hurt; Alice was great at this. Probably best if I didn't over think it.

"His information has proven to be very reliable," Luna then paused and was obviously thinking. Some whispering took up while she sat in silence. When her head lifted, she began to speak again and the whispering stopped. "I can't send anyone in there to help you. How will you defeat Alice? I've witnessed you fight, and Alice is not equal to my children, but still."

"You may not know this, but mind tricks do not work on me. I can see around them."

She grinned; I believe that was the second facial expression I had seen on her. She must really hate Alice, "Really? I doubt she's a great warrior without her mind tricks." A look that I didn't understand washed across her face, "Still, what about the Red Adder? How could you face him in his domain? Even I cannot do that."

I answered this part with more confidence, "Because he will let me leave and furthermore, he will give me the book." Her face washed with confusion. "Before I joined you, I was already working for Alice. The Red Adder had wished me to take his book to Necro Z. I am not sure why, but I bet it has something to do with freeing him. Necro Z is in Las Vegas, and you know the Dark Circus cannot go there."

So far so good, they were buying this made up shit. Well, it did have a little truth in it. Like Alex had mentioned that the Dark Circus could not go to Las Vegas. Most believed that Necro Z was hiding in Vegas, so it should be easy to believe that they were all in it together. Hell, they might be, I could be telling the truth for all I knew.

So I went on with my story, "Alice is gumming up the whole thing. She has realized that she will not end up ruling the world. She is trapped in the Circus, but somehow she holds the book and Adder is furious. If I show up, I can kill Alice, take the book and pretend I'm delivering the book to Necro Z."

Hell, this didn't sound that bad. Luna looked happy, I wouldn't say "Christmas, Happy", but happy. Alice dead, the book in her hands, all in one package. That's when Luke opened his pie whole, "She is lying."

Peter said, "I can't see that."

Matthew even defended me, "She is a woman of God." Well, kind of defended me; no one really wants to be defended by crazy.

Luna spoke, "We will deliberate. If this appears to hold water and you are able to deliver, you will find a place at my table forever. Let us finish our meal. Tomorrow, we will reconvene. The circus will be in LA by tomorrow. I believe it opens by six; if we find no fault in your plan, we will begin right away."

Great, now I had to worry if they bought my stories for twenty-four hours. If they didn't, they might start to whip Adam or his sister. I truly prayed this would work, but I didn't have any other options. The truth would not help me... I knew that much.

Alice once explained that even though some vampires and magic users could see through the lies, it never worked on her. Lies are trying to convince someone of something you know not to be true. So, if you believe it, or at least you believe it possible; then it is not a lie. Everything I said could be spot on because Alex had failed to fill me in on any other details. I was really crossing my fingers on this one.

After dinner, I was glad to be led to my room and then left alone. I was asked nicely to remain in my room. That was fine by me. I didn't have to escape. I needed my plan to get me into the Dark Circus, followed by a miracle from Alex to get me back out.

I flopped on my bed, my mind left to wander. Alice, my evil crazy friend, what is the truth between us, long lost sisters? Or, evil doll bitch and her gullible friend? I trusted David, and look how that turned out. My heart hurt, just thinking about the betrayal. What else might I think about? Adam, lying in a hospital bed, hating my guts. Oh, that's helping… *not*.

I needed something to take my mind off it all. I fell back into myself reaching for my dark gift. It was like going to the library, traveling down a pitch-black hallway. No walls or roof, you couldn't even feel the floor, but somehow I knew which way to go. I could feel different strings of existence, and if I listened long enough, I knew what they were and what they were feeling.

The first string I knew at once. Nicks, he felt tired, I could feel the strain the Necromancers were putting on him. He was in the library, I might have been able to travel to him, but I believed he needed rest. He has faith in me, and I would like to give him good news for once. I felt the next string, immediately I knew this to be Alex. He was deeply intrigued and close to Nicks.

I found Alice's string; it went into the shadows. I could not feel her, nor tell you where she was. The only thing I knew for sure was that she was alive. I found the string I was looking for, Spooky. I traveled down her happiness until I saw what she saw.

At first, I was confused. I was seeing Kathy. Why am I seeing Adam's and Summer's aunt? Kathy was cooking in the kitchen. Spooky picked up a plate and traveled to the dining room. There my sister and her husband sat. They were eating when my brother came flying into the room. My sister started fussing at him for running through the house. Spooky had hidden my family in the city of Queen Anne at Kathy's house. How clever! My heart swelled with some happiness.

This is why I'm glad it took me so long to find out about David's utter betrayal and possibly Alice's as well. I needed to remember this, burn it in my mind. It's worth taking chances on people, even if one is horrible, for one good friend makes life worth living. It wasn't long before my father came in to join them with paper in hand. They all looked so happy. If I died, it will be for them. This world will never be right for me. How can I let it end for them? Just one worthy person might be worth saving the world for, and here are six.

A while passed as I watched my family get ready to turn in for the evening. Spooky started to clean the kitchen with Kathy. The rest of my family had left for other parts of the house. My mother pushed my brother upstairs for a shower, her husband announcing he had to do some work to get ready for his new job. Father finding his place in front of the TV set only to fall asleep on the recliner. No longer interested in watching Spooky and Kathy work, I pulled away from her. As I did, I noticed something, a missing string.

I searched and searched, lost in blackness and could not feel Bow. I had been stuck in the dark for hours, perhaps days, hanging by chains and not once did she come to me. I did not know how, but I knew that Bow had been destroyed. It was the same as my dear friend, Carrie, and, like Carrie, she would finally have found peace. Her only remaining wish was to use her skills that she had built over her lifetime. After living that through me, she was ready to join her husband in the afterlife.

Over the years we spent together, she was able to pass much of her skill to me. I was now a master of the Katana, violin and not too bad at speaking Japanese. She told me on many occasions that I had outgrown her. I will miss her. I will miss the sword. I needed a weapon now; damn it. Luna had destroyed her, I just knew this. How, I'm not sure how, but she did. She would have thought Alice had made the weapon for me using the book.

I was still floating in the dark tunnel between worlds looking in vain for Bow. That's when I noticed it, a different string. At first I thought it was my sister's mom or my brother. It wasn't. I found their strings quickly when I thought about them. It did seem to help that I was thinking about the person who I wanted to make a connection with. I felt this new string, and it was at peace, perhaps sleeping. Wait, it was awake, worried, scared, and happy all floating around in this person's well being, no one emotion ruling this person.

Chapter 36 Switch

This string scared me. Who the hell am I attached to that I do not know? How did they have my blood in them? Who, other than Alice, had fed off me without me noticing? At first I was afraid, then a little mad. I pushed further toward this new connection. I could feel the blood lust. The first question answered - vampire. My eyes opened to a jungle; was this person in a jungle?

The person was female and young. How I knew this, I wasn't sure. I also could feel her panicking; she knew I was with her. She started to move through the jungle, which turned out not to be a jungle. As her eyes moved around the thick greenery, I could now see she was inside. She quickly headed down a flight of stairs. That's when I realized where I was, Michael's apartment.

The panic stopped and curiosity took over. I was in Zoey, and she knew it. I had never spoken to anyone in this form, so it surprised the shit out of me when I heard, "Melabeth, is that you?"

"Yes, yes it is," I replied. It was strange because I had no mouth, eyes or ears. I was in a world of blackness, and yet I spoke, and I knew she understood.

"Is this a vampire power?"

My smart-ass took over, "Only to the daughters of Dracula."

She was really excited about that, "Really, I didn't know you were Dracula's daughter."

"Just kidding, it's because I'm special. Apparently, so are you." My mind wandered from the conversation. She had been created with my blood. I knew this. I remember Michael saying she had cancer, and it was a small miracle she arose. My response was, you must have had hope to steal her body and bury her.

My chain of thought was interrupted. Opening my eyes, I felt my fingers, "What..." my voice was all wrong. I was in Zoey's body, and Zoey was gone. I freaked and pulled back, finding myself in the darkness again.

Zoey was there freaking out, "Holy shit, I was in another body. I found myself lying upon a bed. It took me a minute to realize it wasn't me."

"You did that?" I asked.

"I'm sorry; I saw this place and went there," She sounded dazed.

It hit me. No one had ever really been this open with me. Spooky, Alice, even my sister. They had always blocked me. Zoey was open to this. I could see how it worked for the first time. The spirit inhabits the body, the darkness was the space between life and death. I could feel people and some of their emotions through that space. If I traveled to them, it was like looking over their back. I could see through their eyes, hear what they heard and sometimes feel what they touched. Still, there was not enough room for two spirits to inhabit the same body. The minds could not speak to one another.

Zoey had stepped out of her body, the same thing I had done. She met me in the middle, in the darkness. Both of our bodies were empty. At this point, she decided to enter mine, which tossed me into hers. This power was crazy, but it took an openness that few in this world have.

I was still in the darkness with Zoey; I explained this to her. Of course, I made it sound like I knew it all the time. No reason to scare the girl. I asked her, "Can you do me a small favor?"

I could feel her willingness, "What?"

"I need you to hang out in my body, but it is very important that you do not leave the room. I'm kind of in trouble; I need to speak to Michael."

I could feel her concern, "No problem. I won't leave the room."

"Thanks," I let myself go further down the string. With no one home, I slid right in.

It was so weird, standing in the middle of Michael's living room. My body felt all wrong, like it didn't fit. I walked toward the sliding door to the balcony, which was where Zoey had been heading. I could see Michael leaning against the railing smoking a cigarette. He was facing the chairs that were hidden by plants.

Walking out onto the balcony I was met with, "Hey, Zoey." Several voices said it at once.

Two other vampires were out on the deck with Michael. A male and female were sitting in seats facing Michael. They both were young and hip looking. Tattoos, piercings, and the latest clothes, they were laughing and smiling when I entered. Michael was wearing white sweat pants and no shirt. Oh my, how I had forgotten what a Greek god this man was. His whole back was covered in tattoos, but none anywhere else I could see.

Michael had a warm smile on his face, "Love, I thought you went to bed early."

I realized I had no idea what his relationship was really like with this girl. I was mad at him, so of course I planned on messing with him. I walked up to him without a word. Pulling him into an embrace, he was too surprised to react. Then I pulled him into a deep kiss.

He kissed me back; I could feel the passion in him for this girl. Funny, I felt nothing, well, except for the pain in my heart. The kiss brought me memories of Adam, followed by the sounds of whips. I didn't have to pull away, because Michael pushed me.

"Oh yeah," a voice said from next to us. "Oh, bro, look what time it is."

The female voice added, "Yeah, we gotta go; call us in an hour."

The man teased, "Or like five minutes. You know... whenever you're done."

He laughed at his own joke. Michael waved them goodbye, "Later, assholes."

The door shut, and I seductively said, "Now, we're all alone."

Michael's face was full of confusion, "What has gotten into you?"

"Well, hopefully you will be getting into me." This made him squirm, and I tried not to burst into laughter.

He pushed away from me, even though I could see the need in his eyes. He wanted this girl. He was going on, "Look, I'm your master. I don't think we can..." while he made excuses, my mind started to put things together.

Alex was affecting me. I could see the pieces. I thought Alice had him make this girl, but she would have never done this. An old conversation surfaced to the front of my mind. When Alice told me she had taken my blood, she also told me about samples of my blood to study. At the time, I didn't care. She also told me that once she figured out my blood connected her to me, she destroyed the samples. Alice would not have wanted more souls connected to her. Still, I knew Alice. She was bossy. I could see her telling someone else to destroy the samples, like Michael. Michael kept one. After this girl died, or before her death, he gave her some of my blood in the hopes of saving her. Alice would be pissed to find she was attached to yet another person. Michael had no idea about the connections.

Why would he not want to have sex with her? I could see his feelings. It hit me. Vampires don't have sex without biting. It's why some vampires prefer humans. If you were a free vampire and drank another's blood that was significantly more powerful than yourself, you would be enslaved. If the vampire was more powerful than your existing master, they could take you. If you were close to equal, it was pure pleasure.

He was afraid of drinking Zoey's blood. He was unsure of what would happen. This also meant he had lied to me. If I could show Michael one ounce of empathy, I could understand him. This was the true reason for not wanting me to meet her. He has been a slave to Alice for... I had to think about it for a minute. He turned in 1969, forty-seven years under the care of Alice. I realized his need for freedom. I also realized maybe I couldn't simply count on him to help me. What was in it for him? He would not want to free Alice from the Dark Circus. Had he even believed I was saving the world? Surely everyone has heard someone declare the world was ending. I realized this was a moment for me, one that would alter my course. Wow, I could have never realized all this before. Seeing through the eyes of others; understand their line of thinking so I could see what they believed, kind of cool.

Michael was still talking, "See, that's why it would be best if we waited."

I smiled at him while a wicked plan formed in my head. He looked at me strangely, "What are you thinking?"

"Let's go in," he followed me in mumbling about how weird I was acting.

His friends were heading toward the door with drinks in hand. They must have gone into the kitchen and fixed themselves something else. Michael yelled out, "Hey, the sun's almost up. Why don't you just stay here?"

The man spoke, "Hey, bro, we hate to impose."

The girl spoke to me, "Zoey, you cool with that?"

Michael barked, "Not up to her."

I turned and kicked him in the nuts, hard. He buckled, "I don't mind; you can stay here if you like."

Michael rose with anger in his eyes, "I've had enough." He reached for me, probably to grab me and pull me upstairs.

He wasn't even able to react when I moved toward the wall. Kicking off the wall I spun into an aerial spin, my foot finding the side of his head. His head jerked to one side, and he crashed to the ground.

The man yelled out, "Damn, girl!"

The girl squealed, "Zoey, what the hell?"

Michael stood up. He was pissed. I took a fighting stance, "Bring it on."

Michael was faster and stronger than Zoey's body. I was better trained. I always knew that Michael was not very good at hand-to-hand. Mixed with his confusion and not wanting to hurt me, I was kicking his ass.

I moved around and hit and kicked him at will. He smashed into some potted plants, landing on his ass. That's when I noticed the vampire man was wearing a knife on his side. It was in a long leather sheath hanging off his belt. I moved to face Michael, putting my back to the male vampire. I turned around surprising him, not that they weren't already watching the fight, slack-jawed. I reached around him and pulled his knife out. He yelled out, "Hey!"

Michael had gotten to his feet. I spun the blade around in my right hand. "Bring it on, come on; let's see what you're made of."

Michael was enraged, "Enough games. You've brought this upon yourself, Zoey."

We were slowly circling the room. I knew what Michael would do. He would flash to my left away from my knife. The room wasn't big and, therefore, neither of us had flashed yet. Also, I doubt Zoey was powerful enough to even do it. Before he even went into his flash, I started into my move. I stabbed the blade through the palm of my left hand. Now the blade was covered in Zoey's blood.

He did as I thought and as his body materialized next to me, my left hand had already been in motion. He was utterly caught off guard when I drove the knife clean through his chest. The knife came to a stop when the back of my hand hit his chest. He managed to hit me in the face; as I fell away, the knife ripped free. He screamed in pain.

I ducked to miss another wild swing. I spun around on the floor with my leg out, sweeping his feet out from underneath him. Rolling away, I was now on my feet before he could recover. As he held his chest and worked to right himself, I pulled the knife free from my hand. Sending the knife through the air, it hit his kneecap. Blood sprayed out; he screamed; once again, he fell on the floor. The knife made contact with his knee bone and bounced off, hit the floor, and then slid under a couch.

The other male vampire lunged at me yelling, "This is enough!"

He was too fast for Zoey's body, but I felt strength and speed that was not from her. I stepped back as his outstretched arms traveled in front of me. Grabbing the closest arm by the wrist, I forced it downwards. Combined with his forward motion, he went into an uncontrollable head flip, landing on his back. I grabbed him, picked him up with one arm, and then tossed him like he was a cat. He flew through the vegetation that lined the apartment. His head made contact with the wall and a sick, crunching noise echoed back as his body fell limp to the ground.

I could feel the growls ripping free from my teeth. I turned to see the girl looking horrified. She screamed, "Your eyes! You're the devil!" She turned and ran. I heard the front door slam closed.

Michael was once again standing. Anger was washed away and replaced by fear and confusion. "I think you got some Zoey blood in you." I mocked.

His eyes narrowed, "Melabeth?"

I realized from the screaming vampire girl that my eyes were alight with my reaper powers. This made me realize something. This power is not attached to my physical being. It is a part of my soul, and that is why it is with me at all times. Zoey's body was so much weaker than mine, but I had healed, her hands from the knife's cut in seconds. Increased speed, strength and healing were but a few of the powers my spirit could do without my body. Being a vampire just added to them, perhaps allowing me to use them outside of the spirit world. It explained so much to me in a brief moment.

I walked up quickly slamming Michael against the wall holding him by the throat. I licked his face, then whispered in his ear, "Miss me? Now that you have Zoey's blood in you, you have my blood in you. You want to know a secret?" I didn't wait for him to answer, "I'm Alice's master."

His body stiffened, "I don't understand."

"You used my blood, and now you're a part of the same party as the rest of us. Have you followed your letter's instructions?" Michael's eyes shifted toward the picture that hid the safe, "Haven't even opened it?"

"I was going to," he pleaded.

I laughed, "Why? So you could have Alice back? Or perhaps you were worried about me. I realize it's been hard, but let me tell you another little secret. Unlike Alice, I can find you anywhere and even when you die, I'll be waiting. If you love this girl, you will do what I need of you. Do I dare ask where Ezra is?"

Michael hesitated before answering, "Waiting for tomorrow evening when the Dark Circus arrives. He plans on entering to save Alice."

I laughed, "I see. You planned on us all disappearing. Once you turned me over, Luna had promised to leave you alone. Luna would deal with me. Alice and Ezra would be trapped in the Circus."

A tear fell from his face, "I just wanted to be free with Zoey. I tried everything in my power to stop Ezra; he will never let Alice go."

My voice was soft, "It's ok. Now you're going to do the right thing, because you will never be free of me. I'm not all fear and threats. Even though I could kill Zoey at any time, I will offer you a reward. You prove yourself to me, and I swear to let you and Zoey live your life free of Alice and me."

His eyes narrowed, "You swear it."

I laughed, let go of his throat, and moved freely in the room. "Does it matter if I swear it? You will do as I tell you. I am your master. I will reward you. Have faith in me; either way it does not matter. I command you to follow the letter's instructions to the exact letter." His body stiffened at the command; he had to obey.

I hated doing this to him, but the fate of the world was more important than his freedom. Even if I could understand his motives, he still had betrayed me. I needed him to follow the letter and stop Ezra. In the long run, this would be best for him and Zoey. I wondered if he would ever thank me. I added, "Before I leave, Zoey does not know what has transpired here. She is in my body right now," Michael looked surprised. "Take care of her." I gave him a wink.

I felt burning on my hand, "Ow!" I noticed the sun was streaming through the windows. Michael picked up a remote and shades fell over all the windows. Zoey's arm was all red like she had spent too much time on the beach. "I better fix this; hate to return her body in worse shape than when I borrowed it."

I concentrated on healing the burn, but nothing happened. The sun was up; my reaper power doesn't work during the day. Oh well, she'll live. "Bye Michael."

I concentrated on leaving. Closing my eyes, I headed for the blackness. "Zoey, is that you?"

"Shhhh, Michael, I'm concentrating."

"Sorry Mel," and he went very still.

I held my eyes closed and traveled toward the darkness, "Uh oh."

Michael sounded panicked, "Uh oh, what?"

"My power doesn't work during the day."

"WHAT?"

"My power doesn't work during the day."

"WHAT?"

"My power doesn't work during the *day*."

"WHAT?"

"Holy shit, what have I done?"

"WHAT HAVE YOU DONE?"

My mind was spinning, "Luna is sending me to the Dark Circus this evening. It opens at six. If they send Zoey in before the sun drops, I won't be able to switch with her. I won't be able to see her inside the Circus."

"WHAT?"

"STOP THAT, DAMN IT."

Chapter 37 Not Sorry

Michael had gotten hold of Ezra. Apparently he rented a room across the street from the Circus. He had a bird's eye view of the main entrance. He planned on staking it out for a few days before entering.

Ezra was excited to hear I was there and could hardly believe the story about switching bodies. I hung up with Ezra, but didn't tell him about Michael's betrayal. I couldn't see how Ezra is mad at Michael could help. It was ten o'clock in the morning and I could barely keep my eyes open.

Michael noticed me fighting my eyelids, "Well, there is nothing we can do now, and you may as well get some sleep. Zoey is young; her body will pass out whether you want to or not."

I complained, "I need to get to the Circus. Better now than later."

Michael gave me a dark look, "Absolutely not. Sorry, I don't mean to be an asshole. Melabeth, you don't have any experience being a young vampire. Zoey's body won't last ten minutes out there. Just look at your arm; it's still burned from the morning sun. So, get some sleep already."

I didn't want to sleep, "I felt so helpless. I wanted to do something, maybe…" I knew I was falling asleep. Michael's face blurred as I fell into darkness.

It felt like my eyes had just closed when I awoke to someone shaking me, "Hey, lazy bitch. You need to get your ass up."

I sat up confused, "What time is it?"

The boy laughed, "It's five thirty. Just messing with you, Sis. You still hip to the movies tonight? Do you need me to go warm some blood for you? Well, your highness, get with the program already."

"Movies," my brain was still so foggy, and I had no idea who this was. I had no idea where I was. "Blood… what movie?"

"Damn girl, how much did you drink last night?"

I wondered, "Don't remember. Why don't I just drink from you?" Suddenly that sounded like a great idea. He smelled wonderful, and I could hear his heart beating away. I stood up letting the blanket fall off to the floor.

The boy was laughing until I got out of bed, "Hey, you're wearing nothing but your underwear, Sis. I don't want to see that; save the show for another bro." I was now stepping forward, and he responded by stepping back. "Oh, come on Sis, no fu…" I pulled him to me. "Hey, what's up?"

A very good-looking man stepped in the door. He looked at me and said, "Whoa, stop that." He pulled me away from the good smelling boy, then stood between us, "Hey Tim, didn't you see the note? Not to mess with your sister."

"Yeah, but she is my sister. What's the deal, Michael? She seems really out of it, and she fed late last night so I thought she would be in a little bit of control."

Michael gave him a dark look, "I have told you. Control is hard at first. It will take time; you need to learn some patience and learn how to read notes. Is Rachael here?"

"Yeah, she's downstairs. She knows how to read."

It was all so confusing, "What are we talking about? Just give me the good-smelling boy."

Michael commanded, "Go warm your sister's blood." He left without a word. "Melabeth, you can try a little self control. Zoey would never forgive you if you hurt her brother. The rest of her family is out looking for her; it's a mess. Do you think Zoey's mother could handle her son disappearing too? Get dressed already."

This man was confusing, but pretty, "So, who is this Zoey?"

His face twisted up funny like, "Melabeth, this is no time for joking."

My mind was scared, "Where am I?"

He swore under his breath, then forced me to get dressed. After dragging me downstairs a few minutes later, he set down a glass of the most fantastic smelling blood. I drank greedily, but couldn't help but think about the two beating hearts in the next room. Michael was talking quickly over the phone with Ezra as I drank more blood.

The handsome man looked ready to tear his hair out. "Just got off the phone with Ezra, remember Ezra?" I nodded my head. "Well, that's good."

"I spoke to him last night," I said happily as the blood was beginning to lift the fog off my brain.

"Do you remember that?" I shook my head. "It figures; Ezra reminded me about something that we didn't think of last night. Vampires store their memories in the blood and just animate the brain. You must have transferred all that information, but, when vampires sleep, we stop animating the body. Therefore, you would only remember what's in the blood and apparently you can't access Zoey's memories."

I was dismayed, "I remember talking to him last night. In fact, I remembered fighting you last night. Well, kind of... it's all kind of blur."

Michael shook his head, "You managed to store a few memories in Zoey's blood, which really doesn't help. Can you remember anything from before last night?"

I tried; I really did, so I finally said, "Yes, it seems clearer."

The phone rang, and Michael answered it quickly, "Hello... You have to be kidding." He paused for a few seconds listening. "They already sent her into the Dark Circus. It doesn't even open for another half an hour. Did she seem confused? I mean, wouldn't she have forgotten things too?" He listened to another response, "Yeah, that's true. She might not have slept, Melabeth's body can handle that, and she's probably scared shitless. Still, I wonder how they didn't notice she wasn't Melabeth. Ok, yeah, I'll call you back after sunset." He hung up the phone, "Will this nightmare ever end?"

I asked a question of my own, "Can I have more of this delicious blood?"

He rolled his eyes, "Yes, yes you can."

I was feeling good; still those two heartbeats *really* sounded good. They moved closer, and both yummy-smelling people came into the kitchen area. Michael complained to them, "This is not a good time. Why don't you two go home tonight? Zoey will feel better tomorrow."

The boy looked as if he didn't believe a word he just heard. Rachael spoke, "Hmm, Mike, we would like to talk to Zo."

"Trust me, tomorrow will be better," he urged.

Tim wasn't buying it, "Mike, you said you would never keep her from us. Come on, Zo; talk to me."

Michael was burying his face in his hands. "This has been such a long day."

I looked at the yummy-smelling Tim, "Why don't you come here and let me give you a hug?"

Michael yelled out, "Enough. Tim, Rachael, I know this is hard to hear right now, but shit has happened. Zoey isn't home; the lights are on, but she's not home. She's dangerous, and right now, she wants to eat you. She doesn't care who you are right this moment. You need to leave so I can fix this... leave NOW."

The girl was crying, and the boy was yelling by the time Michael shoved them out the front door. I didn't care that they left; well, it was a shame that I didn't get to taste one of them. I was really feeling good, alive even when Michael announced, "Finally, sunset."

I pushed the fuzzy memories to one side. I didn't need to remember last night clearly; I needed my body back. I stood and looked at Michael, "Time to go." He nodded in agreement.

*   *   *

On the way to the Circus my mind finished clearing. The night had allowed me to re-establish my memories. Michael calmed a little now that he knew I could think straight, but he was so stressed by Zoey being in the Circus that he looked close to a panic attack. We met with Ezra in the parking lot.

Standing before the entrance of the Circus, I looked at its bright lights and shivered. The music played that all too familiar tune. The smell of popcorn filled the air, mixed with dust and sweat. Children spoke in screams, and people laughed. The noises and movements made me want to vomit, and I hadn't even gone in yet.

Ezra was a little upset when I informed him that he would be waiting for my return. He stood behind us and appeared to be pouting. Maybe I was wrong, I looked back at him as we walked; nope, I'm right. Ezra's voice was tight, "Come home safely, Melabeth." It touched my heart because I knew he was speaking of me and not just Alice.

Michael whispered from over my shoulder, "Good luck. Bring Zoey back; I mean it."

"I will," and began my walk forward toward the gates of hell while the two men stopped and watched me walk in.

A large archway with letters that were brightly lit covered the entrance. "Welcome to the Wild Circus" the sign announced. Below the arch a dirty-looking man stood over a big wooden box asking for tickets. He then shoved the stubs in a slot on top of the box. To the right of me, stood another line of people waiting to purchase tickets for entry.

I reached the front of the line, "Ticket, Miss?"

"I don't have one," I said.

His face filled with pain, so much so that for a second I thought he might have hurt himself. He said urgently in a low whisper, "Don't come in here. Go home, please."

I shrugged my shoulders, "I can't." I took a few more steps forward and felt my body passing through some invisible force. I knew that all the king's men and all the king's horses, couldn't take me back again.

I continued to walk forward, and the man whispered mostly to himself, "Stupid girl." I ignored him as I followed the crowd deeper into the Circus. All the while I could feel a power draining me; this place was nothing but a large vampire. The Circus drained the vampires and other magic users, while the vampires and magic users drained the guests. All this power must flow straight to Adder himself. No wonder he was such a powerful Lich.

I could feel Zoey and Alice, and I now knew where both of them were. Alice felt lonely, and Zoey was afraid. Unfortunately, I wasn't able to switch bodies; this place messed with my powers. I was hoping if I got closer, or perhaps touched my old body, I might be able to force the switch. There was only one way to find out. I needed to find myself... wow, that's kind of funny.

I walked past the rides and games. All the operators were vampires, and the men and women that yelled at me to try their games were magic users. I could see them using their magic to cheat the people. No wonder no one ever won. I fought my way through the crowd until I came to a large open area. On one side sat a bunch of picnic tables with the food carts all around them. The smell of all the deep-fried foods made me nauseous. I looked toward the direction I knew Zoey to be in. Crap, she was in the fun house. The fun house had a sign above it saying, "Welcome to the Doll house."

I noticed a man walking slowly through the crowd. He was hard to miss. He was dressed head-to-toe in black and bright red. He wore a tux with long tails and a vest. His shirt was bright red and so was his hanky in his vest pocket. Two chains hung across his vest, one gold and the other silver. Bright red shoes a big black top hat with a red band around it completed his ensemble. Even his cane was black with spirals of red. It was the red that caught my attention, his eyes. His eyes were red, and he smiled, showing his fangs. He had black and white hair poking out of his hat. His thick beard showed lots of white mixed in with the disappearing black. He looked to be in his forties, perhaps.

Nobody seemed to notice this man as he came to a stop a few steps away from me. I spoke first, "Red Adder, I presume."

He gave me a curious look, "You presume well. It has been a long time since a soul has walked in my Circus of their own free will, a long time indeed. And then out of nowhere, young girls, one after the other, are coming to join me. Well, I'll tell you the same thing I said to them. There is always room here and a job for everyone."

My eyes glanced at the fun house. I could feel them both in there. "I think I might try your fun house."

He smiled, "Oh, well, that's different. Most of the time I have to force people to have fun; don't let me stand in your way." He had a wicked smile. I started to head for the fun house when he asked, "You didn't tell me why you're here?"

I kept walking, "No, no I didn't."

He laughed.

I came to the entrance and walked through the door. Inside a clown with giant red hair that matched his nose, smiled down on me. He laughed crazily, "Now you have fun. This is where you will learn what we do with all the troublemakers, and when you have had enough, just call for Uncle Happy." Then, with a dark, menacing voice, "And I'll come right away." Followed by more crazy over the top laughter.

I hate clowns. I pushed my way through different colored curtains, to find myself staring at hundreds of Zoey's. A maze of mirrors stood before me; I knew my goal was on the other side. I walked in with my hand in front of me and slowly started to explore my way through. The Adder appeared in the mirror as if he stood next to me, but he did not.

"Perhaps, if you told me what you're looking for, I might help."

His voice sounded as if there were ten of him standing in a circle around me speaking all at the same time. I answered, "I like blondes. Have you seen one lately?"

"You are risking your life for that poor confused soul? You should have left her to her fate; now I'm afraid you will be joining her." He then stepped out of the mirrors, and it has been just my reflection and me once again.

I didn't dare tell him about Alice or the book, not until I had my body back. I was in no position to fight him in this body. I noticed something new - a door that hadn't been there before. I started to wind my way around the mirrors toward this new door. It looked like a house door; it was light blue and completely out of place.

I was almost at the door when something pulled my hair, "Ow!" I yelled. I whipped around to see an image of Zoey standing in the mirror. Hate was in her eyes, and her arm had come out of the mirror and grabbed my hair. I pulled forward and stepped back as the image grabbed at me. I stepped back straight into another mirror and found arms wrapping around my body.

I fought my way free as the room burst to life. Arms came out from all the mirrors as hundreds of pissed off Zoey's reached for me. They clawed at my skin and ripped my clothes, tearing my hair out. I pulled free and grabbed onto the doorknob, trying to push my way into the door as the hands kept pulling me back. Finally, I broke free and fell through the door, slamming it closed behind me.

My body was full of cuts and my head hurt where they had pulled my hair out. I stood up and took in my new surroundings. I was in a house. Well, it looked like the inside of a house, a house that had been abandoned. Kind of reminded me of a haunted house; all the furniture was still here, with paintings on the walls. There were lights on, but they were dim like they were running off weak batteries. The most ridiculous part was some of the lights blinked, as if they had a short. If it weren't for all the dust and spider webs you might think someone still lived here and needed to call an electrician.

A creaking noise started to come from upstairs. I laughed out loud, "Wow, how corny." The walls began to bleed. I was very unimpressed. Walking through the house, I came to the kitchen. The kitchen was full of body parts and a giant pot was boiling on the stove. Of course it was full of body parts. It felt like Zoey should be standing next to me, but she wasn't. Oh, I know, she upstairs.

Traveling up the staircase, bugs fell from above, and snakes slithered down the stairs like it was a waterfall. Huge, hairy spiders were crawling on me, but I climbed the stairs unconcerned. I was used to this stuff living with Alice. At the top of the staircase, I gave a little shake knocking off most of the bugs and started toward the direction I knew Zoey to be in. It was dark heading down the hallway toward the bedroom door, and Adder stepped from the shadows. "Well, you're a different type of girl. Maybe your friend isn't lying."

I wasn't sure what he was talking about, but I was not about to give him information by guessing. If I was a betting woman, I would bet she told him that it wasn't her body. He could most likely see how powerful we were by just looking at us. She was likely freaking out. I was way too calm.

I ignored him and stepped into the room. There inside was Zoey with my legs pulled to my chest huddled in a corner. She was crying and overall freaking out. "Zoey, sorry about all this," She didn't even give me eye contact; she held her eyes closed tight.

I touched her arm, and the room spun... it took me a second to realize I was now looking up at Zoey. I wiped my eyes clear of tears and stood up, "Nice to be home."

"Truly," Adder said. He had been standing there watching the whole thing. "Now that you are where you belong, enjoy your stay."

"I don't think so," I replied.

Adder disappeared again, and Zoey sat on the bed. She was still freaking out; I really wanted to make fun of her, but how can I expect her to be used to this kind of madness. She lived a sheltered life while sick at home. I blame Michael for dragging her into this hell. It's best that I take no responsibility... ok a little.

I spoke softly, "Zoey, you ok?"

"I think so," She sounded as if she might cry.

"Hey, it's going to be fine. Hate to do this to you, but I need you to hang tough. I'll be back as soon as I can."

Her eyes filled with panic, "Don't leave me."

I hated this, but I knew that she might get hurt following me. "I will be back for you. Do you understand? Do not leave this room," I took her hand. I pulled her into a hug and she cried on my shoulder. "Try not to show weakness, ok? Be strong, and I will return."

I had to push and pull to get her loose. Poor girl, I didn't have time to stand by feeling sorry for her. It wouldn't save her life anyway. Leaving the room while she begged me not to go, I opened my senses for my next target, Alice. Funny thing, she was close and she was heading my way.

I went downstairs, minus the bugs and snakes. It was almost as if the haunted house was giving up on me. It was calm, too calm. I moved through the lower half of the house until I reached a rather large living room. It looked to be a throwback to the eighteen hundreds from the furniture and décor. A large fireplace was in the center of the room, and nothing was modern, not even a telephone. Standing in a dirty, tattered, black dress, stood Alice. She was wearing her black hair in ponytails, and her pale lifeless face lets me know that her power was either not working or she was not using it. Alice normally made people see her as if she was full of life, not death.

She spoke first, "It took you long enough. I certainly hope this isn't some botched rescue."

"Dear sister," I said as I walked into the room. "I'm not sure this is even a rescue."

She misunderstood, "Oh, no plan of escape? Well, that's just great... Well, at least I'll have company."

"Oh no, sis," I corrected. "I have a plan to get out of here. I'm not sure you're coming."

Her eyes narrowed, "Is this another trick Adder?" I said nothing; just stared at her with hate in my eyes. "Why would Melabeth hate me so?"

"Why would my great-aunt turn me over to the son of Luna for a science experiment?"

Alice took a second, her face blank. "How did you...? Never mind, it doesn't matter. What's done is done. Now what, you want an apology?"

I was taken aback by her cold demeanor. "It's true then. How *could* you? Did you know what they would do to me?"

Alice couldn't look at me, "I didn't ask. I didn't care. Do you really want the truth of it?"

I was sarcastic, "*That* would be different."

"You can't handle the truth!" She was smirking.

I couldn't believe she was cracking a joke, "*Really.*"

She dropped the smirk, "No sense of humor. If you have to know, it was a simple reason. You were my last great promise. I had promised my sister before she died that I would protect her daughter. I did better; I protected the line and the power that was passed down through the generations."

I asked, "Then why did you give me up?"

She smirked, "I was tired of keeping track."

I was floored and then I floored Alice. I moved so fast that I took her by surprise as I knocked her on her ass with a solid punch to her stupid face. She slammed onto her back, and her hands rushed to her nose that was now covered in blood. As if she was trying to speak underwater, she exclaimed, "You broke my nose!"

That's not all I planned on breaking, I went to kick her, but she was fast and rolled away onto her feet. I didn't give her a second as I leaped after her. Our vampire powers were diminished in this place; there was no flashing, and we weren't as strong. No matter, we both had mad skills, and the next few minutes would have made any martial arts movie better.

We exchanged a few blows; she kicked me upside my head, sending me head first into the wall. I quickly recovered, surprising her in the process. I bounced off the wall by kicking it, catching her with my arm as I clothes lined her. She fell flat on her back. She spun around and jumped to her feet as my knee smashed into her face, and, this time, she smashed into the wall.

She didn't recover like me; instead she slid down into a heap. Blood covered her face, and bruises and cuts were all over her. On the other hand, I had healed. Apparently this place didn't mess with my reaper powers. She was slow getting to her feet.

I called forth my power and rushed forward with more strength and speed than Alice was ready to deal with. Grabbing her by the neck, I slammed her against the wall. She was pinned against the wall, a few inches from the ground. She wasn't afraid of me.

Her voice was restricted because I was squeezing her throat, "I'll never apologize… and I would do it again. You hear me… I-would-do-it-again."

My anger lost some steam. Was I going to kill her? Should I? I demanded, "Why, oh why? How can you be so evil, and why should I care if you live? Haven't you learned anything?"

Her voice sounded defeated, "I'm glad you're the one killing me."

I let go of her and she dropped to her feet, but did not move from the wall. "I should kill you."

She spoke with an empty voice, "What can I tell you Melabeth? How can you understand four hundred years? Before you, I cared about nothing and no one. Now I care about you. With your blood, you made me care about what you cared about. I'm not sorry. I won't apologize. I wanted this, and if you destroy me, that's just one less thing to worry about."

I looked down at my crazy sister. She had risked her very life and freedom coming here to find answers. I knew she didn't know about the rape, and I doubt she knew that part was even in the ceremony for the spell. How could she? I still needed to know, "What did you believe you would get from turning me over to them?" For the first time ever I saw true shame in her eyes. It was only for a second before she masked behind a childish grin. Still, even her grin fell short. I demanded, "Tell me."

"I don't want to," she sounded like a child.

I reached through the power of my blood. I commanded her, "You will tell me. I command you."

I could see her body stiffen, "You know you're the master. My life is over; kill me now." She was trying her hardest to defy me. In the end, she could not defy me. It came out like water from a broken dam, "I did it for power, wealth and the freedom from my old promise. I had no idea you would be... you."

Her eyes were cast downward on the floor. She was no longer able to look me in the eye.

"I forgive you," I said with a soft voice. She didn't deserve it, but then again, neither had I. It was hard to imagine that anyone in the whole world needed forgiveness as bad as Alice. It's equally hard to believe that anyone deserved it less, but forgive her I did.

"No, you don't," she said on the edge of tears. "I don't want it and don't need your forgiveness."

All the anger and hate that was in me washed away with those words. Killing her would never make her wrongs right. She would remember her sins every time she looked at me. It was truly her cross to bear. I pulled her face up and forward, bringing her eyes to mine. "I forgive you, sister. Now help me figure out how to save the world."

She pulled me into a hug, "Ok, as long as I get to kill people. And, for the record, I didn't, and will not apologize."

"Yeah, I know," I pulled away just as someone came into the room. I asked half fearing the answer, "So, why aren't you sorry?"

Alice grinned, "Because my life has meaning again. I wouldn't give that up for nothing, so therefore, I'm not sorry."

I understood, the years I had spent with Alice I had learned her dark secret. Her power was a gift and a curse. The power to control anyone sounds like a great idea until you have it. Over the years she had become so gifted in controlling others, she soon found herself all alone, never knowing if anyone really loved her, or if it were the simple fact she tricked or forced them to care about her.

Hundreds of years… impossible for me to even imagine being alive that long. How many times had she been betrayed by friends? She trusted no one, not even Ezra. When she gave me up to Richard, it was another sign of her detachment from reality. No longer living within the world, she created her own world, a world with nothing but her and her dolls.

When we first met, I could see around her power. At first she was challenged as to how she might control me. When that failed, she worked on other methods of control; even taking my blood was another trick to control me. It backfired, and she found herself feeling my emotions. It in turn evoke some of her emotions that she had long ago buried. Not being able to control me made it seem impossible to trust me. Then, through my power, she learned she could feel how I felt about us. In the past, she had commented, not directly, but she had wondered how I accepted her and cared about her.

This had been the final secret, the one that in her mind would destroy our relationship. She knew once I understood her part, I would hate her. The fact that I forgave her at all and still loved her, had left her in shock. Even though she stands before me with no apologies, I can feel that she is overwhelmed with relief. I pulled her into my arms and embraced her.

Adder started to clap, and then pretended to wipe a tear away, "Oh, how wonderful, two sisters forgiving each other, truly moving." He snapped his fingers, and the floor broke open beneath me. Before I could react, I found myself landing in a giant ball pit. As the roof above me closed, I could hear Adder saying, "For the record, I'm not sorry either."

Chapter 38 Red Adder

I looked up, and all I could see was darkness. Alice was gone; it was hard to move through all the yellow, blue and red balls. I just kept sinking. I tried to fly, but it felt like my vampire powers had been washed away. Adder's top hat rose out of the ball pit, followed with the rest of him. He stood above the balls as if they made a solid floor. He looked down on me, "Why do you seek my book?"

"I don't; I seek the truth. I only search for the book because it seems to be the root of everything that has happened to me. In fact, I wonder if I shouldn't blame you."

He looked none too happy with my response. "You lie."

I barked, "So do you... I came here for Alice and Zoey."

At this he laughed, "Well, you will have company, while you live out your life in my circus."

I started to say, "We'll see about that." But I was unable to finish when arms reached up out of the ball pit and grabbed me.

I pulled the arms to break free. I sank further into the ball pit, and, at the same time, the arms came out clawing at me. The arms had long yellow sleeves; I fought them off and kept the sharp nails from cutting me. Next, the head of a clown rose out of the balls, with red eyes and sharp teeth. It laughed wildly. I was able to punch and push the evil clown while I tried to move through the balls away from him.

It didn't matter when I realized evil clowns of all kinds of bright colors and shapes were rising from the balls. I really hate clowns, "What is this?"

Adder spoke softly, "A lesson. You will learn, and then we'll *talk*."

"I don't think so," Anger rippled through me. I reached down, deep inside. Adder had crazy magic, in this circus. He could even diminish my vampire power, but not my reaper side.

The first clown came toward me with claws aiming at my throat. I bashed them away and ripped at the clown with my own claws. My hands were huge with long black claws. Using my power, I lightened myself rising up on the balls giving myself more movement. The clowns came at me from all directions, and I fought with speed, strength and skill.

These mindless, fearless clowns came at me nonstop. I fought them off, but the ball pit made it hard to move. A clown jumped on my back. I grabbed his hair to pull him off, but came up with a wig in my hand. He bit my neck; in retaliation I shoved my two fingers into his eyes. Blood poured out as I drove my fingers deeper into his skull. He let go, to screaming and pulled away, falling back into the ball pit.

The clowns were relentless. Another charged me, and I jumped at him, slapping his arms away from the inside. I grabbed his head and pulled it to my knee with everything I had. A satisfying crunching noise came from his face, but there was no time to celebrate. I was already kicking another clown. I formed my dark wings and flapped to stay above the balls, and also it helped me keep the clowns off my back.

Clowns reached up from below me, coming up from the ball pit and grabbing my legs. They kept me from flying away as I fended off yet another attack. Another clown jumped on my back, and this time I got a hold of him before he bit me. With his weight and the pulling on my legs, I found myself being pulled into the balls.

Soon the other clown dog piled on me, driving me neck deep into the ball pit. All I could see were balls as my body was pulled ever deeper. In the pit, my second sight was, at last, blind. I could see nothing but shape, and my eyes witnessed nothing but color. I could hear the laughing of the clowns and feel their hands digging into my flesh, pulling me ever further into a bright hell.

I would not scream. I felt like that is what Adder was after. I fought the hands off. I would fight until I could not. I felt my feet and realized something did not make sense. It felt as if the bottom half of my body was coming out of the balls and hanging. Not long after, my whole body broke free. I landed softly on the ground. The balls hung over me like some kind of freaky ceiling. The laughter of the clowns died off as if they were swimming away through a sea of balls. Clown sharks?

There was not much left of my clothes as I healed myself from all the cuts. I felt weak and no longer could hold onto my wings. No matter, I wasn't going to be flying up into the ball pit again.

Looking around at my new environment, things did not look like they were improving. I was standing on an old stone path. Each stone was a couple of feet square and covered with dirt or moss. The trail itself wound around a corner and out of view. On both sides of me reaching all the way to the ceiling of balls were stone cliff sides. Well, obviously he wanted me to follow the path, and I had little chance of doing much else, unless I wanted to face the Clown sharks; the thought alone made me do a full body shudder.

Following the path, it soon came out from underneath the roof of balls. I walked outside and took in the view. Before me lay vast hills covered with long green grass and outcroppings of gray sharp rocks. The sky was dark and overcast, and for some reason I did not believe the sun was overhead, nor the moon for that matter. In fact, I was sure this was somewhere entirely different.

The path wound alongside the steep hills, steadily moving upwards. I followed until I reached the crest. There the path was not much wider than a foot across with steep cliffs on either side. Winding up the ridge of the hill, I could finally see where it was leading me. In front of me stood a castle, the strangest castle I had ever seen. It looked as if Japanese, Europeans, Egyptians and ancient Greeks engineered it. None of it seemed to match, and sometimes the changes from one kind of construction to the next were sudden and hard to look at.

I had not noticed him a second ago, but there he stood on some rocks that jutted up over the path. Adder stood there with his coat tails flapping in the wind. I walked closer until I stood just a few feet from the base of the rocks. "What now?"

"You've never seen it from the outside," he said with a faraway look.

"What are you referring to?"

He pointed with his cane at the castle, "Go find out." He turned to black dust and floated away in the wind.

It took a few minutes to get there, and the castle was much bigger than I had thought. From a distance it didn't look that far to travel. I arrived at the gate to find the drawbridge down and the gate open. Walking in, I watched for whatever the Adder had in store for me. I moved into a large courtyard with an oversized statue in the center. The place looked dead; vines hung from the walls dry and brown. Leaves piled in where the walls and ground came together. The statue itself was that of a cloaked figured with no face. A large door stood at the end of the courtyard to enter into the castle. The doors were closed with giant matching symbols on both doors. The symbol was of a skull with a sword and spear crossed behind it.

It took me a moment, but the symbols seemed to be familiar. I had seen these before… the library. I had seen this symbol on some old tapestry hanging next to Nicks' favorite fireplace. It hit me; this was the outside of the library. I said out loud, but to no one, "But how?"

He startled me as he spoke from behind me, "Because, my dear, this is my domain and that is his."

The door swung open, and Nicks came forward; he looked older and pissed off. "How dare you! You have no right to touch her let alone bring her into your domain."

Adder spoke to me, not answering Nicks, "This courtyard is the only space where our domains overlap one another. You're special, you know, because you can travel from one side to the next."

"Why?" I started to ask.

Nicks interrupted, "Why indeed? Why are you in his Circus? Is no one able to follow a few simple tasks? Alex knew to keep you away from my brother."

I looked at one and then the other, both with glowing red eyes. Nicks with his long hair, then back at Adder who at this point was laughing at Nicks' anger. Yep, they were brothers. "I don't understand. Why didn't you want me to meet him?"

Adder laughed, "Who does? My brother comes up with rules and regulations for others to follow."

Nicks was still angry, "I can explain it. It is my brother's fault. He is the cause of all your misery."

"Hey," Adder stopped laughing at that remark. "It's not all my fault. It just happens to be the power of love."

"Lust," Nicks corrected.

"Love, my dear brother. Plus, look at her," he pointed at me. "If it weren't for me, she wouldn't exist."

Nicks said every word slowly as if trying to explain something to an idiot, "I did not say she is not worthy to be my daughter. Nor did I say I'm not glad for her. BUT, I would have not wished her trials and tribulations upon my enemy, let alone to an innocent child. Your foolishness has yet another victim."

"You're welcome," Adder responded.

"You need to leave and release Melabeth. More important things are going on than your foolishness." Nicks demanded.

I felt kind of left out of the conversation, "Wait, I didn't come here for nothing. I need Alice and answers… oh yeah, Zoey, too."

Adder gave me a strange look, "As if I would release one fly from my trap, let alone three."

Nicks yelled, "You will release her!"

Adder smiled slyly, "As if you could make me."

I interrupted before they could fight. "Hold up." I was doing my best not to lose it. "You both suck right at this moment. You're supposed to be my father," I then looked at Adder. "And are you not my Uncle? Why not level with me? Are you like God and the devil, and what does this have to do with the book?"

Nicks face lost its anger and instead looked ashamed, "I blame you, Adder. You tell her; you explain this to her."

Adder winked at me, "It would be my pleasure."

Nicks shook his head, "You'll never change."

Adder found a seat on a ledge on the wall around the base of the statue. "This story starts long ago, and, when I say long ago, I mean ten, forty, fifty, thousand years ago. Really, I couldn't tell you, and it doesn't matter. My brother and I remember the first day together. What was before that? We don't know, and we just knew we existed and we were, in a word, happy. We existed here, in this place where you stand now. Once it was much bigger and not so… segregated."

Nicks piped in, "Who's fault is that?"

Adder snapped back, "Do you want to tell this story?"

"I probably should, so it's told right." Nicks mumbled.

"Well… too bad, so stop interrupting." I couldn't help but laugh; this got me a smile from both of them. "I was saying; we existed here, this place before death. Only, at first, we didn't know that there was another place, or that others might pass through here. It was just us. The first spirits who came through were simple enough and after awhile we began to speak with some of them. If they got violent, we would slay them. After awhile we noticed animals, not any kind of animals, mind you, but animals that could speak. They were the memories of those who passed, so Nicks and I learned of another world.

"Humans grew, and they advanced, and, as they did, so did we. The discovery of writing and advancement in knowledge, allowed us to build this library to store all we learned. It wasn't enough, not for me and not for my brother. We wanted to see, to experience this world we spent so much time reading about. Naturally, we figured out how to get there."

"It was easy," Nicks began talking. "I think we were always meant to go there, to help keep balance and move the dead along. We found doors even if they were only open to us during the night. We do not know why."

Adder, for the first time, looked mad. "Is that all brother? Move along, move along." Adder had jumped to his feet and moved his arms as if he were leading people. "I can't help it; I can't help that I feel and you don't. I love while you heard the sheep along."

Nicks just shook his head, "I feel."

"So you say, but do you love? I do... I did. Melabeth, you might understand; she was beautiful. Yet that was not it. I had seen a million beauties. No, this girl was... smart, clever and so many more things, a daughter of an ancient king to a kingdom long lost. Her name was Lilith."

I knew that name, "Not *the* Lilith. I have read books proclaiming she was the first vampire, a female demon, who lived long ago."

Nicks nodded, "That's her."

"I was in love," Adder proclaimed. "All she wanted was immortality so that we might live together, forever. Hindsight being twenty-twenty, I might have made a small mistake. At first, not even Nicks thought it was a mistake. We were happy; we were lovers, and she was everyone's queen. At last, the years went by, one after the other. Humans don't have the... I don't know if there is a word for it. Immortality proved too much for my Lilith, and she turned cold."

"She was always cold," Nicks said harshly. "You turned her into a vampire. She stole life from others so that she might cheat death. Our power only connects with the plane of the living at night, cursing her to forever darkness."

Adder shrugged, "Never said it was perfect. Let me get to what happened next. This part has more to do with Melabeth. My dear Lilith was unhappy, and, of course, I wanted to rectify the problem. She explained that she had no children, and it was wrong that she never bore a child. I came up with a way for her to make children." Nicks started to say something, but Adder quickly amended, "Children of the night, that is. Lilith is not just a vampire, she is so much more, and here children are but shadows of her."

"A real mess, that is," Nicks added.

"For a time, Lilith was once again happy. I don't know how many thousands of years we were together, but if you compare it to marriages now…"

Nick mocked. "As if it were anything like a marriage, perhaps you would not have made the problem even worse."

"My brother's skipping ahead, and it was a marriage of sorts. It was not just sex, but we were partners in the most amazing ways. Time passed, and I had another urge, one that was truly a mistake, but a mistake that I would make over and over again. I wanted children, children of my own and not some creature of the night, for the vampires that Lilith created were even more foreign than herself."

"So you had children with humans?" I asked.

Adder shook his head, "I did. It was not easy, nor what you think. I kept a journal and after recording many magical blunders, I discovered the secret. My family grew before my eyes; at first, just my direct children and then grandchildren. Of course I lived long enough to watch my family grow into many families. That is until Lilith found out about it.

"She was beyond jealous, and she came after my family, killing all she could find. My family ran from place to place. Alice was a part of one such journey; she and other direct relatives of mine had fled before Lilith's wrath. Unfortunately, she turned into such an awful creature. Lilith finally caught up with me and stole my journal; you know it as 'the book'."

"Wait," I said. "How was Luna involved in this?"

"Luna," Adder smiled. "Luna is Lilith; Lilith is Luna, makes no difference what name she uses. She has learned who you really are and now wants revenge on you, of course, only after you make her look good by saving the earth."

"I thought Luna was an elf; she even has the ears."

Nicks laughed, "Sorry, didn't mean to laugh. I didn't even realize that Luna was Lilith; never really kept up with my brother's crazy ex-wife, but I do remember the ears."

Adder looked upset, "There's nothing wrong with her ears. In her tribe it was considered beautiful to have your ears stretched. You always teased her about that. I found her ears breathtaking. I will ignore my brother to answer your question Melabeth. Lilith is so much more than what most vampires are. She realized long ago to call herself an elf; people take more kindly to elves than vampires."

Nicks added, "Elves died out long ago, if you were wondering."

Adder answered for me, "We weren't."

"HEY, I was wondering," I interjected.

Nicks smiled, "You're welcome."

"Oh, you both make me sick… blah, blah, blah, elves are dead. Oh, thank you, now I can act like I know something." Adder was mocking us. "Shall we get into the thick of it; you are the last living member of my family. Not sure if I should let you go. See, I'm not too worried about the rest of the world."

Nicks eyes narrowed, "You must set her free!"

"Oh, must I?" Adder met his stare. "Let's not forget where her body is. It's in the circus, my little hell on earth; after Luna stole my book, she then used its knowledge against me. She trapped me in a kind of bubble. I can move it, but not quickly. Luna called me a Lich and hand feeds me all her undesirables. She comes to visit once in awhile."

Nicks chuckled darkly, "This is where my dear brother cannot keep his story straight. She did not capture him; she killed him, and that is why he is trapped here. That is why he requires the undead to feed from the living so he might maintain his life. It's also why he can never again enter into the library. It is why our realm is smaller and split in two. Look at his half, nothing but hills and broken rocks."

I could see the lost look in Adder's eyes, "They'll kill you too, brother. Then they can challenge God."

Nicks approached his brother. His voice was not harsh. "Then, brother, let her go. She might challenge these evildoers, save the earth and perhaps destroy that infernal book of yours. She can set right what has been set wrong. If they destroy me, do you think they will let you live? Can you protect her in that circus against such reckless power?"

Adder laughed, "You don't understand. The book is nothing but words that I'm sure Lilith has memorized. It is my power that threatens the world, the power stolen from me, the power that once was in the book."

Nicks responded, "And that is why she must get the book back."

Maybe it was Alex's influence working overtime, but I caught something that Adder said. I didn't believe that he meant to say it, but didn't Nicks catch on? "What do you mean by 'the power that once was in the book'?"

Adder gave me a sideways grin, "Clever girl."

Nicks' voice went dead serious, "What are you saying?"

Adder shrugged, then explained, "What do you think? The spell that had been used was to summon my power. When Lilith destroyed me, she found that she could not contain, nor use my power within herself. The spell that her evil fool of a son cast, was to give him the power; he needed someone of my family line. Here I am, trapped, and my power came back to me, all on its own."

I asked Adder, "Something's not right; she sent me here. Why would she do that if she understood?"

Adder grinned at me, "She sent you here for the book. She doesn't understand, because she thought her son screwed up the spell by not using a virgin. And yes, she figured out you were not pure; how she found out, I couldn't tell you. Lilith is unlike any vampire you have ever heard of. She has magic and a beating heart. It's her children that are truly cursed. Richard was not her child by birth, because she has no living child to her name. She adopted him when he was small, due to the fact that he showed such promise of becoming a great wizard. She believed, wrongly - that's because he was human, he might take my power from the book and use it."

Now I understood, "So, she believes that if I bring the book to her, she will someday figure out how to take your power. She still thinks the power is in the book, and I'm some kind of Frankenstein from a bad spell."

Adder laughed, and Nicks spoke over him in a booming voice, "I didn't know… I thought… the same thing. I thought your power was like mine, but I would have never guessed. What a fool I've been."

Adder stopped laughing, "See brother, that's why I'll never let her go. She has what's mine."

A voice came from behind Nicks, "Oh, yes, you will and you are wrong; she is mine."

Adder narrowed his eyes, "How is that? She has my power trapped within her. She is a vampire, or at least partly, which are the children of Lilith. Why is she yours?"

I added, "Yes, I've been a little confused about a few things myself."

Nicks face looked thoughtful, "If I were to have tried to explain this in the past I would have failed. Not only because you would have not understood it, but I hadn't fully grasped how it all worked until this very moment. To understand we must go back to when you died.

"You are a great grandchild of Adder's bloodline, and, through a spell, they should have been able to steal the power of the book and take it for themselves. Adder has not seen the video of your death, so I will explain it. Lilith's child performed an evil spell on poor Melabeth to steal the power of the book, but they did it wrong. Instead, it puts the power into Melabeth, and her body melted away as the power drained into her. In the video you can see an image of me; it was the moment that our worlds collided.

"From my perspective, I did not see the men, nor the spell. What I witnessed was a body repair in the library. At first I thought, how strange for her spirit to lay upon the floor. I almost fell to the floor with shock when I realized I was looking at her physical body. Never before had anyone traveled to the library with their body from the outside world. Even now, Melabeth's body is at your circus while her spirit travels. That day was different, and I could feel her power."

Adder was on the edge of his seat, "What did you do dear brother?"

Nicks went on, "I fell in love. I had been secretly jealous of your success building a family of sorts. She lay before me, my daughter, a gift from God. I knew she was dying, so I gave her my power, and her spirit grew stronger, but her body was still dying. I used every magic potion, every blood, from all types of magical creatures, but nothing stopped her physical body from failing. Still, I knew of one trick, one trick I learned from you, dear brother. You had spent thousands of years designing magic to make a new kind of body.

"I called upon spirits to prepare her body. Once I fused her blood with that of a vampire, I brought her body out of death and back to the realm of earth. As I traveled, she awoke, and my heart was filled with hope. I arrived at the graveyard that I had chosen; spirits had already prepared what I needed. Melabeth was awake, but now the vampire blood would kill her to complete the change. I had no time to explain to her what had happened, and, in truth, had only parts of the story myself. I smothered her and waited for her to rise. It took her so long that I had lost hope, but, when she finally rose, I knew that my daughter was born, so, that is why she is mine."

The door opened in the library; we all turned to see Alex coming out of the library. Adder asked, "Who is this?"

"Alex McDonald," I offered. "He's my ghost."

Alex spoke, "Sorry for being late."

Nicks did not sound happy, "I was not aware you were even coming. Explain why my daughter is in such dire circumstances?"

Alex spoke quickly, "Well, yes, here it is. Adder is going to let her go, because it is what's best for him. He hasn't had time to realize it yet, and neither has Melabeth for that matter, but it will not be too long before Melabeth is controlling the circus. The powers that hold you in here, dear sir, are based off your own power. She not only controls that power, but if she spends enough time inside your circus, she will start to drain the power off, you and your circus. Before long you will be answering to her. Of course, if you kill her, well actually, you can't."

Adder shook his head, "I know that, you little ass." Adder laughed, "I have no ill will against Melabeth; I would never bring any real harm to her."

I was confused, "If you knew this and you were not going to hold me, why the game?"

He smiled while looking at Nicks, "My dear brother didn't know that you had my life power within you. He was unsure of what I might do to get it back, and that was upsetting him. Do you not know the lengths I go through to piss him off?" He was smiling, full of mischief.

Nicks blurted out, "Because you're childish. This is why I can't deal with you. Always have to win, even if you change the rules to the game."

Alex handed a letter to Adder who took it with a funny look on his face. "What is this?"

"Read it," Alex urged. "Don't tell anyone what's in it."

Adder scanned over the letter, "Really. Well then, you have a deal. That is, if you come through with everything in this letter."

"Just do your part and I'll do mine," Alex then turned to me. "Alright, Adder is going to let you go along with Zoey and Alice. That is, if you want to take Alice with you?"

"Yes, she's going with me," whether she deserved it was a whole other question.

"Good," Alex said with a smile. He handed me a letter, "For Alice's eyes only."

"Hey, why can't I ever know what's going on?"

Alex smiled, "Sorry, but some things work better if you're not acting."

Chapter 39 Free

Alice was waiting for me as I headed out of the circus. Still in her messed up dress, she was holding her doll. I didn't see Zoey. I asked Adder, "Where's Zoey?"

Adder smiled, "Don't worry; she'll catch up when the time is right." He waved the folded letter in front of me, as if to say, this was a part of the plan. Adder pointed toward the exit, "Good luck." With that he disappeared.

As we stepped outside of the circus's magical boundary, the Apostles stood awaiting us. They were not alone; behind them stood Adam with an angry look on his face. Now what do I say? If Adam helps them, Alice will be powerless. I don't even think with Alice's help that we could defeat the Apostles. We were weak, but even if we weren't I doubt we could win. No weapons, and all Alice had was a doll, and the Apostles had weapons. It was kind of strange to see three middle-aged men, dressed up with slacks and polo shirts, with medieval weapons.

Peter made a statement, "At last, you are here with our prize."

I pointed at Adam, "What's he doing here?"

Peter said, "He has decided to help, just in case you didn't properly dispose of Alice."

"I will not allow you to dispose of her." I turned, and Alice no longer had a doll in her hands, but the book instead. "What is this?" I turned to Peter once again, "Are you trying to trick me?"

Peter laughed, "It is not me. Once again, she has fooled you. Dispelled by your Adam, you now know the truth."

"Join us," Peter beckoned.

Adam spoke up, "We should destroy Melabeth, too." My heart sank with his words. His anger, his hate, was it all for me?

Luke yelled, "Silence, boy. Just keep Alice's power at bay, and we will handle the rest."

Adam looked none too happy with being told to shut up. He nodded, "Yes."

Matthew spoke to me, "You will save the world through the destruction of the book and all the works of the book. Will you help us complete the Lord's work? I believe you will. So, step aside, and let us destroy your tricky little friend."

I was about to tell him to go to hell, when Alice spoke up, "You now know the truth, sister. I was so close, and I would have ruled the world. You're so easy to manipulate; with or without you, they will never stop me."

Alice tried to flash away, but the brothers responded to quickly. She moved away from Luke's quick hatchets only to barely dodge a stroke of Peter's great sword. After everything that had gone on in the circus... was it still all a lie? Had Alice once again played me for a fool? I watched as she tried to battle the brothers. If I did not help her, she would fall. I was stuck in indecision when Peter finally caught Alice's leg, bringing her down to the ground.

Luke moved in quickly cutting Alice up. She tried to rise up, but Matthew's Great War hammer had found its mark. A powerful blow crushed her back to the ground. Peter screamed with book in hand, "I have it!"

Alice laughed, and Peter turned to look in my direction. Alice was standing perfectly still next to me; she had never moved. That is when I realized my heart had begun to beat. Adam had his power upon me, not Alice.

In my confusion, Peter yelled, "Adam, what are you doing? You will die for this betrayal." He raised his sword and flashed forward only to slam face first into an invisible barrier.

Adam smiled, "Sorry, these whip burns sure do make it hard to concentrate."

Peter stared in disbelief; without another word, he knew he was standing within the boundaries of the Circus. Alice was once again holding a doll. Adam smiled and then pulled out an envelope. "I'm hoping Alex is truly your friend." I couldn't speak. I was too emotional. I managed a head nod.

I was interrupted by screams; I snapped my head back toward the noise. Peter was screaming while hitting the barrier. I looked at Alice, "How?"

Alice beamed at me, but, before she could speak, Red Adder burst forward. "May I answer that question?"

Alice giggled, "I would be honored."

Peter had even stopped yelling as the Adder spoke. "To answer your question Melabeth, I would have to tell you about a letter I received. It offered me a trade, for how can I give up on two fine specimens like you and Alice? Such power to feed the Circus, but the letter promised me three times as much. And now look!" He threw his arms apart while pointing the end of his cane at the Apostles. "Three brothers with great power... what fine specimens they are. They will feed the Circus now and forever, children of my most beloved."

Adder had been standing within the border, of course, because he could not leave. Peter charged him bringing his sword down upon Adder. His thin wooden cane stopped the sword completely. Adder reached up and touched Peter. His touch brought the great knight to his knees and within seconds he passed out on the ground. His brothers were stunned, but now raised their weapons against Adder. They never got the opportunity, they were attacked. Evil clowns came running out of the circus entrance. There was a fight, but in seconds the clowns overwhelmed the brothers and started to drag them kicking and screaming. Their vampire powers would be stripped away, and they had no reaper power like myself. Before long they were gone, to some hellish place that even made me feel a tad bit sorry for them. The feeling passed quickly.

Adder smiled at me, "I will have a truly glorious time with them. Still, I will miss your beauty and radiant smile. Come back and visit soon."

I smiled, "Not likely."

Adam approached me, but I was frozen in place. We were eye-to-eye, and I was speechless. He pulled me into his arms and hugged me with all his might. His voice was strained as he asked, "Will you ever forgive yourself?"

I was crying, "I did."

He was crying, "I have forgiven you. What took you so long to come back? I expect *you* to beg for forgiveness within the week." He was openly weeping.

I hugged him tighter, "I couldn't take you with me. You were safe; at least that is what I had hoped."

Alice yelled out, "You're making me cry! I hate you both," then joined in our hug. We held each other for a while. For the first time in a long time, I felt happy and safe.

I broke free wiping my face of the tears. I still had business to attend to, "Adder, what about Zoey? She's not very powerful, but she means a lot to me."

Adder raised his hand, "Say no more. Three for three and I'm getting the better end. Melabeth, come here for a second."

I started walking forward when I heard Alice say, "Careful." I came to a stop just outside of the invisible barrier around the circus. I could not see it, but I knew it was there.

Adder came and stood in front of me. I knew even if I stepped back into the circus he would let me out again. It would never serve this man to have the world destroyed. He gave me a grin, "If you succeed in saving the world and destroying the book, I will owe you. Zoey is coming, and she carries with her a small payment for the debt. The man who has that book will be able to destroy any spirit weapon you bring but what I have made you… well, let's just say it will most likely last longer than you. One more thing, Melabeth, with this weapon you will carry the hopes and dreams of the living. Carry it well."

Zoey was now in sight, and she had something strapped to her back. She didn't look too freaked out or hurt. Adder waved goodbye to her, but she just narrowed her eyes. I said, "Goodbye, Adder."

We started to head out when a van pulled into the parking lot. At first I didn't think anything about it, but I realized that it was our band's van. The door slid open, and Summer hopped out, followed by Dan. Summer yelled out, "Now we can get this party started!"

Spooky jumped out the driver's door, and, before I knew it, there were hugs all around. Spooky even gave Alice a hug. Who would have guessed? Michael's Camaro pulled up; Michael and Ezra stepped out. Once again the hugging and the "glad you made it" started all over.

Michael started to kiss Zoey; she didn't look like she minded it one little bit. He suddenly broke free, "You are Zoey, right?"

She laughed, "Yes, yes I am." She pulled his face to her, and they began to kiss again.

I looked over, and Ezra and Spooky were kissing, I found Adam's face. He smiled at me and wagged his eyebrows, "Well, what do you say?" I pulled him to me and kissed him deeply.

Alice teased, "Well, Dan, it looks like there's a lot of kissing. What you say, for old time's sake?"

Dan shrugged his shoulders, "Not a chance, but I wouldn't mind a hug, old friend."

Adam spoke to Dan, "By the way, thanks for getting my sister back."

Dan smiled, "My pleasure. It wasn't very hard your sister was clever when she enchanted her hair so that I could track her and teleport her."

Summer moaned; she was the only one not with someone, "I wish I was clever enough to have a boyfriend. This is so unfairish." I broke free from my Adam and walked timidly over to her. Her eyes narrowed, "You gonna kiss me?"

"I haven't had a chance to beg for your forgiveness." I paused, and she waited. "Ok, here it goes. Please, please, please, forgive me. In the short time we've been friends... you've meant a lot to me. What I mean is you're more like a sister. What I did to your father, well, I can't take it back."

She stared at me; her face looked tight as she tried to hide her emotions. "Do you know what it's like to grow up without parents? I'm not like Adam. I'm not ready to forgive *you*."

I nodded, "I understand."

Before I could turn away, she asked "Why? I need to know, and I know it won't make anything better."

I gathered my thoughts, "Well, David and I were fighting the order. He was targeted for making weapons for Order members."

"Ok," I could see her lost in thought.

She had started to walk away, "He didn't die in vain." She turned to listen, and I noticed I now had everyone's attention. I explained, "My life as a vampire started in turmoil. I was raped and murdered, and then I rose from the grave to find nothing and nobody. I murdered a man that night and almost killed his wife. I was a monster full of anger and the need for revenge.

"I found myself hunting down the men who had killed me, but so much shit happened along the way. I found myself in fight after fight. I deserved my revenge, didn't I? People I came to love and care about died for me. Doesn't that mean that I was just? People died for me! I don't even really know when it happened, but one day life meant very little to me, and killing someone meant even less. The Order stood in my way, and that also included your father. When I killed him, I took his last memory. Do you want to know what that was?"

Summer and Adam answered in stereo, "Yes."

"His last memory was the love of his family. He planned on running away with you guys and escaping the war. He was a good man, and his memory convicted me in so many ways. When I look back it was after killing him that I realized I was no longer the good guy. I want to say I changed, but I didn't. Only being burned to death after trying to kill yet another innocent person stopped me. Then I went to Hell." It wasn't truly Hell, but it felt like it. Rather than try to explain it, I just figured Hell was explanation enough.

Summer looked confused, "What do you mean. You didn't die?"

Alice answered, "Yes, yes, she did. Her body was burned to ashes, and her soul was set free. Her blood was now dormant in her sister. When her sister became pregnant, her blood called Melabeth back from the depth of Hell giving her a second chance. I doubt she can pull off that stunt twice in a row, but perhaps there is a higher power. For her sake I would hope not, because if the gods save you, it only means you have shit to do." She finished the last part with a wicked smile.

I laughed at Alice's remark, then I spoke seriously again, "Then they exist, because ever since I returned to Earth, I've been busy. Well, that's not entirely true; I've had some down time. I will tell you this - during my time in Hell, I spent a lot of time thinking about Aaron Reite. Reliving my mistakes, I was forced to remember… no wait, it was more than remembering. I was him, and I lived his final moments over and over again. I was forced to live his death thousands of times. His death was and is my worst nightmare. I hope that in my life, what I do for you will somehow give his soul some peace for what I did to him. In his memory I know that I can never be the monster I was."

A tear fell from Summer's eye. "I never knew, raped and killed, I never knew."

Adam pulled me forward at the same time he grabbed his sister. He pulled us together within his arms, forcing us into a hug. Now that we were all huddled together, he said in a low voice. "Time is short, and death is waiting for all of us. What we've already done has been hard, and it was nothing but a warm up. Summer, forgive her and let's move forward. We don't have time."

I started to argue, "Adam, she doesn't have to."

Summer pulled me close, "No, he's right. I don't want you to die without forgiving you. I want to hate you. It's just hard to forget how you have saved my freak of a brother, and what a superfishly friend you've been to me."

We laughed, cried and hugged some more when Alice finally announced, "Can we leave the parking lot. What's for dinner? Does anyone have a plan? Can I get a new dress? Damn, is it drama time in the park?"

Dan shook his head, "What have I gotten myself into?"

I laughed, "Listen up my strange family. Let's go to Michael's house. There we'll plan."

It took hours before everyone had a shower, a bite to eat, and fresh clothes. Finally we all met in Michael's living room. I first told everyone what I had learned from Luna and how Richard had stolen the book. Dan was furious, yelling about how others trusted her. The conversation soon turned into a back-and-forth. No one knew what we should do, or even who to do it too. An hour into this conversation to nowhere, we started talking about different things, when a guest arrived. Alex formed from a shadow with a grin on his face. He announced, "I'm glad to see all your faces. For those who don't know, I am Alex McDonald, the man who wrote the letters. It is time that I explained to you all the truth of things."

Chapter 40 True Enemy

Alex got everyone's attention quickly. He was forced to answer some of Alice's crazy questions, but it didn't take him long to get the conversation back on track.

He started to explain, "Most of you received letters from me." Michael, Ezra, Spooky and Dan all nodded. Black dust formed around Alex's hand, and another letter formed from that dust. He then presented it to Alice, "A favor."

She took the letter and opened it. Quickly scanning over the letter, a wicked smile formed on her face. "Oh dear, we will get along just fine. This won't be a problem."

Alex replied, "Good. Are we ready to plan our next move?" Everyone responded with a yes. "Great! Let us first discuss whom we are fighting. First, you need to know there was only one plot, and all of us were playing supporting roles. The man we're dealing with is nothing more than a genius with a little bit of luck. Let me start from the beginning.

"We all know now, thanks to Melabeth, Richard's true part in this. We know that Alice played her part." She frowned and crossed her arms over her chest, but everyone ignored her. "So, what changed? Who has the book, and what do they plan on doing with it? This has been the question on everyone's lips. This means no one has any idea who has the book. At first I thought perhaps that Richard had left it in South America for safe keeping. It didn't make sense; the book was safe with him. I was as lost as everyone else as to the whereabouts of the book, until I started comparing stories, then it all made sense.

"Alice was quoted as saying that she recovered the book directly after Richard dropped it. She had found it in the hallway on the ship, right after he teleported away. Melabeth had been chased away by a fire element and later ended up with Peter on an island. Alice, you said that the book never left your side. When Dan came to pick it up, he checked the book with a spell and found out it was under an illusion spell. Angered, he left, an, from that moment on, the book was lost. Alice didn't know where it was, and Luna believed Alice had tricked everyone and kept the book for herself. So, let me clarify. Alice, you had the book with you the whole time?"

Alice sounded confident, "I did."

Alex turned towards Dan, "How long can an illusion spell work, the one cast on the bible?"

Dan replied, "If the caster is strong, a week or two. Of course, the book was in Las Vegas, as most of you might know, Vegas does not have any mana. It might last forty-eight hours in Vegas."

Alice laughed, "That's how we keep it away from the riffraff." Her face changed expressions as something hit her. "I had that book sitting next to me for at least five days. I flew back as soon as I got to shore and was stuck waiting for Melabeth to rejoin me. She was off playing with Peter on an island. Dan took forever to come and get the book, even though it was *so* important."

Dan defended himself, "I had to get away without anyone noticing. It was instrumental that Luna did not believe that I had the book. What I don't understand is, how did someone make that simple spell last so long in Vegas?"

Alex answered, "They didn't."

I remembered that night, and I answered the question before Alex could. "Alice didn't have the book on her at all times."

Alice blurted out, "Yes, I did."

Dan came to my rescue, "You didn't have it the night I came to get it. You sent, I believe, it was Melabeth, to go get it."

I finished where he left off, "I did go get it. Alice had brought it down to my room. She had been very excited to hear about what happened to me. In her hurry to hear the tale, she left it in my room and not alone either. David had been there with my ghost Carrie. Carrie followed us up to Alice's room and left David alone in the room. When Alice requested that I grab the book, I went to my room to find it empty. David was gone. He left a note on top of the book, saying he had something to do and would see me later that day."

Alice growled, "A Gideon's Bible, no less. That snake in the grass."

I added more to the story. "It was after that he started to show great improvements to his magic. He developed Zombies - the animated dead that could survive daylight and run off the power of the trapped soul. You could kill the necromancer who summoned it, but the Zombies would keep on coming. He figured out how to make spirit weapons using souls and later a gas that could kill you and then raise you as a zombie."

Alex finished the story. "He has had twenty years since then to develop weapons. He has also developed a following. It's not much of a leap; you all have most likely figured out that David is Necro Z. He has the book, and I believe he is preparing to end the world." A murmur burst out of all of us. Alex hushed us, "It's worse than you can imagine. I found writing in the land of the dead. Only Melabeth would understand this, but, just understand, spirits leave behind knowledge in a place called the Library. A fellow necromancer named Ralf Pitt, died not too long ago. He was David's buddy.

"I found information, in his mind that uncovered what David is planning to do and why. David wants to kill God and rule both Death and Life. Whether he can do this doesn't matter, because he plans on building an army. He plans on killing every last human and trapping their souls in their bodies and making them into zombies. He believes once he's conquered the earth and turned the world into zombies, he can open a gateway to the land of Death. He plans on marching his seven billion monster army, right into Heaven and overthrowing God himself."

Dan yelled out, "That's crazy!" Everyone yelled out similar things.

"Yes," Alex continued and everyone quieted back down. "It is crazy, but you need to know who we're dealing with. He might be crazy, but he is smart, powerful and has plenty of followers. We can't wait any longer; we must take him down."

Alice stood up, "I have phone calls to make."

The planning went on all night long. It didn't take long to figure out what needed to be done. We needed to take David down, and we would have to go to Vegas to do it. Dan, Summer, Zoey, and Adam would be useless in Vegas. Summer could enchant things, but that took time, and she couldn't enchant in Vegas. Dan would be powerless except for using magical items. Zoey was a newborn and was nothing but a liability. Adam would be little to no help. He might be able to foul a few necromancers' spells, but useless against the army of the undead, spirits and Nosferatu.

We all thought it best they go back to the city of Queen Anne to protect the others. Summer, Alice, Ezra, Michael, Spooky and I would go to Vegas. Dan agreed; he felt that perhaps there could be problems there as well. Plus he needed to deal with Luna. I wasn't sure how he planned on doing this, but I had faith that the old wizard was better equipped to deal with her than us. Luna might make her move soon; it wouldn't take her long to find out about the Lionhearts. Alice announced that we had a small trip first. We needed to go see some man by the name of Dr. Fritts.

Finally, we called an end to our meeting. Adam had been giving me harsh stares ever since the announcement that he would be going to Queen Anne without me. He came over gently taking my hand, "Let's go out on the balcony so we can talk." He led me outside. He had barely shut the door, "I'm coming with you."

I grabbed him and pulled him into my arms. Kissing him deeply, too quickly he pulled free from the kiss. He stared at me awaiting my answer, "No."

His eyes narrowed, "No, that's all you have to say? I am going."

I smiled, "In my heart, I will always be with you."

He really looked hurt. "You're not taking me seriously."

"I am, but you're not listening. I am in command for the rest of this mission, and I already said that you aren't going. I do have my reasons."

He looked like he was going to say something, but thought better of it. "Ok, what are these reasons, Miss Commander?"

I took a second to organize my thoughts. "First, you're a distraction for me. Two, your powers will be useless in Vegas, not in Queen Anne. If they attack or Luna pulls a fast one, I'm counting on you to protect my family... and your sister. Did I also mention that you are a distraction?" I said the last part with a husky voice, rubbing his chest with my finger.

He was trying to remain mad, "That won't work."

Breathlessly, I asked, "What won't work?"

"What you're doing." his eyes said he was lying. They were full of passion, "If you go without me, I'll be stuck worrying about you. I hate that feeling. I worried about you the whole time you were gone, and now I find out I had good reason to worry. How will I sleep knowing you are going to battle?"

My mind slipped back to watching him being whipped. "You worried, but who has the scars on their back? Another thing, you're not healed. You will have to sleep the same way I will, restless. I need you to go, not for me or because I am trying to save you. How will I know that Queen Anne hasn't fallen under attack and all my family is not dead? If I stay with all of you I will be able to protect you. Well, that is for a while. And then Necro Z will rise up an army of dead and kill us all. If I die in this battle, don't worry about it, and you will be close behind me. Don't you see? I can't fail... *you can't help me.* I need you safe; I need to know if I win that you'll be waiting for me there to put me back together again with your love. I also need you where you will do the most good."

He huffed, "I don't know...."

I smiled, "Perhaps we should go upstairs and talk about it."

He grinned, "Cheater."

A few hours later I lay next to Adam, wrapped up tight, our naked bodies covered by sheets. I kissed his neck, "I've been waiting for that. I was worried it might never happen again." He said nothing, but responded by gently touching my face. Slowly his fingers found their way through my hair and down my back. I shivered at his touch as I stared into his purple eyes. "Thank you."

He moved to get comfortable. I spied his torn up back. He looked ashamed, "How bad does it look?"

I smiled, "Scars make me hot."

"I can't believe you don't want to bring me, even if it's just to use me for sex." His fight gone from his voice, replaced with playfulness.

I laughed, "That alone almost changed my mind."

He looked into my eyes, "You're really not letting me go?" I shook my head, "What if the sex becomes so good you can't live without it?"

"I can't, but I'll be with you before you know it."

He shook his head, "I better give it one more shot. It will be the last time to change your mind."

"Oh my," was all I had time to say as he took me again.

How time flies when you're having fun; I stared at Adam as he slumbered. His chest rose and fell with a steady rhythm. Laying my head on his chest made the sound of his heart fill my mind. Instead of hunger, I felt happy as his power kept the vampire in me at bay. I knew the sun had just risen, and my poor body hadn't slept for days. Still, I was too happy to sleep and most likely wouldn't until Adam and company hit the road. The plan had been for them to hit the road this morning.

I heard the light footsteps approach the door, followed by a light knock on the door. Zoey whispered, "May I come in?"

"Yes," I whispered in reply. She heard me and came into the room. She gave me a smile as she looked at me wrapped up with Adam in bed. "Is it time?"

"Close, I just wanted to pack some stuff before they leave." I realized that Adam and I had used her room. I felt slightly embarrassed about it, when Zoey seemed to have read my mind. "Hey, don't even sweat it. I don't sleep at night… not that you guys do much sleeping." She followed that with a grin.

I could feel her as well as she felt me. She wanted to ask me something, but wasn't sure she could, "Ask! You really deserve to ask anything you want after the hell I dragged you through."

She relaxed, "Well, I have so many questions. Listening to everyone talk made it sound like that, perhaps, what you and I did… the body switching? That was not really a vampire thing. What was that? Why do I feel you? I feel like you're my mother or something. Sorry, that sounded stupid."

"No, no, no, that is because I am." Her face was full of shock. "I don't have the time or the energy to start explaining half of this to you. The fact is, Michael made you, but not with his blood. He made you with my blood and I'm only half vampire. Michael has never understood this, so he has no idea what he has really done to you."

It didn't take a mental link to see the thousands of questions building in her mind, "What else are you?"

I smiled, "Angel of Death." I laughed as her mouth fell open. "Don't think about it right now. You'll have plenty of time hanging out with Adam, Dan, and my family. They'll explain more to you later, ok?"

Getting my hint, she agreed to question everyone else to death. She loaded up all her prized possessions into a large gym bag. It really didn't take her long. She asked a few more questions which I answered. She was just about to leave when I heard Dan yelling upstairs for Adam; they were about ready to go.

Suddenly Zoey remembered something, "Before I forget, Adder gave me this to give to you."

She walked across the room and grabbed the long bag she had been carrying on her back when she left the circus. I had forgotten about Adder's little gift. It was a long black bag made out of nylon. I wrapped a sheet around myself as Zoey handed me the package. Unzipping the top and reaching inside, I pulled out a sword, and it was breathtaking.

In my hands was the most beautiful Katana I had ever seen. It was bright red with black accents. The hand guard was black with red cloth wrapping the handle. I could feel the magic in this weapon. Taking the grip, I slid the weapon free of the sheath. The blade was bright shining steel. I moved the sword around me in slow choreographed moves.

Zoey was in awe, "That's cool."

Adam awoke, "Damn, a gift from another man?" I hardly looked at him as he teased me. I slid the sword back into the sheath with great reverence. Adam added, "I might be jealous, of the sword that is."

I laughed, "What can I say? I like sharp things."

I put the sword away for now. I wanted to spend every minute with Adam. Once again, a whirlwind of activities surrounded us as Adam and the rest of his party prepared to leave. Adam grabbed a quick bite, I watched him chew; staring at him like it was the next big thing on TV. Alice made it a point to groan at me several times as I followed Adam around and ignored everyone else, but I was going to make every moment count. Adam didn't say much about it, but I could tell he felt the same way.

Dan came up to me and gave me a hug. He looked at me dead serious, "You stay safe. Our band would suck without you, and we have some gigs coming up."

I smiled, "Right after I purify David, I'll be back to rock the night."

Alice caught on to our conversation, "What band?"

I answered, "PTF, Purification Through Fire. We started a rock band and we went around purifying dip wads who had it coming to them. We weren't too bad at it either."

Summer piped in, "We weren't too bad at the music part either."

We laughed as Ezra said, "Can't wait to hear you guys play."

Dan reached in and pulled out a CD from his bag. He tossed it over to Ezra, "Signed and everything."

Ezra looked down at the CD and truly looked grateful, "Thanks."

Like all things in life, when you want something not to come to an end, it happens quickly. It felt like minutes and my time with Adam and company was over. I watched Michael slide Zoey's coffin into the back of the van. Minutes later, the van was out of sight. We didn't wait around. Quickly we hopped into Michael's darkly tinted Hummer. It won't be safe staying any longer in Michael's house. I was sure that Luna was on the warpath by now.

I crawled into the back seat and before I knew it, I fell into a deep sleep. All the emotions in the world can't keep you up forever.

Chapter 41 Dr. Fritts

"Time to wake up, sleepy head," Alice was shaking me awake.

"Where are we?" I asked disoriented.

I realized we were still in the aircraft that we had boarded that morning. The sun was peeking in through one of the shades. Michael was a corpse along with Ezra. I asked, "What time is it?"

Alice replied, "Four-thirty mountain time. The plane should be landing soon."

"Where is that?" I inquired.

"Texas - that's where Dr. Fritts is. He's not really a doctor; he's a weapons dealer. We need supplies before we attack David. Good chance is he knows we're coming, so we may as well go with as much bang as we can carry."

We sat quietly for a moment; Michael and Ezra still sleeping as the plane hummed along. Alice was sitting there with a thoughtful look. "Ok, so why did you wake me up?" I asked.

Alice shrugged, "I was awake. Spooky is hanging with the pilot. Not that she wants to talk to me."

"Missed me?" I teased.

"Nope, it was nice to get away from you. Since you're here, would you like to play some cards?"

I smiled, "Nothing better to do, deal me in." Why I enjoyed her company was beyond me. She never said nice things to anyone. Still, it wasn't what she said, rather what she did. I was happy the little devil was back...deep down I had really missed her.

Looking at my cards I asked, "So, can you tell me what your letter said?"

She nodded, "It asked me to make phone calls to prepare for your arrival in Vegas." She paused as if she was deciding to tell me the rest. "It also said to make arrangements if you failed."

I thought about it for a second, "Did you?"

"Yes," she replied, offering no more information.

I always knew this might be a one way trip, but to have it confirmed by Alex that he was preparing for the possibility of my death was sobering to hear. "Good," I said.

Alice added, "I made many arrangements. I have a feeling not all of us will make it." Then with a wicked grin, "I will."

The plane had finally landed. I lost every hand, but I was deeply suspicious that Alice was cheating. My second sight didn't allow me to see anything but shape, so, if she had used her power to change the face of the cards, I would not have known.

It was late in the evening by the time we arrived at a crappy-looking pawn shop in El Paso. We piled out of a rented Chevy van. The neighborhood looked almost as bad as the shop. Spooky looked around, "Nice place."

Alice laughed, "Good place to grab a bite. Let's say two hours, and we all meet back here. Dr. Fritts is the owner of this fine establishment and will be expecting us."

Spooky took the van, talking about a nice taco place she spotted on the way in. The rest of us split up since it was faster to hunt by ourselves, and we were on a schedule. It didn't take me long to find a quick bite. It wasn't late only about nine when I came upon a party. It was a Hispanic party with loud music and lots of dancing spread between two homes in a small neighborhood. It was easy to attract boys away from the crowd with the promise of sex. I fed on three young men and left them where they lay, to sleep it off.

I was not hungry, but it had only been an hour. I enjoyed feeding, and, even if I didn't feed, it would be more entertaining to hang out here instead of the pawnshop. It didn't take long before my body fell into the rhythm of the music. The men danced with me, while the women glared. It felt good to let my body just move.

At one point it sounded as if there was a fight as a woman yelled in a language I didn't understand. It took me a second to realize the loud music had stopped, and everyone's eyes were on me. An old lady stood not far from me screaming at me; behind her some gentlemen were carrying in one of the men I had fed off. Blood was still stained across his neck and covering his shirt.

I walked backwards through the crowd as the old lady yelled curses at me. Some of the younger crowd was saying she was loco. I quickly turned around and left the party. Some men yelled, "Senorita! You don't have to go!"

It didn't take me long to find my way back to the pawn shop. There was something about being a vampire that bothered me. The way that lady acted was just one of them - the hate in that woman's eyes. Of course, she had good reason. I had already attacked three men and at any time could have killed one. She was calling me something in Spanish, but I didn't need to understand it, to know she meant vampire or demon.

I went inside the pawn shop. The place was just as shitty on the inside as it was outside. Long metal shelves held piles of crap, precariously balanced stacks of: tools, old electronics, and random junk. At the far end of the room stood some glass counters filled with stuff. Jewelry, guns, and an assortment of valuables that might fit in your pocket, were on display behind the glass. Two men were working the counter, a young man and an old one. The old guy was half sitting on a stool holding the wall up, with a look of boredom. The young man looked to be moving stuff and cataloging.

The old man eyed me, "Can I help you?"

The young boy stopped what he was doing to look up. He was Hispanic, but his English was spot on, "What he means is, can I do anything for you? Cause he ain't moving."

The old man was white, with a big mustache and an old cowboy hat. He said, with no feeling, "That's why we hired you, wetback."

The boy blew it off, "Ignore him; he would be dead if it weren't for meanness keeping him alive."

I looked at the clock. I had arrived half an hour late. I guess I had been shaking my ass a little longer than I thought. No wonder they found one of my victims. I asked the boy, "I'm here to see Dr. Fritts."

The boy no longer appeared to be friendly. The old man answered the question, "Never heard anyone go by that name. Either you're buying, selling or leaving."

I thought for a minute. My heart beat that slow steady beat. I had forgotten how human I looked. I smiled and gave them a good look at my fangs. "My friends should have already come in. So, either you're helping me by calling Dr. Fritts or you're on the menu."

The boy relaxed, "Sorry, didn't realize you were one of them." He then spoke to the old man, "See, what did I say? If they're pretty and come in this shit box, they're dead."

The old man nodded at the boy, then pointed with his thumb towards a door that led further into the building. "There, in the back."

The boy voluntarily led me to the back room, which was full of random shit. He slid a secret panel on the wall to the side that led to a staircase heading down. The boy told me just to follow my way down. I headed down to yet another large door. As I knocked on the door, it unlocked and a cute, young girl ushered me in.

Once inside, I almost fell over. The place was plush and beautifully decorated. Row after row of shelves lined the walls and filled up the center. Instead of piles of shit, there were neatly marked boxes and knickknacks. Everything was labeled and looked to be expensive. I walked deeper into the room and followed the aisle between some shelves. When I reached a clearing on the other side, I could see Alice and the rest of our party talking to who I guessed was Dr. Fritts.

Dr. Fritts was a vampire, not too tall and very thin. His face was narrow, and he reminded me of Sting. His blonde hair was in spikes, and his beard was trying its hardest to grow. He was well kept, wearing a suit while he spoke in an animated fashion about his merchandise. The merchandise he was going on about, lay behind everyone, so it took a moment before it became clear.

Before me lay a pile of weapons; the more my eyes focused, the more I saw. There were more weapons further behind Dr. Fritts and stacks of crates. He was showing a shotgun to Alice, "Now this is an AA-12 shotgun, fully automatic, four hundred rounds-a-minute. It comes with these thirty-two round drums. This rifle fires with the most amazing recoil reduction system. A child could fire it fully."

Ezra commented, "Kind of bulky to carry a lot of ammo." The drum the doctor was holding was kind of on the large side compared to thirty round clips for assault rifles.

Dr. Fritts acted as if he was waiting for that comment, "Yes, but consider this." He pulled out four different colored shotgun rounds out of his pocket. "The first two shells are common enough. Buck shot and slug. These two rounds are special; the red one is called dragon's breath. I won't get technical, but anything you shoot will burst into flames. I know what you're thinking, what if everything in sight just needs to die?" He held up a green shell, "*This* little monster is for you. It shoots a high velocity fragmenting round. In short, it's a small mortar. Now, imagine firing exploding rounds at the rate of four hundred rounds-a-minute."

Alice clapped her hands together, "I'll take two, one for each arm. I want as many exploding rounds as I might be able to carry."

I noticed the young girl sitting in the corner taking notes on a computer. Ezra looked around, "Well have you ever seen Terminator?"

Dr. Fritts' face lit up and in a single breath, "You want a mini? You *do* mean the M134 Minigun, firing 7.62x51 mm NATO, six-barreled machine gun with a high rate of fire at six thousand rounds-per-minute? It features Gatling-style rotating barrels with an external power source, to run the electric motor. " Ezra just shook his head with a grin a mile wide. Dr. Fritts looked over at the young girl, "You heard the man, load it in the van. You know I bought one of those years ago and was starting to wonder if anyone was going to buy it. Well, I think we're done with guns."

I cleared my throat, "I want a few." I looked down at the pile as the young lady slid over yet another large crate. She must have been a vampire, too; Ezra was already opening and eyeing his new weapon with a gleam in his eye.

Dr. Fritts, "I'm sorry, you must be Melabeth. I got so excited I forgot we were still awaiting another person. Now that I look at you… well, it was worth the wait."

I laughed at him, and his smiled deepened. The next little while was crazy as I picked out my guns. I ended up with a pair of forty XD Springfield's with many spare clips and all the accessories to carry it all. I didn't go too crazy with firepower. Instead, I chose an M4 with a red dot, plus mags and ammo. I was glad I was not paying the bill.

Some helpers came in and started to cart our stuff out to the van. I thought this would be the end of it, but then things really got interesting. Dr. Fritts, who I expected was not really a doctor, led us to yet another secret room. This room was different. It looked like I was on the set of Downton Abbey. The room felt crowded with old world stuff, but you didn't have to be magical to feel the magic in this room. In the center of the room was a rocking chair; what was in that chair made the hair on the back of my neck stand up.

On the chair was a doll, a doll that looked just like Alice. Her black hair was tied into pigtails, with a white face with large blue eyes. Alice ran across the room, dropping her old doll on the way, "You did it! You finished Dolly… she's beautiful!"

Dr. Fritts added, "And dangerous. She runs off your blood; you just add it in her mouth. After that she will do what you will. One more thing, if she runs out of juice, you can command her to take a nap. When you do that, don't be anywhere near her. I like to call it 'the final fit'."

Alice smiled wickedly at her new doll. As she lifted it, there were also two long daggers in sheaths behind the doll, "Oh, you finished my weapons... good."

Ezra asked, "Michael and my weapons, did you finish them as well?"

Dr. Fritts smiled, "Ye of little faith." He walked over to a fireplace and picked up a poker. He then tossed it over to Ezra, "Give that a try."

Ezra spun the poker around by the shaft. The next thing I knew, he was holding a large double-sided ax. He smiled at the weapon, "Perfect."

The doctor picked up another metal pole and tossed it at Michael, "They're both the same weapon. You may choose the shape once a day and as long as you hold them they will not break. They pull from your strength to stay strong. Not too many other enchantments hold up in Vegas, so I kept it simple."

Michael had turned his pole into a war hammer with a spike on one side, "That's fine, these will do."

The doctor turned to me, "I heard you don't need anything."

I shook my head. I have my sword. His disappointment was over-exaggerated, but it quickly turned to excitement. He rubbed his hands together, "Time for the big one."

He ran over to the corner and pushed out what appeared to be a mannequin on wheels covered by a white sheet. Spooky, who had looked left out, was even curious. She had no need of guns, because she could be a powerful tiger. Alice squealed, "Drum roll!"

Michael and Ezra started what was nothing short of the world's worst drum roll. They stopped when they realized everyone was staring at them like they had lost their minds. Michael shrugged and Dr. Fritts laughed and pulled the sheet off.

What stood before me was amazing. A suit of armor, held up on a mannequin. The suit didn't look European - instead it looked more Japanese, like a samurai. The metal was glistening black. It looked as if it were wet, it shined so much. I could feel the magic coming off the suit. I wasn't sure who this suit was for, but I kind of wanted to claim it.

Alice beamed at the armor, "It's for you." Alice was looking at Spooky.

Spooky's face tightened, "Me?" She said pointing at herself, "I can't wear that."

Dr. Fritts explained, "Oh, let me tell you about this armor. First, there were only three suits ever made, and only two in existence. Long ago, there was a great enchanter who specialized in armor. Who really cares about him? What we care about is the magical properties of this armor. In short, this armor will take the shape of any shapeshifter who wears it. The seller I bought this from went into great detail on how he accomplished this great feat, but I say let's try it." He gave Spooky a look, "It has padding and is meant to be worn with nothing underneath."

Her face dropped and she gave him a dirty look, "As if."

The Doctor pretended to be taken aback, "I didn't mean I would watch you get into this." Then he said in a lower voice, "Unless you wanted me to."

The doctor was kind of creepy and funny all rolled up into one. He knew that everyone in the room could hear him and laughed loudly after saying it. Of course he was told to leave so she could try it on. Spooky got dressed with Alice and me as we sent all the men to finish loading the truck and play with the guns.

I stood back and looked at her, "Wow, you look scary hot! How does it move?"

She twisted around and moved side to side. Alice and I giggled at her as she made funny stretches, "Seems good, not too constricting. Not heavy either, not like I can't lift a small car. I'm going to shift… if this hurts me; I'm going to hurt Fritts."

Before my eyes she became a large Black Tiger with red stripes. She was huge, bigger than any Tiger I'd ever seen. Her back had stood as high as my shoulders without the armor; with it she looked even taller. The armor had stretched and formed over her new shape, moving with her when she shifted. Instead of black metal, it looked like silly putty as it took its new form. The giant armored cat stood before me, she let out a roar. Alice said what I was thinking, "Awesome."

The next few hours we spent hanging out with Dr. Fritts. He was taking pictures with Spooky as a Tiger. His whole crew had to check her out. Most of his crew appeared to be young women - all vampires - so it was impossible to know their true age. Every girl had different color hair and hung on every word the doctor said. Even the grumpy old cowboy came down. He looked almost excited before heading back upstairs. Eventually Spooky took her human form but was in no hurry to take off her armor.

I heard Dr. Fritts lean over to Spooky, "Glad you like the armor; Alice sure wanted you to have that." He said the next part proudly. "It took every connection I have to get that suit for you."

Spooky asked, "How much did it cost?"

Fritts grinned, "Let's just say, we should be calling you 'the million dollar woman'." Spooky gasped.

She stood up and walked over to Alice who was in conversation with Ezra about who had the best weapons. "Did you really spend a million dollars on this?"

Alice narrowed her eyes at Dr. Fritts, who pretended to be needed elsewhere. "Not nice to ask how much someone spent on you for a gift. Consider it an early Christmas gift."

Spooky eyed Alice, "Why? You've never done anything nice for me before. Is this your way of apologizing?"

Ezra shook his head like he knew what was coming. Alice looked shocked, "Buying someone's affections through expensive gifts is NOT an apology, even if this person were to re-think the way they may or may not have treated this other person. A gift by itself does not constitute an apology in any shape, way, or form." She finished this by crossing her arms across her chest tightly.

Spooky hugged her, "Thank you Alice; I accept your apology." She turned and hurried off to the sound of Alice yelling about how this was not an apology. I laughed, and realized that I couldn't be leading a more dysfunctional group of people into battle. Yet who else was there?

Fritts asked with sly eyes, "Let's talk about payment." His voice promised something wicked.

Alice just smiled, "Bill me."

"Oh, no," Dr. Fritts corrected. "Let's come to terms now. Money is one thing, but that..." he said this part while looking at me and waving his hand up and down my body, "Is another, and I want a little bit of the other." His eyes undressed me as I came to understand his full meaning.

Alice giggled, "Oh Doctor, of course you can have her for one night. One little, tiny, itsy bitsy warning... she doesn't obey me. Good luck!"

Dr. Fritts looked deflated, "Is she dangerous?"

Ezra shook his head and started lying, "Harmless. You go right ahead."

Dr. Fritts narrowed his eyes, "Damn it." He then looked at me, "I meant no offense; have fun storming the castle, or whatever you're about to do." After quoting the Princess Bride, he waved us goodbye. His girls looked relieved that he was not taking me into his bed.

As we left I noticed the young vampire girls looking at me with a strange stare. I suddenly realized I had no idea just how evil this doctor might be. For now, I couldn't worry about it; I had the world to save.

It wasn't long before we were all piled in the van heading down the interstate. My mind was lost in thought as we rode, talking very little. I already missed Adam, but was glad he was somewhere safe. I had no idea what was about to happen, but, if I survived it, I would see my family again - my brother and sister/mother and her husband. I could start a life with Adam and hang out with Summer and Alice. It seemed too good to be true, so better not make plans yet. I still could be killed before all this was over.

Spooky took over once the sun came up. The rest of us crawled into the back of the van and slept. I woke up around three and, thanks to my beating heart and sunglasses, I was able to take over for Spooky. I hadn't driven long before we entered Boulder City. We woke up Alice. She grumbled and told me to go to the Fontainebleau Casino. She then turned around and went back to sleep. For the next hour Spooky and I shot the breeze. Everyone was awake by the time we hit Las Vegas.

We arrived at the Fontainebleau Casino. As I looked up at the building, I noticed it wasn't finished being built. Alice informed me, "That building will never be finished; the company that was building it went belly up. Almost skeleton of a casino stands unused."

Ezra added, "Fontainebleau was supposed to be a $2.9 billion, 3,889-room, 68-story building - a perfect place to stage our operation." Ezra directed me around back where he gave me a gate code allowing me to enter. The road led me through a half-finished building and then down a ramp into an underground parking lot.

I came to a stop when I noticed two soldiers standing there with rifles at the ready. Alice beamed, "Good they're already waiting for us."

It surprised me, but it shouldn't have. Alice had connections with the United States Military. Come to find out, they had been waiting for us. We were quickly led deep within the seemingly endless building. They had a huge headquarters setup. Surrounded by soldiers were stacks of desks with computers, and screens hung from every wall while a fury of activity was happening. All the office workers were in uniform. If they weren't typing into their computers, they were talking into their phones.

I felt really out of place standing there with my company. We got more than a few looks; I mean, how could we not have. I was dressed like a teenage girl. Spooky was not much older looking than me. Alice looked like she just came off the set of some horror movie. Michael looked like he was on his way to shoot for GQ. In fact, the only one of us that didn't look like we were lost was Ezra. He was in a black suit, tall, good-looking and in his thirties, and he could have passed as a secret agent.

A man approached us with confidence, a sense of direction and purpose. He must be in charge. "I'm Brigadier General Morris of the United States Army. I'm in charge of this mission. Which one of you goes by the name Melabeth?"

He was so forceful. I raised my hand, "That would be me."

He looked at me like he wasn't impressed, "Good enough. I will be filling you in with a situational report." He turned and started walking, "Follow me."

Alice spoke as we walked, "The general and I go way back."

The general came to a stop in front of a set of screens, each displaying blueprints and pictures from obvious surveillance. He spoke with no emotion, "Yes, Alice, good to see you as well. Let's get down to business. Alice, some years ago, made us aware of the necromancers and the building of the Luxor. Ever since then, we have infiltrated the casino and have a good idea of what we're up against. We have been aware that they have been working on a weapon. What this weapon is, or where it might be found, we still do not know. I have been led to believe that you, Melabeth, can give us insight."

"Well, in a word, sir,… Zombies." The general cocked his head.

I launched into what I knew about David. The meeting went on for hours. I filled them in, and, in turn, they filled me in. They had been infiltrating the Luxor for years now. They had undercover employees watching what was going on. They hadn't been able to break into the inner circle, so they were down to surveillance, but that was very limited. I had a feeling that the necromancer ghost kept a closer eye on their agents than the other way around. The Army noticed that in the last few days there had been lots of activity around the Luxor. Necromancers had been returning from abroad. Vampires had been leaving town. The rise of Nosferatu attacks was happening throughout the city.

The general informed me of the goings-on underneath the city. The tunnels that were used by vampires and others had been busier than usual. A lot of humans were being invited down into the tunnels and underground structures. You would be hard pressed to find a bum in Vegas; the homeless had gone down into the tunnels in droves. It looked as if food, drugs and alcohol were being offered for free.

Alice realized that the vampires could not be counted on. She said that a vampire could be easily controlled by the necromancers, so they were afraid. The vampires were leaving Vegas like rats on a sinking ship. That's why she called in help from the Army. We would need it to contain this. We started to hatch a plan. In the center of this plan, I would go into the Luxor and face David. Only I had a chance of ending this.

Chapter 42 Luxor

I sat upon the top roof of the Fontainebleau, sixty-eight stories above the ground. Below me the lights of the Vegas strip lit up the night. I could see the solid beam of light rising from the ground; it was the light that shot straight out of the top of the Luxor Pyramid. They say on a clear night you can see that light in California. My mind wandered as the wind whipped my hair up behind me. The cool breeze on a warm night calmed me.

Alice walked up behind me, and then joined me on the ledge, "What's you doing?"

"Waiting for someone to come and annoy me. Oh look, it's finally happened."

Alice giggled, "Miss him? You'll see him soon enough." I didn't reply. "Do you want to go hunting?"

She had been right; I was missing him. I was suddenly angry, "Why me? I don't want to be the hero. I don't want to save the world... barely even see a reason to do it."

She didn't respond right away, "What if we don't?"

The fact she said that reminded me of how selfish I was being. I was not the only person putting my life on the line. I answered in defeat, "We go home, play Uno and await the end of the world. I would rather meet my end on my own terms, if I could help it."

"Me, too," she smiled. We sat quietly together, overlooking the city. I prayed for my family and friends, for if not for them, I would not do this.

I finally broke the silence, "So do we have a plan?"

"Oh, yes. The men in uniforms will circle the problem. Our little party will land at the airport, directly across from the Luxor. There is an access at the airport to the underground tunnels, and yes, I'm sure it's guarded. We will kill, slash, and burn a path straight to the underground entrance to the Luxor. From there, it's just a matter of working through some unknown traps, killing monsters, killing David and saving the world. It should be easy." She added the last part with a big smile.

"Good, I really hate work," I jumped from my perch, and Alice followed me.

It was almost daylight. We went to rest, and, later in the afternoon, we all got up and ate. The army supplied our meals… blood in a bag, yum. After that, we armed up. I dressed head to toe in black leather. I felt like Cat Girl, but Alice demanded that I would be better protected in leather. I think she was lying when I realized she was wearing a dress. Ezra wore a suit along with Michael. Spooky was wearing nothing but her armor. At least two of us looked like we belonged in a super hero magazine.

Alice strapped her doll to her back. Her knives lay flat on her back so the handles stood at forty-five degree angles right above her shoulders. She was holding two AA-12 fully automatic shotguns, one in each hand. Ammo hung from her everywhere. I wasn't much different. My sword was attached to my back, while clips of ammo were attached anywhere I could get them. Two pistols hung from each hip, and my M4 rifle hung from a strap. Ezra looked crazy in his sharp looking suit holding a mini and a large steel backpack holding the thousands of rounds of ammo. Michael was the coolest among us; he looked like James Bond, sexy and dangerous.

We all headed to the roof where a Blackhawk was waiting to fly us to the airport. The operation would move fast. The military would secure all the entrances and exits to the underground while we penetrated the building. Alice had fed them more information than they would have ever found out on their own. There were dozens of secret entrances that she had pointed out the night before. We were secretly hoping that, between all the attacks from the military that David would not know the exact point entry, and this would mean that his forces would be spread out. If not, we didn't stand a chance.

We were all standing on the roof waiting to board the chopper. I took out a small paper cup that I had grabbed earlier. Cutting myself, I let my blood pour into the cup. My cut healed; everyone was now looking at me, wondering. I walked up and held out the cup to Ezra. He took it without question and drank the blood. I asked, "Everyone gather around."

We formed a circle; I could feel each and every one of them. Ezra smiled, and I could feel his loyalty and, surprisingly, his lust for me. It made me smile, and he was filled with joy, not because I was willing to be with him, but because I accepted him. Being bound like this was very personal, not for the light-hearted.

With my friends gathered, "We're about to go against an unknown force. I know this is my task, but all of you have chosen to fight by my side.

I may not be a great leader, but I promise you victory... for anything else will doom us all. They may take our lives, but, they will never take our FREEDOM!"

Boos and hisses erupted as they were all speaking at once. "That's Braveheart," "Really?" "I feel inspired," those were but a few words I made out.

We all laughed, and Alice told me, "That wasn't very good even by my standards... and I don't even have any standards."

We boarded the helicopter, and it started its climb skyward. Michael spoke to me, "If I don't make it, Zoey is your responsibility."

Alice answered for me, "Zoey is her responsibility regardless. Using her blood, you have bound her to all of us. I will not be bound to hundreds of different people."

Ezra yelled out, "Talk about this later; we're almost there. This isn't the time or place." You could see Alice wasn't finished with him, and he knew it.

It was only a ten-minute flight. We landed near the back of one of the terminals. TSA agents were surprised to see our group rushing the terminal. Army rangers flanked us. No one stood in our way as the Rangers led us inside the terminal. We moved into a part of the terminal that most humans never see, the lower half. It led to doors that connected to escalators heading further down. We rushed downward, and, the deeper we moved into the tunnels, the less people we passed. Soon we were alone as we entered into a large shaft that was wide enough for two trucks side by side.

Once we entered, our group fanned out. I took the lead with a Ranger on either side of me. Ezra was behind me with Alice. Michael and Spooky took up the rear with the last two Rangers. Our connection was wide open; we could feel each other's fear, excitement and worry. We also knew what the others needed so we moved without words or hand signals. The only noise I heard as we headed down the shaft was that of the soldiers. Their footfalls were heavy in my ear, and, when they whispered in their mikes, it sounded like yelling. My ears were straining for the sound of our enemies.

According to the map, we were approaching a T-section directly under Las Vegas Boulevard. It wouldn't be much further from there to the entrance of the Luxor. I was just starting to think that it seemed awfully quiet, when I heard the chatter erupt over one of the soldier's earpieces. The fighting had begun. My hearing picked up a new sound, the sound of feet - lots and lots and lots of feet.

They came down the tunnel like a wall of flesh. The sound of gunfire filled the air as the soldiers fired. I yelled, "Shoot them in the head, you're wasting bullets." I had told them earlier, but they were just excited. I dropped to one knee, and the sound of the mini made me cover my ears. Ezra hosed the zombies with bullets. Blood and body parts exploded in front of me turning the tunnel ahead into a nightmare.

The zombies moved only as fast as a human, but they feared and felt nothing. They would not tire nor quit coming. The mini slowed them down because they were now tripping over the fallen zombie bodies. I raised my M4 and took my time putting a bullet into each target's head. I felt the bolt lock back, so I grabbed another clip using my trigger finger to drop the empty one from the gun. Slapping the new magazine in place, my left hand hit the bolt release, and once again, continued firing.

The crowd of undead thinned a little so we surged forward quickly. We had to hurry so the dead bodies wouldn't block us. Plus, Ezra's gun needed to cool down. When we got to the T-section, we had another problem. Zombies were rushing towards us from both directions. We ran toward the Luxor. We needed a minute to blow the door, so Ezra, Michael and I took up the rear to stop the dead.

The soldiers took over for us, continuing to fill the tunnel with bodies. In a sick way it was getting easier because the bodies had clogged the tunnel so badly that the dead couldn't get through quickly. Alice informed us that we couldn't go through in the direction we had planned; time for plan B.

I had never liked plan B. We were about to use a service tunnel back to the surface. We would arise in front of the building, directly in front of the Luxor. We would be fighting in the open; it would be harder to deal with their numbers.

We burst out a door that came out in a guard shack a hundred yards from the valet parking. The zombies had already taken over the parking lot. Our group was instantly fighting our way toward the door.

Alice unleashed her fully automatic shotguns; body parts exploded everywhere. Ezra unloaded his mini in another direction while Michael and I drove our firepower toward the front door. Spooky had turned into a giant Tiger with shining black armor. It was breathtaking. I could feel the pride and confidence of our group. We fought toward and then under the large valet parking area. We had moved under the cover when most of us ran out of ammo.

Alice released her doll and drew her knives. The creepy ass doll came to life and tore off toward the zombies. It started to jump upon them and tear their heads off. We were only about fifty yards from the front doors when they flung open and necromancers flanked by Nosferatu came out.

The Nosferatu leads the way. They had little hair and what they did have was greasy and unkempt. Their eyes were huge with an unnatural yellow color to them. Mouths open wide, with their sharp teeth and elongated canines. Their face looked almost alien in every way and they never changed appearance. It was hard to know how much humanity was in them, but with their look and their hunger for blood they always remained in the shadows. The necromancers had captured and bred them, and now use them to fight their war.

I pulled my sword and flashed upon them followed by Spooky. Alice screamed, "No... do not kill them!"

My sword stopped inches from the neck of the first necromancer. I was about to ask why when I noticed that they were all staring with a strange look in their eyes. The Nosferatu launched forward and attacked the zombies while the necromancers began to attack each other. Two of the necromancers were girls; they looked as if they were kissing when I realized they were biting each other. Blood was going all over the place as they bit into each other's flesh. Alice was laughing away as she sliced down zombies with ease. The vampires and necromancers were stuck in a nightmare, courtesy of Alice.

Spooky ripped the front door down with her massive claws. Without a word, Ezra, Michael and Alice stood up behind Spooky and me. They would hold the door and keep them off our backs. We charged into the casino and fell under attack.

The inside of the Luxor was hollow, making for a gigantic room. The hotel rooms ran up the side of the pyramid's walls so the many balconies appeared to be steps as they climbed to the sides of the building. The center of the building was far from empty. It held smaller buildings within it in a confusing layout, plenty of places for people to take cover with guns. Most of the gunfire was coming from the balconies above us; there were Necromancers with rifles. Perhaps some of them were just humans.

I took cover behind Spooky as we moved into a corner of the wall. Rounds were bouncing off her armor as I tried to figure my way out of this mess. We were pinned down; we had to break free.

Behind Spooky's protective armor, gunfire rained down on us. I shot back with my handguns, but I was under a great disadvantage because of the range. The guns' bolts slid back showing they were empty. I dropped the empty magazines tossing the guns into the air. I retrieved two full magazines and slid them in place as the guns fell back towards my hands. I pressed the bolt releases and then resumed firing.

Three large werewolves came toward us. They were growling with saliva dripping from their mouths. It was going to be difficult to fight them while under fire. The werewolves stopped their forward advance when a small doll walked over to them. The doll stood before the three confused werewolves and said, "Mummy, mummy."

I ducked behind Spooky as the room filled with fire and a deafening sound. The explosion was massive as pieces of werewolves splattered against the wall. The explosion had another effect; smoke filled the air. It would blind the gunmen.

Chapter 43 Las Zombie

I planned on using the smoke and the confusion of the explosion to attack.

I wasn't about to die here. I reached inside, letting my reaper side out. I felt my dark wings burst forth as my hands blackened and enlarged. I could not see myself, but I knew my eyes glowed with power. Jumping on Spooky's back, sword in one hand and gun in another, we charged.

A group of Nosferatu appeared in front of us. Nosferatu were crazed, disfigured vampires, which showed no fear. Bloodlust made them wild and uncontrollable. Somehow the Necromancers were managing them. They stood before me, and, for the first time ever, I witnessed them pause. Spooky and I made a hell of a sight, a woman in leather with giant black wings wielding a sword and riding on a giant armored tiger.

We slammed into the group; I sliced, while Spooky clawed. Seconds later the few surviving Nosferatu ran for it. The smoke was starting to clear, and it would not be long before the gunmen would be firing on us again. I did not wait; I took to the air.

I must have surprised them when I burst free from the cloud of smoke. I flew onto one of the balconies where some of the gunmen were. They got their wits about them and turned to fire on me. I moved so fast that their bullets appeared slow. With quick slices of my sword, three less gunmen existed.

I picked up one of the rifles and quickly dispatched other gunmen before having to duck from gunfire. I flashed and flew, shot and sliced, while Spooky killed everyone on the lower floor. It felt like hours, but it had been more like ten minutes, and the enemy was either on the run or dead.

Out of ammo, I used my sword to cut free all the straps that held the empty magazine pouches. Michael joined me carrying his war hammer. His suit was ripped up and covered with blood and dirt. He looked around, scanning for more threats, "Alice and Ezra have the front door. I came to see if you needed help."

I asked, hoping he might have an idea, "Directions on what to do next, or perhaps David himself?" He shrugged as we both looked around.

A giggle from what sounded like a young girl caught our attention. Spooky came up behind us as a young girl walked in from a side entrance. I had a bad feeling; she moved calmly like she hadn't a care in the world. As she closed the distance between us, I noticed things about her. She was wearing a black dress with a corset. The corset had light blue patterns running throughout. She wore lots of white and black makeup with jet-black hair that was tied up messily. What really caught my eyes were the scars; she was covered with them. She looked like someone had sewed her up after going through a wood chipper.

Michael let out a gasp, "No… it can't be... Lizzie?"

With shock and horror, I realized he was right. Coming to a stop a few feet away from us, she giggled covering her mouth as she had done so many years ago. She was David's baby sister; she died trying to help me. I remember it like it was yesterday. I recalled her death and David taking her body with us. David buried her right where this building was built. He must have planned to raise her, but was she really Lizzie?

Michael started to head toward her. I grabbed him and pulled him back, "Wait." As if provoked, she attacked. Needles attached to strings burst forth from her body.

I moved in a flash, spinning and ducking from the onslaught of pins. My sword sliced through the air cutting the strings as the pins fell to the ground. Michael was nowhere as quick as me. The needles spun around him, wrapping him in the string. As the needles pulled through the air, the string tightened around his body. I flashed over to help him.

I quickly cut the strings, when more needles came flying my way. By the time I dealt with the next attack, the needles had pulled so hard on the strings, his arm and one of his legs were close to coming off. Before I could react, the string around Michael's neck took his head clean off.

I could feel the shared rage of my entire group over Michael's death. I knew, without a doubt, Ezra would be here soon.

Lizzie's voice was full of pain, "Oh my God, Michael. How could you have let me kill him? It's your *fault*, Melabeth. You killed my family and cursed me to a half life… and now you have killed Michael."

Needles flew at me while Spooky attacked. I mentally yelled at Spooky, she wasn't quick enough and was quickly wrapped by strings. The armor protected her, but now I needed to worry about cutting her free and fighting off attacks on myself.

Luckily, I had more help as Ezra joined the fray. His weapon had become a Kukri blade. He sliced through the strings with ease. He was so tall, all legs and arms; his face was full of rage. His son had fallen. Ezra was the Ace of Spades, and watching him fight left no wonder as to why. His long limbs lent to his grace as he moved through the attacking needles like a ballerina on an empty stage.

He fell upon Lizzie and his Kukri found its mark. Her arm fell to the ground. There was no blood, and the needles quickly dove to the ground and into the fallen limb. Putting the limb back in place, it was sewed on faster than it fell away from her. Ezra had cut her two more times, but then he was driven back by all her needles flying through the air. They began to create webs so that it was harder for Ezra to close the distance.

I had freed Spooky and was about to help Ezra. Ezra knew what I was about to do, "I have this Mel. End this; find David."

It was hard to turn my back and let them fight. I had faith in Ezra, turning away from their fight as he drove her down a hallway and deeper into the casino. I decided I would take the high ground so I flew into the air. I started circling the inside of the building scanning for David. I knew he was close; I knew David. He would want to watch and control every moment of this fight.

As I flew, a large circle caught my eye. It was drawn on the ground with many symbols on it. When I looked closer, I could see the dark power at its center. The book was sitting on a stand in the center of the circle. I realized that it was set in the dead center of the building.

Spooky moved into the area prowling and covered with blood. Her black armor mixed with the red, made me think of a dragon. An object blurred from nowhere right at Spooky; before she could react, it was at her side. I felt her pain and confusion as her consciousness faded.

There, standing next to her was David. He had flashed upon her like he was a vampire. He looked up at me with a grin as he pulled his long sword out of Spooky. The great tiger fell into a pile with a bang as her armor slammed against the hard floor. He had slid his rapier through one of the joints of the armor, and, like a great swordsman, hit her heart.

I was stunned.

I could feel the pain of our group as we felt yet another loss, but quickly we all buried it. This was no time to mourn Spooky. I took to the air, landing but just a few feet away from David. He wore no mask this time. He was wearing black pants, boots, and a tunic with bright green highlights.

He smiled at me, "Have you come for your precious revenge?"

The funny thing was, I was mad at him, but I did not hate him. He had become so lost; he was like a rabid dog. "No David, I'm not here for revenge. I'm here to stop you and bring you to justice for what you have done."

His eyes widened and then he laughed, "For what I have done? As if you are any better... you're just jealous. See, you always wanted revenge for the wrongs done to you, but you went about it the wrong way. I will have revenge on anyone I want, for I will be God." He was crazy; his eye even twitched. He reminded me of a villain I used to see on Saturday morning. "If you're not here for revenge for her," he said as he pointed at the human body of Spooky, "Then you must be here to avenge what I have done to you. Or perhaps you don't know."

"I know, and I forgive you, but you must be stopped." I looked down at Spooky's body. "Too many have died due to your madness."

Before he could speak, I attacked.

We came together with a bang as our swords clashed together. The sound of clanging was the music of war. We both flashed, and we both were strong and skilled.

David tried casting several spells, but they had no effect on me. He sneered, "That's no spirit sword. Where did you get that weapon?"

I sliced him with my sword as I answered his question, "Wal-Mart."

More than once our swords cut each other, and I watched as David's wounds healed as quickly as mine. I attacked David with all the savagery of a wolverine and the skill of a Samurai. In the heat of battle David had cut off my wings, but that did nothing to hurt me. My power flowed through me like a river. This place felt as if it might have been feeding me. I knew that it fed David, but I hadn't known that I would feel its power as well.

David came at me with a lunge. My defensive blow was the same as it was the last thirty times I deflected his sword away. This time I threw something new at him. This idea was Bow's... the very idea that her husband had proclaimed was his.

Instead of stepping one little step to the side while holding off his blade, I jumped. My blade was still up against his as I pushed my feet into the air and then into a handstand. As my body traveled through the air and over his head, I grabbed his shoulder. I then went into a spin.

This caught him off guard as he tried to figure out where I had gone. I was still spinning through the air upside down when my sword sliced through the back of his neck. I landed on one hand going into a cartwheel and righting myself. I had cut his spinal cord; no matter how fast he healed, he still had lost control of his body. He fell to the ground, and his sword clattered across the ground.

I flashed in front of him as he was already healing. David rose to his knees, only to find my sword pressed to his chest, right where his heart was, "Don't even think about it," I hissed.

"*Is this* your justice?" His face, hardened, "What now, do you kill me?"

"Yes," I replied.

"What kind of justice is that?" He questioned.

I was calm as I explained, "What do you know about justice? Do you believe it's when you pay back for your wrongs against others? That doesn't make any sense. You can never take back what you have done. You can never make a victim whole again. You have killed so many innocent people; you took everything they had or ever would have. No, justice is not paying for your crimes. It's the idea of rehabilitation, to repair a broken mind so once more they can be returned to society. When rehabilitation fails? We keep them in prison… not to make them pay, but to keep others safe - to keep them from making more victims. There is no hole deep enough for you, and you know it."

David smirked, "I will not fight. You will have to kill me in cold blood." His smirk melted as his face lowered to his chest. My sword had plunged straight through. His eyes met mine and with a trembling voice, "What was I thinking? I knew you would do it."

He almost looked as if he might say more, but his life faded away. I pulled my sword out, and his body fell to the floor.

From there I hurried over to see if there was anything I could do for Spooky. I bent down on one knee over her body. I reached down and removed her helmet. She was dead. I touched the side of her face, "Sorry, my friend. I owe you a life, a life from start to finish."

A low chuckle made me swing my head back up, there in front of me David stood once more. This time he looked bigger his eyes were bright and full of fire. His eyes looked like Nicks', as huge black wings spread from his back. He laughed, "This is not over Melabeth."

The ground shook as the floor turned black, full of cracks, and then shattered like glass. The only part of the floor that remained was the circle. The pyramid walls stayed. I looked down into the darkness and I could see an orange glow from under me as if there was a fire deep down in a cavern.

I looked back at David and realized what he was for the first time. He has been an Angel just like Nicks and Adder. Perhaps he was just inhabited by one; either way I could feel his power. He was so much stronger than Nicks and I realized whom I was dealing with. The strongest of all the Angels, I whispered his name, "Satan."

He smiled with pleasure, for he heard me speak. "I prefer David," He then laughed at his joke.

I had to know, "Has it been you the whole time? Or is David in there?"

He looked thoughtfully, "He gave himself to me long ago. Since I'm about to kill you, and without you *none* of this would have been possible, I will tell you a secret."

I was stunned and not sure what to do, but I still had my wits, "Ok, ready for the monologue."

His eyes tightened, but he really wanted me to know what he had accomplished. "It all began when David found the book and used its powers. In this place, so close to death, he made a contract with me. Not really knowing who I was, he struck a deal. The poor boy was full of fear, because he was in love with a girl, a girl he had secretly betrayed and lied to. He felt, if he had the power to help this girl find her revenge, then she might find it in her heart to forgive him. Is that not wonderful? Of course, what I found out was that you are a mix of both human and Angel. Your blood held the key, and David brought it to me.

"With dark magic and the fact that you are a vampire, we were able to reprogram the blood. Your blood cannot die and because it pulls power from my world and steals power from your world, I finally saw the way to take back what should have been mine. I will raise my armies up to the gates of Heaven and knock them down. Guess what the best part is?"

"The end of country western music?" I guessed.

The devil laughed, "Close, but no. The best part is, you will lead my armies."

"Oh, this is a job interview. Well, hate to tell you, but I don't work well with others, or on major holidays, oh and Sundays are a day of rest."

"When you die, you will go to hell and you will be mine," His face was deadly serious. David's sword flew across the air and into his hand, the blade burst into flames.

I took a calming breath as I raised my sword, "I do not fear you, nor do I fear my judgment."

This made the devil burst into laughter, "Oh my, I had no idea you were so delusional about your life. All the people you have killed and murdered, who could forgive a wretch like you? Let's see," He held up his hand and held up one finger. "First, you have lusted for Michael's body, along with other men. Second, your gluttony has led you to kill for the pleasure of feeding. Thirdly, you have been greedy with your love. Fourth, slothfulness has been the cause of hundreds of deaths. You lay at home while David killed. Fifth, you envied your father's love for your sister and then killed her for it. Sixth, your pride is great, and you cannot deny this. Finally, your wrath has been second to none; it has been your wrath, which has caused all of this." His one hand now held up seven fingers, showing me how I had covered all the deadly sins.

"You forgot being gay, lying, cheating and any other sin you can think of. You are truly the king of lies. I fear no judgment, for I have been forgiven; no hate remains in my heart. If he is my father, then he will find forgiveness for me and accept me with open arms and love. I would do this for my child, and he would do no less for me. If not for the forgiveness and love, I would never be worthy. 'For God so loved the world that he gave his one and only Son, that whoever believes in him shall not perish but have eternal life.' You know that verse right?" I raised my sword and the devil's face hardened. "I'm truly thankful that my deeds are not how I am judged."

The Devil countered, "You will never be forgiven, and you still sin; you are *mine*."

"That's because I am still free, free to make my own choices, and sometimes I choose poorly. I have had a rough road and I'm too quick to kill, but I'm working on it, with love in my heart and support from others that love me... I will grow. Jesus knows my name." I reached deep within myself and never have I believed in myself and what I stood for like I do now.

His face filled with rage, he came upon me with a mighty swing of his fiery sword. I met his attack, for I knew if I fell, so would my family. Our weapons clashed and as our swords met, sparks flew around the room. I wasn't sure what to do against the power that stood before me.

As I fought to hold my own, a light cast down upon me. The light was brilliant and brighter than I could ever remember seeing. I was not the only one blinded by this light; so was the devil. He screamed, "NO, HOW DARE YOU INTERFERE. She is not worthy."

Our swords met, but this time we broke apart like an explosion. We were blown apart. He fell to his knees, covering his eyes. His voice full of wrath, "This is not over. It will never be over. Your blood lives on... it lives in you and others. David assured that many necromancers and wizards have small amounts of it, so they might raise the dead. It may not be tomorrow, but someone will use the power and I will rise once more. Mankind will die from an army of corpses. Do you understand, you have lost."

I thought about what he was saying. He was right; there would never be an end. The zombies would eventually take over the world. I held my sword tight, "Perhaps no one can stop this, but I can stop it for now, and, just maybe, there will be enough good to stop it in the future. I didn't come for the future; I came for now."

He was still covering his eyes from the blinding light, "One day you will serve me no matter what you do. You cannot kill me with that sword."

I brought my sword down upon him with a mighty swing, taking his arms and head clean off. I stepped back looking at the body, "That wasn't the plan. I don't need to kill you; I just needed to send you back to hell."

His head, laughed as it lay upon the floor. David's body began to crawl and pull itself back together. How could I stop him? He possessed his body... then it hit me. I ran to the center of the circle and hefted my sword over the book. The devil's scream shook the room, "*stop.*"

"Time to be purified," My blade came down on the book.

The world exploded as the light filled the room. I found myself lying on my back blinded. When I opened my eyes again, I was looking at a different ceiling, one I was very familiar with; it was the library. I sat up and, directly across from me, sitting on the floor, was Nicks. He was smiling with his young face and eyes full of pride, "You have made me proud. Truly, the world will never know how you gave them more time to find themselves. You will come and see me soon. The doorway here is closing.

David had made his choice; do not cry for him; you have chosen wisely." He said the last part with a wink.

Before I could speak the world once again spun. Finding myself once again inside the Luxor, I was sitting on the floor. The light was gone; so was the darkness as the floor had returned to normal. I knew that the spell that opened the doors to death had been broken.

Chapter 44 Home Bound

With the spell broken, I could hear the sound of battle. Ezra was still fighting Lizzie. I took off to help him, arriving in the nick of time. Ezra was caught within the strings and being cut apart. Without a second to lose, I flashed in, cutting the strings and freeing him.

I could tell he was tired and had used a lot of his power. Lizzie giggled with an evil smile as more strings attacked me. I looked at my old friend as I cut the attacking strings. All my powers were alive, and I could see what Lizzie truly was. She was a spirit trapped within a magical body, a Franken-doll.

I knew what to do. I charged at her flashing and slashing, closing the distance. The closer I got, the more needles, with strings attacked, and the less room I had to maneuver. The strings caught my left arm first, wrapping and cutting. Soon, the needles stabbed through my leg, then began to wrap around my leg slicing through my hip. She was sewing me up alive. No matter the pain, I pushed closer until I was standing within arm's reach. The strings continued to wrap around me, cutting through my flesh.

With one final effort I stretched my arm forward, but it was not enough as the strings pulled me apart from the inside. I was close enough, "Time to go home, Lizzie." My voice could barely make the words as the strings wrapped around my neck.

I freed myself, not from the strings, but from my body. My spirit came forward, reaching, reaching into the abomination that stood before me. There I found it, Lizzie's soul. Grabbing it tight, I sank my claws into her spirit. I pulled until she came free, and, as I pulled, her spirit from her body I drained the spirit of its life. Her spirit came apart, started to turn into blackened ash. She smiled at me and mouthed the words, "Thank you." Her spirit was free. Her body fell limp; dead flesh fell off her very old skeleton as it collapsed on the ground.

The pain was what I felt as my own soul returned to my body covered in strings that were buried in my flesh. I felt freedom as Ezra and Alice came to my rescue. I healed fast, but all this fighting had weakened me. The best I could do was staunch the bleeding. Alice handed me my sword. At first, I wondered why. That's until I heard them; the dead were coming. With pieces of strings and needles hanging from my flesh, I raised my sword once more. My sword reflected my bad mood as I cut through the army of the undead. The necromancers had lost control of the Nosferatu, and now they were running amok. The fact that the military and us, we're able to keep this fight off the streets of Vegas amazed me.

The surviving necromancers were now trying to help us. They had lost their greatest power with the destruction of the book. Now the Nosferatu and undead were attacking them. In the end, few necromancers would survive this night.

There was hope for Michael and Spooky. Ezra rushed Michael's body into one of the Luxor's rooms, once the fighting was under control. There he filled the tub with blood. Michael's body could repair itself. I finished the clearing of another tunnel when I felt Ezra's need of me. When I arrived, he looked stressed. He was sitting on the edge of the toilet looking down at the blood-filled tub. There Michael's body lay submerged in blood, "This is all the human blood I could come up with. Perhaps we should hunt some more humans down."

I didn't respond; he knew that we would have to kill a lot of people for that. The military had supplied him with way more bags of blood than they were willing to give. Alice has a way with people. I cut my wrist and let the blood add to the pool.

Ezra smiled at me, "That will help."

"We will bury Spooky in Queen Anne when we return."

Ezra barked at me, "Why wait so long putting her into the ground?" He took a deep breath, "Sorry, I'm just..."

"Don't worry about it; I know how you really feel, remember? Plus, it's a good question. She has my blood in her, and she might arise. This also means it might take decades for her to do so, if she rises at all. If that's the case, we can't bury her in Vegas; this is a dead place, and now that I closed the door here, there will be nothing to feed her."

Ezra nodded, "You're right. I'm just a little out of sorts. Michael was my son, and Spooky means the world to me."

I rubbed his shoulder, "I know. They both meant the world to me... I have hope."

We were in Vegas for a few days. No one noticed all the military carting off the bodies from the front of the Luxor. It amazed me how the whole city missed all that fighting, but there were good reasons for that. The buildings were almost soundproof, and most people saw what they wanted to. The few stories that circulated, were all about either mob activity or a casino heist.

On the second day we had a miracle. Michael awoke. He was weak, but he lived... kind of. I pulled his bloody body up from the tub and hugged him tightly. Alice and Ezra rushed in from the other room. Michael sounded as if he had laryngitis, "Miss... me?"

"No," we all said in stereo, and then we all laughed. I whispered in his ear, "We are even, my brother."

He hugged me back tighter, and I could feel the relief washing over him. Then Alice screamed; we all jumped in panic. She looked at me in horror, "That's the new dress I bought you. You've got blood all over it."

I yelled back, "YOU DIDN'T BUY IT. You stole it from the store downstairs."

Ezra shook his head, "Why don't you two go somewhere so Michael can get cleaned up."

I hadn't realized that, when I lifted him out of the pool of blood, he was naked. Covered in red it didn't matter, he was one beautiful man. I let out a whistle, "Adam... Adam... Adam, I need to go." Alice and I left the bathroom in a fit of laughter.

It took another day before Michael was strong enough to travel. I could barely sit still in my seat as the plane took off toward Virginia. It was a bittersweet ride home. I was about to see my sister, brother, stepfather, Summer and birth father. Most of all, I would be in the arms of Adam.

The bitter part was the coffin riding in the belly of the plane. We had a funeral planned for Spooky. It made me realize how much she had touched everyone's lives. She had become family with my sister, my brother, my stepfather and my real father. In doing so, they became very close to the cat who could turn into a girl. My brother knew her better than me. We hadn't even met yet. Only through her, did we speak. This was the second lover that Ezra would bury for helping me. Yet I knew he held no grudge toward me. Even Alice formed a relationship with her - if it weren't for our connection, I probably would have never known. She was unable to show any outward emotion. The time in the band had made Summer and Spooky inseparable. When I told Summer over the phone, she burst into tears. I knew Adam and Dan would feel the loss as well. It did bring a small smile to my face when I imagined that we might need to find a new drummer and perhaps that we should find someone who could play the drums. It won't be the same no matter what.

Dan, Summer, Zoey and Adam were waiting in the terminal when we arrived. Hugs and excitement were in the air. I gave Adam a deep kiss and held him tight. Not letting him go, I asked, "I thought they didn't let you past airport security if you're not on a flight."

Dan overhead me and laughed, "I'm a wizard; the TSA is no match for mad skills."

Adam added, "Mad part is right; skills are pushing it."

Summer pulled me away from Adam, "Share some love, girl. Can't believe Spooky lost her nine lives. Still, I'm proud of her… and the rest of you super-flyish-ass-kickers."

I held her tight, "I missed you, thanks for being a friend."

We had a short drive back to Queen Anne. My sister and family hadn't come, but they were awaiting me. I was nervous and excited about seeing them and meeting my brother for the first time. Zoey and Michael were riding in another car with Ezra and Alice. Dan claimed that this car was for PTF band members only. As we drove, I came to learn that it hadn't been quiet in the city of Queen Anne. Apparently David had sent some nasty necromancers to the city. They didn't go into great detail, but wanted me to know that Zoey was a hero. She fought bravely. More importantly, she saved my brother's life. If not for her, I might not be meeting with him. When I could pry her free from Michael, I would have to thank her.

Arriving back at Queen Anne, we entered Dan's home. He lived in a big house, and, as we walked toward the living area, there were plenty of signs of battle. There was broken furniture and pictures, burned marks on the wall and, of course, dried blood. We entered into Dan's large living space where everyone had been awaiting our arrival.

My sister and stepfather rushed me first, followed by my real father. A three-way hug commenced. My stepfather cried, "You're all grown up… I feel like I missed everything." This, of course, started a chain reaction of tears.

After reassuring my stepfather that we would have time to make it all up, I was able to get my tears under control. He had always thought of me as his daughter, and, when my sister had me, he never looked at me in any other way than his very own daughter. My true father was really showing his age and looked to be more like my grandfather now. It was good to see him. My sister was all smiles. I never felt so complete.

My brother stood up from the couch, he had been reclining on. He was visibly nervous about meeting me. Now, standing in the same room, I could feel him, not as strong as my sister or others blooded to me, but somehow, the same. I knew he carried my blood. I walked over to him, and everyone left, leaving us in awkward silence. I took in my brother, I had seen him many times through the eyes of Spooky, but he had never seen anything other than a picture of me.

His brown hair had grown longer since last I'd seen him; it was starting to cover his eyes. I don't know why I said it; I didn't know what else to say, "You need a haircut, Jeffery."

His hand went to his head, and he flipped his hair to one side, "So do you; call me Jeff."

My hair hung to my waist, "It just grows back."

"Oh," was his response. I finally had enough and rushed him, pulling him into a slightly awkward hug. He chuckled, "Damn, you are strong."

"Sorry," I mumbled as I loosened my grip.

That night my brother and I did nothing but talk. He wanted to know what it was like to be a vampire. I wanted to know what it was like to be a teenage boy. It was weird, so much time apart, yet, talking and hanging with him was as comfortable as an old pair of shoes. Jeff had started to nod off while I was talking, "Perhaps we should hit the sack."

"Not tired," followed by a large yawn. We both laughed.

"It's sunrise. You may not be tired, but I am. We'll have more time together tomorrow."

Jeff narrowed his eyes, "You don't seem real to me. I feel like I'll go to bed only to wake up finding out this was nothing but a dream."

That made me kind of feel bad, "I can't wait until I'm real."

"It won't take long," he responded with a smirk. We followed with a hug and then headed our separate ways to get some shuteye.

It was weird being together with everyone and exciting at the same time. I couldn't help but feel like I was constantly being torn apart, wanting to spend time with everyone at the same time. I was sure, in time, that things would fall together. Still, I couldn't help but feel bad because I wanted to spend so much time with Adam, but felt like I was trying to make up time with my family.

Weeks passed quickly in Queen Anne, and my life started to come together as I watched the loved ones around me fall into life's patterns. I even signed up with Adam to go to Virginia Tech in the fall. I was happy and, for now, the world was safe, but only a few people in the whole world even knew I saved it.

Dan had gotten rid of Luna; I was surprised at how easy it was. Dan explained that Luna was full of pride and the most important thing to her was image. The deal was struck; she stayed out of America, and I had to stay out of Europe. No one was allowed to talk about Luna's involvement with the book or me. At first this angered me, but Alice explained that secrets like that spread faster than the truth. Luna would never be trusted by the magical community as she was. In a way this was the closest to justice, we could get without getting into another war. I was ready for peace.

Adam and Summer talked me into going to the beach with them and taking Jeff. It was late August and this would be our last chance for some fun in the sun before school. Except I hate the sun. I would take one for the team. The room was nice, and I could see the beach. Adam kept coming back and checking on me, afraid I was being left out. I finally kicked him out and told him he could make it up by taking me to dinner.

That night we found a romantic little pizza place. We could see the water from our outside table. I was telling Adam, "Thanks for worrying about me, but I was fine today. The room was great; I got caught up on sleep and some reading."

"I just didn't want you to feel left out. Your brother kept telling me that you were fine."

"He does know," I said with a wink.

Adam shook his head, "You could fool him." Adam knew me well. "Plus, I know you can handle some sun even if you don't like it."

I was about to say something when a man caught my attention. He was in his mid thirties, dark hair and of average height. He wasn't doing anything but walking down the sidewalk next to the tables. He looked so familiar; he saw me and then did a double take. He had been in mid stride when he came to a sudden stop; his eyes widened in surprise. I wasn't sure who he was yet, and it began to make me nervous.

He finally snapped out of his shock and changed direction to approach me. He didn't look angry or aggressive. He spoke with excitement, "It is you! Melabeth, you haven't aged a day."

"Sorry, I can't quite place you," He did look familiar.

His face was friendly, "No need to apologize. Unlike you, I've aged. We met twice, long ago. My brother and I gave you a ride up Mile High Road to a party. Then, about a year later, we met in a cemetery. You were," his voice lowered, "Flying, or perhaps landing there. Then you came over to my place to use the phone. My name is Eric, Eric Hood."

I remembered the boy now, "Wow, we met in California. What brings you here?"

"Work, family, better place for my kids to grow up." He paused and looked as if he were thinking about something. He must have decided to tell me. "You know, since that day at the cemetery I have wondered about what and who you are. My brother was an inspiring writer, and we were going to write a book about my chance meeting with you. Unfortunately, he passed away from a brain tumor a few years back."

An idea popped into my head, probably a bad idea. I asked, "Do you write?"

"No, not really, but I love to read."

Adam piped in, "What are you thinking? I know that look."

I explained, "Do you know what Alice and I have been working on?"

Adam snapped back, "I try never to think about what you and Alice are doing, let alone working on."

Ignoring him, I went on, "She has been showing me advanced blood tricks. Or perhaps I should not use the words trick, because there is no trick involved. She has been showing me how to concentrate memories into my blood and remove the vampire. By concentrating, I can push memories into the end of my finger and therefore transfer them to someone else without blooding them."

Eric asked, confused, "Did you say 'vampire'? I'm sorry, I'm not following."

"I know," I replied, giving him my best reassuring smile. I held my pointer finger in front of me and started to concentrate, putting my entire life of memories in the blood at the end of my finger. It was more like a copy of those memories because I would not lose them. Then I said to Eric, "I will give you a gift, a gift for your brother, a story like no other, and you will write it."

He was very confused, "I will do my best I'm sure, but…"

I interrupted him, "Good, that's all I ask. Mr. Hood, so you will drink, then you'll have something to write about." I continued to push my memories into my finger.

I cut the end of my finger and started to pour it into a cup.

Chapter 45 E.B. Hood

Watching the blood from her finger pour into the glass was the last memory I had of Melabeth. It took me years to work out all the memories that filled my head that day. The first memory I had of her was awakening inside a coffin, followed by memories of Alex McDonald. It was all very confusing at first.

It took me some time to understand that, when she took Alex's blood, she took most of his memories throughout his life, changing her forever. I hope that I did her memories justice in this book. Now you, the reader, know why there were crazy changes of perspectives in the books. It was the only way I could show you the whole story as I witnessed it through dreams.

So in short, yes, this entire series is based on a true story interrupted by my dreams, which were given to me by a vampire. I know this is a lot to buy into, but it's my story, one way or the other.

Not long before I finished writing this book, I received a large box on my doorstep. No return address, I opened it like the fool I am. Inside were many old books of different shapes and sizes. On closer inspection, I found that all of them were handwritten with beautiful cursive handwriting. Some books were rather new, and others looked ready to turn to dust.

Stranger still, all the books appeared to be written by the same person who signed each one as A. White. I hadn't noticed the note that had fallen on the floor, but, when I did, I had a chill run up my spine. It was in a baby blue envelope, and it was addressed to E.B. Hood in the same writing that I saw within the books in the box. I opened the envelope and read:

Dear E.B.,

We have not met, but I feel like you are already family. You know many of my secrets and will write them for the entire world to see. I found out about this recently and promptly read your first two books. I found them okay for a child perhaps. They were not completely boring. Still, I found grievous errors concerning me, Alice. I have decided to let you set the record straight. I have sent you all my journals so that you may write a book about me, instead of my boring sister. I will expect a rough draft soon, so that I might give it my approval.

Love, Alice

I am now announcing my next book, The Chronicles of Alice. It's about a wonderful, well-adjusted girl who is turned into a vampire and makes the best of it. In this book we will turn back the pages of history and point out all of history's mistakes while exploring the unique life of a young girl named Alice White. We will begin when she first chooses to be turned into a vampire with some of the first English settlers, what really happened to the lost colony. Travel through her life as she becomes a bloodthirsty pirate and kidnaps her first love. In this adventure you will see how she manipulated world leaders and even got her claws into the United States government from its very inception. Of course, you will also see what a wonderful person she is, too. I'm searching through the journals looking for that so I may add it.

At any rate, you will see this new book soon. I also have been seeing a fortune teller and she has given me some insight into the future. Stay tuned for my post-apocalyptic book series, *The World of Empty Glasses*. The first book will be called *Dr. Weaver*.

Looking at doing a short story about Zoey, so keep your eyes open for the next E.B. Hood story.

Thank you so much for your support, and I hope you enjoyed this story half as much as I did writing it!